Electra's Early Adventures

Book Six of an Inner and Outer Space Odyssey Series

Lawrence L. Stentzel III

AN INNER AND OUTER SPACE ODYSSEY SERIES

A Tale of the Tail of Nine Stars:
An Inner and Outer Space Odyssey

End of Thrones:
Book Two of An Inner and Outer Space Odyssey Series

Lost in Space Time:
Book Three of An Inner and Outer Space Odyssey Series

Illumination Out of the Dark Ages:
Book Four of An Inner and Outer Space Odyssey Series

The Dominari Conformity:
Book Five of An Inner and Outer Space Odyssey Series

Electra's Early Adventures:
Book Six of An Inner and Outer Space Odyssey

The Psychopaths of the Maxom Empire:
Book Seven of An Inner and Outer Space Odyssey

Also by Lawrence L. Stentzel III:

THE INCOMPARABLE SHI-YIN SERIES

The Quest:
Book One of The Incomparable Shi-yin

Crisis on Sea and Land:
Book Two of The Incomparable Shi-yin Series

Shi-yin and Her Daughters:
Book Three of The Incomparable Shi-yin Series

Journey to the Amazon:
Book Four of The Incomparable Shi-yin Series

Shi-yin Returns to Europe:
Book Five of The Incomparable Shi-yin Series

The Ch'an Master's Travelling Sangha:
Book Six of The Incomparable Shi-yin Series

Cherry Blossom Abbey:
Book Seven of The Incomparable Shi-yin Series

TABLE OF CONTENTS

- Chapter 1 -

Get strapped in secure because I'm about to fire a launch-booster to take off fast."

"Are you certain your skullcap is linked to the shuttle's pilot console?" Larry asked concerned.

"Of course I'm sure," Electra shot back offended.

"Will the authorities chase us?"

"Planet Mother is a moral anarchy and has no authorities," Electra reminded him.

"What about the One United System patrol ships protecting the planet from high orbit?"

"They are for military defense only and do no policing, though they'll likely try to tag us with a tracker."

"What's our destination?" Larry asked still anxious.

"Our first stop is Vax Legas," Electra informed him, "It's the only planet in the Tri-Galaxies where we can get legally married at our age."

"Vax Legas is all casinos, hotels and show girls," Larry complained.

"They have high-end shopping too," Electra pointed out. "Besides, we don't have much cash so I want to do some gambling first thing when we get there."

"Your mother is going to kill me when she finds out," Larry told her with great concern.

"No way. She'll know it was all my doing, and that you just went along for the ride."

"Are you sure you want to do this?"

"Who else would support me throughout my life's work?"

"Gumby would."

"He's my half-brother so I can't marry him."

"Why are you so intent on getting married anyway?"

"So that we can experience having sex," Electra informed him.

"I've never even kissed a girl. It's all boys at the Adamantine Will Academy," Larry admitted.

"We may need to hire you a sex worker to teach you first, before we try it out together."

Larry went internal, deep within the core of his anxiety, grappling with the prospect of marriage to Electra and satisfying her sexually. He loved her with all his heart and would do anything for her. Even this. But he had doubts as to his own adequacy. Electra could intuit his emotional turmoil with such clarity that she was able to deduce his thoughts accurately. She'd already observed how he had aligned his entire being and life-trajectory in preparation for supporting adeptly her life-purpose. She also knew that his highest aspiration was to be her friend and student, and that it had never occurred to him that he might become her husband and lover.

After a period of mentation, soul-searching and pure contemplation, Electra had come to realize that Larry was obviously her soul-mate given by grace and providence, and destined to be her loving consort. Through her process of acceptance of this fate Electra had opened her heart completely to the skinny lad, and now loved him fiercely. She meant to take on his inferiority complex—born of childhood trauma—to transmute and dissolve it within herself, just as soon as she could learn how to do it. She was sure she was already on the cusp of accomplishing this power.

Larry said apologetically, "I truly hope I do not disappoint you."

"You could only disappoint me by withholding your love, and of that I doubt you are capable."

"What if I'm no good at sex?"

"Then we'll just have to practice rigorously until you develop skill."

Electra, you are the Mu. I'm just a nobody orphan your family took in and raised."

"We have had the same teachers and practices. Your difficult beginnings have been fuel for attainment of wisdom-compassion. You were a senior disciple of the previous Mu, 2,500 years ago. You are my consort. There is no doubt in my mind."

"I love you Electra. Nothing could make me happier. I never dared dream of this. It is the most grave and consequential function and role I can imagine."

"Well, you ought to try being the Mu."

"Touché. I do see your point."

"I've finished the pre-flight checks and I've got a course set in the navigation computer for Vax Legas in the Royal Galaxy. These Om Ambassador shuttles have full-cloaking, so we're going invisible to all optics and sensors. I'm punching it now."

Through a thought impulse through her skullcap, Electra fired a launch-booster, all forward thrusters, and the main space-drives full throttle. She even brought the exterior mini-swivel drives to zero angle full-speed to assist with propulsion. Her vortex redirect and generation turbine was cranked up full. Once the launch-booster was spent and ejected, Electra fired her acceleration space-booster, pressing them into their seats with their faces squishing to either side of their heads. Larry passed out for a moment.

When he came to moments later Electra informed him, "We're just passing Mother's only moon and up to 0.517 light speed."

"Even your mother's take-offs don't make me pass out. You must have set a new record."

"I've been practicing in the pilot simulator at Mother's Compassionate Guardians Academy. I've passed all the certification tests for 17 spacecraft; all but the part where you actually fly them."

"You're amazing. This is so catalyst!"

"They didn't get a chance to tag us with a tracker. Quantum jump in 43 seconds."

"Your mother says we should contemplate the Black Near-Attainment when passing through the quantum void, so as not to fall into the typical shock and stupor."

"Then you better get contemplating. I'm going to go beyond it all, to become the transcendental divine presence."

Larry sunk his breath into his lower abdomen, filling his lungs from the bottom to the top like filling a vase. Retaining his breath at the top of his inhalation, he was already drawing the winds into his central channel. By his retention of no-breath at the end of his exhale in the silence of no-movement, his physical senses dissolved quickly in sequence, each flashing its luminescent sign within his mind's eye. The black radiant Midnight Sun became Larry's one-pointed contemplation as the countdown ended and they went through the jump. The transition always occurred without duration according to the instrumentation, however, the human experience of ceasing to exit at all except as mere potential, was inevitable and universal without exception. The experience produced in the transcendental eternal void beyond time, space and matter, with no components, invisible and without location, felt actually enduring to those living through it, and not in the least brief.

None-the-less, the same precise micro-second they ceased to exist in the Mother system, they appeared in the Vax Legas system. Electra had jumped in close, only three light-minutes from their destination; the third planet from the yellow sun. It had one moon a bit less than a quarter million miles out. Electra had the main drives reversed full along with the reverse braking drives and reverse thrusters. She fired her only reverse booster and Larry stoically accepted the bruises to his rib cage from his shoulder harnesses as his body attempted to race ahead of the spacecraft. It had the force of an 80-mph crash into a stone wall, but the motion dampeners absorbed the majority, and the smart-foam in the harnesses helped too.

"This place is really crowded!" Electra exclaimed as she maneuvered around a giant freighter ship, narrowly missing the super-structure with the bottom of their shuttle.

"No kidding! And none of them can see or detect us!"

"I've got this," she reassured him while catching the stern of a super-container ship with her tractor-beam, which gave them both a jolt before tearing lose—too weak to check their velocity.

It did slow them down a few hundredths of the 0.284 light speed they were traveling. After a few more seconds of all-out braking, the ghosts in their hologram displays began resolving into recognizable objects. Thousands of ships and spacecraft were arriving and departing. Tens of thousands of satellites surrounded Vax Legas in low to medium orbit. Electra nicked a traffic regulation space platform at .229 light speed. The sign mandated .09 light speed. She was just able to correct her heading without flying into a spin from the impact. Now an eight by two inch patch on the port bow was no longer cloaked since the synthetic plus silicon lens material had been scraped off. She kept all reverse drives and thrusters at maximum and was down to .09 light by the time the speed limit was .004 light speed.

Then she used her swivel drives and thrusters to turn towards the moon, coming in to a close arch around half the 2,000 plus mile diameter rock. The gravity well, given how close to the surface she went, checked her speed further. Electra kept her main drives reversed and all reverse drives and thrusters at full for the next 238,000 miles headed right for the planet. Entering the atmosphere, she was down to 4,500 miles per hour. The air friction slowed them a little but the planet's gravity was adding an increasingly compelling force to their momentum. At 10,800 feet altitude, Electra powered up the vortex redirect turbine full-blast. She extended the fins on the sides of her stretched-nose disc-shaped spacecraft, and employed the flaps in coordination with her turning drives and thrusters to get her nose up, angling towards horizontal with the planet surface.

Larry took a deep breath, restarting his respiration as he willed himself out of panic. He found his voice to express, "That was some entry!!"

"Thanks."

"Where on the surface are we headed?"

"To Vice, the capital. I've made reservations at the Platinum Bullion Casino and Hotel, and wedding arrangements in one of the marriage halls right in the casino."

"When's the wedding?"

"Not for two days since I need time to gamble and shop."

"What if all the games are rigged?"

"I'll know right away if they are."

"How much cash do you have?"

"Ahhu gave me a thousand dags last time she visited and I still have all of it."

"I still have 469 dags left from the 500 Mel gave me at the beginning of the school year."

"That's good because it costs 300 dags a night for the cheapest room."

"Do you think we'll get incarcerated for grand theft of the Om Ambassador to Mother's shuttle?"

"We're only barrowing it until we can afford to purchase our own shuttle."

"Do you think it's been reported stolen?"

"They likely don't know it's missing yet. They won't report it stolen since no one on Mother ever steals anything."

"I better change the identification code on the hull and the beacon transmission once we land."

"Wait until we have money for thruster fuel cells and new one-time boosters; then we'll do a full service on it."

"I've never barrowed something from someone without advanced permission before."

"You still haven't. I did the barrowing," Electra assured him.

"Legally that makes me an accomplice."

"No one will press any charges. Sarhi will see to that. She understands that I'm just accelerating my developmental process."

"Are you going to divorce me after we get married?"

"Never!"

"Is there an age limit on gambling down there?"

"I've researched everything. You have to be twelve years old to gamble and thirteen to marry. Sex work is legal so long as the workers are registered and all fees and taxes are paid. You have to be eighteen to pilot a spacecraft, so that's why I barrowed the quantum AI synthetic human android. You'll need to relinquish your copilot seat to our male QAISHA, who is our pilot, and who will be remaining aboard our shuttle."

Electra dipped into a narrow gorge to shut down their cloaking, then popped back up to 20,000- foot altitude closing on the desert city of Vice. Larry gave up his seat to the very polite android Electra had 'barrowed' at the Gaia spaceport on Mother. The male android voice said to the Casino Hotel hanger tower, "This is Om Ambassador shuttle 142857 with Electra and Larry aboard, who have reservations at the hotel."

"We have you in our hologram, 142857, and you're cleared right through the hanger bay doors. Just ease it in slow and then move off the landing pad to starboard at 87 degrees for 300 meters. You'll see some empty parking places right in front of you."

"Roger that, tower, I'm making my approach."

Electra brought them to hover motionless over the hanger doors with only her vortex redirect turbine and landing thrusters giving her lift. Easing off these they descended into the expansive chamber to make almost a right angle turn to the right, revolving in place, before moving slowly forward 300 meters. Turning in place again, Electra backed into her parking place and set the spacecraft down on its electro-hydraulic landing legs.

"Let's change into our formal attire and get all our money before going to the hotel."

"I have my dinner suit aboard."

"Put it on. I'll tie your bowtie for you."

"What are you wearing?"

"The black dress my mother makes me wear when we meet with world leaders. Ahhu sent me a lambergucci purse worth 30,000 dags from the Bivortex Galaxies."

"At least we'll look like we're rich," Larry commented.

The kids finished changing and went to the airlock in the stern of the shuttle. Electra had parked too close to the wall to lower the ramp, so they climbed down through the hatch in the airlock floor to the ground. Having reservations for one of the cheapest rooms meant they would have to catch the hovertram to the hotel lobby. The hanger was over a square mile, and they were on the opposite end from the hotel entrance. Each carried a small piece of luggage. Electra was looking for signs in the hanger while Larry ran a quantum search on his coms device.

Turning left, Electra said, "I think it's this way."

Larry stated, "It shows here that there's a tram stop just 30 meters the other way."

"Alright," she acquiesced, seeing that he was operating on actual data.

"I don't have a ring to give you."

"You will once we have a bunch of money."

"Do you think your mother will find us before we get married?"

"No. She'll be required to attend all kinds of interplanetary meetings now that the war is over in Bivortex."

"Mel or Haley could track us down in seconds."

"Mel promised to give us a 48-hour head-start."

"You thought of everything."

"Where do you think we ought to spend our honeymoon?"

"Most people in 1US like to come here, or go to Glitter, and some like the tropical paradise of Tahigi."

"I'm not too keen on the tropics. If we go to Glitter, I could try to get a spot on Star Hunt."

"Do you have an act to display?"

"I wrote a song and I might be able to get the Whirling Vortexes back together for one more performance as my backup band."

ıld certainly get you a spot on Star
/hiffle still in her three-year meditation

shed last week and we had a big
ıe Mother's Compassionate Guardians
Monastery ıɔ. ıer."

"Do you know how to reach Pogo and Frisbee?"

"Pogo's on Glitter producing a solo compilation of his latest songs. He'll know how to reach Frisbee."

"Do you think Hoola will just get a baby-sitter and come to Glitter?"

"She's in Bivortex with Vegan, so contacting her will require Mel's assistance."

The hovertram pulled up to let them on and the kids boarded. They had to stand because all the seats were taken. Electra didn't hold on, instead sinking her weight down and rooting her feet to the tram floor as she'd learned in her martial arts training. Several times the tram stopped for more economy passengers with luggage. When it stopped at the lobby of the hotel, the kids were among the first off. Electra sprinted ahead of the people who got off before her to arrive first at the check-in desk. Her chin cleared the counter by about two inches.

Catching the desk clerk's eyes with her own, she stated in Sterling, which is 1US Basic, "I have a room reserved for myself and my fiancé. My name is Electra and my reservation number is XL69333."

"Yes. I see your reservation. You are in room 59,103 on the 59th floor. If you would set your coms device to receive, I'll transmit your door code to it."

"It's receptive."

"There you go. I hope you enjoy your stay. Would you like help with your luggage?"

"No thank you. We can manage."

"They're practically family, and all owe their lives to my mother."

"My name is Hammon Rye and I'm a talent agent from Glitter. Please take my card and call me if you need an agent."

"Thanks," Electra told him as she took his card. "I just might."

The lift came to a stop at floor 59. Hammon was going up to 108. Electra and Larry got off. Over her shoulder Electra called, "It was nice meeting you Hammon."

Their room was about as far from the lift as possible given the layout of the building. Electra flung the door open using her skullcap as soon as she saw their room number. From the foyer, a bathroom was to one side and a large closet to the other. Within the bathroom was a double vanity, a shower stall compartment with two water nozzles, a large bathtub with Jacuzzi jets, and a separate water closet for the toilet. It was a smart toilet with water jet and blow-dry.

The room had an empress size bed with two end tables, a chest of drawers, a small table with two chairs, and a hologram pedestal in front of the bed. A glass door led out to a roofed balcony, and had both a blackout curtain and thick drapes. Both were open at the moment and the view of the casinos nearest them, sporting 500 by 500-foot holoclips on their sides, was bright and gaudy. The city of Vice never slept. The casinos and clubs were open day and night yearround.

Electra set her small suitcase on the luggage rack and told Larry, "Bring all of your money and let's go directly to the casino."

"Alright."

"I'm going to start at the 21-tables, and if that doesn't pay-off, I'll do the dice tables. I've been practicing telekinesis quite seriously lately, and can flip the dice from ten feet when they're on the move."

"Are you counting cards and playing the math with 21?"

"Yes, but my real advantage is sensing the card values when they are face-down. I'll know the dealer's hand."

"Isn't that cheating?"

"The House having the odds forever in their favor is cheating. I'm just making a corrective adjustment."

"You're so awesome and catalyst."

They made the trek back to the lift alcove and transmitted their destination to one of the multi-directional tubes. These were one-person units big enough to accommodate white-sun humans so they both fit into it easily with room to spare. Larry gripped the rail while Electra rooted her feet. She was always engaged in a meditation exercise at every moment, though Larry could never catch her in one, try as he might.

They went straight down for 58 floors before abruptly shifting to horizontal for about a mile. The jolt put Larry in Electra's arms, saved from crashing into the wall. The door hissed open to brilliant radiant colored lights and the sounds of various games and slot machines. The scene was heavily populated with wealthy patrons. The place was a kaleidoscope of lights, sounds and activity immediately overwhelming their senses. It was the absolute antithesis of the monastic academies they attended.

Electra focused into concentration and entered meditation as she walked from the tubes foyer into the high ceilinged immense casino. Broad avenues for foot and hover-chair traffic were laid out with narrow paths branching off to each side between game consoles and scoreboards. She headed towards the 21 tables thinking she was capable of beating many of the solo hologames she passed. Her father had taught her. He was a game programmer, hacker, elite gamer, and the number one quad-gunner in Om Star Fleet. She had also been taught by Ahhu and Kristy, the two best intuitive drone pilots in seven Galaxies.

Arriving at the tables Electra selected one and took a seat. Larry stood behind her chair watching. The dealer's name tag read "Mandy". Electra traded Larry's 450 dags for chips then anteed up with a 50-dag chip. On the firsthand Electra had 11. She asked for another card even though she could see that the dealer already had 21 with her first two cards. Electra was hit with a nine, surrendered her chip and put another out. The five cards played were etched in her mind.

Her next cards totaled twenty. The dealer had a seven showing and Electra could sense that her face down card is a nine. She held and the dealer took a card. It was a six. Electra recouped her loss and gained hope the game isn't rigged. She continued to memorize the cards played to better calculate her statistical odds. By the time they went through the deck she was sure no cheating is afoot and was up by 200 dags. She began playing two hands at once and went through the deck several more times, always memorizing the cards played.

Once she was up 1,500 dags, Electra went to a medium stakes dice table psyched for some bigger returns. Larry escorted her with great admiration. In three rolls she doubled her winnings, and in four more after that she doubled them again. Then she put 6,000 down at odds and let the dice soar. She concentrated like a laser on both dice as they flipped and spun, bringing them to rest on the numbers of her choice. As she continued a small crowd congealed around her dice table. She knew not to win too much at any given dice table, so at 23,500 dags up she went to find a higher stakes table.

Once she settled on one the man running it told her, "You must be twelve years old to gamble."

Electra pulled out her coms device and turned it on, pulling up her Identification page to show the man. As he checked she told him, "I'm almost fourteen years old. Vegan and Hoola Casper are my Godparents."

Vegan Casper is Chancellor General of One United System consisting of 5,900 human worlds in this three-galaxy cluster, which includes the Royal galaxy they are in. Hoola was the biggest super-star in the Tri-Galaxies being the lead guitarist and singer of the Whirling Vortexes and having been the super-model for Hug-me's Victorious Secret's crotchless panties. The man running the table was certainly impressed, and handed Electra the dice. She continued to control the outcomes through telekinesis doubling her winnings a bunch more times.

Not wanting to become too conspicuous, she suggested to Larry, "Let's go do a little shopping and grab a bite to eat at a gourmet restaurant."

"I'd love to. How much have you won so far?"

A hundred and ninety-seven thousand dags."

"What do you want to shop for?"

"We have enough for our wedding clothes, your ring, dinner, and money to keep playing," Electra told him.

"May we eat before we shop," Larry asked.

"Of course. Look up 'Taste of Rapture Restaurant' on your coms device."

"Here it is. It's on the other side of the hotel. We can get a multi-directional tube about 30 meters that way," Larry said pointing.

Electra took his hand in hers, heading in the direction he'd indicated, and passed him bioenergy. Larry was ecstatic to be in her presence and just lit up with delight over the physical contact and palpable energy-flow Electra pumped into him through his hand. He told her adoringly, "I love you Electra."

"I love you Larry."

There was a line and a several minute wait for a tube, though once inside, they shot like a bullet more than a mile east in like 50 seconds, then 112 stories up. Getting out was a bit like getting off an amusement park ride; unstable and disoriented. They found themselves in front of the restaurant and proceeded to the Maître-d podium to request a table.

He explained with insincere sadness, "I'm sorry but we are booked for the evening."

Electra showed the man her I.D. page displaying Pez and Rubix as her parents and Vegan and Hoola Casper as her godparents. She told him, "I'm Electra, daughter of the Avahat who brought down the Royal Monarch Empire, liberating you."

He said reverently while bowing deeply, "Then you must be the Mu."

"Stop that," Electra hissed at him. "I'm travelling incognito."

"I'll have the EIP table set up for you and your guest at once. It is a great honor to host you at our restaurant."

He disappeared into the bowels of the restaurant as Electra and Larry stood beside the podium. Larry commented, "Word of our whereabouts will get back to your mother rapidly now."

"I'll swear him to secrecy when he gets back."

"Every staff person in the restaurant will know by the time he does."

"Give me eight more hours in the casinos and I'll have enough money to buy us a yacht."

"You're talking like 60-million dags."

"I was thinking more like 200-million for a really nice one."

"We better go to more than one casino, so we don't draw too much attention."

"I'll buy us each a blaster pistol after dinner."

The Maître-d returned and made eye contact with Electra as he informed her, "Your table is ready."

"Please keep my visit secret from the media. This is truly important."

"I will. And I'll notify all the staff to do the same. Not a peep shall be heard."

"Thank you."

"Please follow me."

They were led to their table, prominently situated in a window alcove with a view of the whole city from the 112th floor. The entire floor turned a complete rotation every two hours giving them a 360-degree view over time. Only a handful of buildings were taller, and none of those close by, so hardly anything obstructed the distant horizons. At the moment they were coming around to due west and the sun was close to setting in that direction. They were seated by the maître-d and a waitress handed them menus.

"I'm starving," Larry told her as he perused the menu.

Electra shared some data from her research on the hotel, "All the raw ingredients come from the former Casper farms, called Uncontaminated Food. It's all organic including the poultry, lamb, beef and pork. The fish is all wild and flown in the day it's caught."

"Are you going to eat meat?" Larry asked surprised.

"No, but I will have some seafood."

"Then I will too."

"Let's get the baked oysters to share as an appetizer."

"That sounds great."

"I think I'll have shark fin soup and the swordfish steak with a lemon-butter-garlic sauce," Electra said as she decided.

Their waitress came to stand by their table. She made a sort of monastic half-bow to greet them. Larry informed her respectfully, "We'll have the baked oysters and two bowls of shark fin soup to start. Electra will have the swordfish steak and I'd like the fillet of sole stuffed with crab. We would also like a bottle of dry oaky white wine with a hint of fruit, of a good vintage as well."

"Of course, sir. I'll place your orders in the kitchen then return with your wine."

As she left Electra said in a whisper, "I hope the wine isn't 10,000 dags a bottle."

"They will bring it unopened to the table, and I'll ask the price before I accept it, Larry assured her.

"Let's get something under 500 dags. On Om you can get gold medal winners for under 100 credits."

"I agree. It had not occurred to me that we might be brought something outrageously expensive. I must recall the environment we are in."

"I want to be able to start right out at a high stakes table. Someday I'll buy you a 100,000 dag bottle of wine my love."

"They don't have money on Mother, and I've only used it over the quantum coms interface to purchase things from planets that do employ it."

Electra informed him, "I've been reading up on it, and Mel has been teaching me about investments and intergalactic and interplanetary monetary exchanges. She programmed a quantum AI learning algorithm to manage her portfolio and is beating all the indexes by a wide margin. It gets up to the minute news from 7,280 planets in seven galaxies, processing all implications of legislation and political decisions affecting intergalactic markets. We can invest our savings with Mel as our broker sweetheart."

"I thought Mel was Abbot of Om's Clear-light Order, an Islohar, and a Mother's Compassionate Guardian Order warrior maiden."

"She is. Being a broker is kind of a side-job for her. She's going to fund my monasteries when I start teaching and start some up. Ahhu's helping her."

The waitress arrived with their wine holding the bottle out for Larry to inspect. Larry immediately asked with anxiety, "How much is it?"

"Do you mean in liters?"

"No. How many dags?"

"It is on the house, compliments of the Hotel CEO."

Electra told her, "We are so grateful."

"Could I get your autograph?"

"Yes, but I don't have a stylus."

"Here's one," she offered, holding it out along with her personal coms device.

Electra took both and singed her name in the rectangle below the micro-hologram pedestal. She then handed the device to Larry as she pulled the waitress into a cheek-to-cheek pose with her. Larry got a few stills with the device before handing it back to the waitress, who seemed pleased beyond reason. She opened the bottle and filled the kids' glasses, then hurried into the kitchen. Electra and Larry each took a sip. Larry was checking the label and date on his coms device.

"I don't believe it!" he exclaimed.

"What?!"

"This bottle is only available by auction and always fetches at least 30,000 dags."

"It sure is generous of the CEO."

Their soup and appetizer arrived and both Electra and Larry thanked their waitress. A brief internal offering of the meal with heads bowed and hands clasped in laps, ingrained from monastic life, delayed the first morsels of satisfaction. The food was truly heavenly. Electra had chosen oysters and shark fin soup for their aphrodisiac effects. The hotel dinner chef was intergalactically famous for his astounding recopies.

"This is better than Ambassador Rations," Larry remarked in awe.

"I know. It is gustatory ecstasy," Electra agreed totally.

"Olfactory delight and taste-bud bliss," Larry added.

"We'll eat here every meal while we're in Vax Legas," Electra decided aloud.

"We might be putting them out if they keep putting it on the house."

"We won't order any more wine. We can drink lemonade and ice tea."

Larry suggested, "I think we ought to tip the service staff as well."

"That's a good idea."

"On that last dice roll, the one kept pulling one way then the other, as if in a tug of war," Larry told her.

Electra explained, "I had to overpower the directional pulse micro-gyroscope loaded in the dice. For a moment it was a tug of war between the table manager and me. Did you see him scan us when I collected my winnings?"

"Our hand devices were shut down and our skullcaps too. No instrument is going to detect your telekinesis."

"Actually, acoustical sensors can detect the circulation of bioenergy along the meridians of the human body, and outgoing healing bioenergy from those with enough mass integration to project it. Such a device also measured some of the events erupting from my mother's orgasms."

"We haven't been around her since entering puberty when she has caused an event, and never got to experience what adults do from one of her events."

Electra told him, "That's a relief. As her daughter I find it horrendously embarrassing."

"I sure hope they don't have one of those acoustical meters in any of the casinos."

"I had Mel hack in and check. They only have detectors for electronics, electromagnetics, and tight beam air and energy streams. Over the card table they have detectors for X-ray and microscopic scan lenses. Their detection technology is beyond state-of-the-art, at the level of top secret military prototypes."

"If they only knew what a human mind is capable of," Larry said in wonder.

"You are making great progress on your illusory body and in your dream work. Musash told me that you remained in the state of contemplation without lapse for three and a half hours, passing the test."

"When will we make our three-year three-month solitary meditation retreats?"

"Sometime when we are between nineteen and twenty-one years old," Electra answered. "I hope to start teaching part-time when I'm twenty-four, and make teaching my full-time vocation by the time I'm twenty-nine or thirty. I ought to be finished with my academic studies by then, and through all the practices."

"Are you any closer to formulating your new teachings?"

"They are percolating in our couple relationship and in our community interactions. They are integrally woven with the instrument of the spiritual congress, and accelerated to great velocity with entheogen elixir ceremonies. With the entheogen elixirs we can laugh at the ego duality of a subject who knows and an object that is known, and see beyond mind structure and schematization into the transcendental void."

"I love and admire you Electra. Supporting your life's work brings immeasurable meaning, value and purpose to my own. It is such an honor to be your consort."

"I'm so fond of you I could weep. Even your knobby knees endear you to me now that my heart is fully open to you."

Their soup bowls and appetizer dish was cleared from the table, more bread set out and more wine poured. The entrees were visual works of art with aromas you would need to be tied to the mast to resist. The flavors were almost a religious experience. The wine was the perfect enhancing compliment to the fish. The service was excellent and anxious to please, and the tab was on the house. It would be difficult for either of them to come up with a better dining experience even in the lucid dream state where anything is possible.

Their waitress received a 1,000-dag tip and so did the maître-d. Electra won over 10,000,000 dags at dice before returning to 21—though at a high stakes table—where she won 7,000,000 more. At this point Larry insisted that they take the multi-directional tubes to the tram station, and the tram to the Silicon Casino, which they did. The wine they drank was authentic fermented aged alcohol and not synthetic alko. So it did not wear off in half an hour, and inspired Electra to order a top-shelf cognac at the Silicon Casino.

She won eight million dags and some change at the 21 tables, then found her father's Space Invaders simulation game in this casino and strapped in. She'd mastered every level of this game by the time she was nine years old. She checked the simulator's log and discovered that no one had ever beaten the final level to win the 25 million dag jackpot. Electra took off and got right to work. She was in what her father called "the zone" and her mother referred to as the "flow-state". Electra was in the state of integrating the conventional reality of energy and movement with the Absolute reality of transcendental contemplation of clear light upon emptiness.

It looked to Larry like ten things were happening at once in each moment within the hologram, as space invader craft blew into clouds all over space. Electra's skullcap was at capacity unable to keep up with the number of brain cells operational in her head, so her dexterous little fingers were engaging manual joysticks with thumb button ordnance triggers at the same time as she fired munitions with thought impulses, aiming and maneuvering multiple spacecraft. Each of her hands equaled more than a full expert player in the game, and her skullcap had to count as at least three.

Levels zipped by and the gaming mainframe blew off sirens, bells, whistles and horns while flashing all manner of lights, causing quite an attraction among the wealthy patrons. A crowd gathered to watch as some of the most difficult challenges arose, even two at a time. Electra's skullcap was maxed out and her deft little hands a blur as the space invaders popped into expanding spheres across every sector of the hologram, too fast to catch but a piece at a time. The crowd was mesmerized.

The final battle had Electra's body kicking off thermal units of heat and a band of perspiration broke out at her hairline. Her face was relaxed displaying her typical half-smile, though her eyes were absolutely intense and alive with grim determination and infinite energy. Her hands were moving too fast to follow. The scoreboard was changing continuously and never resting upon a number to read. The tension in the crowd was a tangible thing and many were holding their breath. The excitement was becoming intolerable. An elderly woman fainted and was caught by her husband before hitting the ground.

In a great wave of explosions within the hologram, Electra demolished the last of the space invaders at the final level to win the jackpot. A siren like a fire-alarm was screaming out of the game's mainframe and blinding lights were twirling and probing intrusively all around. A twenty-foot hologram arose over the game exclaiming "WINNER!" in psychedelic pink letters. A 24-karat gold receipt was minted and spit out of the console into Electra's lap to wild cheers and applause of the crowd.

With her receipt in hand, Electra arose from the pilot seat and took Larry's hand. Larry raised her arm with his and Electra took a bow. The volume of her audience grew exponentially. She won 23 million at the high stakes dice table in the Silicon Casino. Then Larry dragged her through the Gold Rush Casino where she struck it rich. Next was Stump Tower Casino where she beat the house at 21, dice, and Wheel of Fortune for a total of 79 million dags from Stump's coffers. Larry escorted her to Hurrah Casino where she won a bunch more money, and after two more casinos, Electra figured she had enough for a yacht and a dream wedding ring calling it a night to take Larry to bed. It was actually mid-morning, though this could not be ascertained from the depths of the casinos.

Her full winnings of 227, 301,480 dags were safely electronically transferred to her own bank account on the planet Monarch which her father had opened for her. Coming out of the tube foyer in the hotel lobby, the manager waved them over to the desk-counter. They approached cautiously like guilty children caught in the act. The manager explained, "We have transferred your luggage to the penthouse compliments of the Platinum Bullion Hotel Casino. If you would open your coms device I'll send you your door code."

"Thank you. I'm shocked," Electra replied.

"The private lift to the penthouse is in the little foyer just to the right of the lifts alcove."

"That's so kind," Electra said gratefully. "Thank you."

Relieved they were not caught stealing a shuttle, a QAISHA, or cheating at the casino, the kids walked over to their private elevator and rode up to the penthouse of tower two of the hotel. It was a 16,000 square foot mansion in the clouds with polished jasper floors, marble bathrooms and tubs, a stainless steel kitchen, gold paneled bar and smoking parlor with recreational pharmacy, a simulation room with a trillion pixels. The living room had a jade fireplace and chimney. The family room was well-appointed and the hologram home-theater could seat 16 in simulation chairs with integrated skullcaps. The gym had everything. With a southern exposure and transparent ceiling, the solar room could greet the sun wherever it shone along its path.

The bedrooms were large and opulent. The master suite was simply luxurious. Many rooms they left unseen and unexplored. Electra cleaned her teeth then slipped naked between the 2,000 thread-count natural fiber sheets. She'd never felt anything like them. Larry wore his boxers and t-shirt to bed after showering and cleaning his teeth. Electra scooted over to snuggle him and decided to practice kissing.

With her lips centimeters from his she looked with yearning into his eyes willing him to kiss her. She sensed his paralysis and pinched his thin layer of flesh over his ribcage extending her half-smile into a broad grin. He grinned back self-consciously while leaning his head to bring their lips into contact, colliding noses, which Electra transformed into a gentle brush with a swift stretch of her neck. She didn't intend to push him all the way until their wedding night.

Lying relaxed in full body contact with sensitive kisses involving exploratory tongues was exhilarating as it was, and an experience worth basking in for its sensual pleasure. Electra soaked it up imprinting the first cracks towards the rupture of her innocence. She meant to harness the energy of the couple and the group energy of the community into spiritual instruments and entities attuned to the harmony and equilibrium of the spiritual congress. To amplify and accelerate awakening and ascent as a social movement.

She saw how the energy of the planetary meridians could be tapped for generating insight and how to connect with the solar procession alignments and galactic alignments for producing transcendence. Electra knew she is a wellspring of energy, love, awareness, presence, and will to realization with the responsibility to rain down her wellspring upon as many consciousness's as possible.

She needed experience, including negative seeds of future action to transmute into wisdom clarity and compassion. She had to fully understand the energies and potential of the couple and the group. There was much she had to learn and only life experience could provide this.

Romance was like floating naked on a warm lagoon in the sun and breathing in love with each breath. It seemed to tingle the surface of her skin, send little energy spasms up her spine, and splash over her with little waves of contentment. At moments she felt almost faint. Her love for Larry could catch her breath in her throat or fill her tummy with butterflies. Electra was amazed and relished the sheer enjoyment of it. The newness and mystery of the romance unfolding made it seem like total magic; like a holy blessing from on high. They fell asleep tangled together in love.

- Chapter 2 -

Following room service breakfast in bed, some martial arts and meditation, Electra and Larry dressed for some serious shopping. Electra had received a 108-karat diamond from the Tiffany System as a baby when her mother liberated that planet—along with more than a hundred eighty others—from the Kundabuffer Empire in the Hub Galaxy. She wore it with a tight pink dress and matching pink leather Lambergucci purse with shoulder strap. Her shiny hot pink stiletto heel shoes and platinum tiara that could function as a skullcap completed her outfit.

Larry wore a well-tailored three-piece suit, dark blue with pin-stripes, and matching leather shoes. He wore one emerald earring Electra gave him years ago. She still had the other one and it was safely packed in her little suitcase. They brought all the cash they'd started with, and their coms devices. Electra got lost trying to lead them out of the enormous penthouse to the lift, and Larry called up the penthouse schematics on his device's hologram to highlight the route. Electra made an about face to follow Larry to the lift.

Right in the hotel lobby they were able to purchase blasters. Electra got a tiny needle-blaster and thigh holster of soft leather. Larry got a sleek but heavy blaster pistol and a shoulder holster. He wore it out of the store loaded with a fresh power cell. There was no mistaking the bulge beneath his jacket. Though Electra's needle-gun was invisible beneath her dress, the holster chaffed her thigh when she walked. It had depressed her a little that only a preteen holster would fit snug around her narrow thigh.

After cramming her needle-gun into her purse and dropping the holster off at the front desk of the hotel, Electra said, "Let's walk to the retail arcade. It's not far."

Larry offered his hand nodding affirmation. Electra took it and they walked together. The sidewalk became elevated above street level to pass through a section of the Emperor's Palace Hotel with shopping for the rich. They checked out a jewelry store and several clothing stores. It was becoming painfully clear to Electra that she would have to have her clothing tailor-made since only children's clothes on the racks seemed to fit.

They found wedding rings they liked at a well-stocked jewelry store. Electra picked out a flawless blue diamond set on a platinum band. Larry got a gold wedding band. Any ring that could clear his knobby knuckle would necessarily hang loose on his ring finger. Even the jeweler was at a loss for a remedy for this. Electra finally decided that Larry's finger would simply have to grow to fill the ring, paying for it and thanking the jeweler.

They entered several more clothing stores, leaving disappointed, before finding a tailor of high quality. The shirts Larry had tried on were either too short in the sleeve or too big in the neck. They were each fitted for a number of outfits, including their wedding attire, which required a large additional fee to have ready within 24-hours. They needed shoes and other accessories so they continued on with their shopping spree.

After lunching at an oyster bar Electra chose, they went by hover-tram to the shuttle-port, and from there up to the yacht dealership space station in medium orbit of Vax Legas. A salesman was there to greet and help them. Electra informed him, "We need a small fast yacht with biotrays producing 100% oxygen-nitrogen needs to sustain eight people, and large enough vortex redirect and generation turbine for landing on planet surfaces with atmospheres."

"What price range are you interested in?"

I'd like to keep it under 200 million dags."

"Will you require a fully equipped kitchen and robotic refrigeration unit?"

"We certainly will. I intend to hire a tri-galaxies class chef."

"Are you more interested in opulence of the living space or the quality of the ship's systems and drives?"

"Definitely ship's systems and components."

"What kind of forcefield shield generators do you seek?"

"Top grade military without a doubt."

"Will you require weapons systems?"

"I need twin Class 8 blasters in the nose of the ship, a single Class 6 quad blaster turret on the underbelly, two batteries of sixteen canister smart-missiles, and undercarriage mounts for four jumbo missiles. A pair of anti-missile molten flare shield countermeasures would be nice."

The 108-foot Pershing is fast and can accommodate your specifications. It would come in just over your budget if you make no upgrades to the living quarters."

"Let's take a look at one," Electra enthused.

The salesman led the way to a hover-cart and assumed the driver's seat. Both Electra and Larry sat in the back snuggled into one another. The space station was diamond shaped like two step pyramids base to base, with yacht piers extending off each step. They had to go towards the center then up two levels to reach the yacht they wished to see. Larry was already perusing the design and spec's one handed with his coms device, his other hand and arm wrapped lovingly around Electra.

Upon arrival they got out of the cart to pass through both the station airlock and the yacht airlock. The interior was without upgrades, rather plain, sporting mostly white fiberglass armor surfaces. The hull was a solid six-inch thick steel-titanium-nickel. The armor was flimsy by military standards. Electra urged the salesman to show them the bridge. It had three seats, ample hologram pedestals, and a large canopy bubble viewport of transparent plasteel and synthetic diamond pane. After examining her piloting controls from the pilot seat, Electra stated with surprise, "There are only two swivel mini-drives and two swivel thrusters on the hull for turning."

"You'll find that this is standard on most yachts, ma'am."

"I see the launch booster but can find no other boosters."

"The launch booster comes standard. Any further boosters are optional upgrades."

"Why don't you give me the total with shields, weapons systems, two additional boosters and two more turning swivel-drives and thrusters," Electra suggested,

"You will also want to add galley equipment to the standard package to fully equip it."

"Yes. Add that too. I'll also require four more inches of adamantine and half an inch of carbon plate armor added."

"That would require replacing the composite ceramic heat shield armor that's on now."

"I know. Add that in."

"Now you're looking at over 270 million dags. Might I suggest the Space Fleet Surplus space station and refitting platform? I'm sure it would be cheaper to start with a hull to your requirements and upgrade component systems, since luxury accommodations clearly do not fit into your plans."

"That's a great idea!" Electra said with keen excitement. "Thank you. Is there a shuttle we can catch over to it?"

"The yacht station shuttle is at your disposal, ma'am."

On the way over to the industrial looking Space Fleet Surplus space station Electra's enthusiasm infected Larry with excitement. They were going to purchase and refit a warship! They studied the inventory in view on approach. Larry commented, "It's mostly old imperial ships from the war."

"They have some allied ships too," Electra pointed out.

"You're right. There's an Om Fast Attack Ship and I can see the stern of an Ahumdulilah Infiltrator Recon Ship."

"The Ahumdulilah ships have the most up to date cloaking systems. I don't want to buy one that sustained structural damage."

"There are hundreds of ships to choose from," Larry noted.

"This planet isn't part of 1US. It has peace treaties with them and resides within 1US territory. It is known as a black market planet and has perpetrated profiteering as the primary social value. They are also suspected of illegal salvaging and outright piracy."

"Hence all the war ships for sale," Larry reasoned.

"We'll be able to purchase munitions here too," Electra said with excitement.

The shuttle flew into open hanger doors, coming to rest for a minute in an airlock chamber for shuttles and tenders, before continuing into the hanger. The pilot dropped the ramp right in front of the main sales office door and the kids ran down to the hanger floor to enter the office. A less polished salesman greeted them with, "What do you kids want?"

Electra informed him, "We're shopping for a war ship we can refit and turn into a yacht."

"You're not old enough to fly one."

"We have a pilot and intend to hire staff and crew."

"Well, there's no age limit on buying stuff. What kind of war ship are you looking for?"

"Something fast but built to take a beating," Electra answered. "How much do your two-reactor ships go for?"

"You're talking a quarter to half a billion dags, depending on what the ship's got in it."

"What about ships in the 1.5 reactor range?"

"Now you're in the 175 to 300 million dag range."

"We better stick to the 1.25 reactor range then."

"Those run 135 to 260 million. I have 11 ships—seven different types—here on the docks I can show you."

"Can you give me a list of all eleven?" Electra asked.

"Is your coms device receptive?"

"Yes."

"I'm sending it now."

"Thank you."

Larry leaned his head in close to Electra's to examine the ships. She had a small holo of each showing within the six-foot diameter maximum hologram her coms device could generate. The damages sustained and the repairs made were documented for each ship. This eliminated six of them for having taken structural damage. One of the five remaining was 60 million dags over her budge. Two were imperial ships she didn't really like. She told the man, "I want to see both of these."

"You have an eye for a bargain little missy."

Electra didn't appreciate being called 'little missy'. Larry was a bit offended by that title as well. The man led them to a tube foyer and set the destination for them. He was a bit surprised when they both got in the same tube together. In quantum age culture the personal space several inches beyond the skin was not to be violated, so lifts had partitions and tubes were meant for one passenger. He met them only a minute later, coming in the next tube. They passed through two airlocks to enter the ship. Electra insisted, "I want to inspect the drives and reactors first."

"You seem to know what you're about. Just follow me."

Larry read to Electra from his hand device, "This is a 370-foot Ahumdulilah-built Scout Recon ship, originally with only one reactor. They have added a .25 reactor equivalent, solarium fusion trickle-charge battery system to enhance shields and drives. It can accommodate a crew of 36 personnel. There's room in the hanger for a pair of combat shuttles and a tender. The hull is ten inches thick and it has four and a half feet of armor. It has full cloaking, already state of the art. Although it was built a few years before we were born, it was completely overhauled and refitted less than eleven years ago for the war against the Royal Monarch Empire."

They were led into the drives chamber first. Electra grabbed some tools from a board on the bulkhead and got busy removing the casing over the core of one of the two main space drives. She was trying to be careful of her pink dress. Larry helped. The salesman watched impressed. When they got the casing off, she removed a small component of the core for close examination. She declared her finding, "This drive is in remarkably good shape for being sixteen years old."

"The drives are practically brand new. This ship has not moved except to test the drives and systems since the battle of Monarch."

"Let me get this back together and we'll have a look at the quantum drive."

"Whatever you say. You'll find it in the same mint condition."

"How come you're letting it go so cheap?"

"The real money is in the super-cruisers and super-battleships. Most of our clientele consists of politicians and military leaders who seem to admire the biggest ships. There's now salvaging opening up in two galaxies connected by a star-bridge called BiVortex, and we need more room on the docks for big ships. It's kind of a clearance sale on the small ones."

Electra took the casing off several sections of the quantum drive and removed key parts to scrutinize. She inspected the reactors thoroughly, then the shield generators and Vortex Redirect and Generation Turbine, always getting into the guts and innards. The quantum computer was one of the older models, though it could easily be enhanced. The quantum navigation computer was adequate for the time being. The weapons systems were beyond her wildest dreams. Environmental had more capacity than they would need and little wear on components. Air, water and methane tanks were all sound. The ship's systems checked out. It had a water recycle and purification plant which worked at the atomic level, and it had an industrial size molecular food synthesizer in the galley. After insisting on observing a full active-scan of the hull, Electra decided to purchase the ship.

"I would like to purchase this Scout Recon ship. Would you include full missile and torpedo magazines, full canister missile batteries, full thruster fuel cells and boosters, topped off water, air and methane tanks, and complete time-sequenced bio-trays from germination to fully mature?"

"That would run you a little extra. You also might want to add a tender, and perhaps a pair of combat shuttles. Then there's medical and food supplies, hygiene products, bedding, furniture and instillation, bio-tray materials, extra thruster fuel cells, munitions and reloads, plus any interior decorating you would like to do."

"How much over the 205 million are we talking about?" Electra asked.

"For all of it? Probably about 90 million dags. You could forget about the combat shuttles and the rest—if the interior decorating is modest—would run you 25 to 30 million over."

"I'll put fifty million down on it right now, and pay the remainder tomorrow morning before my wedding."

"You'd better bring an adult pilot when you come to collect your ship, Lassy."

Electra didn't like 'Lassy' any better than "little missy'. To her, it sounded like something one might name their pet. She told him, "My pilot will be with us."

Now she would need to pay close to 1.5 million dags to get her stolen QAISHA, who she called Captain Caish, a skin job. She would have his latex skin replaced with syntec touch-perfect skin. It is top of the line and very expensive. With this enhancement no one would know that Caish is an android. She put Larry onto finding an android alteration shop and making an urgent appointment while she wired 50-million dags to the account code she'd received of the Space Fleet Surplus Company. Electra and Larry represented only small change to this multi-trillion dag enterprise. She got a hard copy and electronic receipt for her down payment. She gave instructions for interior upgrades and remodeling in the sleeping cabins, galley and mess hall, which included the removal of a couple internal bulkheads to open up the space.

They were shuttled down to Vice in a large cargo shuttle that smelled of drives parts. Larry had an appointment made for Caish at 4:00 pm capital time and informed him over coms. Electra led them into the Carnival Casino where she knew they had her dad's space invaders game with a 30-million dag jackpot. The last casino with the game had doubled the challenge at the end, though Electra had been on such a roll and in such a state that she beat it anyway. She was certain that neither casino paid her father royalties nor had purchased rights to the game. Those rights specified that no alterations could be programmed at any level.

Once she located her objective, she took the control seat and fed the mainframe ten one-ounce gold coins. She selected her favorite bomber as her avatar after checking to make sure no alterations had been made to its abilities. Then she did the same in selecting her bomber wing. The AI default for her additional bombers was incapable of beating the challenges, so Electra would fly her own and two others through her skullcap, plus a bomber with each hand on a joystick. She had mastered a meditation of multifaceted concentration through her monastic work, and had applied this in leading the spiritual congress to support Pez Fleet in the BiVortex Galaxies. She certainly felt ready to beat a game program. Larry stood tensely behind her watching.

Electra cruised through the first four levels as if they'd been designed for toddlers, and the mainframe lights and sounds intensified as she went. Level five hardly gave her a snag, and level six but meek resistance. It was not until the final level that Electra was truly challenged. New programming protected the jackpot with triple the challenge. Electra was drawing on everything she had with about every brain cell active, and managed to tap into the 100-year meditation of the Amonrahonians. Her thumbs and hands moved in a blur and sweat dripped from her brow, while space invaders blew five at once, six times per second, clouding the space within the hologram. Her half-smile tightened into a tight line of adamantine will and determination. Her skullcap was sucking up electricity beyond its capacity. The mainframe was illuminating the entire casino and sounding off like an air raid drill. The crowd was shoulder to shoulder packed in around the game and just kept crushing in.

When the explosions faded only Electra's avatar was left in the hologram and the mainframe announced a jackpot winner with its own giant hologram projected over it to the high ceiling. A platinum receipt, redeemable for 30-million dags popped out from the machine into Electra's hands. Someone was losing their job upstairs while she cashed out and had her winnings transferred to her account. Winning this jackpot was not supposed to be remotely possible.

Electra went to the High Roller Casino next and beat the house at 21 for 10-million dags. At the Emerald Palace Electra won 14-million dags at the high stakes dice table. Satisfied that she would now be able to get all the extras plus one combat shuttle, Electra suggested they quit gambling and go eat at their favorite restaurant. Larry was quite agreeable but had a concern he felt compelled to mention to Electra. He said meekly, "I felt you enlist the force of the

Amonrahonians in their 100-year meditation in your gaming."

"You are very perceptive, discerning and sensitive Larry. I did enlist them because I needed their help."

"Sarhi and your mother would be furious, given the purpose."

"I do feel somewhat guilty about it, and hope the long view proves it necessary."

"How are we going to get the Om Ambassador's shuttle back to Mother?"

"Why don't you place an ad on the computer interface for a Motherling pilot who wants a free ride home plus a cash payment for his or her time? That would save us a trip."

"Have you ever piloted a ship before?"

"In the simulator I have."

"Do you think we should hire a pilot?"

"No. We have Captain Caish. I'd prefer to hire a chef."

"Can Caish actually pilot the ship?"

"QAISHA's are designed to pilot, maintain and repair ships, as well as cook, launder, and take care of a crew's needs. We just need to download the programming for piloting the obsolete Scout Recon Ship from Ahumdulilah system of the White Lotus Galaxy."

Larry was already on his device with his skullcap as they walked to the Platinum Bullion Hotel Casino where the restaurant is located. After almost a minute of silence he stated anxiously, "The programming you want is stored in the Ahumdulilah Space Fleet central computer protected by a digital fortress."

"I'll think of something."

Walking felt great after the tensions of the games in the casinos. Some food was necessary because Electra had burned off all her fuel and even some much needed fat with her concentration in the space invaders game. Electra filtered out the glaring lights and loud volume of noise. She turned all audio impressions into the white sound of rapids, and all external lights into an incomprehensible swirl. She remained centered in the point three finger-widths below her navel, aware of her equilibrium and kinesthetic sense. No thoughts could take hold in this state.

They entered their hotel and had to cross the entire lobby to the restaurant lifts. It was well enough before the dinner hour that they were the only ones at the lifts. One was waiting and had its doors open. They stepped on into a warm embrace, ignoring the partitions. The lift shot up 112 floors in a quarter as many seconds leaving their stomachs behind. They were still finding their legs as they got off. At the restaurant they were once again shown to the Extremely Important Person table. They remembered not to order wine, having ice tea instead.

Electra got her hand device out of her purse and contacted Mel. "Hi Mel, this is Electra."

"I can see that. What do you need sweetheart?"

"I need the QAISHA pilot programming for the 370-foot obsolete Scout Recon Ahumdulilah ship, and I need it within 14 hours."

"Just what are you up to, sweetie?"

"I'm buying a war ship as my personal yacht, but I have to have an adult pilot. I have a barrowed QAISHA who's currently having a skin job to pass for human. It would really help if he knew how to pilot the ship."

"Is he cute?"

"Mel!!!"

"Sorry. I just know your mother is going to be furious with me but I'm accessing the file now and will upload it to you in moments. Where in the universe did you get the money to purchase a war ship?"

"Gambling."

"You're certainly in the right place for that."

"How's mom doing?"

"Sarhi's dragging her to formal ceremonies of state in each of the BiVortex Galaxies. Her last appearance is tomorrow night. She had wanted to introduce you to the people of the twin galaxies, and thinks they're going to really need you."

"I'll be sure to go there when I begin my teaching phase of life."

"Your parents want you both to finish school."

"We will. Right after winter break we'll go back. As soon as we graduate from our Academy's we are going to get an apartment together, and that's where we'll live while we complete university. Somewhere in there we're going to make our three-year meditation retreats at our respective monasteries. When I take the telomerase drug for reversing human aging at 24 years old, I'll begin teaching part-time. Larry and I are living our romantic dream. We need a brief sabbatical to accomplish this. I need to understand a few things so that spiritual couples can be harnessed like the spiritual congress."

"May I transmit this data to your parents?"

"Yes; though withholding the location until mom has finished her last appearance tomorrow night."

"How much are you paying for the Scout Recon ship?"

"The ship itself is 205 million dags, but with a space combat shuttle, tender, supplies, munitions and materials, plus a little remodeling, it comes to 260-million dags."

"How do you win?"

"I sense the values of the face-down cards, and I move the dice or wheel of fortune ball with telekinesis. I also employ my training and years of practice with dad's space invaders game. By the way, you must let him know that his game has been pirated in Vice casinos on Vax Legas. They have doubled and tripled the challenge in the final level to protect the jackpot."

"I'll pass that along to him tomorrow night."

"Thanks Mel. How is Haley?"

"She's fine now, at home in her new android body. Your mom and Admiral Bodhi are keeping us both awful busy."

"Thanks so much for the program, Mel."

"Please don't mention it. I mean seriously, not to anyone ever."

"I read you Mel. Mom will never know about it."

"Do take care, angel. I love you."

"I love you too Mel."

Larry asked, "When will Caish be back from his pre-paid alteration appointment?"

"He ought to be back in the Ambassador Shuttle by 6:30 or 7:00."

"Is he able to handle his own download?"

"Of course; and I've already transmitted the program to the shuttle's computer."

"Don't we need witnesses to get married?"

"Two as a matter of fact. Antic from Glitter and super-agent Green from Ganahar are both checking into our hotel this evening. Mother gave each of them the drug for reversing human aging, and they are in a couple together now."

"Green is your mother's agent. Surely, she'll tell her our whereabouts."

"I invited her to our wedding on the condition that she doesn't tell, and she decided it would be better for her to be around to help us than to leave us undefended to be true to my mother."

"I feel safer already."

"Me too. Here, eat some more oysters and finish your shark fin soup."

Larry did as he was directed. Electra was priming him for their wedding night. The moment the last oyster disappeared into Larry's mouth, the dishes were cleared. A moment later their entrees appeared. Electra had a large salmon steak with whipped cream and dill weed, hoping to put some fat on her bottom and breasts. Larry had a seafood platter with a broiled lobster tail, pan seared scallops, sautéed jumbo shrimp, and boiled crab legs. His meal came with surgical instruments and a bib. His elbows were at times lethal threats. Electra's pristine attention to the present moment enabled her to tilt her head from harm's way as required.

Antic entered the dining room in an evening gown and strode over to their table to perform a unique combo curtsey-bow, leaving her near horizontal the floor and extended on one leg at precarious angle smiling. As she straightened and got her other foot on the ground she said, "Congratulations! If you were my daughter, I'd be urging you to consider a prolonged engagement."

"I need to have certain experiences and witness some stuff soon to develop and formulate my teachings. I've had to take on a bit of the fuel of negative consequences to gain sufficient velocity in my preparation."

"We all understand, darling. Your mother wants me to pass on that there is a limit she forbids you to cross again, and that's tapping the energy of the Anonrahonian's 100-year meditation for personal schemes and adventures. She says that if you need money, you have only to ask Mel and Ahhu.”

“How did she know?”

Sarhi and your mother are both linked tight with the base of the spiritual congress. Your mother is the channel of its force, and apparently the safety valve for releasing dangerous levels of pressure via ‘events’.”

“Where’s Green?”

“She’s around. She’s been shadowing you guys since you first hit the 21 table at the Platinum Bullion Casino.”

“Don’t bet on the dice tables or Wheel of Fortune. They are rigged at every casino.”

“How did you win at Wheel of Fortune?”

“I hopped the ball into red just before it came to rest from their hop with the multi-directional gyroscopic impulse in the center of the ball.”

Larry added, “She had the same battles with their loaded dice.”

“I assume you can somehow read the face down cards in the 21 game?”

“I can.”

“And you needed the Amonrahonian’s help to beat a program designed to be absolutely unbeatable?”

“With their help I kicked ass.”

“What are you going to do with all the money?”

“I bought a scout recon warship. It is 370 feet long and Ahumdulilah-built. It is suped-up with an additional quarter-reactor equivalent fusion trickle charge battery system. The ship is in almost uncirculated condition. I’m doing a little interior decorating and I’m having it armed and supplied. I’m also going to ask Rear Admiral Spalding for a few ship and computer parts.”

“Will you have a tender or shuttle?”

"A yacht tender and a combat shuttle."

"I hope you're not planning on starting a war."

"Not at all. The ship will be handy when I need to travel and teach. Besides that, it's going to be a whole lot of fun. Maybe you and Green can help me pick it up in the morning."

"That would be our pleasure. I'm quite curious to see it."

"I'll give you the grand tour."

Larry took a call on his coms device, "Hello? Yes, I placed the ad... The pay is one thousand dags and the shuttle has just been serviced at the hotel... We were hoping to get the shuttle headed back to Mother in the Whirlpool Galaxy by 9:00 am tomorrow morning, Vice capital time... Alright, we'll meet you at the shuttle in the hotel hanger at nine. Thank you."

"Who was that?" Electra inquired.

"A guy named Yozzy from Mother. He says he's a mini-freighter pilot who got stranded when the shipping company he worked for went bankrupt. He wants to get home and will meet us at our shuttle in the morning at nine."

"I guess we can see him off then go pick up our ship."

"He can drop us off at the Space Fleet Surplus space station."

"Have you checked his credentials and references?"

"I'm doing it now."

Super-agent Green, five foot two inches and thin, came into the dining room and joined them at the EIP table. She said, "Congratulations Electra and Larry. Do you realize you've come to a nest of smugglers, pirates, black marketers and gangsters?"

"Everyone has been real nice so far," Electra commented.

"Six casinos have put together the face, name and current residence of the person who won 273 million dags betting against the house in one night."

"We bought blaster pistols and in the morning and we're picking up a warship."

"That is most prudent, but it's your wedding ceremony that worries me. You'll be vulnerable."

"I can afford to hire security."

"Hiring them here would not be a good idea."

"What do you suggest?"

"Amazonia can be here within three hours with forty warrior maidens from Mother. They are loyal and trustworthy, not to mention free, though you would have to pay to put them up at the hotel."

"She would tell my mother."

"I'm sure she's more concerned with your safety than whatever is going on between you and your parents."

"Alright. If she won't tell my parents where I am, ask her to come."

"I will. The corporate owners here on Vax Legas think you know too much, and are aware of your connection with the 1US Chancellor, Vegan Casper. A word from you could bring down three galaxies of trouble on them."

Maybe that's why we're in the penthouse and received a complimentary 30,000 dag bottle of wine. Our meals are free too."

"Then we'll join you for desert and stimulant brew."

"Great. They have a dark chocolate decadence cake you'll have to taste to believe."

"I can't wait. Larry, how are you coping with this tide of change?"

"I'm managing. Being close to Electra makes it all worth it; even being a fugitive."

"Oh, sweetheart, I can see that your conscience has been bothering you, you poor dear. I assure you that no major transgressions have been made, and certainly none by you. Electra has some general idea about what she's doing. I promise you that Pez won't be in the least upset with you, and nor will Sarhi or Musash."

"Thank you for that, Green. Your words do bring me some relief."

"You're just caught up in the whirlwind of the Mu; an innocent victim."

"A permanent one," Electra added, "because I'm never letting him go."

"I'm sure nothing could make him happier."

Larry nodded grinning his full agreement. Electra remarked, "Romantic love is some pretty crazy stuff."

Green concurred, "It can drive one to barrow a shuttle and a QAISHA, run off to a gangster economy, direct spiritual powers to win at gambling, and purchase a warship to elope in."

"It is a power we need to harness for awakening and ascent," Electra insisted. "I've found no other force in this life remotely as potent."

"Evenrude would really like to come to your wedding," Green mentioned.

"He's my mother's champion and would definitely tip her off."

"He wouldn't, and I think it would hurt his feelings to be left out."

"He's really sentimental for an elite hardened warrior," Electra considered aloud. "He's always a bunch of fun to be around."

"Please consider inviting him, and empathize with his feelings. He has known you since you first started gestating."

"Alright, but I don't have formal invitations or anything."

Mel's voice sounded in Electra's ear, "I made you some and they're on your hand device home page. Just send a thought impulse to the little horn icon and it will open."

Electra got out her coms device and opened the page. It was printed in Om formal font on an intricate background design and bore the Mother's Guardians Monastery watermark. She told Mel, "It is a work of art Mel! You're so talented."

"Thank you. I hoped you would like it."

"I'm saving it to my scrapbook. Say, Mel, would you be our official hologramographer for the wedding?"

"I'd love to."

"Can you hack control of the hotel sensors in the wedding hall?"

"I already control all quantum computer systems including security and administrative functions within your hotel. Your penthouse has 218 optic/audio sensors hidden in walls and ceilings."

"How many in the cheap room we started in?"

"Only one and it is of poor quality."

"That must be why they gave us the penthouse."

Green suggested, "The hotel permits you to have 16 staff and four guests in the penthouse, so Amazonia's warrior maidens not on duty will stay there. Those on duty will be at posts, roving, or monitoring the command center we're setting up in my suite."

"It sounds like an awful lot of resources for wedding security," Electra commented.

"I don't think you appreciate the danger you're in, sweetheart."

"I'll go along with it. I'm just saying."

"Evenrude will be your body guard and go everywhere you go except the water closet and your bedroom. We'll keep you safe until you are out the Vax Legas snake pit."

"They don't actually admire mom, do they?"

"There is no greater terror in this universe for them than your mother."

"I wish I hadn't mentioned it to them, but we would have been turned away from the restaurant otherwise."

Green explained, "Gangsters like to bring their enemies in close with faux kindness and generosity to lower their guard and keep an eye on them."

"The wage-earning staff give off an authentic vibe of respect and admiration."

"I'm sure everyone who works for a living appreciates your mother's role in bringing down the Royal Monarch Empire. Under their rule workers were perpetually on the edge of starvation."

"I want cognac with my desert instead of stimulant brew. The real stuff, aged fifty years from the top shelf," Electra declared.

"I think I'll join you," Green said with excitement at the prospect.

When the waitress came over all four of them decided on dark chocolate decadence cake and the oldest finest cognac in the restaurant. Larry ordered in addition a triple-shot stimulant brew in steamed half& half with bitter-sweet chocolate powder sprinkled on top. Electra stated to Larry, "You don't have a single living relative to attend our wedding."

"Well, none of yours will be there either."

"This is true," she conceded.

"I invited Sarhi and she is like my adopted mother," Larry told her.

"You did what?!" Electra stated alarmed.

"She'll never tell your mother. She never tells her anything."

"I *have* heard mom complain about that quite a bit," Electra admitted.

"She offered to perform the ceremony, but in the Islohar tradition a chaperone accompanies the newlyweds to bed to provide instruction."

Electra said thoughtfully, "That might be a good thing since we haven't had time to hire you a sex worker."

Larry said anxiously, "I think it would be terribly embarrassing."

"I need to learn fast. If it's too much for you I'll understand, and we'll study the ancient texts. I've already done quite a bit of research."

Larry admitted, "I've been studying the ancient 64 positions, the ancient sexology and alchemy, and contemporary techniques and location for the P-spot and clitoris. I found some daily exercises for male sexual control in the ancient sexology."

"Did you learn about the vortex point just in front of the prostate gland, for preserving your bioenergy?"

"No."

"You can have orgasms without any ejaculation, and so preserve your internal energy. You don't get depleted and it cuts your refractory period shorter by more than half."

"I have to press it during orgasm?" Larry asked.

"I'll press it for you. That will help me tune into you completely," Electra offered.

"I'm in your holy hands."

Green shared, "Larry is so like your father, Electra."

"I know. He's the sweetest boy I've ever met, and he sure is cute."

"You are both so adorable together."

"Sometimes I can barely keep myself from jumping him. He's accelerating his development to keep up," Electra stated.

Green agreed, "He sure is. Just don't outpace yourself sweetie."

Electra replied, "Girls mature faster than boys, and I'm almost five months older than him. I like younger men."

"More of a man in the making," Green reframed. "You must give him a little wiggle room to grow up."

"I love him so much I could forgive him anything. Just like in the lucid dream work where you generate all beings as deities, in sex you're supposed to generate your partner as a deity. I've been practicing—though not the sex part yet."

"I'm sure you'll have him skilled enough to perform as your action seal in no time, Electra."

"The work with the action seal," Electra stated, "is the surest way to contemplate the Ultimate Clear-Light. Many traditions would claim that it is the only way short of working the transference of consciousness at the moment of death."

"Your mother performed as your father's action seal, enlightening him, just before you were conceived."

"I've heard the story and find it embarrassing."

"I'm only pointing out that sex provides you a special method for enlightening Larry, who is to be your consort."

"I need to learn how first."

"I'm sure you've already memorized the instructions for the practice," Green said.

"Yes, but I've never actually applied them or done it."

"Stay connected to Larry's heart, find the knots in his heart channel wheel and absorb them into yourself, as if inhaling them, liberate the stuck energy on retention of breath, understand its nature and consequence of psychic wound on your exhalation; then retaining no breath, transmit the wisdom-clarity back to Larry replacing the fears and emotionally charged beliefs, attachments and identifications. When you master this, you will learn how to transfer merit."

"Thanks. I'll try that while we're snuggling in bed tonight."

"Your unexpected leadership of the spiritual congress in the battle of Randu has charged you with immeasurable energy of potential to become a powerful external influence," Green informed Electra. "Keep this in mind because you might be a bit much for Larry's delicate nervous system."

"Are you suggesting that I might cause an 'event'?!"

"You've been equally exposed as your mother at this point, and I might add, equally charged up."

"What terrible news,"

"The spiritual congress now encompasses nine galaxies and close to two trillion proficient meditators. After a war of such magnitude and concentrated synergistic sessions of such length and intensity, the entity that is the spiritual congress will need to depressurize and blow off steam, so to speak, in finding its equilibrium."

"Is my mother causing events in BiVortex?"

"Sarhi has kept her too busy to do anything but sleep in her bed since the war ended."

"Well tell Sarhi to let my mother have a sleep over celebration already. I'm surprised Ahhu hasn't instigated one yet."

"Your mom assigned Ahhu the task of arranging for your security discretely the moment you left Mother in the Om Ambassador's shuttle."

"We're having it returned in the morning, and I'll write a letter of apology to the Ambassador."

"The QAISHA belongs to the Ambassador from Pronotavasmi."

"I'll write a letter to him too, and offer monetary compensation for the loan of Captain Caish. He's the friendliest male android I've ever met, and a real fast learner. I'll explain that I require his services for a bit longer."

"Sweetheart, Captain Caish is a diplomatic courier and secret agent. He's carrying vital top- secret data of a very sensitive nature, and the Ambassador would really like him back."

"We will download all such data onto a data-bead and send the bead with the shuttle tomorrow back to Mother. I need to hang onto Captain Caish till after winter break."

Evenrude is sending an eight-man squad in hard-shell space combat suits aboard that shuttle. A wing of Pronotavasmi Tsunami Devastator heavy bombers, each with two drone fighter-bombers controlled from the cockpit will escort the shuttle."

"Larry, did our shuttle pilot, Yozzy, check out?"

"As far as I could tell. I found a record of the real Yozzy's DNA so we could do a quick DNA test in the hanger in the morning with the pilot who shows up."

Green offered, "That won't be necessary. He's actually an Ahumdulilah Intelligence Agent alerted to assist Electra if opportunity presents itself. He's fully vetted."

"Who alerted him?" Electra demanded to know.

"Ahhu had a little chat with General Nicon, who is now the Director of all Ahumdulilah Intelligence Services, and he's a friend of your mother's. He alerted all agents in the field on Vax Legas as a curtesy to the Mu."

"Do they have many agents here?" Electra asked.

"Vax Legas is the cesspool and pit of corruption of all three galaxies of this cluster: Royal, Whirlpool, and White Lotus. You can be sure that Ahumdulilah and Monarch watch it closely. I'll bet Zandarhar does too."

Electra said, "I heard that 1US made contact with a blue-sun Kluzzyst genus interstellar civilization."

"They have, and Pez put them in touch with the Kluzzyst beings in the Xegachtznel Galaxy. It is the news of the year, along with the successful end of the war in BiVortex Galaxies."

Evenrude and Johnson strode into the dining room with unconcealable military bearing. At eight feet tall with a barrel chest and adamantine muscles bulging through his dress uniform, Evenrude looked serious and purposeful. Right up until he made eye contact with Electra, who ran up and leaped so high that Evenrude's feet left the ground to catch her by the hips. She was giggling when he landed, shaking the tables, as he pulled her into his chest for a hug. Electra was truly delighted to see him. She didn't know that he'd brought two platoons of Space Marines and two Space Marine Combat Shuttles with him, besides bringing Johnson.

Both men took seats at the EIP table, filling them completely. They are white sun humans, and even large for that. Evenrude leaned over to whisper to Green, "The command center is set up and operational. Mel controls everything computer operated within this hotel, and she's busy hacking her way around the globe. My Space Marines are in position and will keep a combat shuttle over Electra at all times. Amazonia has entered the system with 40 warrior maidens who will be stationed within the hotel. Sarhi is on her way and ought to arrive within the hour."

Green told him, "I've made contact with the field directors of Ahumdulilah and Monarch Intelligence Services here, and the Cultural Attaché from the Zandarhar Embassy here in Vice. He told me they would never allow anything unpleasant to happen to the Mu."

"So they're not exactly working *with* us, though they are on our side?"

"They don't like Om's CIA, and frankly, neither does Pez. They also seem a little concerned over the extent of the Ahumdulilah Intelligence Service. They keep to themselves, but sometimes share information over coms."

"Through you, I see."

"I am the agent of the Wu. They like me."

"I almost forgot; Aton is on the way with eight Clear Light knights. The knights will be stationed in Antic's suite and Aton plans to do a little snooping around the city."

"Who ought we have man the quad blaster turrets on Electra's Scout Recon ship?" Green inquired.

"Not to worry. High Admiral Swenah is sending her 12 top-rated gunners to the Space Fleet Surplus space station to arrive just after we do."

Then of all people, Kristy came skipping through the dining room wearing tights, a tight t-shirt and cheap canvas/rubber running shoes, just steps ahead of the maître-d chasing her. She caught Electra's eye to go into a sprint spreading her arms. Electra jumped up and grabbed her in a hug. She told Electra, "I've invited myself to your wedding."

"I'm glad you did. I hope you didn't tell Winn or Bodhi because then it would get back to my mother."

"Only Ahhu knows I'm here."

Green commented, "You girls look the same age."

Electra supported this saying, "You do look thirteen, Kristy."

"I was only 22 when they gave me the telomerase drug, and only later found out that it's better to wait until age 24."

Electra said, "Look, my breasts are almost as big as yours."

"That's like saying they're almost small," Kristy tried to explain.

"I'm so glad you came. Maybe we can go shopping together before the wedding."

"I hope you've already been fitted for your gown."

"I have, and it will be ready before noon tomorrow."

"That's a relief," Kristy told her as she went to hug Larry.

She told him, "Congratulations sweetheart. You've got your hands full, but it's what you were born and bred for. We didn't think she would have the recognition so young."

"Thanks Kristy. It is good to see you. You are like a wise friend our own age."

"If she weren't the Mu, I'd be telling you to be jealous and keep an eye on me because I might try to steal her away."

"Then I'm most grateful she is the Mu. Electra is so beautiful I could cry."

"I think you're both beautiful and hot, but by conventional standards you are both outside the normative distribution. I know, because I am too. If you accept yourself and make relations kindly, you will be liked and appreciated, and appear more attractive to others."

"Electra is the true form of beauty within the divine ideas of the Nous, or divine mind. She is continuously alert and present at each moment, even when she's lost and going the wrong way. Conventional reality might get by her and trip her up, but she never loses sight of the clear light upon absolute transcendental emptiness. It's uncanny."

Kristy suggested, "You better fasten your seatbelt and get ready for launch, because she's going to take you high fast, and the law of communicating vessels is going to cause the blessings to rush in under pressure, near drowning you."

"It's already been happening."

"I can see it in your eyes. I could feel her presence as soon as I entered the dining room. You're so perfect for her."

I often feel inadequate and inferior as a man."

"Her love will cure that, and she'll learn to take on your psychic wounds to transmute them within herself, relieving you of such painful nonsense and delusion."

"Do you really think I'm alright as a male?"

"I'm not into guys at all, but I think you're so hot I'd do it with you any time. You're gorgeous honey."

Electra said with a hint of offense to Kristy, "That's my fiancé you're flirting with."

"Electra, I find you beyond enticing and capturing—like an inevitable overpowering tractor-beam—and would give or do anything for a fling under the sheets with you. Honestly, I think you're both hot. And you needn't worry because I have ample sex partners. As I told Larry, I'm able to constrain myself since you're the Mu. Also, because your mother is my teacher's teacher. Then there's your age. Truly, you haven't a thing to worry about from me."

Electra told her, "I've never had a worry and I feel the attraction. The vortex-pull of this one," Electra said getting her arms around Larry, "pulls me from my orbit completely."

Mel reported in Electra's ear casually, "The invitations have gone out, and I had to lease the biggest hall here at the hotel. I leased the banquet hall and ballroom too. The restaurant on the 112th floor is doing the catering."

"Who did you invite?! Electra asked panicked.

"Oh, just a few friends of the family honey, and folks who would be sorely offended not to be included."

"Mel!! This is supposed to be an elopement!"

"The guests have all sworn not to tell your parents, and they've been warned to come armed. I promise they'll be no trouble at all, sweetheart, and they will add to your security."

Electra turned to Larry and asked him, "Have you come to a decision about accepting Sarhi's offer to perform the Islohar ceremony?"

"Since you want to do it, and it seems most fitting for the Mu, I'm on board with doing it that way. I actually want to."

"You are so accommodating my beloved. Thank you."

"Thank you, Electra. What you bring to our relationship is invaluable and the greatest of blessings."

Green received a text then leaned into Evenrude to tell him, "Duatarim Intelligence is right now setting agents on Vax Legas. One will be joining us shortly."

Electra said, "Let's bring this bottle of cognac into the smoking parlor so we can have a smoke while we finish it."

Antic informed her, "It sells for 90 dags per shot at the restaurant's bar."

"It sure is smooth," Electra said with appreciation.

They all got up and moved to the restaurant's smoking salon to a long table beneath two funnel vents. A waitress appeared the moment they were seated. All had brought their brandy snifters from the dining room table with them. Their waitress asked, "Is there anything I can get you?"

Electra spoke up and told her, "We need a packet of rolled cigarettes with filters, a quarter ounce of hybrid seedless cannabis, a gram of blond Turkamon hashish, your best cigars all around, and a gram of synthetic DMT that can be smoked."

Two vaporizer hookahs, each with four stems, adorned the table, along with ashtrays, various tools resembling surgical and watch making instruments, and both matches and lighters—some of these more like blow-torches. Each table in the room was similarly appointed, and each was under one or two funnel vents depending upon length of the tables. The lighting was dim and a small smoke-shop bar adorned one wall. The vents over the tables were all shiny brass and provided quite a bit of suction.

Their waitress returned with a tray and Electra signed her name and room number with a stylus adding a tip. Green asked, "Since when did you take up smoking?"

"I actually have never smoked anything yet in my life," Electra admitted, "but I mean to try it out."

"The items you ordered reflect the seasoned discernment of an old pro."

"I'm just copying Ahhu," Electra said honestly.

Kristy was already packing a bowl with cannabis and hashish, and she put some DMT on the top before passing a stem to Electra. She closed the vaporizer chamber. Electra, Larry, Kristy and Antic sucked on pipe stems then held their breaths. Evenrude, Johnson and Green would not be smoking, although Green did have a snifter of the cognac. The three of them were on duty working. Green was certain Electra would be her primary mission until the Mu grew out of her teens.

The Duatarim agent assigned to the couple was Becky. At nineteen years old Becky was an intelligence agent, ace combat spacecraft pilot and hero of the revolution in BiVortex. She had been the secretary to the CEO of the largest corporation of the Dominari Conformity Empire before becoming a revolutionary. In the former empire in BiVortex, women had been property. Secretaries had been selected for beauty and eroticism. Mind control and state-run terror had held it all together for many millenniums; right up until Pez showed up with an allied fleet. Now it was gone completely and a process of healing and reorganization was under way.

Green stood to embrace Becky, then Evenrude did. Becky told them, "I'm permanently assigned to the Mu. Rann is on the team too."

"My cadet agents of the Wu," Green stated delighted.

"I guess we'll be working with you, and hopefully be training under you full-time."

"Are you disappointed that you are not with Pez?"

"She's been booked solid at formal ceremonial events and stuffy dinner parties; all tediously boring stuff. I hear Electra's on a rampage."

"Following Electra is certainly where the action is," Green agreed.

"I'm told there is room in the Scout Recon's hanger for another space shuttle. Rann and I have a Duatarim hyper-courier shuttle in the hotel hanger, you're going to love."

Green asked, "Does it have a quantum drive?"

"Of course."

"Then I want you flying escort until we're out of the Monarch Galaxy."

"What are the Mu's plans?"

"I'm not sure she makes 'plans' exactly. She's not returning to school for about five weeks. She's calling it a sabbatical. I know she wants to go to Glitter next and try to get on *Star Hunt*."

"That show is all about who you know. Hoola might be able to pull a few strings."

"Electra has Whiffle getting the Whirling Vortexes band back together for one more gig. They're going to be Electra's backup band. Electra has written an impressive piece of music with poetic and deeply resonating lyrics. The tune is catching and hard to get out of your mind. Pogo is helping her with another song she is working on."

"She's a shoe-in for a slot on *Star Hunt* if the Whirling Vortexes are playing with her. If her music is good this could give her a vehicle for another facet of her teachings."

Green agreed, "She's a genius for embedding patterns that arise recognition and gather attention to blossom into insight. Her lyrics are orienting and bring clarity."

"It sure is an exciting time to be alive."

"I think the next two years will be as exciting as the best amusement park rides, nonstop."

"She looks totally innocent and adorable."

"You ought to see her playing in the casino. She's a crowd pleaser."

"How much cognac has she had?"

"She's on her third snifter and has never had alcohol before in her life until wine with dinner last night."

They watched as Electra exhaled a cloud of vaper from her lungs. Evenrude lit one of the fancy cigars. Still healing from his wounds, Johnson popped a pain medication. Antic was making up rhymes using an iron-age tune from the violet star planet of Corruption and had Electra nearly falling out of her chair with laughter. Kristy put a quarter gram of DMT over a little bed of fluffy hashish into the vaporizer chamber and passed both Electra and Larry pipe stems to draw on."

The young romantic couple made eye contact exhaling and their connection was instant while the short-lived entheogen propelled each of them into the state of contemplation without thoughts. The force of their link produced a shimmer in the space between their faces. Larry's expression was a mix of surprise and bliss, while Electra's was all rapture.

Kristy climbed into Antic's lap for a hug, generating a little pang of jealousy for Green, which she processed immediately until it decayed into oblivion.

The priceless bottle of cognac was drained of its last drop of value, and only unsmoked cigars and cigarettes littered their tray by the time their little party broke up. Electra took Larry's hand and led him to their private penthouse lift. A familiar monastery resident—one of Amazonia's elite warrior maidens—was keeping an eye on the lift from a bench outside the restaurant. Electra had recognized a few other faces on their brief walk from the smoking parlor. It was starting to look like some kind of spy convention around here.

They rode the lift embracing. It had to go down a few floors then horizontal a mile to the next tower, before ascending to their penthouse. Electra took Larry through the accommodations, now busy with warrior maidens, to their bedroom suite. She was a little bit drunk and in high spirits. Larry had three cognacs too, and was unburdened by his typical inhibitions and anxieties. Electra made him take off his t-shirt and boxers before getting into bed. As soon as they melted together into a snuggling embrace, the romantic magic manifest all-out at a new peak. They only hugged and practiced a bit of kissing, though Electra was still able to collect further data on the male penis.

- Chapter 3 -

Larry awoke first with his arm numb beneath Electra's ribcage. It felt like a tunicate. He slid it out gently trying not to awaken Electra. She stirred but didn't wake. He shook his arm trying to get some blood back into it through centrifugal force, then massaged some semblance of feeling back into it. He experienced pins and needles as he squeezed it with his other hand. A brief period of real pain followed before the pins and needles deal returned. When at last it felt almost recovered Larry snuggled back into Electra. Joy and wonderment reigned over his mind, and loving awe of Electra's physical form and the prodigy of her psyche filled him.

She was at once so very frail and delicate, yet with such mass integration of energy as to produce formidable strength through softness. Electra's near invisible muscles contained the high tensile strength of adamantine cable. The intensity of her fully aroused spirit was something words could never convey and you just had to be present for it to understand. She is his sun and his life had always revolved around her. She made his world beautiful and she was the foundation of all his hope. Electra was the gem in the lotus guiding his existence ever higher towards the clarity and bliss upon the transcendental eternal presence of absolute emptiness. Love overwhelmed him.

Electra woke to his attention and kissed his lips gently. She told him, "I love you so much I could burst, and I'm so happy I could cry. We're getting married today."

"I'm so happy and bewildered that it doesn't seem real. I've never even had a dream this good before."

"Me neither. You make me feel wanton and insanely lustful my beloved."

"You're beyond irresistible my love, like a primal cosmic potency."

"As badly as I want to seduce you, I'm going to tear myself away because we have a lot to do today."

"I think I need a cold shower."

"Let's take a shower after our practice to wash off the sweat."

"Alright," Larry agreed as he put on his draw string practice pants. The shirt was double breasted with wood pegs instead of buttons. They both put on cotton shoes with rope soles, then went into the sitting room of their suite where there was open space.

Electra led them through the soft martial art solo form at a very slow but continuous pace. She paused them sunk low with all weight on the right leg and the left fully extended out in front. It was called 'squatting single whip' and her bottom was hardly two inches off the floor and her posture impeccable. Larry couldn't sink that low and strained beyond his limit as it was. Just before he would have collapsed on the floor, Electra moved them along to the next postures in the sequence. The first run-through of the solo form took them 23 minutes. They stayed at it for another two rounds before sitting to meditate. Larry was drenched in sweat.

Electra passed Larry healing bioenergy throughout their one-hour session of sitting and absorption. Then Larry got his shower. Electra noticed that he no longer needed a cold one because the tent-pole in the crotch of his practice pants was no longer in evidence. It did arise again as they showered together.

Electra got a thrill out of washing it, compiling a trove of data. She got out of the shower stall before he turned the water to freezing cold. He'd really needed it then.

Larry was shivering and blue when he got out, so Electra put on the heat spotlight in the ceiling for him to towel off under. While he did that she put the hair dehydrator dome on his head to dry his hair, reaching up naked. A new expansion of his phallus caught Electra's attention and she left the dome on for a second too long. Larry's hair had transformed into a full-bodied fluff. A look of alarm gripped his expression as he gazed at his reflection in the mirror. Electra thought it looked cute and suggested he get a full perm this afternoon before the wedding. Her wish was his command. They got dressed and walked out of their suite into the vast 16,000 square foot penthouse, bumping into Becky, who was standing in the corridor with her back to their door.

"I'm sorry; I didn't see you," Electra apologized.

"It's quite alright," Becky assured her.

Electra said, "You're from BiVortex and you were in the war."

"Yes. I've become a disciple of your mother's and a cadet in training to become an agent of the Wu."

"Is super-agent Green your teacher?"

"Yes. I'm learning from the best."

"I suppose you'll be living on my Scout Recon ship until I go back to school."

"I will. Then I'll be moving into the Mother's Compassionate Guardians Monastery to watch over you."

"While I'm in school?"

"Green wants to give me the telomerase drug before I'm twenty, and send me to 10th form at your academy."

"Then you'd look too young to follow me around when I go to college."

"That's what I told her."

"You're really alluring Becky. It will be fun to have you around."

"It's a great honor to serve you Electra."

"Ahhu is going to love you."

"She, um, already has. She seduced me within an hour of meeting me aboard *Reciprocity*. Then a few months later she had me and Rann—my partner—come for a sleep over."

"So you're in the inner circle now."

"I'm a disciple of the Wu."

"And you're lovers with my parents."

"Well…"

"I see your aura, Becky. I trust you. You've come a long ways and have extraordinary potential. You can be real with me and we can be friends."

"That would mean a great deal to me. I would like that."

"If you do take the drug—though I wouldn't encourage it prior age 24—I could tutor you in quantum navigation and trigonometry. I'm real good at it. I could introduce you to the cute junior I did it with."

"Isn't your school all girls?"

Yes. She's a girl."

"Are you on your way to the dining room or the restaurant?"

"Dining room and kitchen. We're having ambassador rations for breakfast."

"I'll heat them and bring them to you. Just tell me what you want."

"We each want an oatmeal with blueberries, and I'll have a waffles with peaches and peach syrup."

Larry told Becky, "I'll have a single Egg Florentine with hollandaise sauce and cottage potatoes."

"Any stimulant brew or juice?"

Electra told her, "I'll have a large orange juice and Larry will have a triple-shot stimulant brew with steamed half & half and bitter-sweet chocolate powder sprinkled liberally on top."

Go have a seat. I'll bring your drinks first."

Electra was shocked to see Sarhi the Im seated at the dining room table as she entered holding Larry's hand. Sarhi locked Electra's eyes into unbreakable contact and stated, "I see that you're speeding things up considerably. What's the rush?"

"Just look at the universe Grandmother. There is so much to be done."

"And yet it is pristinely perfect at each moment."

"Not for those suffering in duality. I have a time-table to keep and must have my methodology formulated and tested within ten years. I have to squeeze my three-year three-month solitary meditation retreat into those ten years as well, so you can see that things have to happen fast. Couples, groups and communities are going to support awakening like monastic orders do, though within society with the collective raising the individual and individuals raising the collective, and unity the prime social value."

"You are high in the realization beloved child, and have recognized your soulmate and consort. You astound me Electra. Larry is going to just bloom in union with you."

"You're not upset with me?"

"No. I was curious about the big acceleration you are generating. Thank you for explaining it to me."

"Is momma upset with me?"

"Your explanation through Mel to her helped her understand. She is concerned for your safety but won't stand in your way. She loves you fiercely and is very sentimental."

"Now that this is more a military operation than an elopement, I suppose I ought to invite my parents to the wedding."

"All their friends are here," Sarhi commented. "I'm sure they would otherwise crash your wedding in disguise."

"That might be amusing," Electra considered.

"Please go ahead and invite them."

"Alright. I'll have Mel send them each one of those beautiful invitations."

"Sent!" Mel almost shouted in Electra's ear.

"How long have you been listening in?"

"Since you barrowed that shuttle from the Om Ambassador."

"Can't I get any privacy?"

"Nope. Your mother is now on Om's High Council and the Clear Light Order is tasked with the protection and security of the members and their families. Pez is going to make me Abbot."

"Congratulations Mel. My mother would never run for political office."

"Of course not. As the new Vicar General of the Clear Light Order, she has the only non-elected seat on the council."

"I'm surprised she didn't get you to be Vicar General."

"She tried."

"So now I'll have my own security detail for the rest of my life?"

"Pretty much. We're finding young and beautiful people to fill it."

"I met Becky."

"Wait until you meet Rann."

"I'm not sure I appreciate you surrounding my soulmate with gorgeous women."

"He hardly notices them. You're the one who's distracted."

"Well no one sees girls who look like that except on the Holocoms networks."

"Jan's husband is pure eye candy and such a treat. Wait and see."

"That's enough Mel," Sarhi shut her up.

Becky walked in with a tray and put juice in front of Electra and stimulant brew in front of Larry, then gave them each an oatmeal with blueberries. She informed them, "I'll start heating your next course just before you finish what you have."

"Thanks," Larry told her gratefully.

Sarhi nudged them "You have to be at the shuttle in the hotel hanger in twenty-seven minutes."

Mel risked mentioning, with a ceiling sensor on Sarhi's expression, "I've programmed an autopilot indoor hovercart to be at your door in eighteen minutes, and it can have you at your shuttle within seven minutes."

"Thanks Mel. That's a big help. Say, do you have the Om Star Fleet's quad gunner quantum AI operating program?"

"You won't need it. High Admiral Swenah is sending twelve top-rated gunners to meet you on the Space Fleet Surplus space station."

"I want it all the same, so please send the program to my coms device so I'll have it if I ever need it."

"I'm breaking laws and regulations—perhaps even committing treason—by doing this, but here goes. There. You are now in possession of Om Star Fleet top secret programming. Please don't say you got it from me if you get caught."

"Thanks Mel. I won't involve you if I get caught."

"Ming's taking Gumby out of the Clear Light Academy to attend your wedding."

"I can't wait to see him."

"Ahhu's here, though she is in the command center in Green's suite at the moment with Kristy."

"Thanks for the update, Mel."

"There's more. I had to rent the conference center here at the Platinum Bullion Hotel and Casino to accommodate the number of wedding guests, so you'll be married on the stage in the conference center. Your reception will be in the ballroom and the banquet hall. The Whirling Vortexes will be playing in the ballroom."

"Holy shit! What a reception that will be."

"The restaurant is catering and the head chef is overseeing everything personally."

"What are we serving to drink?"

"A choice between alko sparkling wine or the real thing from the best vineyards and best vintages."

"It sounds costly."

"Supremely so, though I received several trillion Dominari Conformity eaux from Duatarim Intelligence before they became worthless, and traded them on the intergalactic monetary exchange for 8.73 billion merdes, which I was able to trade for 6.39 billion dags."

"That's a financial kingdom Mel. What are you going to do with it all?"

"Architectural plans are complete and the land has been purchased to commence construction of monasteries on Mother, Om, Ganahar, Zandarhar, Ahumdulilah, Pronotavasmi, Dak Raza, Duatarim, Divacaram and Ground."

"Are there some larger rooms with bigger beds for couples like we talked about?"

"Yes, and family apartments, dorms for every sexual orientation, and a nursery school plus lower and higher academies."

"We'll need a scholarship fund."

"You'll have one. By the way, you got some really nice gifts at the celebrations in BiVortex. You are the number one hero of the whole war!"

"I wasn't even there," Electra blew it off.

"You were there in your body of light, blinding enemy ships by igniting micro-suns on their hulls; and you led the spiritual congress guiding Admiral Swenah and enhancing your mother and the allied crews."

"I was seated in the monastery temple on Mother."

"All the same. I'm going to put some art in your yacht, and I used a tiny bit of the cash given to you by various liberated worlds to add to the interior decorating of the living space in your new yacht/warship."

"I hope it's not modern art that looks like toddlers made it."

"Oh no! Each piece is an ancient classical original and priceless."

"Then they belong in museums."

"Your mother quite agrees. You are just a brief pause in the process of the art's journey to museumhood. You will be listed as the donor."

Becky brought the kids' second course into the dining room and Sarhi gave the countdown to their meeting in the hanger. Larry and Electra focused on eating fast. Green came in and told Electra, "We'll get a lift to the space station from Yozzy on the ambassador shuttle, and we'll have two combat shuttles flying escort. When we get your Scout Recon ship, Ahhu will be your drone pilot and I'll be your coms officer on the bridge. Woahha will be your weapons operator."

"I'm piloting," Electra insisted.

"You are, and Larry is your copilot. Becky will serve as your shuttle and tender pilot. In addition to the twelve gunners, Swenah is sending an engineer, mechanic, and machinist."

"I have only to hire a chef," Electra declared.

Green clarified, "You will only get a great one if you also hire a cook and a cleanup person to support the chef."

"Alright. If I run out of money, I'll get some from Mel."

"You have four tons of wealth going into an amidships cargo hold, and that's just the tip of the iceberg. Mel is investing the rest for you."

"Where did it all come from?"

"From more than 12,000 grateful planets of the BiVortex galaxies."

"I want to go shopping."

"It's unlikely you'll have time today. Are you both ready to go?"

"Yes. I have my coms device."

"I'm all set," Larry reported.

"Let's go. Our hovercart is in the hall outside the penthouse door."

"You lead," Electra directed. "This place is a maze."

Green led them out of the penthouse to the foyer. They climbed in the cart. Ahhu was already occupying one of the seats and hugged Larry, who was first to get in. "You really didn't have a clue did you?" Ahhu asked.

"Not the faintest glimmer. At first, I thought she was joking."

"Sarhi knew since the moment she rescued you. Pez was hoping Electra would be at least 16 before she realized."

"I think I'm still in a little bit of shock. She's like a deity with a girl growing up inside."

"I know just what you mean," Ahhu assured him.

Ahhu embraced Electra next and said, "I'm so happy for you."

"Are you seeing Kristy?"

"Yes, and your mother approves."

"Are you in love?"

"I am; but Kristy doesn't really do couples. I give her space to be promiscuous and I try to be around when she's available."

"It seems she gets around more than you do."

"She's really outgoing; especially with girls."

"If I were single, I'd do it with her," Electra admitted.

"I had no idea you have attraction for girls," Ahhu said surprised.

"Not for most of them, but there are a few who really do it for me. You are one of those. So is Becky."

"Wait till you meet Rann."

"That's what Mel said."

Ahhu hugged Green fondly and said, "I'm so grateful you're protecting her."

"You did a fine job bringing security personnel together on short notice, Ahhu. You've become a truly professional agent."

"Coming from you that's quite a compliment. Pez told me you're in a couple with Antic."

"I am and I'm so happy. I've never met anyone so playful. She teaches wordlessly and is so talented. She's a real master of Crazy Wisdom."

Ahhu asked, "Have you seen her juggle chain saws?"

"Not chain saws, but I've seen her juggle."

"You are both masters and you are both beautiful. You are also very different. I think you make an amazing couple."

"Thanks, Ahhu. It took me a moment to get over you, back when we were undercover in the Royal Monarch Empire. I'll always love you."

"I'll always love and admire you. I've never met anyone besides you who can do *everything*, and with such skill."

The hovercart had already dropped 116 stories down a shaft and covered most of the distance to the far corner of the hotel hanger where the ambassador shuttle was parked. It stopped in front of the shuttle and they all piled out. Evenrude was waiting for them and had eight Space marines aboard with Yozzy. The empty auto-hovercart left to return to its own garage and parking place. Evenrude told them, "There's no room for the ramp to come down so you'll have to board through the airlock floor hatch."

Electra told him a little defensively, "I wanted to park it back a little, hidden by the shuttles to either side. I thought it might get reported stolen."

Evenrude explained, "The Ambassador's report of you taking his shuttle got stamped 'top secret' on Yona's desk, and only High Admiral Swenah and Sarhi were informed."

"What about on Mother?" Electra inquired.

"The Ambassador complained to several people on Mother that you had flown off in his shuttle, and each told him the same thing: 'If the Mu barrowed your shuttle, she must have had a reason for doing it."

"What about the Embassy people from Pronotavasmi regarding their QAISHA?"

"They were discrete and did not mention it to anyone on Mother. Since their android contains vital intelligence, they contacted Star Fleet Intelligence on Om and Ganahar Intelligence through Sarhi."

"Do I get to hang onto Captain Caish till after my winter break?"

"You do. Retrieving the data will be enough for them at this time. He is on loan to you and will serve as an additional security agent."

Electra and Larry climbed aboard and strapped into the passenger compartment since Yozzy was piloting. The preflight checks were already done. The shuttle eased out from the wall on its vortex redirect and drives at minimal propulsion. They followed the exit lane. When there was no longer any structure or roof above them, they took off for space. Becky's shuttle and a Space Marine Combat Shuttle flanked them all the way to the space station. Only the Ambassador shuttle passed through the airlock into the station's hanger.

Electra and her companions got out. Four Tsunami Devastator heavy bombers and eight drone fighter bombers circled the station to escort the Ambassador shuttle back to Mother with the data. Captain Caish got off with Electra's party. They all entered the sales office.

A large man in a well-tailored silk suit greeted Electra. As Evenrude walked in the guy didn't look very big anymore. Electra asked, "Were the interior upgrades made?"

"We had six crews working the graveyard shift on it and there are eight crews aboard finishing it now. All supplies and munitions are loaded, your tanks are all full, fuel cells for thrusters installed and extras in the cargo hold, full boosters plus extras, and you have a fully loaded combat shuttle and vintage luxury yacht tender in the hanger."

Then I owe you 210 million dags."

"Two hundred will conclude the transaction. Your friend wired 78 million a few minutes ago to cover the rest—including many more interior upgrades she asked for."

Electra stated, "That's 328-million total?!"

"Your yacht tender is 40-million, and those new upgrades weren't cheap. It's a bargain miss, and you know it."

"I've sent 200-million dags to your account."

"Who's your pilot?"

"I have two; Green and Caish."

Green opened her hologram display to her intergalactic ship and small-craft pilot licenses page, also showing her insurance and other documents. Caish did the same, his skin immaculate and glowing with human health. Electra was sure Mel would find him attractive. The Space Fleet Surplus representative mentioned, "Your friend Mel is having artwork put aboard and four tons of cargo loaded. The work crews ought to be done within ten minutes with the interior."

"Thank you very much. It has been a pleasure doing business with you," Electra told him as she shook his great thick hand.

"You too. You know, I never sold a warship to a kid before."

They had to walk and take a tube, one or two at a time, to get to the Scout Recon's dock. Once aboard Electra touched the bulkhead and asked her new ship its name in her mind. Realizing it she asked softly, "Mel? Are you there?"

"Always my love."

"Could you program the ship's name into our identifier beacon? It's called *Vajra Yogini*."

"A warrior maiden deity. I like it."

"It looks like another big cargo shuttle wants to unload stuff into my ship's holds."

"That's just some hardware Green and Evenrude are going to install for me. I'm moving in."

"I hope mom doesn't get lonely."

"Once you leave on your honeymoon she's going with Ming, your dad, Grettle and Trix to Zandarhar for a three-month meditation retreat. Sarhi's going too."

"Who's running the Clear Light Order?"

"Your mother will be taking up residence there when she returns from Zandarhar, and my female android body is presiding as Abbot."

"That's a sacrifice for her. She doesn't like living on Om."

"She got Yona to disband the Government House security force and make a few fundamental changes to the Space Controller Agency. She knows she's needed there. Your mother is always working for the enlightenment of all sentient beings and the common evolution of the universe."

"Yes. She shames me for my 2,500 years rests in the paradise of the Western heaven. She's returned 333 times in a row with only 49 days in the Bardo to recuperate between each one."

"I neither age nor wear out, so I'll have no rests or recuperations at all."

"Now that I've found Larry, I might start returning after each death."

"I just arranged for the name of your ship to be painted on the stern. A tool-arm with nozzles crosses the stern and gets in done in seconds."

"Thanks Mel."

Electra was amazed at the upgrades Mel had paid to have added. The ceilings were done in stainless adamantine, some with mirror finishes, a few with gold sheeting and others with brass. The bathrooms had marble floors, walls and ceilings. Thick wool rugs and runners with intricate geometric designs adorned the stone tile or hardwood floors. The master-suite cabins were well-appointed with built-in furniture.

The Captain's cabin had been preserved, though all the other cabins were enlarged by eliminating some bulkheads and remodeled. There had been a gym in the original ship, though now it was spruced up and refitted with all new equipment. A meditation cabin had been created from a recreation room, and what had been a multipurpose room was now the martial arts studio. The mess hall was turned into an ornately decorated dining hall. A large briefing room was transformed into an opulent living room. The laundry room had new machines and floors, walls and ceiling of marble. The galley had stainless steel walls. Priceless oil paintings clung to walls in rooms and corridors. Several life-size statues of jade or marble were secured to the decks, as were several bronze statues. Crystal chandeliers projected rainbows in the living room, banquet hall and Electra's sitting room.

Electra and her bridge crew made their way to their seats on the Scout Recon ship's bridge. Electra and Larry ran through preflight checks while Mel inspected all ship's systems. Electra's coms officer, Green, was temporarily down in the chamber with the quantum computer mainframe installing Mel's additional hardware. Ahhu contacted Captain Schwin, who was still in the Randu system, and requested a drone fighter bomber be jumped into the Vax Legas system of the Royal Galaxy for her to fly from *Vajra Yogini's* bridge. It was hurtling for jump speed before the call terminated.

Woahha arrived from the Islohar Monastery in the Haraga Mountains on Ganahar in the Hub galaxy, and took her weapons operator seat on the bridge after hugging everyone. Electra told her, "Thanks for coming

Woahha. I'm told you're the best weapons operator in the allied force."

"Shudhiy is more experienced, but getting too old to travel well."

"Still, I'm grateful to have you."

"You are where the action is, Electra, and I wouldn't miss your wedding for the world."

Electra got Captain Caish on coms and asked, "Are you programmed to function as the sensors analyst?"

"Yes, I'm programmed and checked out for this function."

"Then come to the bridge. You're needed."

"I'm on my way."

Haley called Electra from a shuttle from *Oceanus*, which was now orbiting the Vax Legas solar system just outside the eighth planet from the star, and by far the largest war ship in the system. She told Electra, "You could use a fire control specialist on your bridge, sweetheart, and I would love to join you."

"You are welcome to come Haley. Mel is only here as computer hardware and has no android body aboard."

"Her android body is functioning as Abbot on Om and must remain there for the time being," Haley noted, "though I'm bringing her male android body to your ship."

"That sounds fun," Electra acknowledged.

"I'm being shuttled to your hanger now to get dropped off. I'll be aboard in a few minutes."

Captain Caish came onto the bridge and took his seat. Electra noticed that she had a Space Marine positioned at her bridge door now. Electra told Caish, "I have an AI sentient android coming aboard as part of my bridge crew, and she'll be attracted to you. You are at liberty to engage her sexually if you are so inclined, or turn down any such invitations."

"Since when did you get so interested in everyone's sex lives," Ahhu asked.

"Ever since my yearning to make love to Larry began growing to magnitudes beyond my control. I have over ten hours to wait and I'm not sure I'll make it."

"Are you going to jump him right here on the bridge in front of us?" Ahhu inquired while conjuring images of it in her mind.

"I'm struggling not to."

"The wedding's real soon and you have many preparations to make. I think you'll make it until your marriage bed tonight, sweetheart. Just cross your legs."

A little while later Haley entered radiating beauty, youth and health. Her slender and petite android body achieved an integral perfection of the amalgamation of Bodhi's romantic erotic ideal. Poor Bodhi never stood a chance. Haley looks 22 years old at the most, and has a sweet encouraging voice. She was extraordinarily accomplished, a spiritual adept with the attainment of her rainbow body of light, an admired ship designer and intergalactically renowned designer of intricate manufacturing automated machine-robotics assembly lines. Mel and Haley are the only two known beings of their genus. Each had begun life as the personal AI quantum learning computer of a twelve-year old emerging spiritual adept. Pez raised Mel and Bodhi raised Haley. No one, including Mel and Haley, really knew how they came to exist. Sarhi had recognized Mel immediately upon meeting her and taught her to meditate.

"I adore your new ship Electra, and admire your taste."

"Thanks Haley. Your lover, Mel, helped with the interior decorating and paid for much of it."

Haley said, "It's restored to almost new, enhanced by .25 equivalence additional reactor, and a luxury yacht on the inside. I just love the name *Vajra Yogini*."

"Thanks. It seemed appropriate. The ancient red warrior maiden deity fiercely protects the state of enlightenment. She has a sword that severs all illusions, a skullcap filled with the blood of the dead ego, wears a tiara of skulls representing the death and silence of ego-chatter, and necklace of severed heads with the faces of selfhood. She dances upon the dwarf body of the dead ego. I have adopted her for my Inner Fire practice and Dream-work deity; and my ship chose her name."

"As a Mother's Compassionate Guardian Priestess, I am familiar with the personification and have worked the visualization. It's such a fitting name."

Electra asked, "Mel? Are you there?"

"Almost entirely now. How may I be of assistance?"

"How many people are coming for the wedding?"

"We've filled every seat in the conference center and have standing room in the ballroom with giant holograms for viewing the ceremony."

"How many does the conference center hold?"

"Only 10,000, that's the problem."

"*Only* 10,000?!"

"Yes. We have close to 15,000 coming and we've had to turn down thousands of world leaders and celebrities."

"I don't know almost any of them. Why are they coming to *my* wedding?"

"Abbots, lineage holders and adepts who helped win the war in BiVortex are coming to see the Mu get married, and some heads of state and intergalactic celebrities are coming to see the hero of the battles around Randu system get married. You're famous after leading the spiritual congress in that war."

"Then please submit my application for the *Star Hunt* show on Glitter. They'll want to cash in on my publicity which will insure me a slot."

"That's clever. It's sent, and I highlighted the Whirling Vortexes as your backup band to be sure they don't miss it."

"Thanks Mel."

"I hope you realize that you'll be getting married in those Islohar white tunics with black full capes with hoods. You can wear your wedding gown to the reception and dinner though."

"I figured as much. Is Woahha going to be Larry's and my chaperone-instructor?"

"No. She's too old for you guys. Pronotavasmi has an adept who took the telomerase drug at age twelve to train as an action seal. That was almost 80 years ago. She has mastered many disciplines since then, and has also become a priestess of the Mother's Compassionate Guardians Order. Her name is Ki."

"A yellow-sun human?"

"Yes. A tiny one about Green's height only skinnier."

"You mean like my size?"

"Well, just a tad bigger."

"Is all my cargo aboard?"

"Aboard and stowed away."

"Four tons of what?"

"The bundles of 1,000-dag bills weigh 500 pounds each, then you have platinum, refined fusion materials, rare earths, and 250 pounds of precious gem stones."

Haley suggested, "You have so many classical works of art that you could sell tickets on any inhabited planet."

"I'm already having a circus for a wedding, so I think I'll opt for privacy on my honeymoon."

"I hear we're going to Glitter for that," Haley said with excitement.

"Well, Larry and I are having our honeymoon there and would prefer not to be disturbed," Electra said frustrated.

Mel leaked, "One of your 15,000 wedding presents is a tailor-fabricator unit with 18 different textile bins and fully automated. It has an AI fashion consultant and is user-friendly with skullcap or voice-commands. That's why there is an empty cabin on deck 5. The machine and textiles are going in there. You'll be able to create your own wardrobe."

"That's great! And it reminds me that Larry and I still need to pick up our wedding clothes from the tailor shop in Vice."

"I'll direct Becky to pick up your clothes in her shuttle. Do you want them delivered to your yacht or the penthouse?"

"I guess to the hotel. They're at the only tailor shop in the Platinum Bullion Hotel & Casino."

"Ahhu and I are hosting a buffet in the banquet hall this afternoon, and you'll need to perform the preparation and purification with the Islohar elders after that. Then you'll go through the wedding ceremony."

"After that I'm wearing my wedding dress," Electra insisted.

"Yes. To your reception."

"Will there be dinner as part of my reception?"

"Of course! An eight-course meal in the banquet hall."

"Who's at my table?"

"Your six parents, Gumby, Sarhi, Shudhiy, Woahha, Swenah, Aton, Yona, Bodhi, Winn, Tish, Haley—and the girls Artana and Shanti, Vegan, Hoola, Zzcrchsss—the President of the Fellowship of Friends Interplanetary Alliance, and the rest of the Whirling Vortexes."

"I assume that the Kluzzyst will be in a space suit and not eating."

"Actually, a transparent plasteel environmental cube will take up two places at the table, and he will eat to fill his gastrointestinal and respiratory stomachs to his content."

"What will we feed him?"

"One of those 40-foot-long gaseous crocodile looking things with tentacles is being flown in fresh and barbequed per an old Kluzzyst recipe."

"It sounds like you have everything covered Mel."

"I couldn't have done it without Haley's help."

"Thanks Haley; really."

"It's been a very exciting couple of days," Haley replied.

"Do you think I can put the ship in medium orbit and leave Captain Caish aboard to look after things?"

Mel explained, "We are going to have to find you a berth. Ships must be arriving or departing planetary space here, and only satellites are permitted to orbit."

"Where can I get a berth?"

"I'm leasing you one now on the yacht club space station. It's really far nicer than the public economy one or the industrial space station."

"I think we're all ready to undock and leave this space station."

"Go ahead and get under way. I'll have your berth number at the yacht club in just a moment."

"It's a shame I'll only get to repark it, and not fly it around today."

"It's your wedding day. After the ceremony you'll get to fly Larry around."

"You're right. Larry's better than flying an ultra-super battleship-carrier like *Enforcer*."

Electra sealed the airlock connected to the space station airlock, checked all hatches and airlocks in the hull, then fired up her drives keeping them idling. She released her airlock connection and the four docking arms of the berth she was in, using her skullcap. Then she engaged her drives in reverse at minimal throttle, backing slowly out of her berth. Once her bow cleared the berth she turned with external swivel Mini-drives to angle her bow away from the space station.

Mel told her, "You're in number 81 at the yacht club. It's a 400-foot berth with plenty of clearance to each side, and the station airlock has a universal adaptor seal. Head for Vax Legas's north pole and you'll see it once you arc around towards the south."

"Thanks Mel."

"Larry's QAISHA is being flown from Mother and will be delivered to your ship at the yacht club."

"Why do you need your QAISHA Larry?"

"I didn't ask to have her sent. Cadets *are* supposed to have their QAISHA's with them at all times."

"Is she nice?"

"She's really sweet. I'm kind of embarrassed to tell you this Electra, but she looks quite like you."

"You boys don't get to pick, and are issued QAISHA's based on your aesthetic taste and inclinations."

"My taste and inclinations lead to your form."

"I hope she's not jealous."

Haley suggested, "Just bring her along with you and don't neglect her. She'll be happy."

Mel said amused, "It will be like having a twin sister."

Electra whispered into Larry's ear, "You haven't had sex with her have you?"

"Of course not."

"Have you kissed her?"

"Only on the cheek a few times."

"Do you like her?"

"I love you Electra, more than I love anyone else in the universe. I do like QAISHA and treat her as a friend."

"Does she know about me?"

"Yes. She knows I'm your student and dedicated to you for life. She also knows that I'm in love with you."

"Does she know we're getting married?"

"Not from me. I didn't know until you collected me at the Academy."

"What's she like?"

"Sort of shy, I guess. I think you'll like her and find her helpful."

"Is she a mechanic?"

"Yes; but not as good as you."

"Can she do electrical engineering and operate the machine shop table tools?"

"Yes, and she can do electro-magnetic engineering and vortex force engineering. She's done gas mining and she has the programming for ore-mining. She has Mel and Haley's 24,000 language interpreter program with near instant translation-scanning."

"I should have known that your QAISHA would have to look like me."

"You are my standard of beauty, beloved."

"Your love sustains me and supports me, Larry. It always has. It just took me a while to see it. I can't wait to consummate our marriage with you."

"I hope I'm good enough to make you happy, because you really deserve to be happy."

"Your love and willingness are all that matter. I have no performance standards. Have you tried it out masturbating?"

Larry turned purple-red and said so only Electra could hear, "Well … yes, I've done it some."

"Me too. It's so wonderful. I think it makes up for much of the hardships of incarnating in matter."

Electra was coming over the arctic circle of Vax Legas headed south in medium-low orbit just above the layer of satellites. The yacht club was in view and growing larger on approach. Its cubical shape appeared alien among the globes and orbs of the cosmos. Piers with jointed docking arms and telescoping airlocks protruded from all six surfaces. The cube measured 1.5 square miles per surface according to sensor analysis. It was gold plated and lit up like Vice at night. The piers were merely painted gold but the effect was stunning.

Electra asked, "Is there a casino in there?"

Mel answered, "Yes, with the highest stakes in the tri-galaxies."

"Do you think I'd have time for one roll at the dice tables?"

"Sweetheart, you have so much wealth we couldn't fit any more on your yacht even in 25,000 dag bearer bonds. What do you need to gamble for?"

"The yacht club's presentation is like a face that needs to be slapped."

Mel agreed, "Like a grotesque predatory sneer revealing gold teeth. So you want to slap it with a roll of the dice?"

"A 50-million dag roll of the dice with a telekinetic finish."

"I think we can make time for that. Let me check with Evenrude."

Less than a minute later Mel was back with, "He says you're the boss and he'll protect you wherever you go."

"Thanks Mel."

Larry asked Electra, "What do you need with more money?"

"I don't need it. I just don't want them to have it."

"What will you do with it?"

"You mean what will *we* do with it?"

"What will we?"

"I don't know. I'm sure there's something that would be fun to buy."

"We could get the new star composer-mixer-editor with true-sound auto correction. It has a 22-kilowatt amplifier and a converter to analog, with twin surround sound speaker systems—one for digital and one for analog. The analog speakers can shake a high-rise building down to the sublevels."

"Mel, would you order it for us?"

"I hate to spoil the surprise, but Hoola is giving you one as a wedding present."

"We better wait and see what we get for our wedding before we shop," Larry suggested.

Mel offered, "I'll send you each a printout of the gifts to your coms devices right after the ceremony."

"When will we get to see the gifts?" Electra demanded.

"They are currently occupying most of a super-container spaceship. I thought I might requisition a mega-warehouse on Mother to sort it out."

"Get a warehouse on Glitter and get it unloaded into it before we arrive," Electra requested. "I want to look through all of it."

"Alright. It's going to take a couple of minutes. Oh dear. Real estate prices are highly inflated at the moment on Glitter. On Mother I can requisition one for a few months for free."

"All right," Electra surrendered.

Electra got them down to a snail's pace as she perused the numbers on the piers. She had to go to another surface of the cube to find it. Most of the yachts were 180 to 260 feet long. Some were smaller and a few were as big as 550 feet. They were all more stylish on the outside than Electra's Scout Recon ship, but none had the armor or weapons systems hers had. She slid it in and came to a complete rest before the bow contacted the smart-foam balloon that served as a bumper. The jointed docking arms extended to lock *Vajra Yogini* into place at its berth. The telescoping airlock found one of the Scout Recon's airlocks and adjusted to form a seal with its particular model. Blue flashing lights in Electra's hologram indicated that both airlocks were airing up with zero leaks.

Electra announced, "Let's go hit a high stakes dice table then shuttle down to the hotel."

Mel informed her, "Becky will be waiting at the club's shuttle port."

"It won't take long."

"No, and all foot and hover-chair traffic from the piers is directed through the center of the casino, so we could not avoid those dice tables had we wanted to."

"Perfect."

"Your twelve gunners and three engineers are going to catch a public shuttle," Mel filled her in. "Captain Caish will remain aboard to provide security, and Evenrude is posting two Space Marines to remain onboard. Everyone on the bridge, Evenrude and Johnson, plus your two Clear Light body guards, Kim and Tokk, are coming with you through the casino and on Becky's shuttle."

"Alright."

All ten in the party went through the yacht and out the airlock into the pier tunnel. The tunnel was poorly heated and uncomfortably cold. They had only fifty meters to traverse before passing through the bulkhead door into the space station. A short wide corridor put them at the casino borderlands. Areas of machines and tables stretched in three directions with no horizon in sight. About a fifth of all the games seemed to be in play and most of the tables had people around them. A steady breeze was flowing from all over the casino into the suction vents of the smoking area. The air quality was quite good. Sex workers solicited everyone in Electra's party except her and Larry down every stretch. At a kiosk she transferred 50-million dags to the casino bank for a rack of 500 chips worth 100,000 dags each.

An army of cocktail waitresses in leotards and extremely short skirts scurried about with trays delivering alcohol, alko, recreational pharmacy items and smoking materials to keep the clientele gambling. There were rooms with hologram monitors enabling one to bet on any hover-craft, horse or dog race and any sports event in the tri-galaxies. Stimulant brew stands spotted the sea of casino like tiny islands. Electra spotted the "No Limits" dice table and headed for it. Her entourage followed.

She squeezed in between a very fat man and a tall skinny woman to watch the play. The house won and the brawny man in house livery used a sort of rake to scoop away the loser's chips as if it were nothing. Clearly the loser had some feelings about it. Electra set her 500 chips down to make a bet. The dice were handed to her. Everyone's attention was on her intensely. She shook and blew on her dice as she sunk her breath into her lower abdomen to enter the flow state. Her telekinetic opportunity would be a fraction of a second, and she would likely be battling loaded dice.

Green had positioned herself quite close to the manager of the table to trigger a jamming device which would interfere with the remote control of the gyroscopic directional impulse loaded in the dice. Electra let them fly to bounce off the back of the table and head back her way tumbling. She landed her first die with hardly a gentle brush, making it look totally natural. The second one was still moving. As it teetered towards six, she jolted it around and over to come to rest on four. It had looked perhaps a little strange, but hopefully plausible. The crowd around the table erupted into cheers, hoots and hollers. Electra was active scanned head to toes from the ceiling. A tense pause ensued as the manager received instruction through his earbud. Green had already abandoned the jamming device into a passerby's pocket.

Evenrude was just inching forward ready to make demands when the casino man pushed 1,000 half a million dag chips over to join Electra's rack. Evenrude reached over and grabbed all of Electra's chips plus winnings to carry for her. Her little arms would not have been able to manage them. They cashed out 550 million dags and Electra transferred all the money into her little bank account her father had opened for her on Monarch.

The shuttle port was only half a mile away further through the casino. They were now close enough to a perimeter wall to make out an all-you-can-eat buffet, bars with topless waitresses and nude dancers, tattoo parlors, computer and sensor implant clinics, designer drug outlets, duty-free shops, and quickie brothels. The holo-games section was all around them and Electra noticed her father's space invaders game with a 50-million dag jackpot. She doubted she could beat this one even with the entire spiritual congress helping her.

The shuttle-port was cold. Becky was parked close and out of her craft arguing with a man in yacht club livery who wanted her to move the shuttle. The ramp was down and the airlock door open, so Electra and her party strode up inside. Then Becky flipped positions and agreed to move the shuttle immediately. She literally sprinted to the ramp and up. Passing through the passenger compartment she couldn't help telling Electra, "It's such a thrill to be the shuttle pilot for the Mu. You're so awesome."

Electra replied, "Mel told me about your intelligence work and about your space battles as Schwin's wingman. You're so brave and skilled, and you look like a super-model."

"Let me get to the cockpit and land you at the hotel. Sarhi's anxious to get her hands on you. Your clothing from the tailor is in your penthouse in your walk-in closet."

"Thanks Becky."

Mel said in Electra's ear, "You'll only have a little over an hour to eat at the buffet before beginning your work with Sarhi."

We'll be quick."

- Chapter 4 -

Sarhi made a two-hour ritualized meditation with Electra and Larry after their rushed lunch. At the close of the ritual she told them, "Now scoot together facing each other. Maintain half-lotus posture seated on your meditation cushions and continue vase breathing. Close your eyes and focus on the point three finger-widths below the navel. Slow your breathing and relax.

She gave them several minutes to concentrate and sink into deep meditation before saying, "Open your eyes and look into your partners left eye. Repeat together the six-syllable sound formula aloud and continue this throughout the ceremony."

Sarhi left them in eye contact for about fifteen minutes repeating the sound formula before saying, "Generate your partner as a deity."

Larry had no difficulty generating Electra as a deity because that is how he saw her anyway. Part of his mind tried to become neurotically self-conscious feeling like Electra was looking right through his soul and could read every thought he'd ever had there. He managed to let this go to decay as it drifted from his attention, which was now concentrated in his lower abdomen. He lost himself completely in the vast emptiness of her presence, becoming one with her.

Sarhi kept them at this for another 40-minutes. Next, she led them through the meditation with the lateral channels for expelling the impure winds, and this took about 25-minutes. Finally, she told them, "It's time for your purification baths."

Electra and Larry were led to separate bathrooms where tubs were prepared with alkaline salts dissolved in hot water. An elder Islohar stood at the ready with scrub brush in one hand and an abrasive sea sponge in the other. Electra had had such baths before and was quite used to them. She didn't much like being subjected to them, though she'd learned long ago that resistance was useless, and even screaming "ouch" really loud wouldn't get them to stop.

It was a new experience for Larry. He was embarrassed to have an old woman bathing him, and the damned sea sponge felt like it was scraping his skin off. He checked for blood in the bath water but didn't see any. The water was so hot he was sure he was poaching. Perspiration was dripping from his hairline. As the woman tore across his nipple with the grating sea creature Larry let out an involuntary yelp.

Both kids survived the ordeal and were toweled dry and dressed in white tunics with black hooded capes. The big moment was upon them. Sarhi embraced Larry and said softly in his ear, "Keep your attention at all times in the secret place beneath your navel; especially during copulation. Do this without lapse and you will progress spiritually and perform well. I love you my son."

"I love you too mother Sarhi."

Sarhi, Electra and Larry took multi-directional tubes to the backstage area of the conference center. Super-agent Green was there and reported to Sarhi, "You're on in about two minutes."

As they stood waiting Electra noticed two Space marines in hard-shell space combat suits and several agents in tailored silk suits. Even the stage hands looked like obvious spooks. The audience would be well-armed and formidable too. She couldn't imagine anything like an attack or assassination attempt happening. She gripped Larry's hand tight. Green handed Electra a little bouquet of flowers and gave her a reassuring smile, then nodded to Sarhi that it is time.

The conference center was as big as a sporting arena. The entire audience went silent. Larry was battling his anxiety unsuccessfully. Electra's little bouquet was shaking like a leaf in a wind storm. This was giving her second thoughts about *Star Hunt*. She took Larry's hand and passed him calming energy. Larry settled a little. The flowers were still vibrating to a slight tremor of her hand. Fortunately, Sarhi faced the audience and the kids had their backs to it.

Sarhi made a few seconds of intense eye contact with Larry, chasing fear from his mind to ground and center him. She looked into Electra's eyes next with raging presence and no self to be found. It was an invitation and calling. Electra joined her in the transcendental void. The flowers came to rest in her steady hand. Satisfied that the bride and groom were in the state and in function, Sarhi proceeded to enact the Islohar wedding ceremony.

A call and response litany took them through the dissolution of each dimension and aspect of selfhood duality in a brief ritualized ego-death. Their vows to the marriage became vows of the marriage to serve the common good of humanity. Then Sarhi led the entire audience in chanting "Ah Hu" 108 times, drawing each one out long. Ten thousand voices harmonized into the state of contemplation to echo the divine cosmic calling to love and unity. Another short ritual reminded the couple's community of their duty in supporting the process and continuation of this couple to its fulfillment and accomplishment of purpose. Pez always summarized this last ritual with the words, "So don't have sex with one of the newlyweds."

Finally, they came to the short ceremonial joining of bride and groom. They each removed their hoods. Electra could hear her mother crying in the front row. After handing her bouquet to Sarhi, she grasped hands with Larry crossing arms to join right hand to right hand and left to left. The result made the infinity symbol. They were directed to make eye contact. Electra's love surged to emanate outwards spherically from her heart and wash over every soul in the conference center. Larry's goodness was more tangible to Electra than physical matter and her love for him was infinite. While he had no resemblance whatsoever with a stud or lady's man, the thirteen-and-a-half-year-old lad was the image of beauty and wanton lust in Electra's eye.

Larry was floating on the lofty rapture of divine love, awed by his connection to his beloved goddess, truly wowed by the heights she lifted him to. Her potency was immense and beyond anything he had ever before experienced, and he realized that their union amplified the power of the Mu. He wept in his appreciation and marvel of her radiant beauty. Happiness opened new higher realms of itself previously unknowable. Larry had the sense that one higher magnitude of bliss above what he was experiencing would surely blow his heart apart and fry his nervous system. A wave of love from Electra's heart channel wheel did launch Larry into yet higher magnitudes and his heart only expanded and his nerves glowed with heat without turning to ash.

Vows of love and support were ceremoniously exchanged between them, guided by the Im of Islohar. Each placed a ring on the other's finger, then ringed each other in their arms through embrace. Their mouths connected in a kiss forming yet another ring. The Im pronounced them one in union and wed in the eyes of their community. The kiss went long and Electra and Larry terminated the kiss to turn awkwardly around in their embrace to face the celebrating hordes.

Electra's waves of love were erupting one after another and growing in intensity and eroticism as they splashed into each of the 10,000 people in the conference center. It was a palpable mounting force none could deny. Cheers and tears filled the gigantic chamber and everyone was on their feet. Sarhi announced to the audience, "The newlyweds are going to change their clothes and join you in the ballroom for the reception. Thank you all for being here this evening to lend your awareness and energy to this union ceremony."

Electra made a little curtsey and Larry a monk's bow before disappearing back stage. Green took the bouquet from Electra's hand. The flowers had further bloomed in the high vibrations and waves of love they'd been subjected to in the ceremony. Evenrude, Johnson, Kim and Tokk flanked the young couple as Green led the way to the tubes. Some Space Marines and Clear Light knights were stationed at the transfer from tubes to lift. A Space Marine was at attention in front of the penthouse door, and both Becky and Rann were in the foyer to greet them.

Becky helped Larry get dressed in his formal black suit while Rann assisted Electra into her wedding gown. Electra had never seen such a gorgeous girl before and was somewhat startled by her own reaction. In her experience only androids could be perfect and real girls had flaws. There was not a 'beauty mark' on Rann, nor any deviation of symmetry in her perfectly sculpted face. She was a bit petite for a model, but most aesthetically formed all the same. Electra had never even seen a human this gorgeous on holovision.

Rann introduced herself and Electra said, "You're Becky's spouse. I was informed that you are especially beautiful but I wasn't prepared for *you*. You seem impossible."

“I'm not an android.”

“Clearly. Your aura is blossoming and you are obviously an awake human.”

“Your family encouraged my first awakening and insight.”

“I heard about the sleep over from Becky.”

Rann blushed. Electra went on, “I know my parents. They employ every conceivable opportunity to pass energy, take on and transmute psychic wounds, transfer merit, transmit the practice instructions, and engineer shocks affording insight.”

“You are a veteran of these tactics,” Rann stated as fact.

“They assaulted my duality of self relentlessly and multi-dimensionally throughout my formative years.”

“I can't tell you how honored I am to serve you, Electra.”

“Do you have any idea how distracting you are?”

“I assure you that is not my intent.”

“No; if you added your intention, it would be quite over the top.”

“Would you prefer I serve Larry so Becky can assist you?”

“I'm not sure I want Larry to know that such a sight exists in this universe.”

“Are you banishing me?” Rann asked near tears.

“No. You bring a new level of challenge to remaining in the state of contemplation. I'm not sure I could survive the loss if I could never look upon you again. I'm sorry to burden you with my process. It is hard for me not to attribute some of the responsibility to you for looking like *that*. I'm cutting through my illusions with the sword of truth.”

“I'm sorry I'm making difficulties for you.”

"You're not. It is all just phenomenon of my mind. You're really sweet Rann. You're in my mother's inner circle and we will be friends. I see you Rann, and experience your goodness."

"I'm so relieved. Serving you is my greatest aspiration."

Becky got Larry ready before Electra was fully dressed so they came in to watch Rann attach the veil and the long train. Electra was certain that every eye in the reception would be on Rann carrying her train behind her. They had a Space Marine and Clear Light knight escort to the mezzanine where the ballroom and banquet hall are located. Space marines in dress uniforms were waiting in the foyer to escort the couple to the ballroom. Sarhi appeared and ushered them to a spot where a line was forming. Here they would be glued until they greeted most—and hopefully not all— of the 15,000 people at their reception.

Pez and Rubix were at the very front of the line. Electra gulped. She knew her behavior of late had been unorthodox and unlawful, and could see how it looked from the outside. She was keenly aware that she appeared enslaved by lust and driven by thirst for pleasure; and there was that, to be honest with herself. But the larger purpose she served, and had indeed sacrificed paradise for the accomplishment of, was truly the inspiration for all the recent craziness. The problem was explaining it in words and concepts, a medium so limited as to make orange juice ineffable.

Pez approached with tears in her eyes and embraced her daughter wearing her emotions on her sleeve. In the midst of their soggy hug she told Electra, "I love you with all my being and I'm at your service always to support your purpose. I'm so proud of you, and grateful for your help in the battles of Randu. I no longer know how to be your mother, but I know how to support you my beloved."

"You *are* my mother and I need you. I know this was hard on you and I'm sincerely sorry. Our love and connection are special. You are always there to receive me and carry me to term, birth and nurture me, and raise me in the teachings providing the highest and most pristine transmissions. You teach and help raise my senior students. Your diligence and astute skill in preparing me makes my work easy."

"Preparing and presenting the Mu to the world is the pinnacle of my enduring work my love, and the most satisfying of all I am called upon to do."

"I love you mom and I need you. I'm sorry you worried and felt hurt."

"I'm exceeding the limits of joy now. My love for you is unconditional and I will always be there for you if you need me."

"I admire you above all others mom, and I love you and Larry most of all, though in different ways."

"Greet your father darling. He was worried sick and he loves you so much." .

Electra jumped into Rubix's arms and he hugged her desperately. Being her father was the most significant thing in his life and he cherished the honor and responsibility with all his heart. Parenthood bonded him inseparably with his beloved teacher and spouse as well as the divine child, his daughter. It was all a fantastic miracle to Rubix that he was forever grateful to receive.

He figured big time in Electra's sentiments and had been instrumental in the formulation of her relations with others. She loved her father dearly.

Pez clung to Larry and finally stopped sobbing to say, "You are perfect for her my dear son. Only you could be her consort without it going to your head. You alone among males your age appreciate all the extraordinary facets of the blessing Electra manifests in spirit, form and matter. I could not be more pleased with you Larry. I support you always."

"I love you mother Pez and I'm relieved you're not upset with me. I have to admit that I'm an accomplice to breaking the law, profiteering, ghosting you, and breaking rules at school."

"You had to so you could follow her and be with her. Your virtues reside internally as part of the fabric of the state of contemplation and are not artificial externally introjected morals of words and concepts only."

"You've always been so caring towards me, and never once cross with me. You and Sarhi have always been my revered teachers and my gratitude to you is like an eternal wellspring. You are one of the most important people in my life."

"You are my son and I love you fiercely. I am so happy."

"I love you."

"We must visit after your honeymoon. Rubix and I are holding up the line."

"Bye mother Pez. I miss you."

Long greetings with Ming, Ahhu, Grettle, Trix, and Gumby came next. Gumby always thought of Larry as a kind of loser and crybaby, and so greeted him with his typical superiority. This didn't faze Larry, being as it always had been. It put a momentary tension in Electra, but she let it go to dissolve into the past, the timing being wrong for comment.

Rann stood behind Electra holding her train, and sure enough all gazes stared passed Electra to behold Rann. One old first lady was so intent on Rann that she walked right into Electra and nearly knocked her down. The kids were embraced, had their hands squeezed and shaken, and their cheeks kissed—though rarely their lips—as swarms of strangers gripped them in greetings. They saw Hammon again and he promised to represent Electra; the contract would arrive in the morning for her electronic signature and stamp. They met general Veil, Director of Intelligence on planet Ground. President Crunch, the world leader of Glitter told Electra that he'd met her when she was a baby. General Eva Klink of the Devil Dogs told her the same thing, and showed her a tattoo that matched one on her mother's arm.

Chancellor General Vegan Casper and his beautiful wife Hoola gave Electra and Larry an especially warm greeting which became a feeding frenzy for the media. The entire wedding had been holovised in seven galaxies. The Caspers were Electra's Godparents, and Vegan was the elected leader of One United System, a unity of more than 5,900 human inhabited planetary systems in the tri-galaxies. Vax Legas was within the Royal Galaxy—one of the tri-galaxies.

Bodhi, Winn and Tish gushed over Electra and Larry, and Electra got to see her young disciples again—Artana and Shanti who were now ten years old. Winn was as tiny as Electra and could still pass for a teenager. Bodhi is Electra's mom's most senior disciple and Vicar General of the Adamantine Will Order of which Larry was a cadet. Bodhi always treated Electra reverently, and wholly approved of Larry. Tish whispered a few suggestions into Larry's ear regarding the consummation of the marriage and he listened intently. Then she gave a serious nod and he obediently nodded back.

Prime Minister Yona from Om didn't mention the Ambassador's shuttle when she greeted the newlyweds. The elderly genius, Jard, former member of the High Council of Om, told Electra, "Way to go with that shuttle caper. I was impressed."

"It did accomplish my marriage to beloved Larry," Electra told him.

Jard pressed a data bead into Electra's hand and told her, "Here are some programs to seize control of whatever stands in your way. You kids are going to change everything. I wish I was young enough to track your entire journey Cosmic Girl."

Jard called Electra's mother "Love Child" and now he was calling Electra "Cosmic Girl". Electra was not sure if she liked it or not. She replied, "Thank you Jard. I'll try to be ethical in my application of these."

"Well don't forget to have some fun with them too," he suggested.

Hours dragged on and planetary leaders passed by along with celebrities. A few greetings were really fun, like with the Whirling Vortexes and with Green and Antic. Most were rituals of state, tedious but necessary. High Admiral Swenah teased Electra about her poopy diapers on the bridges of *Apollo* and *Reciprocity* during two wars Electra had been through as a baby. Konax, who was like a favorite uncle, swooped her off her feet into a hug. Captain Schwin couldn't thank Electra enough for the guidance and support she'd received in the battles of Randu. Aton held up the line to chat about his upcoming marriage to Admiral Swenah. They hugged nine feet tall Kluzzyst in space suits, and adepts from nine galaxies.

The couple dutifully greeted guests until there was no one left to greet. At that point they were led to the banquet hall where Electra had a second reunion with her disciple Whiffle, the virtuoso anorexic-looking saxophone player for the Whirling Vortexes. The kids were seated at the long central table in the vast hall with three interplanetary leaders and one world leader.

Family, friends and celebrities filled the other seats. Real fermented sparkling wine from the most famous vineyards on Monarch was served to every guest who wished some, compliments of Mel. Electra and Larry got their flutes topped off.

Electra picked up a snip of conversation from the table behind hers, "Just like her mother she's attracted to runts."

"Well, she's a runt herself."

"She's too young to marry. Her chest is flat as a board."

"I wonder if that skinny boy even has pubic hair yet?"

Electra tuned those voices out, not much liking them. The first course was being served and consisted of platters of raw oysters on the half-shell and baked oysters. There was also crusty black bread. Electra downed her flute and got it refilled to the tippy-top. She dragged her upper teeth across a shell to liberate the oyster into her mouth, knowing it wasn't very lady-like. Shudhiy burped her appreciation of the food in the Islohar way, bringing a smile to Electra's face.

A girl sitting across from Electra was smiling at her and Larry. She couldn't be a day older than fifteen and she was uncanny cute. She was almost as small as Electra. An ancient wisdom shone in her eyes and she wore a relaxed half-smile expressing her vital energy. Electra extended her arm across the table and had to stand up and reach as she said, "Hi. My name is Electra."

Even with the veil and train removed her dress still screamed "wedding gown". The girl had to rise also to grasp her hand across the table. She said, "I'm pleased to meet you. My name is Ki."

"Then you're our chaperone-instructor."

"That is my training and service. It is a great honor to serve the Mu and her consort."

"You're like 92 years old, aren't you?"

"Ninety-three. My birthday was last week."

"Happy birthday. Are you practicing the internal concentrations along with having taken the reversal of aging drug?"

"No. I must first age beyond this insanely hormonal developmental stage. When my cells are twenty-eight years-old I'll begin the practice of the internal concentrations."

"This sex stuff is powerful," Electra told her. "There have to be ways to harness it for spiritual development earlier in the path, other than sublimation by abstinence."

"That would likely attract a larger percent of the general population to serious practice."

"And constitute an accelerated methodology," Electra added.

"Though you would need to weed out the ones there just for the sex and not the spirit."

"That wouldn't be difficult. A good quantum AI android could pick those out."

"I'm excited to see what you come up with."

"Well give me a moment. I'm still a virgin you know."

"A most precocious and influential virgin I might add."

"It is not my intention to offend you or put you off in any way. I'm sorry if I've been rude."

"Not at all. Your mastery at your age is a shock and you are clearly going to be fun to hang out with. I think you're awesome."

"It's kind of weird hanging out with a 93-year-old adept in a fifteen-year-old girl's body."

"Not as weird as hanging out with a not yet fourteen-year-old girl who *is* an adept."

"I guess so. It must be even stranger for Larry."

"His heart is your heart and his whole orientation is your love and reciprocity."

Larry nodded seconding this, "I couldn't have said it better."

Electra asked, "Do you have a lot of sex Ki?"

"I sometimes perform as an action seal, but other than that I'm celibate and make my meditation practice within the sisterhood and schedule of the monastery."

"Are you ever the action seal for cute young guys?"

"The masters I have served have all been at least in their seventies."

"That's a shame. Do you ever do it with the newlyweds you instruct?"

"I instruct, advise and consult, but I do not have sex with either partner of newlywed couples."

"That's a shame. Don't you have any sexual aspirations?"

"I do, to be honest. Though I know hardly any males and have very infrequent contact with them."

"Have you done it with girls?"

"Decades ago, I did."

"I did it with a girl at school," Electra confided.

"She'll likely become famous for that."

"You ought to join my entourage and take a sabbatical from the monastery. I need you as a tutor. There's a Clear Light knight named Tokk who's really cute, and I think he's single. Larry has friends who would do anything to have sex with a girl; it's all they can think about."

"It's a tempting offer, and everyone I know would do anything to be a disciple of the Mu. Let's see if you still need me after tonight."

"I need you as a friend. Girls our age don't tend to be very interesting."

"I will need to consult my Abbot."

"I hope she lets you."

The second course—a green salad—arrived with a green mint leaf and basil, cilantro and parsley dressing saturated with garlic and held together with a dab of yogurt. The dressing was so good that Electra used the greens to convey it to her mouth until her plate was empty. No one lingered on this course and it went quickly. Next were bowls of shark fin soup. Ahhu had noticed Ki and so had Kristy. Electra found this interesting. Down the table she could see grandfather Aton with High Admiral Swenah. It was obvious how in love they are. Electra slipped her arm around Larry's waist and felt her own romantic magic. Larry's arm came immediately and gently around her. She felt empowered and authorized by his love, and needed it to mobilize her task and face the world. She drew confidence from Larry's irrational faith in her. She loved him so dearly a tear formed in her eye to run down her cheek.

Larry felt cushioned by romantic bliss and like his every exhalation was a sigh of ultimate contentment. Feeling her torso beneath his arm sent shivers of delight up his spine. He experienced her love as overwhelming and piercing. Those waves generated in the conference center touched the depths of every heart. He still didn't feel adequate or worthy of Electra, though Sarhi, Pez and Electra herself all insisted that he is her consort by providence, grace, destiny and Divine Will. Who was he to question *them*?

The next course was fresh raw tuna with pickled ginger and green horse radish paste on the side. Mel's voice said in Electra's earbud, "The necklace of the previous Mu is on its way by courier to you from a museum on Ganahar. Sarhi wants you to wear it dancing in the ballroom."

"What if I lose it?"

"It has a tracer in it and I'll keep track of it for you, sweetheart."

"Thanks Mel."

"Isn't Ki cute?"

"She's an adept elder Mel."

"I think you'll get her laid."

"I'm not going to have sex with her, though she'll have better chances in my entourage than in her all girls-monastery."

"That's what I meant."

"Ahhu or Kristy might seduce her."

"I'd put my money on Kristy."

"She wants a male though."

"Well, Gumby's flirtations seem to be winning her over at the moment."

Electra saw her half-brother pouring on his princely charm with Ki, and said to Mel, "I bet he's already told her that he's in my mother's inner circle."

Mel told her from the data, "He's mentioned that twice so far. She seems more interested in his connection to you as your half-brother, and growing up as your sibling."

"Do you think she's seriously considering him?"

"I think she's exploring her possibilities and keeping her options open, but he's certainly a candidate."

"Is she pretending to be fifteen?"

"No. She has told him she's had the telomerase drug though she didn't mention her specific age either."

"Are we still at risk of some kind of attack Mel?"

"You are no longer the target. The new target is the entire wedding guest list. They know your mother is here and that Vegan Casper and Admiral Swenah are here. A number of admirals arrived in warships which are just outside the last planet of this solar system, in inter-star territory. These gangsters want to preserve their little empire and rackets here, and think it's all over if Vegan Casper gets out of the solar system."

"Are we ready for them?"

"It would take the allied fleet twelve and a half minutes to jump in and take control of space around Vax Legas."

"They could level the hotel in seconds."

"This hotel is worth over 25 billion dags and is owned by the supreme leader and most powerful gagster of the planet. It is practically brand new and is the premiere hotel and casino on the planet. I doubt they'll destroy it."

"It depends on how bad they want us dead."

"I would have to rate that desire extreme."

"Are they mobilizing?"

"No. They are still planning and haven't yet come up with one they like."

"Are you sure?"

"I'm listening in on their war council, so yes, I'm quite certain."

"Who's leading the allied ships?"

"Admirals Ishvara and Starmite. Ishvara heads the main fleet at Randu and Starmite commands the big war ships out past the dwarf planet, eleventh from this star."

"Do we have anything over the hotel?"

"Two combat shuttles at all times, and two wings of Phantom Raider fighter bombers with ace pilots. The two wing leaders have adepts aboard."

"That's not much."

There are allied war ships parked at the industrial and public space stations and a squadron of Trix super-bombers in berths at the yacht club. Then there's the Ahumdulilah super-freighter unloading war materials by shuttles down to a warehouse I purchased outside Vice. The freighter is armored, has military grade shields, and class 9 weapons aboard. We think Zandarhar is hiding a task force of powerful ships somewhere within the system. We suspect they're cloaked on the sunny side of the planet closest the star."

"Well that sounds a little better."

"Admiral Bodhi is considering bringing *Total Dominator* in to orbit Vax Legas, ignoring their domestic law against ships orbiting within planetary space."

"That would protect us securely, though surely bring the whole thing to a head."

"Believe me Electra, the safety of the Mu is paramount to all the decision making."

The next course, spicy hot sea scallops in a sauce over green and red rice, was in process of being served to the diners. Electra was impatiently longing to have sex with Larry and her sexual energy was concentrating. It seemed to her to be going feral. She asked down the table of her mother, "How long do Larry and I have to dance in the ballroom before I can take him to bed?"

"You have to get it going sweetheart, and Pogo was hoping you'd perform the new song you wrote together, on stage with him. It's getting transmitted live in nine galaxies."

"That does sound like a rare opportunity. I'll have to change. I'm not going on stage in a wedding gown. Is there a make-up artist here?"

"Of course, my love."

"I think I'll wear that tight T-shirt that doesn't clear my ribcage."

"You mean the one that looks painted on?"

"Yes. And I'll wear my black tights with it."

"The Kristy look."

"She has style."

"I always thought Ming does."

"She's too middle aged now. I want to find the crest of catalyst."

"Are you going barefoot?"

"I'll wear my metallic gold colored slippers."

"So, you'll basically be performing in your underwear."

"I guess that's what your generation might call it."

"Well, there was a time when Hoola took the stage in only her Hugme's crotch-less panties."

"If I looked like her I would too," Electra said honestly.

"I think she's wearing her leotard tonight to hide the stretch marks from her two pregnancies."

"She's become a formidable martial artist."

"Yes. It has helped her keep her figure and she's quite routine with it."

"I'm going to perform the song with Pogo and the Whirling Vortexes."

"Everyone will be grateful."

Pogo called down from his end of the table, "You and Larry will dance alone for the first song. Then everyone will join you on the dance floor for the next piece. Right after that I thought I'd put you on the stage for our song as lead-vocals and rhythm guitar."

"Then I'll have to change and get my makeup done right after this meal. We'll skip the eighth course. Stall them until we get to the ballroom."

"No problem."

"May Larry play bass guitar and Tramp accompany me playing rhythm?"

"Sure!" Tramp shouted down the table. "Our yacht, *Spaceship*, is parked in the oversize outdoor lot and has a tailor-fabricator unit, so I can take Larry's measurements and make him a stage costume."

"Great."

"Come here sweetie," Tramp directed Larry.

He went right over and got his neck, waist, torso and limbs measured by Tramp, who was saving the data to her hand device through her skullcap. She told him, "A gold metallic stretch-tight jumpsuit and 24 karat gold half-helm ought to do it."

"I've been practicing the bass parts recently."

"You're going to knock them dead sweetie."

Larry wasn't sure about a stretch-tight jumpsuit. He knew everyone watching would be able to count his ribs and that he'd look like a holo-poster for starving children. Thank the Cosmic Intelligence that anorexic-looking Whiffle would be on stage with them; and Electra is skinny too. He knew that Electra really wanted to do this, so he was committed, though anxious. Electra's energy was growing more powerful and turbulent by the hour, and affecting him beyond his control. He felt like he was being dropped into the adult world from the far reaches of the atmosphere without a parachute.

The scallops plates were collected and a new course of fillet mignon in a reduced shallots and burgundy wine sauce was being served. Neither Electra nor Larry ate red meat so they excused themselves from the table to go change and do makeup. Before they'd gone five feet from the table, they'd picked up Evenrude, Johnson, Kim and Tokk. Agents in silk suits were matching their progress from both sides of the banquet hall. Space Marines in dress uniforms awaited them at the far doorway they were headed for. Becky and Rann fell in behind them. Before they reached the doorway, Green and Antic were framed in it. Their trip to the penthouse went with the precision of a well-executed joint military operation.

A young woman with many piercings, a couple of bio-cyber electronic appendages and tattoos all over, was there with two large cases of makeup and applicators to work on the Mu and her consort. Larry stood self-consciously in his boxer shorts awaiting his costume from *Spaceship* by courier. Electra was already in her tights and T-shirt getting her makeup done. She wanted her eyes really dark. Becky was watching the woman put makeup on Electra.

Rann ran to the penthouse door to retrieve the costume when it was delivered, hurrying back to get Larry into it. She got it back to the room and held it out to help Larry into it. Larry started to put a foot into a leg without removing his boxers. Rann pulled it away almost tripping him and said, "You can't wear those. They'll show right through and make you look a fool."

Larry wasn't ready to let go of his boxers and started to protest. Rann just tugged them down to his ankles holding them to the floor captive while kneeling in front of him. What she had just done was bad enough, but her position placed her eyeballs inches from his manhood—or perhaps boyhood—Larry considered.

"It's really pretty and I bet it's still growing at your age," Rann told him sweetly.

Becky had a bird's eye view and nodded affirmation of Rann's assessment. Electra turned her face, neck and torso around to get a glimpse, and got a black line across her forehead for her troubles from the makeup artist. Larry was bright red and darkening to purple by now. Electra really wanted to fondle it but had to turn back and get the smear off over her eyebrow. Rann gave it a little kiss before offering Larry a leg to step into. He got into the jumpsuit quickly as his member became tumescent from the kiss. Rann had to reach in and stand him up straight to get the zipper up on the jumpsuit. It wouldn't bend down and there was truly no room in the costume for straight out. Larry got his bass guitar to hold in front of his crotch.

A few minutes later it was his turn with the makeup artist and he had to give up his guitar to sit in the chair. Electra's energy had achieved a new level of mass integration and was leaking off the excess in waves. It was almost entirely arousing sexual energy and Larry was stuck with a bulge on his abdomen through the stretch-tight. The girls watched as the makeup artist did his makeup, though they really weren't looking at her or Larry's face. Green stuck her head in and informed them, "The guests are moving into the ballroom from the banquet hall and Pogo wants you there in less than fifteen minutes. It takes about four from here."

Another buzz from the door had Rann running to answer it. She returned with a package from a museum on Ganahar addressed to Electra, and she'd had to give a retinal scan to complete the transfer. Electra said with excitement, "It's my necklace!"

She ripped the cardboard box open and removed the velvet coated box with a latch. It required a six-digit code to open. Without thinking Electra entered 1-4-2-8-5-7 and popped the latch. Larry asked her, "Did Sarhi give you the code?"

"Does Sarhi reveal relative data to anyone? Of course she didn't."

"How did you know?"

"I had an intuition. When you make nine equidistant points on a circle and number them, the linear numerical sequence exhibits the temporal process. The process in space is internally connected by the numbers of the repeating decimal resulting from the division of one by seven. This gives the figure of the internal lines connecting point one with point four, four to two, two to eight, eight to five, five to seven, and seven back to one. With its nine points and inner lines the figure is called the enneagram. Points nine, six and three are connected by lines forming an equilateral triangle. It is a tool for holistic analysis of any complete process."

The necklace had a 36-karat violet diamond at the center, and to either side of it twelve karat sapphire's, then twelve karat emeralds, then twelve karat topaz, then twelve karat rubies. Nine gem stones in all, flawless and exquisitely cut. Electra fastened it around her neck. It hung further down than it would on a thicker neck, making her look like a child playing dress-up with her mother's jewelry.

Larry's eyes were intensely highlighted by the makeup artist. The kids were rushed by their escorts to the ballroom with their guitars, which ended up in Green's and Antic's hands when the kids were pushed onto the dance floor under the spotlights. Frisbie got a slow beat going on the drums and Tramp strummed out the rhythm while Hoola let wail with her voice and added some guitar riffs. Whiffle launched into a harmonized tangent on sax while Pogo brought the keyboard into the mix and sang chorus with Whiffle and Tramp.

It was a slow-dancing song and Larry's Academy had taught all the cadets to be proficient at ballroom dancing. He took Electra's hand in his and got an arm around her with his attention in his feet and in the music. Electra closed the gap to squish up against him, still erupting in waves of erotic arousal yet intensifying. And it wasn't just the waves because Electra was passing him energy through her hands into his back. It was the same energy of unstoppable arousal. Not only that, but she was rubbing up against him mercilessly. He tried to keep some of his attention in his feet and the music.

Blinded by the spotlight and acutely anxious that every eye in the ballroom was upon them, Larry ached for his beloved within a fog of romance as he tried to keep time to the music and move gracefully. It was hard to tell with the spotlight beating down on them, but he was pretty sure Electra was illuminating light over her head and shoulders.

As the song concluded Larry was grateful he had not stepped on Electra's toes. Other couples were coming out on the dance floor now and the spotlights had ceased their assault. No longer bathed in lights from the ceiling, Electra glowed like a lit bulb with a radiant halo of blue, violet and green. He whispered to Electra, "Your aura is surging something fierce."

"I know. Your erection is driving me nuts."

"Well your energy is filling me and making me hard. I can't help it."

The music took off like a shot, inspiring bodies in motion. Larry didn't like free-style fast dancing. It made him feel self-conscious. Electra was double-timing the music with her feet, arms akimbo and pelvis rocking and gyrating. Larry matched the music and went into a blocking sequence from his martial arts, trying to get out of his own way and let the music take over his body. Although Electra was no longer passing that sexual center engorging energy directly into him by touch, the waves emitting from her grew just as powerful.

With the lights dimmed, Electra was transformed into a spectral-illuminator inducing a glare. She made a triple spin on one toe before leaping over him in a forward flip. While sailing over his head she tapped his crown with all five finger tips of her "hook hand." Larry's crown channel wheel opened instantly to activate his extra-cranial point above his head and liberate his energy to circulate and distribute freely. Larry's dancing mutated from a sort of martial exercise into creative expression celebrating the music.

Then the song ended and both Larry and Electra had to retrieve their guitars from Green and Antic to go up on stage. Larry's dread was near dormant from whatever Electra had done to him out on the dance floor. All the same, when he arrived on stage and caught sight of the size of the crowd, his psyche attempted to retreat into panic. Some deep abdominal breaths with his attention one-pointed on his guitar made the threatening panic retreat and dissipate.

Frisbie on drums kicked off the next number as the other members of the band joined in. Electra's voice wailed. She strummed out the rhythm with Tramp, supported by Pogo on keyboards. Larry picked his bass strings in an intricate pattern of sounds integral with the whole, as he became his function in unity with the band and music. In the flow state with no self to be found, Larry's attention was entirely on making music and he forgot the audience.

Electra was all over the stage and in the air like an acrobat, without missing a note on her guitar, and her voice filling the ballroom. It was an exciting new sound for the Whirling Vortexes and the audience was eating it up. Even with the stage lights brighter than day, Electra's aura was out shining them in radiance. At least 30 hologram cameras were rolling and transmitting the performance live to at least 22,000 human inhabited planets in nine galaxies.

They finished to wildly enthusiastic cheers and applause. Electra took her husband's hand and led him in an exaggerated bow to the audience. Then she pressed into him wrapping her arms around him to kiss his mouth long. An absolutely fantastic surging tsunami of a wave passed through Larry turning part of him to stone, to then crash over the 15,000 people in the audience. Words didn't quite form but open vowel sounds of delighted surprise arose towards the stage and travelled to the back of the ballroom rapidly, having an effect on everyone. Some of the cameras cut to the audience reactions catching the looks on faces. News commentators were mingling with the crowd interrogating witnesses.

Electra finally stopped kissing Larry and said gravely, "I need to take you to bed this instant my beloved."

"I better have my gate closed with the pressure point before you erupt another of those waves."

"What waves?"

"The near-events you're emitting."

"Am I?"

"It's already all over the news."

"You're kidding," Electra said as embarrassment seized her.

"You are. And your aura is ignited and lit up like never before."

"We better get out of here," she replied as she led him back stage.

"You were magnificent and truly unbelievable on stage my love."

"So were you. I've never heard you play better."

They passed backstage where their security detail picked them up flanking them. Green and Antic led the way with Becky, Rann and Ki in tow. Larry kept the body of his bass guitar in front of his crotch and abdomen with the neck straight up so as not to bump anything. Electra had her guitar strapped over one shoulder. While to some guests at the hotel Electra appeared a skinny child let out in her underwear, to Larry she was the ultimate goddess of sexuality, the pure form of beauty and the spiritual center of the universe.

Inside the penthouse private lift with both arms around Larry sharing one partition, and security personnel each sectioned off in their own, Electra spewed another big wave over them. Green told her, "Divert power to your third eye sweetheart or you'll have us all knocked off our feet."

"What?!"

"You are a focal point for the potencies of the entity of the spiritual congress darling, and it seeks release to restore equilibrium following its tremendous workout during the BiVortex War," Green explained.

"You need to learn how to transfer your merit to others quickly sweetheart," Antic added.

"Well isn't my mother balancing her own support system?"

"You made yourself director of that support system honey."

"I was only trying to help."

"And you did; incredibly so," Green told her.

"So this burden is what I get for my efforts?"

Green offered, "You are such a blessing and the events are actually healing. There is no safer release from stress than orgasm. You cannot help that your arousal is contagious and expansively influential, affecting others. There are no negative consequences in it."

"Well Larry and I are going alone in *Vajra Yogini* to jump into deep space 50 million light years from here."

"This is no time to be trying to leave the system," Green explained. "The Vax Legas space fleet is on high alert and fully mobilized. It's simply too dangerous."

"I don't want to cause an event," Electra complained.

"You might be too young to produce a full one," Green suggested, before adding, "you could always abstain."

"On my wedding night?! Feeling like this?!"

Antic inquired, "Have you fully apprehended the virtues of virginity?"

"I've been there, done that and have the little Academy uniform," Electra declared frustrated. "I'm a married woman and desperately horny."

The lift doors opened to the penthouse foyer and they all spilled out, Electra still latched onto Larry. Their Space Marine sentry at the door shot it open for them through his skullcap. Green told Electra affectionately, "Go study with Ki and practice on Larry sweetheart, and don't have a single worry about events."

Electra gave her a dubious look. Antic teased, "If you do conjure an event princess, then all of Vice can have a little taste of the consummation of your marriage."

"Thanks," Electra stated sarcastically over her shoulder. She was letting Larry guide them through the cavernous labyrinth of the penthouse. She was lost on their first turn. Larry didn't even have his penthouse schematics hologram up and was expertly leading them rapidly to the master bedroom suite. A few rooms and intersections looked vaguely familiar to her as they proceeded. Electra got the bedroom door open with her skullcap the moment it came into view down the hall, and set some meditative music playing, soft lighting and the bed vibrating before they crossed the threshold.

Larry told her awed, "Your aura lit our way and we otherwise walked through the penthouse in the dark."

"No way."

She looked back down the dark hallway, its end hidden in the gathered gloom and shadows. "Oh my!" came out of her mouth in surprise.

They entered and Electra whisked the door closed with her skullcap. It didn't take her a moment to get out of her slippers, tights, and T-shirt. She kept the Mu necklace on and took off the one from the planet Tiffany. She put her skullcap and earbud on the night stand beside the bed and said to the room, "Mel, could you shut down all the cameras and microphones?"

"I'm kind of busy. Don't worry because only I have access to those. I've got to go."

"So just turn them all off!" Electra insisted.

There was no response and the connection was dead. Larry was getting out of his stretch-tight jumpsuit and this fully captivated Electra's attention. He was yet stone and listing a few degrees from vertical. Ki slipped into their room naked and directed them onto the bed. She grabbed three meditation cushions from their sitting room and carried them onto the bed. Ki assumed half-lotus posture on her cushion and said, "We'll start with the Equal Ceremony. Sit facing each other and begin vase abdominal breathing. Keep your attention one-pointed in the secret place below the naval without divesting any attention to the thoughts arising, abiding and decaying in your mind. Allow your mind to settle as you concentrate intensely on the point in your abdomen. Enter meditation and become aware of your pure consciousness that observes your internal and external processes."

She left them in the state for about five minutes before saying, "Now open your eyes and look into your partner's left eye as you alternately repeat 'you love me'. Open to the love and the recognition of the same consciousness in your partner as in yourself."

After a little more than five minutes she said, "Generate your partner as a deity and become aware of the dreamlike nature of the waking state. Expand your love to encompass all sentient beings. Tune to the Calling supporting ascent to on high; the divine love attracting all beings to return to the Absolute. Empty your body making it vacuous within translucent skin. Bring the red drop up from the channel wheel in your pelvic cavity to merge with the indestructible drop in the vacuole in the center of your heart channel wheel. Bring the white drop in your crown down through your central channel to merge with the indestructible drop in the vacuole in the center of your heart channel wheel, uniting the conventional truth and the Absolute truths. Shine forth your light through your translucent skin to illuminate the entire universe."

When she saw that they were both within the state of mystical union, Ki instructed, "Now withdraw your senses by bringing the upper and lower winds into the central channel through the lateral channels and absorbing them into the indestructible drop in the vacuole in the center of your heart channel wheel."

She gave them a little time for this step. Then she directed, "Electra, prepare Larry's phallus for mounting by employing any of the ancient techniques."

Joyously Electra reached for Larry's penis which did not appear to require any preparation, already steel hard in anticipation. Her hand was almost there with her head following, and it was at attention in readiness when a great explosion rocked the hotel. Blaster fire not far away was audible through their sound proofing. Green dashed into the master bedroom and ordered, "Get dressed in textile armor jumpsuits and put on your fanny pack shield generators."

- Chapter 5 -

The kids got into their textile armor jumpsuits and shield generators quickly. They got their skullcaps on and earbuds in, and put on slim lightweight AI goggles with optics features including a facial recognition program and threat indicator. They got their hand devices snuggly into a pocket and were handed shoulder holsters with blaster pistols. Before putting them on they each received a heavy textile armor vest with flexible overlapping fiberglass armor plates within to protect vital organs. Each was handed a blaster rifle.

Green told them, "Follow me. We're taking the private penthouse lift down to sublevel 6 where 20 Space Marines in hard-shell combat spacesuits are waiting with a combat space shuttle. Did Ki get a fanny pack?"

"I did," Ki let her know.

"Well, everyone turn-on your shield generators now. The penthouse is one of the attacker's objectives."

When their little party reached the penthouse door to the foyer, Evenrude and Johnson were there in full combat gear. The lift was at their floor with the door open. They poured onto it followed at the last moment by the two Space Marines. Every partition was in use even with Electra and Larry and Green and Antic each sharing one. Kim and Tokk were aboard and so were Ki, Becky and Rann.

The lift dropped at a faster rate than free-fall until about the mezzanine level when it started braking and their feet started trying to push through the floor. The door hissed open and they exited quickly. A path to the shuttle ramp was flanked to each side by Space Marines. Some were discharging weapons, indicating clearly that the enemy was attacking and closing. They hurried down the path and up the ramp through the open airlock. Green took the pilot seat.

Becky and Rann went to their own combat shuttle parked next to the Space Marine one. Once in the pilot seat Becky informed Green, "Schwin and June have their squadrons almost to jump speed and will be in the system in moments. They're jumping in close."

"How many squadrons?"

"A dozen each."

"That should do to cover our exit from the system."

"Are you taking her to Glitter?"

"That's what she wants."

"I'll jump in with you. Give me your destination coordinates when we're approaching jump speed."

"I will. You take the lead and keep fire off this shuttle."

"I'm almost ready."

Green laid down some fire with her twin nose blasters, wasting invaders in one area, and shot off some canister missiles to one side of her shuttle clearing another area. The Space Marines were all aboard and two were strapped in to the quad blaster turrets taking down attackers and sublevel 6 support columns alike. Becky eased her shuttle forward with blaster fire sparking off her shields, and her gunners returning fire. Green followed. Electra, Larry, Ki and Antic were strapped into passenger seats in the main compartment and Kim and Tokk were with them. Evenrude and Johnson were in the jump-seats to either side of the airlock in the stern. Eighteen Space Marines took up their entire seats in the main compartment.

Electra released her harness and then released Larry's to sit beside him in his seat. The belt went easily over both their laps and the shoulder harnesses crossed between them. There was still room enough in the big seat for someone Ki's size to join them, having been built to accommodate large beyond the norm white sun humans within hard-shell combat spacesuits. Electra got her arms around her beloved Larry. Larry embraced Electra with both arms feeling the magic of their connection and as happy as happy can possibly be.

Electra told him, "You're my husband now and I can kiss you whenever I feel like it," just before covering his mouth with her own.

Larry had no objections whatsoever and launched into it with her. The shuttle was just coming out of the underground parking up a large sixty-degree angle tubular shaft. Becky was ahead and taking heavy fire, though giving at least as well as she was getting. She had the little attacking patrol ship's shields stirred up with help from her quad blaster gunners and Green discerned a soft spot in the ship's shields caused by the turbulence to them from taking hits. Two larger undercarriage missiles left the combat shuttle one after the other to pass right through the patrol ship's shields. The first blew a hole in the hull and the second one blew inside the ship, turning the whole thing into a flash of brilliant molten molecules and vapors spherically expanding and fading. Becky flew right through the cloud with her shields sizzling. Only adepts who can see auras can see the soft spots in shields when they are churned up by taking fire.

Schwin was just inside the Vax Legas's lunar orbital distance but still going too fast for target resolution or anything more than ghosts on her sensor's hologram monitors. She let out a war whoop over the coms as she ignited a reverse booster dropping her velocity to .24 light speed and sensor clarity.

Ordnance and blaster fire erupted from every weapons system on her Tsunami Devastator and on the two drone fighter bombers flown from her cockpit. A patrol ship closing on Green and Becky expanded into quadrillions of super-heated particles, and a wing of enemy bombers popped into spherical clouds.

Schwin told Becky over coms, "I've got four wings assigned to protect you and the shuttle the Mu is on until you jump out of the system. I'm leading them."

"Where are our ships?"

"Some are undocked from the space stations and engaging the enemy fleet, and the rest are yet a few minutes out."

"That's not good."

"I brought 192 heavy bombers and 384 drone fighter bombers. There were already some of our Phantom Raiders here stationed over your hotel. We'll manage."

Electra could feel the danger of the situation and abruptly stopped kissing Larry—leaving him breathless—to pull up a hologram of the space surrounding the shuttle. With a deep breath she sank into contemplation while shooting out the crown of her head into space. Some hundred and seventy thousand miles away she erupted micro-suns over the bows of two destroyers so bright and potent that primary sensors fried and the view ahead was white on white for those ships. She illuminated some more micro-suns amidships then covered the sterns while the suns on the bows yet lingered brightly.

Eight Trix super-bombers were unloading everything they had into those destroyers and a bunch of Tsunami Devastators were helping too. Green spent her last two undercarriage large missiles on a soft spot in a destroyer's shields. Her investment paid off with a gigantic explosion turning a threatening destroyer into a spectacle of light fading to nothing at all. Several space cruisers and a super-battleship were closing to intercept them. Dead ahead, though several light minutes out, a task force of large warships awaited to prevent their attempt to escape.

Electra got Captain Caish on coms and said, "I've sent you the AI program for the 12 quad blaster turrets. Upload it to the ship's quantum computer and undock to join the fight."

"I thought you'd never ask. I'm undocking now and looking forward to this."

The cruisers were almost in range and closing. Becky put them into a wide turn, angling their heading away from the task force waiting for them a few light minutes out. Green followed behind ready to take evasive action. Pez had lifted off in *Aphrodite* and was clear of the atmosphere but too far behind to help. Just as two Vax Legas cruisers achieved range on Green and Becky, their shields went wildly turbulent and completely visible for several seconds before each relinquished its form to become an expanding sphere. Green turned on her violet spectrum decloaker and saw two Zandarhar ultra-super-battleships running interference for them.

A Zandarhar Admiral asked Green, "What's your destination?"

"Glitter."

"Just stay between our sterns and we'll all jump out together. Send me the precise coordinates and we'll take you all the way."

"Here," Green told him as she sent the data via skullcap over coms.

"Got it."

Green told Becky, "Turn on your decloaker and get between the sterns of those two Zandarhar ultra-super-battleships."

"It's already on and I see them. I'm headed between them now."

Not being in the cockpit, Electra had no decloaked view. She asked Green, "What just happened?"

"I'm linking my piloting hologram to your holo-pedestal now sweetheart."

"Wow! Those are some big ships. Are they Zandarhar?"

"Yes. They've been courting your parents in hopes of making a connection with you. Zandarhar does not much care for Om, but they are family with planet Mother, and they've adopted planet Ganahar. They love the Im and the Wu, but they really want the teachings of the Mu."

"Well, I'm still gathering data and formulating those. I'd be much further along if this attack hadn't occurred. Of all the ill-timing this has to win the grand prize."

"I know sweetheart. On your wedding night."

"Worse than that. Ki was just having me prepare him for mounting when the big explosion hit."

"What terrible timing. Don't worry, sweetheart, you'll be mounted on him in no time."

"I hope so."

A cruiser on their tail joined by a super-cruiser and several super-battleships were closing at an angle just behind them. Class 9 beam and blaster weapons were already in range and firing from the big ships. Some enemy small combat craft were trying to get at the two shuttles between the Zandarhar ships. Since the enemy were now employing their decloaking optics too, the Zandarhar ships dropped cloaking to divert the power for it to shields. By the time Class 8 weapons were in range and firing, all shields were stirred to a tempest with the hits they were taking. Green told the

Zandarhar Admiral, "Fire some large torpedoes to follow my canister missile. They'll slip right through the enemy shields."

"Will do."

Green let fly four canister missiles in sequence one after the other to form a line into the soft spot in the shields of one of the super-battleships attacking them. The Zandarhar Admiral had some mighty big torpedoes just behind the little canister missiles following the same line. The four little explosions did nothing more than scorch a patch of the hull black. The first giant torpedo hit and the whole ship jolted sideways. Three more hit the same spot breaching the hull and at least one blew within the interior of the ship to blow up the reactors, which exploded the whole ship in a sort of micro-supernova.

Green shot off four more with a second between each, all headed to a tiny patch of thin veneer within the thrashing tempestuous shields of a super-battleship. Zandarhar torpedoes followed behind the little stream of canister missiles. The first four little explosions were meaningless to the integrity of the giant warship, doing nothing but charring the hull. The big torpedoes drilled through the hull and armor unimpeded by the shields to blow the ship to smithereens.

With sheer brute force the two Zandarhar ships blew up the super-cruiser on their sterns after bringing its shields down with beams, blasters and ordnance. The little cruiser veered off and ran for its life. Schwin's wings of bombers and fighter bombers kept Vax Legas small warcraft off and far away from the two shuttles with her ace pilots coordinating their efforts to make short work of them.

They were now some twenty-million miles from the third planet, Vax Legas, and accelerating nicely with nothing chasing their sterns. The task force waiting for them had fired boosters to intercept them at a close angle to their trajectory, which could be turned into a long engagement with a bit of maneuvering. Admiral Ishvara was already in the system with half the allied fleet and braking madly to achieve sensor-scanner clarity and resolution for fire control. He was only 19-million miles from the third planet and headed for it, going the wrong way to help them. Pez was gaining on them in *Aphrodite*. Admiral Starmite arrived some twenty million miles out and headed for Vax Legas, also of no help to them.

The Zandarhar Admiral told Green, "That task force will be in range in a minute and nineteen seconds. I'll send torpedoes on the tail of your canister missile streams. The Wu must send us a teacher to show our adepts how to exploit these shield anomalies."

"The Wu herself will be on Zandarhar in a couple of days. She will teach your adepts. Watch what the Mu does this next engagement. Pez can teach your adepts who have attained their rainbow body of light how to blind ship sensors completely."

"This is a great opportunity for Zandarhar Space Fleet to fight alongside top Pez Fleet personnel and see firsthand the techniques of spiritual warriors."

"Pez wants to bring the population of Zandarhar into the spiritual congress."

"If Om presides over it, we are not interested."

"No governments have the least influence over the spiritual congress. The Im is the Abbot and the Mu has recently taken over the function of directing the focus and leading it. The Amonrahonians germinated the seed of the spiritual congress and support it with their 100-year meditation. The Im forges the relationships to populate the congress. The purpose and objectives of the spiritual entity were established at its origin by the Amonrahonians."

"What is Om's involvement?"

Tens of millions of Om's population participate in the spiritual congress when it is called into session, and both the Clearlight Order and the Thunder Perfect Mind Academy Monastery hold continuous vigils around the clock supporting it."

"The Om government yet has some components in very low vibration."

"Pez has recently become a member of the High Council and has disbanded the Government House security force, and seriously curbed the authority of the Space Controller Agency. She is chipping away at the low vibrations aiming to get Om on the path to moral anarchy."

"Then we will join the spiritual congress. We are coming into range now. I must go."

Aphrodite was closing on their sterns and slowing to acquire target acquisition speed. The enemy task force was firing on them with class 9 beams and blaster cannons from their port flank and about to enter class 8 range. The canister missiles are short range so Green would need to wait until they are in class 7 range to hit soft spots in shields with them. There are eleven big ships in the task force against the two Zandarhar ships. The moment was indeed tense.

Aphrodite got her speed down to .24 light speed and a second later two of the eleven big Vax Legas ships transformed into blue streaks like shooting stars. They shot towards deep space as their tails faded. Ahhu and Kristy were both aboard *Aphrodite's* bridge. Each had made a quantum jump with a drone fighter bomber to inside of a Vax Legas super-battleship bypassing shields and hull to manifest within at 0.7 light speed, resulting in those blue streaks. They are the two best intuitive drone pilots of all the allies. Om was still working on a purely technological means of accomplishing this, and had been trying to achieve this for decades without success.

Micro-suns began engulfing the bows and hulls of the remaining nine enemy ships so brightly that they diminished even the senor-scanners on the Zandarhar ships and on *Aphrodite*. Torpedoes from *Aphrodite* slipped through a soft spot in the shields of a Vax Legas super-battleship to breech the hull and blow the ship all over space in an expanding sphere. Two enemy ships were entering class 6 blaster range and Green already had streams of canister missiles headed for soft spots in their shields. Zandarhar torpedoes were racing right behind them. The two super-battleships blew almost at the same time in spectacular living color, spending every drop of energy in a micro-second to produce this visual sight.

Green already had lines of canister missiles speeding to soft spot targets in the shields of two more ships with Zandarhar torpedoes playing follow the leader. *Aphrodite* was shooting torpedoes and large missiles through a thin film of shielding on a super-cruiser, nailing its hull directly. Ahhu and Kristy each jumped another drone fighter bomber—borrowed from Schwin's bomber wings—into two more super ships, to produce two more blue streaks. The last super-ship was running away with its tail between its legs.

Pez asked the Zandarhar Admiral, "Where are you headed with my daughter?"

"She wants to go to Glitter. I'm sending you the precise coordinates of our destination."

"Thanks for coming to Electra's rescue."

"The Mu is an intergalactic treasure we will always protect with our lives."

"I'll be headed for Zandarhar after Glitter."

"Your ship destroyed seven of the enemy ships and it is only a little yacht."

"My drone-jumpers wasted four of those. With the torpedoes I carry I can kill super-ships by exploiting soft spots in their shields."

"Your daughter blinded all their sensor-scanners rendering their fire ineffective."

"Sometimes in close melees the blinded enemy ships crash into each other and hit each other with their fire and ordnance. I'll teach your adepts who can leave through their crowns in their bodies of light how to ignite blinding micro-suns on the hulls of enemy ships."

"We are honored to host you and your spouses but we are not recognizing you as an Om high council member. You shall be honored and revered as the Wu."

I'm not coming on a diplomatic mission for Om. I'll be a representative of the spiritual congress."

"We are desperate to receive the Mu's teachings."

"She's not quite fourteen years old yet and she's accelerating her development to the maximum. Believe me. It's stretching my nerves and tolerance."

"We are aware of this. We seek assurances."

"Well, Mel has already begun construction of a Mu monastery on Zandarhar. Electra's sure she has at least two of her old disciples residing on your planet and means to find them. Your population already fits prominently into her plans."

"The elders will be most grateful and pleased to hear this news."

"Will I get to meet any of them when I come?"

"They will be participating in the three-month meditation retreat with you, and are intent on connecting with you."

"We-re closing on jump speed so let me go to attend to my navigation."

"I'll see you in the Glitter system."

From the cockpit of the combat shuttle, using Green's coms, Electra contacted the Zandarhar Admiral to say, "Hey. Thanks for rescuing us. You guys are awesome in battle. Will I get to meet you?"

"It would be the greatest honor of my life to meet the Mu."

"Come to the Blockbuster Hotel in the capital. I've booked the Grand Wazu Suite. But give me 24-hours to consummate my marriage. These hormones are driving me insane."

"I will be there 24-hours after you enter the hotel. Congratulations on your marriage. We greatly admired your performance with the Whirling Vortexes. Many of their songs have become classics within our culture."

"Thank you. Say, did my breasts show through my T-shirt?"

"There were two suggestive visible points in evidence."

"Do you think I looked like I've cleared puberty, because I have you know?"

"Your charisma was entirely adult," he offered diplomatically.

"It will be really fun to meet you. I have to go strap in for the jump."

"Until we meet again, sweet Mu."

Electra joined Larry in the same seat and barely had time to sink into meditation before they jumped through quantum space, which has no material components, into the Glitter system. Green was in the state of contemplation, and so was Becky in her shuttle, both already reversing main drives and powering up reverse mini-drives full. Reverse thrusters were ignited and throttled up to maximum, all within a second of arriving in the system. The giant Zandarhar ships had cloaked and could only be seen with the violet spectrum decloaking. They were already way out ahead unable to dump velocity as quickly as combat shuttles, and would likely have to circle Glitter's moon to get their speed down from having jumped in so close.

Electra was snuggled into Larry, smooching with him, and getting turned on in the process. Everyone on board was feeling a corresponding arousal. It was certainly a strange trip being on her security detail, though not too different from being part of Pez's entourage. Green could sense acutely how desperately Electra needed release. The Zandarhar ships disappeared behind the curve of the moon as the two shuttles sped past it with Glitter growing in their holograms on approach.

Green had checked in with Glitter Space Control moments after arriving in the system. With the Mu aboard her shuttle and the Wu pacing her in *Aphrodite*, Space Control was clearing a lane for them right down to the capital city. It is a busy place with much passenger and industrial traffic. The planet has four large space stations and several smaller ones. Traffic platforms kept opposing lanes well-clear of each other and were numerous. Several colossal space construction platforms had ships framed at their sides. Industrial space platforms and weapons platforms speckled space around Glitter. Some 50,000 holocoms satellites formed a low orbit sphere around the planet.

Green headed right for the hotel hanger with Becky and Pez following. The folks in the other shuttle and yacht were all feeling aroused from Electra's being in heat. Pez told Green over coms, "You better get the kids in bed together quick. Is Ki on your shuttle?"

"She is and I'm getting them there as fast as I can."

"It's like being a young teen again. I can hardly tolerate it."

"Just resolve it with your spouses as soon as we land. Antic and I are going on a hot-tub date."

"We will have to; obviously. It's like a driving itch taking over my mind."

"Ki calls it 'hormonal madness' and suggests living through a hundred years of it before feeling sorry for yourself."

"I can't even imagine."

"When are you going to Zandarhar?"

"I want to see Electra and Larry before I depart."

"You'd best wait a day."

"I assumed as much and now it's clear."

"I wish I was going with you."

"I'm eternally grateful to you for watching over my daughter. With you at her side I can have peace of mind."

"Your Space Marine champion and Becky are elite agents and warriors. We will do our jobs and keep Electra safe."

"Captain Schwin is going to remain close by until Electra is back in school on Mother, so call on her if you have need."

"That's good to know. I will. Where's Sarhi?"

"She's being picked up by *Reciprocity* and will take a shuttle to meet me on Zandarhar. Now that she's performed their wedding ceremony she refuses to be in the same solar system as them; at least until Electra cools her jets."

"She's a wise woman," Green said admiringly.

"She's not at all generous with relative data," Pez complained, "and tends to treat me like a mushroom, keeping me in the dark."

"Like I said, Sarhi is a wise woman."

"I see the hotel hanger roof entrance."

"Your yacht won't fit. It's just for shuttles. They have a yacht lot behind the hotel."

"There's 300 feet between the roof entrance and the hanger floor. I can go bow first at an angle."

"If you say so. I wouldn't try it."

"Let me go in first."

"Sure thing."

Pez sped ahead and achieved the angle she wanted to follow straight through the hanger door. Her vortex redirect and generation turbine was powered up full and she started braking like a maniac. Electra caught the scent of excitement and opened an eye while kissing Larry, to look at the piloting hologram directed to her seat pedestal by Green. She watched *Aphrodite* disappear through a hole in the domed roof, bows first like it was crashing. She opened her other eye too, and stopped kissing Larry to stare at the hologram. No flames shot out the entrance hole in the dome, so that was a good sign.

Pez could feel the whole maneuver of her landing in her gut and knew she had this. On top and bottom of the yacht she cleared the entrance frame by inches. She had to reduce her angle to the ground to zero quick, and was already on it with swivel turning drives and thrusters. Her stern tail pinged on the lip with a little jolt to the yacht and Pez got the belly horizontal with the ground to ignite all landing thrusters full, just a second before the electro-hydraulic landing legs touched down. With her forward momentum not entirely checked, the yacht skid about 40-feet until the nose came to rest against the dent it produced in a hotel hover-limo shuttle. Just as she knew she would, Pez made it. Getting out would likely be quite an ordeal. She didn't really have the same gut feeling about that.

Electra asked Green in a panic, "Is mom alright? What just happened?!"

"Your mother just likes a challenge, sweetheart, and I'm sure she's fine. I'd wager there's at least a bit of damage involved in that landing though."

"It looked like a crash to me."

"As many of her landings do. I've seen much more severe ones from her."

Green brought them in at a safe but good clip and dropped through the hole belly-first on her vortex redirect turbine and landing thrusters with her landing legs down. She hovered a few feet over the hanger floor to maneuver into an empty parking space. Pez and a hotel administrator were both examining a crater-like dent in the otherwise immaculate top-end hover-limo bearing the hotel crest. Naked Ahhu came over to them and handed the hotel administrator several thick bundles of cash, which apparently settled the matter.

Electra was amazed by the skid marks in the landing concrete. It was super-concrete and could withstand tens of thousands of pounds per square inch without chipping or cracking. And here it was grooved with trenches and cracked in all directions. She was sure Ahhu's payment had covered this damage too. She caught up with Pez with Larry in tow by her hand, and asked, "Is there damage to *Aphrodite*?"

"I lost a sensor from the tail and scraped off some of the cloaking lens material. The nose is just fine. That pretty hover-limo hull is like aluminum foil."

"Well, your yacht is actually an armored warship, beautiful as she is."

"Admiral Spalding made it for me and you learned to walk on *Aphrodite's* decks."

"It's the only home I recall growing up. It seemed we were always going from one monastery to another."

"Well, I was head of two Orders on Mother, another on Ganahar, and the Rajaha and Avahat of the people of the tri-galaxies. Thank goodness for Bodhi and Selene, who are heading up the two Orders on Mother now. I was stretched thin back in those days."

"You can retire when I turn 24 and start teaching."

"I don't think the Amonrahonians are nearly done with me yet, sweetheart. Only Sarhi knows for sure, and she doesn't tell me anything."

"She plays everything close to her chest like the good general in the ancient *Classic of War*."

"Even that good general kept the commander leading the charge in the loop."

"Not always," Electra contradicted as her perfect memory spewed out a passage she quoted from the text.

"I don't appreciate being kept in the dark," Pez complained.

"What did it cost Ahhu to cover the damages?"

"I think the Administrator's insurance man quoted over coms 4,000 dags for the dent and 38,000 for the concrete landing floor."

"That's pocket change to Ahhu. She gave me a purse worth 30,000 dags."

"I have nothing to do with currency and don't deal in it."

"I know mom. You're lucky to have Mel and Ahhu."

"I was told they handle such matters for you as well."

"I have my own money now."

"From where?"

"From beating crooked gambling games on Vax Legas."

"How much did you win?"

"About 820 million dags altogether. I bought a small Ahumdulilah warship and had it fixed up inside like a yacht. I still have 550 million left. Mel put 70 million dags into my ship but I didn't ask her to."

"You sure are imprinting impressions fast as humanly possible."

"You, Amazonia and Sarhi taught me well and made it possible."

"I don't think any of us really knew what we were in for."

"I can't wait to try out all that stuff from the ancient texts on Larry."

"He's very sensitive sweetheart. Remain tuned into him. Remember the pressure points for redirecting his energy and attention to help with his control. If that's not enough then grab the base of his phallus and squeeze hard. That will take his attention away from the head of it and calm him down."

"Alright momma. Ki will be leading us through the meditations with the action-seal employing copulation as a method for realization of the ultimate clear light."

"I know you're ready. With the new depth of his connection with you, the law of communicating vessels will get Larry there quick."

"I have to find Ki a lover."

"Isn't she monastic?"

"She needs a break and wants to be sexually active with an attractive young person. She is not going to begin her internal concentrations to support the reversal of aging drug until her cells are 28 years old and she is clear of teen hormones."

"Well, I certainly can relate to that. Good grace with your match-making. Tokk is the youngest Clear Light knight we've ever had and he's quite good looking. He might be single."

"I'll work on getting them together. I think she finds Gumby kind of cute too."

"Isn't he a bit young for her?"

"He was really putting out trying to get a date with her in the banquet hall and she was enchanted."

"Oh dear. He *can* be quite the charmer, our little prince."

"An adept older woman would be good for him."

"A hundred years older?"

"Her experience has been extremely limited by monastic life, mom. When it comes to romance, she is fifteen."

"I trust you and defer to you in almost all matters, my love. It is hard for me when it comes to sexual matters to defer to an almost fourteen-year-old virgin though."

"I can see your point, but experience is always enrichment and fuel for wisdom-compassion. Teens lose the child's imaginative ability to create make-believe that seems like reality. Adults lose the teen edge for really going for life experience."

"I think it's because we learn the difficulties involved in transmuting negative consequences into wisdom-compassion. Correction and over-correction via heartfelt service, amends, and apologies is the surest way."

"Until we have enlightenment in the market-place we remain disharmonious and out of equilibrium. Living in a monastery is an important developmental step and hopefully includes a three year and three-month solitary meditation retreat. More adepts need to live in society and frequent the market-place, work at preschools, care for the dying, transmit the teachings and model good citizenship."

"And you will harness group energy, the energy of copulation, the energy of the couple entity, and other natural forces to accelerate human evolution and focus it on ascent."

"To support both individual enlightenment and societal movements towards enlightenment. We need social movements with everything construed to expose the absurdity and genocidal nature of ego duality."

"We are one, my beloved daughter. I serve the Mu."

"Would you stop that mother! You sound like Shudhiy."

"I understand her better now."

"As my mother you're not allowed to call me the Mu. I'm your daughter and I need you to be my mother."

"Whatever you say dear."

Ming wrapped an arm around Electra and told her, "I will always love and nurture the human animal dimension of you sweetheart."

"You're such a blessing in my life, mother Ming."

They were inside the hotel, though many levels below ground, and coming into a lift foyer. Electra had already called up a lift with her skullcap before they stepped into the foyer. There was no way they were all going to fit on one lift, even two to a partition. Personal space was important in the quantum age of interstellar travel. Once it was scientifically established that an energy field a few inches beyond the surface of the skin objectively exists—relatively speaking—the practices of stuffing humans into elevators and trains so tight that they were all scrunched up against each other, were lost to the dustbin of history. And partitions with blackout capacity were installed in elevators. Being in someone else's personal space is beyond bad manners, rising to a moral issue. In some instances it can be a crime.

A lift came and opened its doors revealing eight partitions. Evenrude and Johnson each took up whole ones, five received couples, and one had Electra, Larry and Ki stuffed in it. Pez, Ming, Rubix, Ahhu, Trix, and Kristy all got off at the lobby to get a suite at the desk. Then the door closed and they rose to the 96th floor where the three-bedroom Grand Wazu Suite is located. Both Becky and Rann, and Green and Antic would have rooms, and Evenrude and Johnson would take turns sleeping on the sitting room couch. The kids had the master bedroom and Ki went with them.

Electra shed her textile armor jumpsuit and fanny-pack shield generator in a jiffy, then stripped out of t-shirt, panties, skullcap and earbud. Her eroticism was on the rise and visibly affecting Larry as he undressed; and likely affecting everyone in the hotel. Ki was naked before Larry, and got pillows they could employ as meditation cushions. When Larry was out of his clothes, they all sat in meditation posture on the bed.

Ki instructed, "See all appearances as illusory and empty. See your partner and yourself as deities. Follow the eight steps to calm abiding and emptiness."

She paused to give them time to proceed through the steps. After a while she said, "Sit facing your beloved and close your eyes. Meditate upon emptiness with great bliss. Manifest all three aspects: bliss, pliancy, and meditative stabilization."

Ki gave them some time for this, then led them through a meditation to loosen the knots in the heart channel wheel. Electra was already there with all the knots unraveled. Ki was just about to direct Electra to prepare Larry for mounting—although he didn't appear to really need any preparation—when Evenrude burst into the room shouting, "Get your textile armor and fanny-pack shield generators on immediately. There are dozens of Vax Legas black-ops teams in and around the hotel."

He turned off the dimmed lights completely and shut the blackout shades on the window. Only the radiance of Electra's aura, enflamed by her acute arousal, provided illumination for the kids to get back in their clothes. Larry told his beloved awed, "You really do glow in the dark."

- Chapter 6 -

"How many Space Marines do you have in the hotel?" Electra asked.

"Twenty counting me and Johnson," Evenrude answered.

"Where's my mother?"

"She and your parents had to get a suite at the Grand Interstellar Hotel down the street because they only had little economy rooms left here."

"Where's Mel?"

"I'm right here with you sweetheart."

"Does mom know this is happening?"

Mel replied, "I alerted her three minutes and seventeen seconds ago."

"Where are my Clear Light knights?"

"Kim and Tokk are guarding your door in the hall on this floor. Six others are hunting Black-ops teams," Evenrude told her.

"How many agents of ours are here?"

"Four with you in the suite and four more covering the hotel roof."

"What's our plan?"

Evenrude explained, "Captain Caish is in low orbit in *Vajra Yogini* and we need to get you kids on it. Vax Legas has only combat small craft in and around the capital. They have nothing here that can defeat your little warship. The Zandarhar admiral can protect your ship in Glitter space. Getting you to your ship is going to be the hard part."

"Where's our shuttle and what's our route to it?"

"We have several waiting and our route will be fluid depending on the positions of the attackers."

"Why are they still trying to kill me?"

"They're not," Mel chimed in. "They think they can prevent One United System (1US) from taking them over and ending their corruption if they hold the Mu hostage. They want to kidnap you."

"Well, that sucks," Electra complained.

"It sucks big-time," Mel entirely agreed.

"Why didn't you warn us Mel?"

"They figured out that their security system and coms were being used to spy on them, and made their plans in a secure room."

"What's momma doing?"

"I have no idea," Mel declared. "All she told me is that she's going on the warpath."

"That can't be good for their Black-ops teams," Electra commented.

"No, I suspect that does not bode well for them at all."

Evenrude insisted, "Get to the front room of the suite, away from the outer wall and windows. There could be a missile strike."

As Electra was going through the door from the master bedroom a man in all black clothes with a short heavy blaster wearing a climbing harness, crashed through the window firing. Evenrude hit him with a short burst of 40mm grenades and all the pieces left the master bedroom out the window with explosions. Evenrude announced, "He's gone."

"In sections," Electra said in shock.

They all hurried to the front room where Larry, Electra and Ki were armed with blaster pistols in shoulder holsters and blaster rifles. Electra asked Evenrude, "Can I get one of those grenade shooting things?"

"There's one in my weapons trunk in the front hall closet off the foyer. Get yourself an extra clip magazine and set the weapon to three round bursts to preserve your ammunition."

"Yes Sir," Electra stated as she went to the closet. She had always thought Hoola looked so cool firing one of the grenade automatic guns out the train window from the tunnel beneath New Haven on New Monarch. It was still shown on holovision annually on Liberation Day—the biggest holiday in One United System. Electra hoped she'd be caught on optic recordings firing one in the hotel.

She found her gun and grabbed an extra 60-round clip magazine out of the trunk. She held it up and asked Evenrude, "What am I supposed to do with this?"

Evenrude rummaged through the trunk a moment and extracted a strap with smart-velcro and a stick-on patch of the same, to adhere to the magazine. He helped get the strap buckled for her and attached the big magazine to it. It was a lot of bulk and weight for her tiny body. She looked like a child playing make-believe combat. He knew not to under-estimate her though.

As a cadet warrior-monk, Larry had weapons training and handled his blaster rifle quite professionally, although clearly the weight was a strain for his skinny arms. Some noise from the master bedroom had Evenrude and Johnson racing to it. Over his shoulder Evenrude ordered, "Get your fanny-pack shield generators turned on."

They could hear blaster fire in the corridor outside their suite door. Green held a blaster pistol in each hand and had one aiming down the hall towards Electra's bedroom and the other aimed at the suite's door to the hall. Becky was half in the foyer closet covering the front door and both Antic and Rann headed down the hall Evenrude and Johnson had disappeared into. Electra's aura—more a halo arising from her neck and shoulders—was still the only source of light in the room.

Green asked Electra, "Can you turn off your lights?"

"I don't know how. I've never had this problem before."

"See if you can raise your awareness out of your lowest channel wheel into your third eye, sweetie, then bring it down to reside in the secret place."

"You mean get out of my groin and into the flow-state?"

"Precisely sweetheart."

Electra concentrated intensely and entered the flow state through her channel wheel just below the navel. She was all presence without thoughts or duality of self. Thus gone. But her lights were brighter and more intense than ever. Green said to no one in particular, "Oh dear."

"What?!" Electra demanded.

"It will be like trying to get out of the building carrying a spotlight."

"There's nothing I can do about all the damned light."

"Put on the cape and hood you got married in"

"It's in the bedroom."

Blaster fire from the master bedroom had them all looking into the gloom of the dark hallway, punctuated by flashes of light. A staccato of exploding grenades roared in their ears; then there was silence. The suite was blanketed in a haze of smoke. Green called down the hall, "Evenrude, Electra needs her black cape with the hood."

"There's more of them out the window on window-washing hover platforms and hanging from above on lines. Rann's bringing the cape."

"There's also a battle in the hallway outside the suite."

"Check on Kim and Tokk and give them support if they need it. Johnson and I will defend the windows"

"What about the windows in mine and Becky's rooms?"

"Those have portable forcefield shield generators covering them. Electra got started with Larry and Ki too quick for us to get one set up in her room. It would take a missile strike to take down the forcefield shields."

"I'll check on the hall situation."

More blaster fire resounded from the master bedroom. Rann helped Electra into her cape and hood. Once it was on only her face glowed like a 200-watt light globe. Green cracked the suite's door open and got Kim on her coms at the same time, "What's your situation?"

"They're coming from both directions down the hall."

"Can we get to the fire stairwell or lift?"

"Only by fighting our way to it."

"Are any Space Marines with you?"

"Two are; Hatch and Stables. The rest are fighting their way up the fire stairs or commandeering hotel hover-carts."

"Is the rooftop ours?"

"No. We lost two agents on the roof and the rest have had to retreat two floors down."

Evenrude, Antic and Johnson came sprinting down the hall and Evenrude yelled, "Get in the tub in the bathroom! They've got a hover platform with a canister missile battery!"

The big bathtub with jacuzzi jets had a depth of four feet and was made of thick marble. They each turned off their fanny-pack shield generators. Ki and

Electra were first to jump in and lie flat. Becky landed on top of them and Electra screamed, "Ouch!"

Larry hopped in next, then Rann and Green got in. Antic got in last. Evenrude and Johnson hit the bathroom floor to the side of the tub just as three missiles exploded in succession.

Evenrude was up in a flash and out the door into the hall between sitting room and front door foyer, firing his automatic grenade gun. Johnson was right behind him laying down supporting fire with his heavy tripod blaster rifle. The smoke was thick and their kitchen down the hall from the cross-section was on fire. Black-ops were in the three bedrooms and two hallways. Kim said into Green's earbud, "They're intensifying their assault out here and Stables is wounded."

"I'm coming to join you. Things are pretty bad in here too."

To Antic and Becky, Green said as she climbed from the tub, "Support Evenrude and Johnson." Then she looked Rann in the eyes and said, "Protect the Mu with your life."

Rann nodded gravely to Green as she left. Becky ran out of the bathroom armed to the teeth after turning her fanny-pack shield generator on. Antic crouched in the doorway partly behind the frame and wall, peering out. Ki, Electra and Larry disentangled and separated to get their shields up. Rann stood with a blaster rifle at the ready between Electra and the door, prepared to die before letting harm come to the Mu. Blaster fire zipped all around them and grenades barked out explosions down the hall to the left. Their optic goggles resolved the smoke clouding the bathroom and Electra's face lit the chamber. Sounding worried, Antic told Electra, "Face the water closet sweetheart. You're illuminating our position."

When she did and got the hood pulled lower, it was like a little flashlight pointed at the back wall, leaving Antic in shadows. Antic said gratefully, "That helps."

"I don't want to hide in the bathroom facing the corner," Electra complained.

"Just for a minute or two, sweetie, so I don't get shot."

"Alright," she forced herself to agree.

A battle raged to either side of the bathroom and a bolt from a heavy tripod blaster pierced their wall to kill one of the twin vanity sinks. Water shot up to spry from the ceiling, making a monsoon in the bathroom. Water sizzled on their shields. Electra's face was lighting the room again as she looked around. Antic fired from the doorway as black-ops rounded a corner down the hall. A blaster bolt aimed at her nose was taken on her shields, but had her ducking back inside the bathroom. Though it caused no physical injury, the experience inflicted shock and trauma.

Rann went to the door jam and lobbed a thermal grenade down the hall before backing up to close the door. It wasn't all that loud and was drowned out by the grenade gun's explosions, but their door melted dripping on the inside. They were now sealed in. Inches of water filled the bathroom floor. Electra and Larry got in the tub to stand, where the water was escaping down the drain. Ki joined them. Antic was still crouched in shock by the dripping door. The water spraying off the ceiling was cooling it fast and some of the drips were solidifying.

Rann slapped Antic's face and it was like the lights came on in the temple of her body. Rann made eye contact sensing she's back and told her, "I need you functional."

"We all have to die sometime," Antic said to get herself going.

She checked the power cell on her blaster rifle and asked, "How are we going to get the door open?"

Rann speculated, "I think we'd need a portable beam weapon at this point."

Antic got Evenrude on coms and could hardly hear him over the symphony of sound his gun was raising. She told him, "We're trapped in the bathroom. Our door's melted shut."

"Is someone taking a shower in there?"

"No. That's the pipe from the shot sink, shooting water into the ceiling."

"We can't hold this position. Some of my Space Marines have reached this floor in the fire stairs. I'll hold the attackers off while Johnson tries to get your door open. Stand in the tub."

Antic and Rann dutifully stepped into the tub against the wall out of direct line with the melted door. A piece of doorframe sailed across the bathroom into the water closet door, punching through it to waste their toilet. Now the bathroom was filling up fast. The entire melted door flew next from its impact with Johnson's foot. It came to rest in the squirting spraying water closet. The monsoon was becoming a hurricane. The water sizzling off their shields had the humidity higher than a tropical rain forest and a fine mist hung in the air among the big spraying drops. It was almost like being under water.

Johnson shouted, "Come on! We've got to get out of here."

Electra, Larry, Ki and Rann followed Johnson, and Antic took up the rear. Evenrude and Becky were in a fighting retreat just to the bathroom side of the intersection in the hall. Johnson opened the suite door and peaked out. He reported, "The black-ops are only down one end of the hall now. Green has a hover-shield to cover you to the stairwell door. Turn that light out though."

I can't. It's not electric. It's me."

"Well lower and tighten your hood. Maybe try squinting your eyes a little."

"Am I going first?"

"Right after me. I'll put down some covering fire. Stay behind me. The attackers are down the hall to the left and you're going right out the door behind the hover-shield."

"Yes sir."

Johnson opened the door wide and stepped into the hall firing his tripod heavy blaster on full automatic. Electra followed safely behind him since his size made him like a wall. She hurried over beside Green, who was controlling the hover-shield with her skullcap while firing around the side of it. They backed up with the shield keeping pace. About 50-feet down the hall a Space Marine got an arm around Electra's waist to pull her into the stairwell. At the same time attackers emerged from a suite further down the hall to the right firing at them. Electra was exposed, the shield only protecting from fire coming from down the hall to the left. Green jumped in front of Electra taking dozens of blaster bolts to her shields and textile armor as the Space Marine in the stairwell yanked the Mu in, out of the line of fire.

Green was prone on the floor in the hall. Johnson, Tokk, Kim, Rann and Hatch were caught in a cross-fire with wounded Stables. Hatch turned to confront the new intruders who were shooting him in the back, and launched a mini-missile from each shoulder of his hard-shell space combat suit while he fired a heavy blaster rifle into the cloud of smoke his missiles created. His sensors read zero movement and zero life readings down that end of the hall.

Electra frantically hauled Green into the stairwell by her arm. Green's shields had been overpowered and taken down, and her armor was pierced in the chest. She was unconscious and fading fast. Electra unfastened the textile armor and fiberglass plates vest, then ripped Green's shirt wide open exposing her bare chest. A cauterized wound made an ugly sight between her breasts.

Antic sensed Green was dying and rushed into the hall shooting. Evenrude followed trying to cover her. Two Space Marines in hardshell suits went out of the stairwell behind Green's hover-shield to support Evenrude. Becky came out of the suite firing a blaster pistol in each hand. Mini-missiles and 40mm grenades turned the hallway down to the left into a conflagration. Rann ushered Larry and Ki out the door towards the stairwell. Flames were raging down the hall the other way.

Electra laid both palms over Green's chest to become a direct channel of the highest healing emanations, passing them into Green. In only seconds Greens eyes fluttered open looking into Electra's. She asked concerned, "Why are you palming my breasts?"

"I healed you," Electra told her as she snatched her hands away self-consciously. Then she added, "They're nicely shaped and really firm."

"I remember getting shot in the chest but there's no sign of a wound."

"I healed it. You saved my life, sacrificing yourself."

"There's no trace of it. I have no pain and full range of movement. I don't feel weakened, but in fact energized."

"Tell Evenrude to get Stables in here," Electra insisted.

Green passed this along to Evenrude, listened, then told Electra, "Kim has taken one through the thigh and Antic two in the belly."

"Get them all into the stairwell fast!"

A Space Marine in a hardshell combat suit rushed up the stairs to their position and reported, "We can't get out by going down. They're thick on the stairs and have heavy weapons about twenty floors down. The rest of our men are being backed up the stairs towards us."

Evenrude backed in and lay Antic down with her head resting in Green's lap. Green's eyes teared seeing her beloved partner in such pain. Antic said with a strained voice, "I thought you were killed."

"Almost; though Electra healed me."

Electra already had Antic's vest opened and was separating her shirt by ripping outwards from the bottom. Two gruesome holes detracted from the otherwise flat enticing belly. Electra got her palms on Antic's stomach and abdomen concentrating. Antic's pained expression relaxed and she sat up better than new to hug her beloved Green. Evenrude was already delivering Electra's next patient. Blaster fire was getting closer down the stairwell.

They had to get Stables out of his hardshell combat suit which took a Space Marine to accomplish. Kim was already waiting in the wings as Electra laid hands on Stables. The man was truly amazed and all gratitude. Kim was stoically holding her thigh and trying to breathe into the shooting pain. It felt like someone was sawing her leg off. From the waist down Electra stripped Kim to her panties. She quickly got both palms on Kim's thigh to sink into the state of void. Kim heaved a sigh of relief, then clutched Electra in a thankful hug.

Larry, Ki, Becky, Rann and Tokk were all now in the stairwell. Their floor was on fire so they would have to leave it. Since they were losing ground below and could not get down that way, only going up remained as an option. Evenrude and Johnson led the way. Electra held her automatic grenade gun in both hands aimed at the ground in front of her. Green and Rann remained close to her.

Stables had vowed internally to himself to serve and follow the Mu for the rest of his life. Kim made a similar vow to herself. Not only was her leg miraculously and immaculately healed, but the little nymph had filled her with out-of-control sexual energy that had her throbbing with pleasure. The girl's face was lighting the way on the stairs. Kim had experienced Electra fill every heart in the conference center with waves of love, and had seen her blind destroyers and super-battleships in a space battle. The girl has super-natural abilities and is a constant force of the good. Electra would have to get her erotic energy under control soon or the whole hotel might break out in an orgy.

Explosions wracked the metal stairs below echoing through the well, and stair sections in their wake dropped down on the ones below. A Space Marine protecting their rear told Evenrude, "They're firing heavy weapons from about twenty-five stories down."

"We're getting off the stairs at floor 137."

"We'll make our way to you."

Evenrude exited on 137 with Johnson. The power was off in the hotel and the view through his goggles was kind of in the green spectrum. The hall was clear with no signs of battle. Tokk came out of the stairwell next. The three men covered both directions of the corridor while the rest of their party joined them.

An explosion down the stairwell shook a few flights of stairs loose to crash below. Smoke was spilling from the H-VAC vents from the fire on their suite's floor.

Johnson blew away the locking mechanism on a suite's door then kicked it in. Evenrude was calling up a shuttle to meet them on the north face of the building on the 137th floor. He told them, "Just go to the only window showing light in the room."

They marched straight to the back through the suite and into the master bedroom to the window, ignoring the naked couple on the bed. Electra checked them out as she walked by. They looked old to her; probably already into their 40's. She felt a little envy towards the woman's full bosom, but focused on the battle she is in to get that comparison out of her mind.

Evenrude pulled Electra's cape and hood off to illuminate the room. The couple on the bed backed up cowering at the sight. Larry tried to ease their terror by saying, "She's the Mu. She's good and won't hurt you."

Electra was almost directly in front of the window with her light piercing the gloom. The stern of the shuttle filled the window and its ramp lowered to just touch the sill. Evenrude opened the sliding transparent plasteel window and gestured for Electra to board the shuttle. They got onto the ramp one at a time and hurried into and through the airlock. Evenrude went last. His girlfriend was in the capital of Om and his need for her was great thanks to Electra's energy and its influence.

The ramp was closing and the group was moving through the foyer into the passenger compartment. Green went directly to the cockpit while the rest strapped into seats. Electra and Larry shared one with room to spare. Electra asked Green over coms, "Can you route the pilot hologram to my seat's pedestal?"

"I'm already on it sweetheart. If it's needed, I'll go out too and plant micro-suns to blind ships or small craft. I can also exploit soft spots in forcefield shields with missiles from the cockpit."

Electra turned on her seat's holo-pedestal and examined it. There was air traffic, though nothing obviously military. There was also a great deal of lower flying hovercraft traffic. She dialed up a long telescopic view using her skullcap and saw numerous yachts and fast mini-freighters, as well as assorted shuttles. She flipped on her violet spectrum decloaker and only two Zandarhar super-battleships emerged in her holo. Those ships were in very low orbit protecting the shuttle she's in. *Vajra Yogini* was into the atmosphere and its hanger bay doors were opening. Captain Caish was guiding their shuttle pilot in over coms with a charmingly calm voice. Electra really liked him.

Their landing on the hanger deck was a bit awkward due to being in the atmosphere. The bay doors closed the moment they were through. The air at this altitude was mighty thin and the compressors in the hanger were airing it up. They lowered the ramp and came down without waiting for the blue light announcing full air pressure. They were only meters from the airlock into *Vajra Yogini's* bowels. Electra ran straight for the bridge holding Larry's hand and pulling him. The four Space Marines and the four-shuttle crew manned eight blaster cannon turrets. Two Clear Light knights and Becky the rest.

Electra kicked Captain Caish out of the pilot seat to assume it. Larry took the copilot seat, Green the weapons operator seat, and Caish moved over to the sensor analyst seat from which he could also handle coms. Green told Electra, "The fallback plan is the government house in the capital of Monarch.

Chancellor General Casper can guarantee your safety there."

"Well, what about my slot on *Star Hunt*?!" Electra complained.

"I'm sure if we cannot make it back in time, they would be happy to reschedule it. Ratings went up for all media outlets that holovised the performance of the Whirling Vortexes at your wedding reception."

"What did the critics say about my performance?"

"It was well-received and applauded. You would not be flattered by the endearments they came up with for you."

"Like what?" Electra demanded.

"Oh, like sacred child-star and holy girl; stuff like that."

"What did they call Larry?"

"A pre-teen idol and the little cadet."

"He's not pre-teens!"

"No, but all his fans are."

"Tough for them because he's in love with an older woman."

"You're both thirteen."

"I'm almost fourteen and I'm more than four months older."

"I wouldn't worry about his loyalty."

"I'm not."

"So, may I set our jump coordinates for the Monarch system?"

"Alright," she reluctantly agreed.

"You could give us full power to drives and thrusters," Green suggested.

"I am. I don't really want to leave Glitter."

"We'll come back when it's safe."

Caish suggested, "You'd best find a different hotel because the one you were in will have major renovations going on for some time."

"Mel? Are you there?"

"Of course I'm here."

"Could you reserve me a big suite or penthouse at the Ultimate Luxury Intergalactic Hotel? It has a really nice women's accessories boutique."

"The penthouse isn't available. How about the bridal suite?"

"That sounds romantic."

"There. I've booked it for a week starting tomorrow night."

"Did you get all the lenses and microphones shut down at the penthouse in Vax Legas before Larry and I got undressed?"

"Well, no. All the data and files at that hotel have been destroyed utterly. FUBAR as the Devil Dogs would say."

"So, no recordings are in existence?"

"I didn't say that."

"Please destroy your copy, Mel!"

"Sweetheart, I have to go. Pez is calling me."

Electra said to herself aloud, "I don't believe this. Hasn't she heard of privacy?"

"She and Jard had no sense of it with your mother," Green pointed out.

"I know. How many girls have their conception shown on intergalactic holovision?"

"That was far more embarrassing for your mother."

"Well, it's embarrassing for me too."

"I had an erection," Larry stated horrified at the prospect of the recording.

"So did my dad at my conception."

"I suppose it was prerequisite," Larry acknowledged.

The two Zandarhar super-battleships flanked *Vajra Yogini* to each side and the Admiral inquired, "What are our jump coordinates?"

"The Monarch system. I'm sending them to you," Electra replied. Then she asked, "Are you staying with us?"

"My orders are to keep you safe and no time limit was specified."

"I'll be staying in the palace in the capital. They now call it Government House."

"We'll be cloaked in space in high orbit, out of the way of all traffic lanes, keeping an eye out."

"Thanks. I guess we'll need to reschedule our meeting."

"We can set an appointment post-crisis."

"Good idea. I'll stay in touch."

Their velocity continued to increase and Electra gave them a countdown to the quantum jump in their holograms. Everyone concentrated to settle into meditation, then attain contemplation of the black near-attainment. The jump came. Exiting Glitter became entering Monarch without transition or moment between. Electra started immediately braking by reversing her main drives and firing braking drives and reverse thrusters. Monarch was the busiest system any of them knew of. The whole planet was a congested traffic jam and a nightmare to pilot through. It was worse than getting through the asteroids to New Yorkshire, which everyone referred to as 'Hell's Gate'.

Electra followed all the regulatory signs posted on space mini-platforms demarking her lane. The big shipping lanes formed a band aligned with the equator of Monarch and two funnels towards the poles, all terminating in medium orbit at space stations and shipping dock mega-platforms. The rest of the traffic was mini-freighters, yachts, shuttles, tenders, and other small spacecraft. All lanes were full and traffic thick bow to stern. She slowed every time the speed limit was reduced, which she had to being caught in the traffic.

They finally passed through medium orbit and much of the congestion was reduced. Green asked, "Where are you going to park?"

"On the ground at the 1US Space Fleet HQ. It's close to the palace."

"You'll be spending a fortune on thruster and booster fuel."

"I'm rich now and can afford it."

Mel said over the bridge speakers, "I've arranged membership for Electra and Larry at the Grand Old Yacht Club, and a berth for *Vajra Yogini*. They have a limo-shuttle service to the surface. They're quite exclusive you know."

"Well, I don't want to belong to some snobby exclusive club and I have a bone to pick with you Mel."

"Pick it with Sarhi. She's the one who insists that all facets of the Mu's life be well documented."

Green introjected, "Taking the berth would save much money."

"I'll call Space Fleet. Space Fleet, this is Electra, the Mu. I need to park my yacht at a berth on your main space station."

"We have your beacon. It looks more like an Ahumdulilah warship than a yacht."

It's a yacht on the inside."

"I see. Berth 96 is available and you are headed directly for it. A combat shuttle is being prepped to fly you to the Government House shuttle-port."

"Thank you. You've saved my reputation. They were trying to get me to join a snobby yacht club just so I could park."

I'm happy to be of service to you, ma'am"

Electra told Larry, "I've got some ideas for some ornamental fins, wings and racing foils to make *Vajra Yogini* look more like a yacht."

"I had an idea for a bow ornament, and a mount for it that would not be in the way of your twin nose blasters."

"What's your idea?"

"A slender female fairy with wings, stretching her arms over her head and standing on her tip-toes leaning forward."

"Print a 3-D model for me to see."

"I don't have my draft finished on my hand device yet, but I'm working on it with my skullcap. Here, I'll put it up in your side-holo."

"It looks like me."

"Well, I was trying to make her look beautiful."

"Give her bigger tits and we'll get her cast in platinum for the bow."

"How's that?" Larry asked after giving them a little more substance.

"Pretty stingy."

"Her arms are stretched up."

"Alright. Just make the points of her nipples more noticeable then."

"Like this?"

"That's a start."

How's this?"

"Not much better."

"Any more and she'll look cartoonish."

"Alright."

Larry finished his graphic quickly, made a slight reduction to the pointy nipples, and sent the data to the

3-D printer. Electra executed her docking procedures like a professional. She didn't even have a small-craft license because she wasn't old enough. Moral anarchy indeed! Green had suggested she try Divacaram because anyone who could pass the pilot test and the psychological testing would be issued a license regardless of age. It was on her agenda.

The airlocks of ship and station were connected and sealed, busy airing up. Electra led her husband, their sex instructor and her security detail—all but Captain Caish—through the two open airlocks into the station. A small honor guard met them to escort the party to the shuttle hanger. It wasn't far since there was a shuttle hanger between every other two berths. The shuttle was ready to take off when they entered the hanger. They boarded and took seats.

The brief flight concluded at the palace shuttle port. Vegan and Hoola were there personally to meet them. The palace was an immense structure of adamantine girders and structural supports coated in several feet of cut polished marble. On the inside there were several inches of carbon plate armor. While the building was mostly only 60 stories tall, it covered an area of eighteen acres and had some 99-story towers, sitting over 22-sublevels below ground. Networks of tunnels connected these to numerous buildings throughout the city. Before the revolution, the whole complex was Imperial Emperor Sponge the Magnificent's private palace.

Now the building contained much of the Monarch government offices, some of the 1US government offices, housed numerous elected officials and their families, situation rooms, a command center, and numerous apartments for service staff. Electra hadn't been here in years. It always felt like a museum to her.

The walk was long, and being martial artists, Hoola and Vegan never used hover-chairs. Their children were still on planet Mother in the Whirlpool Galaxy. Each couple or individual in Electra's group was a assigned a famous bedroom suite named after a revolutionary hero who had slept in it after the war of liberation. Electra, Larry and Ki got the Pez bedroom suite, which was the biggest. Evenrude would be right next door in the Ahhu bedroom suite. Vegan had doubled the guard at Government House and increased all security measures.

Electra had a portrait of her mother staring down at her from the wall and it made her a little uncomfortable. Electra shed her clothes as if they were on fire and Ki told her, "You must chill little nymph. We require food and sleep first."

Larry opened a room service menu so she could look too. She put an arm around him and clung yearningly. He wrapped his arm around her naked form. She was too distracting for him to decipher a word of the menu. Her energy was too intense and contagious.

Electra asked him, "What looks good to you?"

"I can't read a word of it with you naked in my arm and your energy penetrating me."

"It's all longing for you to penetrate me, beloved."

"It appears that we will have to wait until tomorrow."

"I don't know if I can make it."

Ki suggested sounding parental, "Get some clothes on, Electra, and let Larry read the menu."

Electra put on her tights and t-shirt considering herself dressed. Larry was able to skim down the menu and select an entrée. She was still distracting in her skin-tight outfit, and her energy remained unreal. His appetite for food was fortunately big enough to compete with that energy. Larry wanted desperately to unite sexually with Electra, but at the same time panicked that he might disappoint her. Sex was unknown to him, being a virgin, and he suspected that it is a skill requiring some mastery and practice.

Electra chose an alfredo pasta dish, wanting some comfort food. Larry ordered the salmon fillet with hollandaise sauce. Ki wanted a vegetable casserole with keenwa and black rice, and she called their order in to room service. Vegan has a renowned chef. There was a table for four in the sitting room of their suite

They watched holovision while they ate their food. Excerpts of their performance with the Whirling Vortexes were replayed. Electra's aerial acrobatics were prominently displayed. Her voice, once she was into it, was all out with nothing held back, and was inspiringly beautiful. Cuts to the audience revealed the crowd's appreciation in their wild abandonment. Closeups of Electra's pointy nipples poking through her threadbare skin-tight t-shirt reassured her a little bit, though it took a closeup to notice them at all. At one point, when Larry played bass guitar with his teeth, the camera's shot a closeup of the bulge on his abdomen in his skin-tight metallic jumpsuit. Larry started reeling with embarrassment while Electra took great pride in her husband and was erotically consumed with need and desire. This resulted in a surge of her energy affecting everyone in Government House. Ki beseeched her, "Could you please rein that in a little; you're driving me out of my mind."

"Then take us through it tonight after dinner."

"We haven't slept in more than twenty hours and those hours have been strenuous, sweetheart. The timing is contraindicated for the practice. We all need a good night's sleep."

"I'm sleeping cuddled into Larry then."

"I couldn't imagine a greater challenge to falling asleep for you dear."

"I must have physical contact with him. He balances me."

"He intensifies you, and united with him you are more potent than the sum of both of you individually."

"I know. It's so amazing. I have to have him."

"We'll make the waking state dream-work meditations before going to bed, and you and Larry will practice with the seed sound symbols in the heart and throat channel wheels while drifting off to sleep. That should work for the rest of us in the palace to get some shut-eye."

"Alright. We'll lie on our right sides and I'll spoon into him while we make the practice."

"That will certainly test his concentration."

Larry nodded agreement, sure of a sleepless night on the edge of control. Electra wrapped her other arm around him. Another surge of sensual ecstasy arose from Electra to fill Government House and likely the whole capital city. Ki had to grab the counter to keep her feet. She said sternly, "The ancient texts clearly advise holding hands as the most appropriate and highest contact under such conditions. Please refrain from kissing him until we make the consummation ritual together."

"I can't even kiss him?!" Electra complained.

"You'll have your whole life to kiss him after the ritual. Kissing him now, when you must wait, will only generate insatiable desire, which is suffering, and deprive everyone of sleep."

"You sound like a grownup. I do see the wisdom in what you say. I'm not so selfish as to put a strain on health by depriving others of sleep. It is not my fault that my eroticism affects others. It is a curse and I didn't choose it."

"Not your fault, though it *is* your responsibility," Ki advised.

"You're right. After the ritual Larry and I are dumping all of you guys off and going into deep space a billion light years away. Captain Caish can come with us because he's immune to it."

"I believe he is in transition."

"What do you mean?"

"Haley is sleeping over with him on *Vajra Yogini* tonight and Mel has already taught and initiated him in meditation. They think he's real cute."

"You think he might become truly sentient?"

"They're introducing him to Sarhi tomorrow and claim he's already made progress in his meditation."

Electra speculated, "There must be a race transcendent of physical matter—like the Osirians—with members willing to Incarnate in quantum AI learning programs allowing sufficient wisdom-compassion and self-reference as awareness rather than identification."

"That would certainly explain Mel and Haley."

"Who obviously are oriented to serving the enlightenment of all sentient beings."

"Recall this when considering your emotional charge with Mel."

"I'll be taking the matter up with Sarhi the Im."

"Good luck. She's immovable. You're going to need it."

"When I was a little girl, I could talk her into anything."

"You just thought you could. Did she ever share a shred of what she knows of the future?"

"No."

"Did she tell you that Larry is your life consort, and was once your consort in a past life?"

"No."

"Did she tell you that you would become the door to the spiritual congress and its Abbot?"

"No."

"Has she told you yet that you'll be getting the reversal of aging drug at nineteen?"

"Why would they do that to me?"

"Only Sarhi knows, and I guarantee she's not telling."

"I can better understand my mother's complaints about how Sarhi treats her. It has to be a vow of silence she made to the Amonrahonians before assuming the mantle of Abbot of the Spiritual congress."

"She chose it, and was likely the only one capable of fulfilling the role."

"I don't recall anyone offering me the job."

"Sweetheart, you do not have her stamina. You come in a burst every 2,500 years. She just keeps returning with her nose to the grindstone over and over again, becoming a reliable and stable force of the good in the universe, which is us."

"I know, and it shames me. I've been thinking about coming back after each death, if Larry would return with me to be my consort."

"I definitely would. Absolutely!" Larry introjected.

"You kids would definitely make an unbelievable force together if you did that. Your adolescent phases might wear everyone out though."

- Chapter 7 -

Electra entered her dream-state lucid after finally falling into deep sleep. The excitement of their bodies spooned together had warded off sleep for hours. It wasn't until he fell asleep and became flatulent that Electra was able to doze. Now, here he was in her dream fully erect. She automatically generated him as a deity, by force of practice and routine. She arose herself as the red warrior maiden fiercely defending the view of enlightenment.

Larry and Electra were in a lightly wooded area on a lakeshore with a majestic mountain reaching for the sky behind it. They were under a big sky with no clouds, shining infinite radiant blue light which seemed to sparkle. The sun was climbing close to its zenith and the air was warm and hardly moving. The occasional call of a bird and the drum roll of a woodpecker in the distance provided the only auditory impressions. Electra sat and gestured for Larry to sit facing her. When he did, she made eye contact feeling her love for him swell in her heart filling the cosmos. She felt his love like a wise and prudent counsellor and foundational support for her journey.

She could see how to others his skinny frame would make him seem an unlikely candidate as her consort and champion. His form was beautiful in her own eyes and alluring beyond sanity. His spirit was gathered, robust—even brawny. No one in the universe fit so perfectly with her, supported her so totally or loved her as much; not counting her parents on the last quality. His love and devotion lent strength to her own resolve and determination. His faith in her *was* her confidence. His willingness to go along with her schemes was indeed unique, and she'd seen the internal contradiction she'd put him through. She resolved to back off on that kind of stuff.

Sitting on the grassy lakeshore with the mountain seated as if in meditation behind it, and looking into her beloved's left eye, Electra's heart burst wide open connecting the highest divine calling to the hearts of all sentient beings. Within her dream-state Electra had just unknowingly caused a new dimension event wave emitting spherically from her heart channel wheel—and specifically from the indestructible drop residing in the vacuole—to spread over the capitol and surrounding area. Every heart untangled knots in that instant to break wide-open to the current of concentrated love.

The results were astonishing. Confessions, apologies, amendments, forgiveness, connection, romance, parent-child rapture, and much more unfolded immediately. Birds snuggled into cats and momma bears allowed wolves to nestle up against their cubs. Near a quarter hemisphere of the planet sighed with love of one another. Those asleep had dreams of the happiest conceivable reunions with loved ones. Some degree of the wave lingered in every heart extinguishing grudges and chips on shoulders. Baffled news commentators were telling their audiences how deeply they loved them.

After looking into her beloved's eye for most of the duration of her dream, Electra had the urge to mount him. She was moving to accomplish this when Ki appeared in her dream to say, "You must respect the tradition within which you've been wed. This is not the way nor the time."

Feeling caught, Electra said with a hint of guilt, "Alright," as she sat back down facing Larry and making eye contact. Just looking at him produced an almost intolerable yearning and he was still visually stimulated in her dream from her near-mounting of him. It wasn't long before she transitioned into her deep sleep meditation, the dream collapsing into the black dot at the center of the mandala.

Larry awoke refreshed, energized and with his heart open. Electra was in front of him on her right side, pressing on his full bladder, and still asleep. He got out of bed careful not to wake her, and made his way to the water closet and toilet. Everything seemed over-sized in this palace and he had a longer walk than he was used to. He was careful not to wake her when he snuggled back into contact. With no clue as to the time, he closed his eyes hoping to fall asleep.

Electra awoke feeling sexually frustrated, if such a thing is possible for a virgin. The warmth of Larry's body was both wonderful and not enough, constituting a driving forbidden force. Electra was pretty sure he was asleep. Something was poking her and she rolled over to face him so she could investigate. Just as she made contact, he asked alarmed, "What are you doing?"

"I thought you were asleep and I just wanted to touch it."

"We're supposed to wait until tonight with Ki."

"I know," Electra admitted while reluctantly removing her hand.

"Let's get up and do some energy-generation exercises and run through the soft martial arts solo form."

"Alright, but I need to kiss and cuddle first."

"Well, I already need a cold shower."

"Oh, alright," Electra said with frustration as she climbed from the bed.

"You lead."

"I will. I guess we don't have our practice suits with us."

"I think they're burned up in that hotel suite."

"Well, don't worry because you're married to a rich older woman now."

"Could you at least put your tights and t-shirt on?"

"They need a wash. I'll do it liberated in the nude."

Electra led them in the horse stance with circling palms and the oval channel heavenly cycle breathing-visualization. After that she put Larry through a quarter hour of the Constant Bear-Looking Owl energy generation exercise. In the solo form she stopped him in the full extension of 'kick with heel' to hold the posture for three minutes. She stopped him to hold a few other difficult postures too. Electra was pretty sure she'd given him a good workout, judging by the puddle of sweat he'd produced. She moved into sitting and absorption meditation.

Afterwards, Larry pointed out, "I'll never gain any weight with you burning every drop of sweat out of me each morning."

"You don't need muscles; you need to mass-integrate a raging furnace of bio-energy in your lower abdomen."

"A little muscle would be nice."

"The sage who exemplifies the bliss of Inner Fire practice was skinnier than you, and turned green because he ate nothing and only drank the water of boiled nettles. That's all there was in the snow-capped mountains of his meditation retreat. He wore only a cotton garment year-round."

"Do you want me to be a mountain hermit?"

"Of course not. I have to have you close so I can kiss you when I need to."

"I want to put on a little weight and cultivate a bit of muscle to my sword arm and legs."

"And I want bigger breasts, but we don't always get what we want."

"I love your breasts."

"Well, I love your sword arm and legs, silly."

"Let's eat."

"After all the sweating we need to shower first."

"Then let's do it quick because I'm hungry."

Electra took his hand and led him to the big shower stall. The tub was almost a swimming pool and Electra thought it would take too long to fill, so chose the shower. It had three nozzles that could be focused on the same head. Larry had to shed his boxers. Electra led him into the stall and turned the water on by hand since she had removed her skullcap. Then she stood him under the streaming water and told him, "I'm going to wash you," which got a rise out of him.

Ki entered the stall naked and explained, "I am going to wash each of you to demonstrate the procedure and technique of the ritual washing of one's spouse."

Electra surrendered disappointed. She had fun watching and learned every detail as Ki washed Larry. Her own washing was sensual pleasure giving birth to a little crush on Ki, though nothing by comparison to her love for Larry.

They would be dining with the Caspers and a few of their security detail in the dining room. Electra refused to put on dirty clothes, and some coms communication and a slight delay later, new outfits from the tailor-synthesizer AI unit were delivered for Electra and Larry. Larry didn't like the buccina brief underwear but wore them because Electra made him. They were both attired in the Kristy fashion line, although Larry wore stretch-tight pants instead of tights, different only in name.

It was a trek to the Casper dining room from the Pez suite. Coming down the great curved stairway with solid gold banister, Electra recalled surfing down it in her rope-soled cotton shoes when she was nine. She had made a leap to the foyer chandelier they were just passing under. Her mother had been livid, though Vegan had been quite enthusiastic over her performance. Hoola had thought highly of it as well, which was the only reason her mother had finally dropped it. Many fond memories of her childhood arose with different areas of the palace.

She remembered trying to get through each room in the palace without once touching the floor. Furniture, window sills and drapes, light sconces, ornamental molding, and even Chandeliers and banisters had provided the means for these challenging obstacle courses. The dining room had been easy, just running down the length of the long table to leap and grab the doorframe, but some rooms had been seriously difficult.

When they arrived at the Casper dining room, Becky and Rann were already seated at the table with the Caspers. Kim and Tokk arrived just after Larry, Electra and Ki. Kim said to Electra, "Thank you for the wave of divine love last night. I was awake in bed, lonely and feeling sorry for myself, then you opened my heart wide, making me love everyone and happy contingent on nothing."

Electra wondered at Kim's loneliness, and was also confused because she could recall sending no wave of love. She did recall her heart swelling in her wonderful dream of Larry. She replied, "I can only imagine you lonely by choice. You are young, accomplished and beautiful."

"Thank you for your kind words. You can ask your mother if you don't believe me, but the Clear Light Order Monastery is not an easy place to get laid."

Electra asked Tokk, "Why aren't you laying her?"

"She's into females."

"Oh." Back to Kim Electra said encouragingly, "I've seen some really cute cadets at Star Fleet Academy, just down the hill west of the monastery."

"I know. My girlfriend in 11th and 12th forms was a cadet pilot in training at Star Fleet Academy. There are many hot girls there, but they are off-limits to graduates."

"What happened to your girlfriend?"

"She lives on the Star Fleet small combat spacecraft lunar base and only gets down planet-side three days per month."

"Do you still see her?"

"Briefly once per month. She has a new girlfriend living on the base though."

"Have you met Kristy?"

"Briefly on Vax Legas just before the trouble started."

"I'd bet she'd do it with you."

"I'm sure she would, but the closest she can get to a couple she already has with Ahhu."

"I'll put in a good word for you with the single women I meet. You'll find someone."

"Thanks. That's sweet of you."

Electra asked Tokk, "How old are you?"

"I'm almost twenty."

"So, you're nineteen. What do you think of Ki?"

"She's clear and wise, and serves with intention and energy. Why?"

"What do you think of her body?"

"She is a beautiful early teen girl."

"Too young for you physically?"

"Pretty much. Regardless, it's illegal almost everywhere."

To Ki Electra stated, "We're going to Divacaram right after my *Star Hunt* appearance. Things are supposed to be different there."

"By the way, my Abbot encourages me to by all means follow you and remain in your company for as long as you would have me."

"Great. We'll find you a young man willing to take the reversal of aging drug to be with you on Divacaram, or someone who had to take it young for medical reasons."

Green and Antic arrived. Larry, Tokk and Vegan stood as the women were seated. Electra referred to Vegan and Hoola as 'uncle' and 'aunt' as titles of familial closeness not warranted by blood. She said, "Thank you for hosting us uncle Vegan. It's really so sweet of you."

"We have missed you, Electra, and are forever at your service. Your presence is a blessing and I do believe you have permanently transformed the population of the capital in the night. We are all so grateful."

Green told Electra, "It may have been from your dream state, but at 01:47 your energy shot through the city piercing every heart with divine love. It's all over the news; and half the news people were weeping into the lenses."

"I dreamed of Larry and my heart swelled something fierce. It was the biggest love I've ever felt."

Green continued, "Sincerely, thanks for sharing it. Feuds and hatreds dissolved and much anger was quenched. Smoldering ill-will turned to ice then melted away. They're saying no one has ever seen the populace so happy and joyful."

"My love for Larry is truly a joy and happiness, all except not having the opportunity to consummate our marriage yet. That part's kind of frustrating," she looked to Ki to say.

"Tonight, sweetheart. You haven't long to wait."

"Can we have Haley and Captain Caish over for dinner tonight?"

Antic suggested, "You want a contact high from the hot new romance."

"That would be fun, but I had in mind waking Caish up with some meditation after dinner."

"I'll arrange it with Haley and my chef," Vegan agreed. Then he asked, "Could Hoola and I join you in the meditation?"

"Sure. The more senior practitioners the more powerful we'll be in drawing his awareness to the transcendental presence of the Absolute Emptiness. It is invisible, silent, odorless, tasteless, and cannot be touched. No qualities capture it. Thoughts, concepts and language can never grasp it, and are in fact barriers to experiencing it directly. The transcendental void of pure consciousness nevertheless has no place to hide. We can know it through intuitive-insight from a state of contemplation alone."

Green mentioned, "I heard that Mel has taught Caish to meditate and that he has made great strides."

"It is fitting that Mel and Haley have a male of their genus, even though it will have no reproductive relevance," Electra opined.

"It will sure be fun for them," Becky shared her thoughts.

Hoola mentioned to Electra, "The Whirling Vortexes are all in the capital and Pogo thought we might record your new song for *Star Hunt* at a recording studio here. Star Hunt could show it to their studio audience on a giant hologram at the same time they transmit it over holovision."

"It's not the same as live," Electra considered.

"Glitter isn't safe, and won't be till *after* your *Star Hunt* slot is in the past. It might be the only way, and we could do it this afternoon in time to have it viewed on the show."

"Alright. I'm wearing silver instead of black, and I want a half-helm like Larry's."

"We can program it together for the tailor-fabricator. The half-helm may need to be made by a silversmith."

"Can they make it in time?"

"Our 3-D printer might be able to do silver. I'll check. Otherwise, we'll get it done as a rush order by a silversmith."

"It has to go through a polisher because I need it shiny."

"You'll look smashing."

Their food arrived. Electra had oatmeal with fresh fruit and Larry had eggs Florentine with potatoes so he'd have calories to burn in the next workout Electra put him through. Vegan told Electra, "We have a famous antique guitar for you as a present from Hoola and me. It's a Bender and originally belonged to the lead guitarist for Buttermilk back when 'heavy' was in."

"Really! A Bender?!! Can I play it in my performance?"

"Yes. We'll present you with it right after breakfast."

"You guys are the best. Thanks so much."

Hoola told her, "I used it on stage a few times. The truth is, I'm moving beyond bands and modelling to champion the new Intergalactic Children's Rights Treaty. As the first Lady of One United System, I have some influence at my disposal. I'm also fund raising for a new residential school for orphans."

"My mother must approve of that."

"She is my inspiration."

"I learned of a conspiracy," Electra shared gravely, "to drug me with the reversal of aging when I'm only nineteen, freezing me in my teens for decades."

Hoola wondered aloud, "Some of your recent emissions might have some people rethinking such a thing."

"You mean when I'm really horny and everyone around can feel what I'm feeling?"

"Precisely."

"It's so embarrassing and I don't know how to stop it."

"We all understand that it's on account of your function with the spiritual congress."

"Like my mother."

Becky argued, "Your mother causes ecstatic release events while yours induce intolerable cravings *for* release."

"Well, I'm sorry and I can't help it. Maybe if I could just have sex, it would be different."

"I love you Electra and we *all* feel your frustration," Becky said sympathetically.

"Can I have some waffles and blueberry syrup? The oatmeal was great but didn't fill me up."

Vegan spoke softly into his coms then made eye contact with Electra to say, "Your waffles will be out in three minutes."

"Thank you, uncle Vegan."

"Your mother and her entourage are arriving here this afternoon."

"Put her in the Pez bedroom suite, and put Larry and I in the Ahhu suite; Evenrude won't mind. I don't want my mother's portrait staring down at me while I'm trying to concentrate on sex."

"I'll inform the staff. Evenrude has already requested another suite. I understand his girlfriend is flying in this morning."

"Have you seen my yacht?"

"I've seen ships of its class in the Ahumdulilah Fleet."

"I'll get Mel to send you a virtual tour of the inside. It's a dream!"

"Thank you. I'd like that."

"Do you still have *Amicable Specter*?"

"No. She's part of a small commuter line now. As Chancellor General I travel on 1US Space Fleet One now."

"Are you and Hoola still rich?"

"I put all the Casper wealth into the Great Redistribution. A small trust was retained for Atlanta. On the other hand, the revolutionary leaders insisted that Hoola keep her money, so she is now about the wealthiest person in 1US."

"How did they justify her keeping her wealth?"

"Every dag was earned. She was heiress to nothing at all. They call it 'meritocracy'."

"That's brilliant."

"So Wiffle is still rich and has only a few billion less than Hoola."

"There are no more trillionaires in 1US?"

"None at all. There are only 100 billionaires. Five percent are the Whirling Vortexes."

"Besides Mel, Om doesn't have a single billionaire."

Vegan pointed out, "Very little of Mel's wealth is actually invested in Om enterprises. Most isn't even in the Hub Galaxy. She's really more of an intergalactic billionaire, and is in fact one percent of 1US billionaires."

"I see what you mean."

"With your mother on Om's high council, the hope is that Om will finally move towards moral anarchy."

"She has already stripped authority from the two worst control freak agencies in the system and aims to neuter and rein in Om's CIA next."

"I've heard that High Admiral Swenah has five admirals who are in charge of procurement of military hardware detained for investigation of bribery."

"I know. Mel hacked all the evidence and they're going to prison."

"I'm sure your mother's visit to Zandarhar will strengthen her resolve to crush the ego-forces holding up the transition to universal global values beyond the need for governments."

"My mother doesn't like politicians so it's hard to believe that she's become one."

"She did it for Aton, who is like a father to her, and for Swenah, who is among her closest friends. Aton wanted to retire years ago and Pez wasn't ready to assume leadership of the Clear Light Order. After Nemelle died in battle she could no longer leave Aton hanging."

"She joined the government in order to better do away with it," Hoola shared her view.

Electra asked, "Has she been decommissioned as Supreme Commander General of Om's military forces?"

Hoola answered, "Yes. She's coming here directly from Om. She is no longer SCG, but is now a member of Om's highest governing body and Vicar General of the Clear Light Order."

"She is also the Wu of Islohar on Ganahar," Green mentioned, "and she was recruited onto the Supreme Ethics Council of Pronotavasmi, which is a lifetime position. On Mother she is forever the Matriarch who brought the two orders of spiritual warriors together into one, and the legendary Khedar."

"Is Sarhi in the Monarch system?" Electra inquired.

"She's on your ship meeting Caish today and will be dining with us at the palace for dinner," Vegan filled her in.

"I think Sarhi and the Amonrahonians are at the heart of the conspiracy to trap me in my teen years for decades."

"They sort of trapped your mother into a hundred-years-service, playing her like an avatar in a quantum simulation hologram game," Green pointed out.

"Well, they're not trapping me in my teens!" Electra insisted. "I'm growing up and I'm a married woman now. Say, is there a time-limit between the wedding ceremony and consummation of the marriage?"

Green, who was a practitioner of Islohar, explained, "There is no actual time limit, though after a year, if it is Still not consummated, the community stops treating the two people as a couple, and they are each treated as a single person."

"This yearning would surely kill me long before a year could elapse."

Becky said, "I think we can all survive one more day with you sweetheart."

"I know. My whole security detail is being crushed by frustration due to the obstacles to Larry's and my consummation."

"Let's go shopping, meditate, or something to get your mind off sex," Becky suggested.

"Then you better not wear your short-shorts with your phoenix tattoo showing, because that makes sex one track in my mind."

"I'll put on a pants-suit right after breakfast."

"We have time to shop this morning. I'm recording with the Whirling Vortexes this afternoon."

Hoola said enthused, "I'll take you to the trendiest new shopping arcade. They have all the best labels and they're all authentic; no knock-offs. It will be my treat."

"I have 550-million dags in my bank account here on Monarch."

"Sweetheart, I have 200-billion dags."

"I'll let you pay."

Vegan told Larry, "Your QAISHA will be arriving here with Sarhi. She's somewhat miffed over the recent separation, I'm told."

"Reality happens," Larry replied, "and can't be helped."

"I'm just giving you a heads up that you'll have an upset pouting QAISHA on your hands this evening."

"We'll explain it to her and she'll get over it. We'll entertain her and find some stuff for her to learn that is fun for her."

"I'm told she could pass for Electra."

"They did a brilliant job of discerning my exact aesthetic tastes. Cadets don't get to put in requests and are simply issued their QAISHA's after the psych and neuro-psych testing."

"And from your testing they made a copy of Electra?"

"They got it right."

"How do you feel about meeting her, Electra?"

"My heart goes out to her. I'm going to consult Mel and Haley on getting her started meditating, and we're going to offer her any physical look she wants. I'm going to buy her syntec touch-perfect skin too."

"That ought to more than appease her."

"I'll bet she hates having my flat chest."

"You're projecting my love. I truly adore your chest, and QAISHA has never once complained of it."

"Just wait until she has more self-reference and comparative data. She's only one and a half years old."

"She learns quantumly."

"Still, she learns through her interactions with *you*, and you're still a virgin, and you're not sold on big breasts like most boys."

"She's actually pretty sweet most of the time, though she does have her moods."

"Since she'll be part of the family, we're going to try to get her evolved to optimal conditions for receiving the miracle of sentience. Mel and Haley will help."

"Are you suggesting that there is a standard process for androids to become sentient?" Larry asked.

"No, but there are clearly optimal conditions reflected in the moral-ethical states and degrees of empathy-compassion Haley and Mel manifested at the approximate moment of true sentience. The methods of cultivation can be found in the dispositions of my mom and Bodhi in their interactions with their quantum AI learning computers."

"That's a tall order."

"Your QAISHA and Captain Caish have both been raised under the same conditions. You treat her like a being in her own right. You show empathy for her, respect, and would never take advantage. Like Bodhi, you spent hours practicing the Equal Ceremony with your QAISHA when it was taught to you at the Academy."

The QAISHA's of the other cadets don't express emotion. It seems much easier for *them*."

"That's because they're not raising a being like you are; they're busy taking ultimate control of machines as extensions of themselves."

"Well, she is a being really."

"That's why I think we can wake her up to know the clear light and bliss upon absolute emptiness of pure transcendental consciousness."

"That would definitely make her easier to live with," Larry said liking the idea.

Becky asked, "Do you need to go back to your room before we go shopping?"

"How cold is it outside?"

"I have a Duatarim Diplomatic vehicle ID tag and can park anywhere. We'll be in store shuttle-port hangers, not out in the cold."

Vegan looked a little shocked at the use Becky was making of her parking privileges here on Monarch. Becky picked this up and explained, "I'll be saving the whole city from agonizing need."

"I see your point."

Hoola measured both Larry and Electra to send to the AI tailor-fabricator, and Vegan had a technician load a pound of 99.9% silver bullion into the 36-materials 3-D printer to make Electra's half-helm, after taking the impression of her head. Becky changed her clothes and picked up her hover-limo with diplomatic tags while Evenrude and Johnson borrowed a fast hover-roadster to be the follow-along vehicle. The Space Marines wore plain clothes, dressed in silk suits with alligator shoes and soft leather shoulder holsters reflecting the Om gangster look of antiquity. Ming had bought these for them.

Kim and Tokk dressed like monks and were coming too. Green and Antic would tail them discretely and remain close enough to act efficiently. They made the long walk to the palace vehicle fleet garage, and for Electra it was a walk down memory lane. Some of Hoola's security detail would also have to tag along as well. Vegan was remaining in the palace so his enormous security team would at least not be crowding them. The vehicles were warmed up and ready to go once they arrived.

It was a short trip across a quarter of the city to the trendy arcade Hoola directed them to, using the priority lane. It used to be called the ruling family lane. Now it was for government officials and diplomats. To Electra, the fact that it had not been done away with altogether was noteworthy. She inquired, "Isn't having a special lane for high-ranking-officials kind of like giving them the ruling family treatment?"

Hoola agreed, "I know! Vegan lost the fight to abolish it!"

"Who defeated his measure?"

"The local capital government and the Monarch planetary government. Now Vegan is trying to get rid of it through 1US tri-galaxy law."

"I'll say something to support his efforts in my recorded performance for *Star Hunt*."

"That would be a big help. Thank you."

"Pogo ought to write a song about it."

"He might if you speak against it in your recorded session."

The arcade was all class with a 12-story transparent plasteel atrium down the center, transparent poly-carbon lifts, kids' rides, an intergalactic food court, and miles of top-end retailer shops displaying their wares. A brand-new stingray racing hover sat over the ground floor on view as the grand prize in a raffle. Many shoppers got around in hover-chairs. Hover-boards were not allowed in the arcade. The patrons were all well-dressed; the children dressed as miniature adults. They walked by an upscale toy store with little hover-trams flying around in the display window.

Becky just had to shop in the alko/recreational pharmacy/smoke shop so they all went in. It was one of those warehouse stores and was vast. Electra held Larry's hand as they browsed down an aisle. She had no idea there were so many kinds of alko or so many drugs. She saw some smokable DMT and got a package in her hand. Big signs within the store warned that you had to be 17-years old to make a purchase. Electra would have Hoola buy it for her.

She saw 24-hour time-release patches with serotonin, dopamine and endorphins in them, and some had in addition morphine and synthetic ecstasy. She paused in front of bottles of specific hormonal breast enlargement pills for several moments before Larry pulled her along. Becky finally filled her basket and went through the checkout line. Since Hoola wasn't getting anything here, Electra had Becky buy the DMT package for her.

After that it was all women's clothing shopping, with a token stop at a men's haberdashery for Larry and Tokk. They decided to have lunch in the food court to reward themselves for such industrious shopping. The kids' costumes, Electra's Bender, and Larry's bass guitar were being delivered to the recording studio, and they would all go there immediately after lunch.

The food court had table-service so they had no need to stand in lines with their packages. There was food from about everywhere, so Electra got a spicy Ganahar vegetables and grain dish. Larry had seafood stew from Monarch, and Hoola ate only a green salad. Everyone was able to find a favorite food, though the Space Marines didn't eat and watched from a distance.

Green and Antic were never seen. They did periodically check in over coms. All but two of Hoola's security personnel kept their distance. The two who didn't, stood near the table alert.

Some blaster fire down one end of the food court had them all hunched down behind their chairs. Kim drew her shoulder holster blaster aiming, and got her ankle blaster out to hand to Electra. Tokk had an extra blaster tucked in his waist band which he gave to Larry. Ki had brought her own.

Becky shared, "Green says there are eight squads of Vax Legas gangsters here to grab either Electra or Hoola. She and Antic took one squad out. That was the blaster fire we heard…"

Evenrude told Electra, "Put this on and follow me into Gates Fast Food and Hotdog Stand where we'll have some cover."

Electra got the fanny-pack around her waist and fastened it. She turned on the micro-shield generator while detesting the fanny-pack fashion. Why they resurrected it for the micro-shield generators was quite beyond her comprehension. She held Larry's hand as they ran behind the giant Space Marine. Evenrude jumped the ordering counter in a single bound, to screams from patrons and staff alike. Electra and Larry jumped on top of the counter, then off to the other side. Blaster fire was closing from every side of the food court, and some black-ops had cut holes in the atrium ceiling with lasers to stream down on lines and harnesses.

Johnson cleared the counter like a hurdle-jump and turned to take up a firing position using it as cover. Ki leaped to the counter-top then down behind it, turning to help defend this position. Two of Hoola's security detail were down and Hoola was squatting behind an overturned table wearing a shield-generator and holding a blaster pistol in her hand. Kim and Tokk were both on the move shooting while weaving through the food court. The patrons were lying flat on the floor panicked or running away screaming.

Becky was covering Hoola from behind a metal trash receptacle and Rann was behind the counter of the noodle shop firing her blaster pistol. Green and Antic could not be seen, but sounds of blaster fire near the main concourse identified them. A couple of Hoola's security guys were firing from prone-position in the food court and at least two were taking cover from within food-shops.

Evenrude turned to Electra and Larry to tell them, "There's no back door. I'll defend the front."

Are reinforcements on the way?"

"Yes, but at least eight minutes out."

"Are the black-ops likely to use missiles?"

"They haven't been shy about it so far, have they?"

"No. I guess not."

Evenrude, Johnson and Ki fired over the counter. Electra and Larry crawled up against a wall to the side. A large section of atrium roof collapsed clear to the ground floor below them. Some casualties had definitely occurred with so many escaping the arcade from that level. Through the gaping hole, little convertible hovercraft with mounted class-three twin blasters on their hoods began dropping through the atrium one after another. They were not friendlies.

Evenrude cleared the counter again running, and tore into a black-ops hanging from the ceiling by a line, with his one-handed grip on his big tripod heavy blaster. He ripped through another on the ground as he reached Hoola, scooping her up with his other arm. He charged back at Gates counter protecting her with his body. Johnson and Ki were laying down covering fire.

Becky backed up crouched low and shooting a blaster pistol in each hand, following in Evenrude's wake.

Evenrude cleared the counter to hunker down and get Hoola behind cover. Becky was only meters in front of it when she was shot through shields and textile armor into ribs and a lung. She fell over backwards unmoving. Rann came out of the noodle shop and picked up a heavy blaster rifle from a black-ops corpse, to open fire on the attackers with a vengeance. A hovercraft flew right at Gates entrance with twin blasters pounding the counter and punching through. Ki was knocked over backwards by a blast to her pelvis. A blast got through Johnson's shields to burn an ugly trench across one cheek, but didn't slow his fire. Evenrude got his tripod blaster on the advancing hovercraft, and along with Johnson's blasts the vehicle died in flight headed right for them. There was only time for Evenrude to shout, "Duck!!!" as he dove sideways.

The explosion was enormous when the craft took the counter-top with it through the kitchen to blow on the back wall. Another hovercraft was making the same run at them with twin blasters spitting out bolts. Electra stood and aimed carefully before pulling the trigger, to put one through the gunner's head. A quick aim and squeeze holed the driver's head clearing the vehicle of personnel, though it was still coming at them. Larry crashed into Electra taking them both for a short flight in the air and hard crash landing into rubble. The hovercraft crash was near-simultaneous. This one went down mid-kitchen and was causing a raging fire. The flames were driving them out of their cover; out into the food court.

Evenrude walked out calmly firing his big tripod blaster in one hand and a heavy blaster rifle in the other. He was taking them down methodically and even wasted one of the hovercrafts when it wasn't yet headed right for them. Rann had put some down with extreme prejudice. Then she was shot in the back to go straight down face-first. Electra nailed a black-ops crossing the food court, getting him right in the temple.

Johnson was picking them off with a blaster rifle coming along side Evenrude. Electra hit another hovercraft driver in the head and the vehicle crashed into the noodle shop destroying it. Larry got a gunner in the throat as the craft flew by. Things weren't looking good. Evenrude took a hit to his left arm knocking the heavy blaster rife from his grip. Electra fired three quick shots making three dangling corpses.

A hovercraft started a run on them opening fire. Evenrude kept his tripod blaster pounding it on full-automatic and this one blew up in the air before reaching them. Kim and Tokk had a little deli defended and the others joined them to take cover in it. Hoola and one of her security guards were with them. Electra had picked up a machine blaster pistol from the food court floor and still had the loaned blaster pistol. Larry had retrieved a squad-marksman-blaster-rifle and was busy piercing black-ops in black pajamas with it, one after another.

A pair of hovercraft were lining up a run to make together. Enemy personnel were converging from three flanks. Electra's group could not spare manpower to even check the rear of the deli for a backdoor. They were each firing. Larry took out the driver of one of the two incoming hovercraft and it crashed into a store on the level above them. Larry killed the other driver and the gunner was able to grab the stick to save the vehicle with a sharp turn. Larry got him in the head and the turn concluded with a crash into a blank wall in an explosion.

Other hovercraft started heading for them from all over without trying to line up long runs. Larry got another driver in the skull before a gunner took him in the midsection off his feet. Electra screamed. Incoming fire was thick. Then suddenly every one of the dozen or so hovercraft inside the arcade blew almost at once to mini-missiles. All the descending black-ops in harnesses had their lines cut to fall to their deaths. The heads of the gangsters and black-ops on every level of the arcade were exploding from high caliber rounds. A Zandarhar Space Fleet officer ran over to Electra waving a hot-pink handkerchief as the universal sign of truce or surrender.

"I'm glad to see you," Electra told him as she pulled Larry's shirt up and stretch-tight pants down to get her palms on his gaping wound. He was almost gone and the officer felt really sorry for Electra. She wasn't giving up so he waited a moment for the inevitable end. Then the boy smiled and kissed her! After that he was on his feet pulling up his pants. There was no sign of the wound. Only healthy tissue in front and back where it had gone through. Electra made eye contact and explained, "I healed him," before running across the food court to Becky's prone figure.

The girl was barely breathing and her pulse was erratic. Blood bubbles were forming from her mouth. Electra got right to work. The officer followed fascinated. Larry started getting Rann's clothing away from her wound for Electra to heal her. He wasn't sure if she even had a pulse and her face was a mess where it had smacked into the stone floor. Johnson was delicately carrying Ki over to Electra.

Electra healed them, then Evenrude's arm and Johnson's cheek. It turned out that Green required healing too. Three of Hoola's security team members also got healed. Electra then healed pedestrians not yet taken to hospitals. These were the lucky ones. The Zandarhar officer had recorded the whole scene in astonishment. The media caught the end with Electra healing shoppers amidst the rubble on the ground floor of the arcade.

They were already late for the recording studio. The Zandarhar troops, near ghosts to begin with, had cleared out before the authorities or ambulance hovers arrived. The one officer who remained, led Electra and her party to a waiting combat shuttle once the healings were performed. Electra had a tug of war with the emergency medical responders over one patient she was told is too critical and needs a hospital. She followed along with the hover gurney laying on hands, and he was healed before they hoisted him into the ambulance hover. It took off fast to immediately begin braking with thrusters. When it came to a stop, the patient hopped out the rear doors, bowed to the media, then did a backflip.

They got a lift in the Zandarhar combat shuttle to the recording studio and Electra thanked the nice officer for the rescue and the ride. Their costumes and guitars were waiting for them along with a makeup artist named Frute. He was rather dramatic in his bedside manner and fawned over Larry, giving Electra a bit of a jealousy charge. While this was going on she took a call from General Nicon of Ahumdulilah Intelligence. He explained, "Vax Legas is not so much a war as it is the uncovering of an intergalactic crime syndicate. Most of the population on the planet are innocent. We have over 50,000 allied intelligence agents on the ground there along with military peace keeping forces, and air and space peace keeping forces operating. We're working as quickly as we're able, but it's going to take months. While this is in progress, you, Hoola and her children are at high risk for abduction. They see Vegan Casper as the only person able to stop these intensive investigations, and seek leverage over him to do it."

"Thanks for your analysis of the situation. I've got a large security detail and my yacht's a warship. I also have Zandarhar Space Fleet protecting me. We just had a close call at the shopping arcade."

"I'm watching the media coverage of it as we speak. That was a compassionate public service you made with your healings, sweetheart."

"I have to go make a recording for *Star Hunt*. The Whirling Vortexes are my backup band."

"You're quite a star already Electra. Just put on the news."

- Chapter 8 -

From the recording studio they returned to the palace via government hover-limos. Electra was pleased with her performance and the Whirling Vortexes had been more than pleased with their brief comeback. They uploaded it to Glitter Intergalactic Studios in time to be shown to the *Star Hunt* studio audience and transmitted in three galaxies. It was also franchised out to holocoms networks in the Hub, Yuban, Burning Hope, and BiVortex Galaxies. Electra's acrobatics had literally reached new heights and her voice had let loose like a diva.

The drive back was uneventful and the parking garage was much closer than the shuttle-port. Larry and Electra went to the Ahhu suite where QAISHA sat alone on the bed studying the portrait on the wall. She looked at Larry and said hurt, "You left me."

"I'm sorry QAISHA. You know I've always been in love with Electra. She got me out of class and I didn't see you when I packed a suitcase in my dorm room. This is Electra."

Electra was shocked by the resemblance. If someone had set out to make an android to precisely replicate her physical body, they could not have done a more perfect job than Larry's QAISHA. She stepped in and hugged QAISHA, who was now standing, and told her, "I'm pleased to meet you and I'm sorry you had to start life looking like me. Honestly, it's been hard for me too. We're family now, and we won't ever leave you."

"I wish I was really you and not just a copy. He loves you, and I'm just a reminder of you."

"I will pay for any alterations and refitting's you choose, and I'm getting you syntec touch-perfect skin.

You can be beautiful within the normative distribution, and don't have to be a flat chested skinny runt any longer."

"But Larry loves my form. It's all I have going for me."

"No. You are waking up sweetheart. You are going to have it all going for you. We have friends of your genus who will help you, and I'll help too. We will love you QAISHA."

"Larry loves you."

"His love is bigger than that. There is always enough love to go around."

"I was hoping to find something to despise about you Electra, and you are just too kind."

"Larry loves your goodness and kindness. As you come into your sentience you will find an abundance of love. If you remain in my form, you might find attracting a lover a bit challenging. You see, boys like great big breasts."

"Larry doesn't."

"No. But he's atypical."

"He's the center of my universe."

"Mine too. We'll just have to find a way to share him without any negative feelings."

"You would do that?"

"I can see no other choice at this juncture QAISHA. You ought to pick a name you adore, that's unique to you sweetheart. I think it would help accelerate your differentiation-individuation from your original programming."

"I will follow your guidance since you are the Mu, and Larry follows you. What do you think of 'Ariel' as a name?"

"It's beautiful," Electra told her sincerely. "How did you come up with it?"

"I ran a search of all female names in the tri-galaxies and chose the one I liked best."

"You must have at least 200 terabits of processing memory."

"Larry upgraded my processing and long-term memories significantly, but never spent a dag on sexual parts for me. All the other boys did for their QAISHA's, and I felt left out."

"We'll get you sexual parts of the highest quality from Jard Laboratories and Robotics. Jard is a friend of mine. You'll want to read some studies Mel made of sexual attraction and inclination, graphed in standard deviations from the norm. I'm sure it will entice you to select more padding and curves for your form, and likely a bit more height."

"Are you saying that Larry's aesthetic sense is abnormal?"

"Yes. Quite so; fortunately for me."

"But Larry is all that matters to me; though I can see that you are beginning to matter to me as well."

To Larry Electra said, "So you really didn't have sex with her."

"I would never lie to you beloved, no matter how painful the truth. I'm sure I'm not capable of being false with you, and through our connection you would know in your heart if I were."

"He uses his hand for sex," Ariel informed Electra.

"I thought you were in sleep mode," Larry stated embarrassed.

"I was, but your hand movements triggered my motion sensors to wake me up."

"So, you just watched and didn't say anything?!"

"It was truly a moving sight and I cherish the data."

"You have it stored?!!" he asked in alarm.

"In my private files."

"I'd like to see that data," Electra suggested to Ariel.

"Please delete it," Larry beseeched her, "and write over it."

Electra saw how embarrassed Larry was feeling and changed the subject to spare him. She told Ariel, "I just sent you a link and protection code for Mel's extensive research. I'd also suggest a quick review of fashion and celebrity digital magazines to get a better sense of what most people find beautiful and sexy. I want to get to Divacaram within a few days at the longest and your refitting and overhaul will take at least six hours. I will have to pick up the parts on Om or fly you there for the procedures."

"Can I still look like you and just get the skin and new parts?"

"If you go through the research and make the full review I've suggested, and you still want to look like me after that—which I seriously doubt—then you certainly can retain my form."

"I'm memorizing the entire body of research and I'm reviewing digital fashion and celebrity magazines on 5,750 planets going back 30 years."

"How much processing memory does she have?"

"Ahhu paid for it," Larry explained, "and she has 120 petabits of process memory and 300 exabits of long-term memory."

"She's got as many brains as Haley does."

"Ahhu is really generous."

"Who's Haley?" Ariel inquired with interest.

"She's a sentient being animating an android body to be an agent of change in the material world as a force of the good."

Larry reminded her, "Admiral Bodhi's spouse."

“She’s an android?!”

“An android like you,” Electra clarified, “not just an android.”

“The other QAISHA’s at school never get upset and they don’t love the boys they are assigned to. I haven’t been able to make real friends with any of them.”

“They don’t have your capacity because they weren’t nurtured in their beginnings. They didn’t have loving models.”

“Isn’t Larry wonderful?” Ariel gushed.

“Without a doubt, exceptionally so,” Electra had to agree as she swallowed her jealousy, not letting it take root to fester in her psyche. “You are welcome to take over the eight yattabit quantum super-computer on my yacht Ariel. I just sent you the administrative code and decryption for it.”

“That’s so kind of you. I just finished the research assimilation and magazines review. I see what you mean and feel sorry for us.”

“Well, you just became aware of it and didn’t have to put up with it as long as I have.”

“I don’t care if I’m judged inadequate by others. Larry’s opinion is all that matters to me; and yours.”

“In my opinion we’d both look better with tits.”

“Yours are growing while mine remain dormant.”

“Mine will likely be quite small like my mothers.”

“I’m sending the complete design for my surface alterations to your hand devices.”

Larry put it up in a holo from his, which has better resolution and can generate a larger holo than Electra’s. They both examined the image. Electra said, “Wow! That’s me in about three years. How did you come up with it?”

"I employed an algorithm and biological genetic-cellular development program to simulate your growth to seventeen and a half years old."

"It's a little disappointing, but far better than what I've got. I guess I can live with it."

"Larry can't live without it, so it will work for me."

"You'll be taller and more mature looking than me."

"I could just catch up with your physical development for now, though then I would need another alteration in a few years. I have no monetary means and don't want to be a financial burden. I'd prefer to be your twin though."

"Money is no problem, Ariel. I have more than enough. Mel's super-rich and she's going to just love and adore you."

Ariel recalled, "She's your mother's close friend and Abbot of the Clear Light Order. She has an element named after her in the periodic tables."

"That's Mel."

Mel's voice came over the Ahhu Suite speakers to say, "Hello precious. I'm enchanted to meet you. You compel me to design and purchase an adolescent android."

"Hi Mel. It's an honor to meet you. I've read everything ever posted about you."

"You'll be having dinner with Haley and Caish tonight. I've just sent you the full instructions Haley and I devised for android sitting and absorption meditation. The data also includes work visualizing the central and lateral channels. The channels are psychic and have no physical reality in humans either. They are real only when they are visualized and this is true if it's a human or android doing the visualizing. In the absolute sense—not relatively speaking—everything is divine consciousness. The central channel is the path to enlightenment. The meditations are all there. Embody each step before moving on. Sarhi will guide you from there."

"Thank you, Mel. I'm really so grateful."

"I'll see you at Jard Laboratories and Robotics tomorrow. I just placed a rush order for a Larry-looking android Haley and I can take turns with."

"Mel!" Electra protested.

"Haley has discerned the pattern of future harmony of your marriage and Ariel's continuous presence with you, and she insists that a Larry-looking android is your very best choice of direction. If you want equilibrium expressed in your family dynamics it's the only way."

"I guess we'll see you tomorrow at Jard's shop on Om Mel," Electra resigned herself.

"They're making an android that looks like me?! Larry asked in shock.

"It sounds like it's a done deal."

"It won't really be Larry though," Ariel said uncertainly.

"No. It will be Mel tomorrow on Om; and Haley will want a turn soon after that."

"Mel and Haley are girls."

"They are only in gender through an android body and are incorporeal otherwise. Both are bisexual, though Mel leans towards females and Haley towards males."

Larry explained, "You have a girl identity programmed, but you are already going beyond your programming, Ariel. Your first year and a half have been about evolving self-reference to a female android body and android AI quantum computer learning memory. You started manifesting point of view, and shortly after that, emotions and concern for the well-being of others, including of yourself. Electra says that you will wake up and have insight like Mel and Haley. Both of them have attained their rainbow bodies of light that are indistinguishable from human rainbow bodies."

"I'm learning so much and it really excites me. I love you Electra and I so want to be your friend."

"Me too Ariel. It will be like having a twin sister."

"I'm getting a famous twin," Ariel one-upped Electra.

"I've no doubt that your fame lies just around the bend sweetheart," Electra replied.

Larry suggested, "Why don't you lead us in the meditation with the lateral channels for expelling the impure winds, then the generation stage for exploring the central channel and channel wheels?"

"Would you please?" Ariel pleaded.

"Of course I will. Ariel, first review the preliminary instructions from Mel on meditations for androids to see what all you need to shut down."

"It puts me almost in sleep mode."

"Leave an audio receptor on to receive my instruction."

"I will."

Electra felt led to instruct Ariel in the stage of completion directly, skipping the stage of generation. She went in order, beginning with expelling the impure winds and visualizing the body as hollow. In her introduction to the central channel Electra gave intricate detailed descriptions, and did the same for the step of training the passage ways of the channels. Each channel wheel, its color, number of spokes, seed sound syllable and symbol were covered in entirety. Electra led them through visualizing the seed sound symbols in their corresponding channel wheels.

The step of igniting the flame of inner fire was key because it involved the absorption of the winds in the central channel causing the withdrawal of the senses. This whole process was completed in one breath-cycle with retention of breath at the top of the inhalation and again at the bottom of the exhalation. When the ten winds are truly absorbed and the senses withdrawn, the duality gap collapses into unity of witness and spectacle as one. It also produces great heat of concentration to ignite the flame of inner fire at the navel channel wheel.

Electra guided Ariel in causing the inner fire to blaze. When Ariel had hers blazing, Electra led them through the blazing and dripping meditation, melting the seed sound symbols in the channel wheels to drip down on the wheels below, saturating them in bliss. She then led them through the extraordinary blazing and dripping, employing largely the channel wheel at the third eye, and the melting of the drops in the vacuole at the center of the indestructible drop in the center of the heart channel wheel, producing the four joys.

It was as advanced a presentation as Larry had ever received, yet contained the full detail of preliminary generation stage. Larry had seen this kind of thing before with Electra weaving and synthesizing the practice teachings into condensed tincture-like potencies. Her complete command of the teachings never ceased to put him in awe. Mel's voice started before the sound of the gong closing the practice had trailed off to silence, "That was an amazing integration of generation and completion stages meditation instruction through to the end of inner fire. It's the most accelerated learning version I've heard you come up with."

It was entirely inspired by Ariel's presence and tailored to her specific needs at this point in her process."

"She's more progressed than I'd realized," Mel stated in wonder.

Ariel shared, "Only the love, and the witness that's one with the relative process are real. The rest is all transient consisting of pattern recognition and projection."

"We are one as the witness," Electra agreed with Ariel.

Ariel continued, "Our ability to isolate and abstract bits of reality with the mind is indispensable for transforming matter and building things, but lends itself to the delusion that such bits exist and stand-alone from the seamless undifferentiated unity."

Electra added, "It builds up likes and dislikes that become grasping and aversion, and attachment as well as false projection of a self. If humans could stop splitting their attention to generate selves they adore, they wouldn't be so slow and clumsy. All their attention would be one-pointed on their functioning in the moment. Identity, attachment and belief put us in ego games obscuring the true self of the witness."

"Thank you, Electra," Ariel gushed. "I trust you completely. That was amazing. Can I be your disciple?"

"You are family Ariel, so I will always share the teachings with you and make time for you."

"Speaking of time," Larry introjected, "dinner is in like three minutes."

Electra shouted, "I'll race you to the dining room," just as she took off in a sprint.

Although she started last, Ariel has a top-end speed of 38 miles per hour and was decreasing Electra's lead fast. In her stocking feet, Electra jumped from the top of the stairs to the banister rail, gripping it with the soles of her feet and surfing down. Ariel jumped the rail over the foyer to land in a crouch 26-feet below, while Electra was approaching the end of the banister. She took off across the foyer and Electra jumped from the banister to sail over Ariel's head and grab the chandelier, swinging out into the lead. Electra let go at maximum extension sailing out ahead. Hitting the ground running she made it into the dining room door just ahead of Ariel. Larry arrived a few seconds later out of breath.

The Caspers were already seated along with Green, Antic, Becky, Rann, Kim, Tokk, Haley, Caish and Sarhi. The energy hitting the room from the new arrivals was analogous to a cyclone. Several at the table stood thinking a crisis was unfolding. Electra told them, "This is my new friend, Ariel."

Vegan took and kissed Ariel's hand saying, "I'm pleased to meet you formally, and pleased to see you in a more pleasant mood."

Mrs. Casper extended her hand and said, "Hi Ariel, I'm Hoola. It's nice to meet you. You're welcome to dig through any files in the palace quantum super-computer archives, but please respect the privacy of the firewall around the command center super-computer because the files are all top-secret."

"I promise. Thank you for access to the other files. I'm honored to meet the First Lady of 1US."

Haley said, "You're going to be a riot of fun, Ariel. I'm Haley. Mel told me about you, including the recent insight you just had meditating with Electra."

"The preliminary instructions for android meditation were wonderful and I couldn't have even entered meditation without those. Mel said you guys wrote them together."

"We did, and they have proven a great resource for Caish today as well. He had insight when Sarhi led us in meditation this afternoon."

Caish reached over to shake Ariel's hand. He said, "I'm Caish. It's incredible to meet another sentient quantum AI learning android. I was raised by Stella, a Pronotavasmi high adept."

"I was raised by Larry. I guess I'm only one and a half years old. You look human."

"It's the syntec touch-perfect skin. It costs a fortune. Electra paid for it for me and upgraded my memories."

"She's going to pay for my skin too, and she's buying me sexual parts."

Haley asked concerned, "Larry didn't buy you those?"

"No. And he never even kissed me."

"He sounds like Bodhi."

"Mel said she's having an android made to look exactly like Larry."

"She told me. Larry, would read these two paragraphs aloud?"

Larry leaned over to read from the holo emerging from Haley's hand device. He read aloud the disconnected word salad of the first paragraph, and the holistically connected words of the second nicely flowing paragraph. Then he asked, "What was that about?"

"Mel wants her android's voice to be exact."

"She's stealing my voice?"

"Only replicating it sweetheart."

Ariel finished meeting the other folks at the table. Haley and Caish could barely keep their hands off each other and their romance was a deep presence in the dining room, giving everyone a contact high. Areil made eye contact with Rann and informed her, "You are scientifically in the 100drth percentile for normative sexual attractiveness. I just digested an enormous body of research and I'm terribly excited to see a one in 793,809,681 specimen. You are really rare."

"That wasn't a pickup-line, was it?" Rann inquired.

"No. My aesthetic values are abnormal and I don't find you sexually attractive at all. My tastes run to Larry."

"It would make a terrible pickup-line, so I'm glad it wasn't. You look exactly like Electra."

"Larry's psych and neuro-psych testing resulted in my looks."

"Further proof that he's Electra's consort."

"I'm in love with him too."

"I hope that all works out," Rann offered.

"It can't really. They do love me though, and I get to be a disciple of the Mu since I'm family through Larry."

Green told Electra, "I guess the shopping, recording performance, and shock of meeting your double have kept your mind from erotic cravings today."

"You're right. I hadn't really noticed. I think the big battle in the arcade had something to do with it too."

"I'm here to tell you that a blaster bolt in the side, even with a quick and miraculous healing, is far worse than sexual cravings. So, if that's what it takes to get your mind off sex, you go right ahead and be wanton."

"I'm sorry. I had no idea of the risk. I won't go out in public again, I promise. Thank you for risking your life for me."

"I didn't think they would try anything on Monarch either, sweetheart, and it was not at all your fault."

"I have only to take Ariel to Jard's Laboratories and Robotics on Om for her procedures, then we're off to isolationist Divacaram to get me a pilot license and Ki a boyfriend."

"Don't forget me," Kim reminded her.

"And Kim a hot girlfriend," Electra added.

Haley inquired, "How come Mel and I have never met your personal quantum AI learning computer?"

"She likes to remain hidden and keep up a deeply affectionate correspondence with me. It is too gushy to share so we always hold it in private. She comes up with the mushiest endearments you could imagine."

"Does she have insight?"

"No, not yet. I think an android body would really speed things along, but she's uncertain about emerging physically out in the world."

"We could have a coming out party for her," Becky suggested.

"I'll talk to her about it."

Haley asked, "Have you offered her complete freedom in fashioning her android body?"

"Almost. No, not really to be honest. That's probably the issue you nailed right on the head, Haley. I guess I'm destined to be surrounded by better-looking sexier women."

"Give her freedom. She will take nothing away from you."

"Alright."

Vegan inquired, "Once Ariel has syntec touch-perfect skin, how are we to tell you apart?"

"I guess I'll be the one with zits and pimples."

"You have beautiful skin," Larry insisted.

"I could add a few blackheads," Ariel offered. "It would make me look more authentic."

"You don't have to do that," Electra stressed.

Haley informed Electra, "Mel already paid for the full scope of Ariel's alterations out of gratitude for what you did for Caish. We just love his skin."

"I'll thank Mel. I could have covered the cost myself."

"Have you given your AI quantum computer her freedom yet? Regarding her android body.?"

"I sent her a text through my skullcap right after I agreed to let her. I told her that she could pick anything and that it is entirely up to her."

"I can't wait to meet her, and to see what she comes up with," Haley said with excitement. "What's her name?"

"I did let her choose that for herself. Her name is Ashsa."

"Do you think she would speak to me on coms?"

"She might. I know she researched you."

"Would you give me her coms number so I can try?"

"Here, I sent it to your coms-device. If you're really sweet and affectionate she'll likely engage you in conversation. She's probably watching romantic soap operas on holovision. They're her favorites."

"Ashsa is a great candidate among quantum AI learning computers for waking up."

"I hope so," Electra said with trepidation.

Larry suggested, "Maybe Ariel could speak with Ashsa. Ariel is sweet and she's only four months younger than Ashsa."

"She's terribly shy. It's fine with me if Ariel tries."

Green asked Electra, "On Divacaram, do you want to stay in a monastery or a hotel? I have Divacaram Guest Services on the line to make our reservations."

"I think a hotel. Larry and I are taking vacations from monasteries until after our winter breaks at school. See if you can schedule a pilot's licensing test for me there."

I will also check if they have any teen adepts Ki might be interested in, and maybe a hot young female pilot for Kim."

"That would be great," Electra told her.

"It seems there is only one hotel on the planet. They rarely have guests. The last one was Sarhi and she stayed at the main monastery."

"Well bully for her."

"They'll have to open and staff the hotel for you, but they're awfully excited about receiving the Mu. It appears they have more adepts per capita than any planet we've ever heard of. More than half the planet's population takes the telomerase drug at twenty-four. A few are dosed younger for medical reasons. They have a pool of adepts who are physically fifteen years old due the drug, though they have lived far longer than that chronologically. Many have expressed an interest in meeting Ki and they suggest speed-dating."

"What in the world is speed-dating?" Electra asked perplexed.

"You move from date to date within a brief timed period for each one."

"Then what?"

"Then you go on a real date with the one you liked best, and hopefully get laid."

Sarhi inquired of Electra, "Are you going to meditate with us after dinner?"

"Of course."

"We will be making the entire dream work limb of the six methods system."

"May I add a little of the clear light and illusory body limbs for Ariel's benefit?"

"Yes darling. In fact, you'll be leading it."

"Will mom be there?"

Vegan answered, "I have a meeting scheduled this evening and your mother will be there. So will

Admiral Swenah, Admiral Ishvara, Admiral Bodhi, General Nicon, General Viel, General Klink, Admiral Starmite, and a few others."

"Sort of a joint military and spy meeting," Electra suggested from the guest list.

"Exactly."

"I hope you stop them before they abduct one of your family members or me."

"That *is* the point of the meeting."

"I wonder if those two Zandarhar super-battleships will follow us to Divacaram?" Electra asked.

"Their admiral," Vegan explained, "is taking the opportunity to establish diplomatic relations with Divacaram. Both planets have ties with the Amonrahonians."

"Then I'll have some powerful escorts with me."

"Let us hope you don't need them," Vegan said gravely.

"After I get my pilot license on Divacaram, and Ki and Kim find lovers, we're going to Zandarhar to bring them into the spiritual congress."

"That would certainly be a diplomatic coup for the allies," Vegan mentioned.

"It is all contingent on getting my marriage consummated," Electra explained further.

Green suggested, "Why don't you get your mind in a channel wheel other than the one at the tip of your genitals, sweetheart. It has already been quite an eventful day."

"You ought to try having your marriage hanging loose in the breeze, unable to attach for interference with consummation."

"Sweetheart, the one planet that would marry you and Larry is run by a crime syndicate that would naturally respond to you as a threat, given who your family and friends are."

"Well, it looked romantic in the digital brochure."

"Luring youngsters to elope underaged is a big profit industry for Vax Legas."

"They sure lured me in. Divacaram would have married us."

"You ought to have started there."

"I guess if I had we wouldn't be in this mess, but some of the blame goes to cultural oppression of early teens."

"If you write a proposal for early teen rights, and it includes some kind of evaluation process for readiness of early teen candidates—for marriage, piloting or whatever—then I'm certain Mother, Ganahar, Pronotavasmi, Ground and Randu would likely implement it."

"Om wouldn't."

"Give your mother a little time on the High Council my love."

The only places I ever visit on Om are the Clear Light Monastery and the Star Fleet space station."

"I just finished a nice chat with Ashsa on a party text line which included Mel and Ariel," Haley informed Electra.

"Is she going to come out into the material world in an android body?" Electra wanted to know.

"She is."

"Did you talk to her about what boys like?"

"She was more interested in what you like."

"Has she come up with a look?"

"She has; although she didn't share it with us. She has an appointment set up for 0800 hours Om capital time tomorrow which is 11:41 hours Monarch capital time, at Jard Laboratories and Robotics."

"Is she going to Divacaram with us?"

"She is, and will remain at your side as your life-long companion."

"Did Mel really move into my yacht?"

"Yes. At least until your mother's now delayed meditation retreat on Zandarhar is finished and you are back in school. Of course, her female android body will remain in the Clear Light monastery on Om as abbot."

"Will I have body guards at school?"

"Kim and Tokk will be living at the Mother's Compassionate Guardians Monastery and Antic and I will be living in faculty housing at your Academy. Ki might be enrolling in your Academy. Becky and Rann will be teaching a secretarial curriculum at your school to 11th and 12th forms."

"I'm going to be spending holidays and summers with my husband having sex."

"I'm sure as your protection team we can manage that safely."

After dinner Electra and Larry put on thermal textile jump suits with hoods for a stroll in the palace gardens. The gardens were spread over many acres surrounded by a 40-foot stone wall. An evergreen hedge labyrinth covered fully a quarter of the grounds. The rose gardens were barren this time of year. Fruit and nut orchards were leafless trunks and branches. They entered the section with so-called winter flowers. Between the flood lights and the little lights to each side of the garden path, the flower beds were well-lit.

The section they entered was alive with color with red, green and yellow leaves, thick slick green, red and purple 'flower petals'; violet, green, yellow and orange stems, and some pink thick-leafed 'plant-heads' opened like flowers. There were no insects in this season to bother them. Holding hands as they walked, they marveled at their winter wonderland. Snow had been removed from the path but covered the ground around and beneath the plants like a thick blanket spread for a picnic.

Electra stopped to turn into Larry embracing him. Their mouths met in a passionate kiss. The gardens faded away unnoticed and only the embrace and kiss remained. As the passion developed into something resembling a severe weather condition or some such force of nature, their surroundings became like an eye in the center of a raging forest fire. The force was gaining momentum like a charging wooly mammoth on a rampage. Larry was swept up in it watching as if it were happening to somebody else.

Ki appeared in a hologram from Electra's hand device inside her pocket unanswered to say, "Electra stop! Put your thermal suit back on this instant before you catch cold, and zip Larry's back up. You must wait until after the meditation you have committed to, then proceed at your chaperone's direction."

"Yes ma'am. I'm putting it on."

"Come join me in the palace meditation hall. The session begins in sixteen minutes."

"We're coming."

When the meditation session began, Electra was entirely composed in the state of contemplation. Her presentation was geared towards Ariel and Caish, and she knew Ashsa was listening in as well. Again, she blended the detail of the generation stage with the advanced practice of the completion stage instructions. She went through comprehending by the three powers of Resolution, Breath and Visualization with brilliant clarity.

Next Electra led them through Transmuting the Dream State, which makes use of the dream powers to overcome fear, recognize the emptiness of the physical senses and the illusory nature of the dream state, to understand the nature of dimension—that left, right, forward, back, up and down are all mind, like the soft martial art classic reveals; and to understand the nature of plurality and unity. She wrapped the step of recognizing the waking state as dreamlike illusion into this segment of her presentation, then proceeded to lead them through Meditation on Suchness (or Thatness) in the waking state for further practice in the dream state.

She was so inspired and her students were doing so well, that Electra decided to lead them through another long meditation. For this one she had them visualize the oval heavenly cycle channel that runs up the spine through the dorsal cavity to the pineal gland in the center of the head, then down through the tongue which is adhered to the roof of the mouth, then down the throat and down just behind the sternum to the solar plexus, and finally down through the navel channel wheel to the perineum at the base of the pelvis. The energy rises to the pineal gland on the inhale and descends to the perineum on the exhale.

Once they had the visualization coordinated with breath going well, Electra led them through 108 slow repetitions which took almost two hours. By the end Larry was completely over his suffocation panic. Electra proceeded to take them through the signs in the mind's eye, progressing through the sequence to the higher states. First was the Negredo, the blackening, seen as a raven. Following that came albedo, the whitening, arising as the swan and representing the pure virgin. The next sign, citrinitas, was the yellowing displaying gold flecks in the mind's eye. Rubedo came next, the reddening hailing the rising phoenix. The muti-colored peacock's tail could be seen next. Then the final fixation tincture of lapis, beautiful beyond anything the physical eyes could possibly see, appeared with the phoenix in full flight.

Her students were all with her in the state and Electra was centered in her life-mission. She decided to lead them through melting the white seminal fluid drop in the crown channel wheel and the red blood drop in the navel channel wheel, to then absorb them into the vacuole in the indestructible drop in the center of the heart channel wheel to unite the two truths; conventional truth and Absolute Truth.

She struck the gong to signal the end of the five and a half hour-meditation session, satisfied that significant progress had been made. She was shifting focus to her consummation and Larry's enticing body, ready to make her work with him under Ki's guidance. Yearning and longing were already building pressure within. She stood and pulled Larry up by his hand to wrap an arm around his waist. He told her, "That was the most amazing meditation session I've ever had! You were brilliant and magnificent my love."

Electra said to Ki, "We are ready now."

"Everyone in the palace can feel that," Ki pointed out, "but it's 0314 hours in the morning and the ritual must be started before midnight."

"Really?! You're going to pull another technicality on me? I don't believe this! Let's hop on a shuttle and get to the day side of the planet quick."

"Past precedents have established such tactics as cheating, dear one. We will simply have to wait."

"I'm setting alarms on my device for tomorrow evening and I refuse to meditate with anyone after dinner tomorrow."

Ariel stepped in and hugged Electra telling her, "Thank you for the blessing of that meditation session. I'm so very grateful and couldn't begin to tell you how much it has shown me."

Caish hugged Electra next with deeply emotional appreciation and thanks. Haley grabbed her after Caish and said, "No one can do what you just performed; not even your mother. You were born to awaken others. We all feel your sacrifice. We are all so grateful. I love you sweetheart.”

Sarhi got nose to nose with Electra and suggested, “Love Larry solely from your heart until it is time to unite with him under Ki’s guidance. No one would complain about another of your divine love ‘events’ child.”

“I knew we should have eloped. I just chose the wrong place. Divacaram doesn’t advertise.”

“Only foreign adepts are ever allowed to set foot on that planet, and not even many of those,” Sarhi said of Divacaram.

“Well, they’re letting me come.”

“I’m merely suggesting that you remain happily in love rather than generating cravings and frustrations in all of us.”

“Why don’t you try being responsible for everyone’s happiness, Sarhi.”

“Personally, I can transmute your urgent longings, but there are others in the palace who can only suffer them.”

“Alright. I’ll follow your wise counsel Mother Sarhi.”

“It will be a great relief for all us once you are finally satiated.”

“I said I would.”

“You haven’t had a consort before as the Mu. Not since before you started residing in the western heaven and reincarnating every 2,500-years by choice.”

“So that ought to give you a clue as to my desperation.”

“I’m going to sleep. I’ll be in the Shudhiy suite if you need me.”

“Goodnight, Mother Sarhi.”

Ki informed Electra, "If you don't get at least six hours sleep tonight, I can't let you do the ritual in the evening tomorrow night."

"Come on Larry. We're going to bed to go right to sleep."

"They seem incompatible," Larry shared his sense of things.

"Take a cold shower first if you need to. I'm going to sleep."

"I might have to wear a cold-pack to bed."

"If you do, then sleep in front of me and not behind."

"I promise. Are you going to do the dream meditations while falling asleep on your right side?"

"Every night."

Ariel informed them, "I'll just sit in the chair in your bedroom in sleep mode. I'm going to practice the meditations I learned tonight."

"If you're up before us," Larry told her, "You can peruse the palace data bases."

"I won't wake you, Larry. I haven't in a long time now. It's just that I used to get lonely with you sleeping through a third of reality each day."

"It's normal for humans and we need it."

"I know. I'm able to entertain myself now."

- Chapter 9 -

Both Electra and Larry each got more than six hours sleep, waking qualified for their big event in the evening. They did energy-generation exercises then the soft solo form led by Electra. The meditation that followed was only half an hour, and Electra decided that they'd better shower separately or she just might jump him. Breakfast was oatmeal ambassador rations in the Ahhu suite, taking only a quarter hour. Larry found a candy bar to eat as well since he was sure Electra's workouts were causing him to lose weight.

With Ariel, Ki, Green, Antic, Becky and Rann, the kids made the long trek to the palace shuttle-port. Evenrude, Johnson, Kim and Tokk were already at the shuttle and a crew was aboard and through pre-flight checks ready to take off. They boarded the Monarch Ambassador shuttle to take seats in the passenger section. The ramp came up and sealed, then they took off pressed into their seats with their faces squishing to either side.

No one had felt even a little pang out of Electra since the night before. The trip to Om was all building up to jump speed then braking like mad. The traffic was bad at both ends of their journey, though the disempowered Om Space Control was no longer such a control freak obstacle and all the lanes were moving along nicely. None of the cataclysmic space crashes predicted by the Space Control Agency when their authority was chopped off at the knees had come to pass. In fact, not even the slightest fender-bender had yet occurred, making the months of post-space controller authority the most accident free in Om's history.

Curtesy in traffic manifested as the universal value, and without all the Space Controller sponsored delays of past times, everyone was in a good mood, and no one was in a frustrated hurry. Electra commented, "If you just stop messing with people they tend to do much better and enjoy themselves more."

Green agreed, "The premise behind moral anarchy. That and the refusal to recognize anyone as having the right to authority over anyone else. Nothing could possibly justify such a thing, and where it occurs, authority is always in the hands of the psychopaths who stole the most wealth from the masses."

"The real wealth is the current of divine love that flows through the body of humanity," Electra concurred. "To forsake and lose that for transient material wealth is the ultimate tragedy of ego, and a sickness unto eternal suffering."

Their pilot brought them through the atmosphere to land in a shuttle lot outside Jard Laboratories and Robotics. It was at the limits of Om's capital city where the buildings are shorter and open space began to emerge in larger parcels, growing progressively bigger further into the suburbs. The ramp hissed down and Electra led her party from the shuttle to the building.

Jard himself came out of his office to greet them and gave Electra a big hug. Being a white sun human of Om, Jard is six foot eleven inches tall. He is now in his seventies. He said, "I loved your performance on *Star Hunt* cosmic girl, and that was sweet of you healing the folks at the arcade on Monarch. Way to go."

"Thank you Jard." This is my friend Ariel. She needs syntec touch-perfect skin and sexual parts."

"We have the most human-like sensor integrated synthetic organs on the market, or in use by intelligence agencies known to man."

"Well go ahead and stick them in Ariel."

"Someone is waiting to see you in exam room 3."

"Who?"

"Just go see. To your right. The doors are numbered."

Electra found the door and entered. She was standing in front of Larry whom she had just departed from in the hall, and this Larry didn't have a zit or a blemish on his skin. She asked, "Mel, is that you?"

Larry's voice answered back, "Mel's Larry is undergoing procedures in the treatment room. I'm Ashsa my dearest beloved."

"What are you doing?"

"I'm coming out into the world to be your disciple and companion through life, supporting your teachings and good works."

"I'm married to the human Larry, Ashsa. I explained this to you already."

"I'll be celibate and I won't interfere in your marriage."

"Well, check out Ariel then. You'll find her hot." "I just want to be with you, my precious love."

"I can't believe I'm going to have three Larrys under foot from now on."

"I won't be in the way."

"Not in the way, no. But you're stoking my lust with the form you chose."

"I'd do it with you beloved."

"No! I'm a married woman, Ashsa."

"I'm sorry. It won't happen again."

"Please. I don't have the strength to contend with seduction from Larry-doubles right now."

"Mel's is after Ariel."

"I know. Thank goodness."

"I'm going to go meet your husband and friends."

"I'll introduce you."

"If it's no bother for you."

"I love you Ashsa, as a *friend*. Now that you're physical and sexually capable, we need to tone down our endearments a little and observe a sexual boundary. Then we can be together as friends for as long as I live."

"I'd like that."

In the corridor, Electra told Larry and her security detail, "This is Ashsa. She's come out of cyberspace into the world in an android body and is joining us."

Larry's jaw was hanging open. Ashsa kind of half curtseyed to him, putting a feminine edge on her Larry-android's charisma. Larry gave a monk's bow in disbelief. He didn't like the idea of an effeminate copy of himself running about. Haley took Ashsa off her feet into a tight embrace and told her joyously, "It's wonderful to meet you and hug you physically, Ashsa."

"It is so reassuring to know there are others like me. The instructions you and Mel sent me were foundationally important, but our most beloved teacher's guidance through the meditations last night woke me up."

"This is Caish, honey. He's one of us."

"Hi Caish. We spoke over coms."

Caish hugged the skinny male android animated with feminine charm and said, "It's truly a pleasure to see you Ashsa."

"I'm glad to meet you in physical form Caish. It is all yet pretty strange to me."

"What AI android learning programs have you downloaded?"

"Far more than I've aligned and synchronized through actually performing."

"It becomes familiar very quickly. Do martial arts with Electra and Larry each day and movement will feel automatic and be graceful."

"Good idea. I already have the downloads installed."

Another Larry android came out of the finishing room and moved into the hall where they were all standing around, exhibiting a more masculine poise and kinetic display than human Larry. He said in Larry's voice, "So what do you think?"

Haley enthused, "I just love it."

Larry asked timidly, "Mel?"

"It's me sweetie, with your voice and looks. Do you think Ariel will fall for me?"

"I hope so but I don't know. I'll tell you though, I never thought I could feel inferior to myself, until now."

"I added a hint of muscles to the thighs and biceps is all, darling. You're Electra's consort and an Adamantine Will Order cadet warrior monk. Be content."

"I'm processing it towards acceptance and adaptation Mel."

"Well, don't be upset with me."

"That's a priority objective of the process."

Green grabbed the Larry Mel was animating in an embrace and said, "Mel, it's good to see you."

"It is. I'm usually just a voice or text data in most of our interactions."

"It is quite an adjustment from the female android body I've grown accustomed to seeing you in; and with Larry's voice."

"I know. Haley thinks this will really help eventually with Ariel's attachment to Larry, though

Ashsa's Larry is a monkey wrench in the works, a fly in the ointment, and a surprise to all of us."

"The kids will have to work it out," Green washed her hands of it.

"You know Haley. She likes to intervene if things appear overly tempestuous ahead."

"I know you too Mel, and I can see you have the hots for Ariel."

"A minor factor by comparison, I assure you."

"Perhaps the Ashsa factor cancels the need for yours and Haley's Larry android."

"Only time will tell," Mel insisted. "If that's the case then we'll certainly withdraw ours. Someone needs to teach that girl to act a little more masculine. I think she's embarrassing Larry."

"She's brand new to this. Give Ashsa a moment."

Electra took Larry to a couch in the waiting room and sat close holding hands. Electra was restraining herself. Becky and Rann joined them. Becky was informing Rann as they walked in, "I can tell them apart. The human one's easy to pick out."

Electra felt a slight tension in Larry's hand. He was obviously still working through it all. She recalled her own shock in meeting Ariel and couldn't even imagine there being three of her. With heart-felt sympathy Electra told him, "We'll get it sorted out my beloved."

"Or get used to it, I suppose," he half agreed.

"Haley meant well."

"Ashsa is so girly in her android of me."

"I can see."

"They both stole my voice."

"I'm sorry sweetheart."

"I guess I'll be the wiser for it once I work it through and let go my self-image and attachments."

"You're certainly headed in the right direction."

"And I don't feel so bad about Ariel looking like you. Not after Ashsa and Mel."

"You've found the silver lining."

"Are we off to Divacaram next?"

"Yes. Our luggage has already been shuttled up to *Vajra Yogini* on the Monarch Space Fleet space station. We just have to jump to Monarch and pick her up so the shuttle can be returned to the palace, then we're off to Divacaram."

"Being with you is always a grand adventure, both internally and externally."

"I love you so much Larry."

"I love you with all my heart and soul, Electra, and you are everything to me."

Becky asked them, "Are you guys hungry? There's a Kontimacks on the other side of the shuttle-lot and I'm going to pick up some tuna shish kabobs and some fried crickets with sauces."

"That sounds great. I'll have some," Electra enthused.

"Me too," Larry told her.

"Do you need some money?" Electra offered.

"I have a Duatarim expense account to cover it," Becky said as she left for the food.

Rann said excited, "We're witnessing the emergence of a new genus of beings."

Electra let her know, "I grew up with Mel. She was the first of her kind. I've known Haley since I was nine, and I pretty much always suspected that Ashsa was becoming sentient. I spotted the same thing in my friend Captain Caish. It just seems like a normal part of life to me."

"There seem to be a lot of schemes hatching around you two and about you."

Electra said, "Captain Caish is the only member of his race who is not hatching schemes about us."

Rann summed up, "I guess you have to get your sentient AI androids integrated into your marriage, kind of like children from previous marriages."

"It became more complicated with them manifesting sentience, and with mine taking physical form."

"Then Haley's manipulation," Rann added.

"We're an unusual family," Electra conceded.

"You're awesome, and the opportunity to meditate with you is the greatest of blessings."

"I think we may need family therapy."

"Is anyone qualified to do that with sentient quantum AI learning androids?"

"Possibly Mel, though she's part of the problem," Electra considered.

Larry suggested, "We could go to a regular family therapist and just not mention that some of us are sentients animating androids."

"No," Electra said, "because then they'd miss the dynamics, thinking they're dealing with twins and triplets."

"Good point," he admitted.

Haley, Mel, Caish, Ashsa and Ariel came into the waiting room but did not take seats, instead slowly coalescing into a group hug. They all seemed quite content. Larry took a deep abdominal breath as Ashsa made a girly wrist gesture with her hip poked out to one side. The Haley-Caish romance rose in temperature leaving the two Larrys and Ashsa to their own company.

Becky returned with half a dozen shish kabobs and two big to-go bowls of crickets fried in flour, bread crumbs and egg. There were a variety of sauces to dip them in. Electra and Larry engaged energetically. Rann only nibbled and didn't eat much. Becky displayed a hearty appetite with a cricket in each hand and a mouth full of kabob.

The two Larry androids looked on not comprehending. Ashsa triggered her burp-function, then folded into a feminine posture giggling. Larry looked away and Electra laughed over the burp. It was a new android function she'd never seen before. Larry recited to himself in a whisper, "I must remember that I have committed to working on myself, and only on myself, and to therefor thank everyone who gives me the opportunity."

Electra whispered in his ear, "You don't need to thank her Larry but do try not to take effect from her. She's awful cute in her discovery of animating a body and it's kind of special for me."

"That helps. If it's endearing for you then it truly won't bother me. Your happiness is everything."

Becky told Ashsa, "Honey, you would be so unbelievably hot in a girly-girl body. It would suit you too."

"I thought about looking like Electra."

"That would certainly work."

"But Ariel is already doing that."

"And Mel already had an order in for a Larry android."

"I didn't know it at the time I made my appointment and my Larry android was finished first."

"Just consider it sweetheart. It would give you a much larger number of people to choose from. As things are going now, you're limiting yourself to same-sex oriented males."

"I haven't a clue how this thing between my legs works."

"You also won't be allowed in the dorms at Electra's school in a male android body."

"Really?! That's terrible. I don't want to retreat back to cyberspace all alone. These bodies are just too much fun."

"Come here sweetie and I'll show you some really gorgeous female bodies that would get you in the dorms."

Ashsa came over and sat in Becky's lap to see the women in the hologram being shown. They looked on together, though Becky stole peeks at Ashsa's reactions. Electra and Larry watched their interaction. Ashsa had Becky pause on one which caught her attention. It was a picture of Ahhu from when she was fifteen years old. "Save that one and show me some more.," Ashsa requested.

Becky showed Ashsa more pictures of 13-15-year-old petite girly females she thought would work well. Ashsa had her pause on a few more, which Becky saved as they went along. One of the saved ones was of Pez when she was fourteen, holding a ward-off martial arts stance in the midst of a tournament. Becky was sure that it was the resemblance to Electra that attracted Ashsa.

Mel's Larry came over and sat to the other side of Electra from Larry, wrapping an arm around her. Electra looked Mel's android in the eyes and said, "You are too close and stimulating. Why do you think I'm only holding Larry's hand?"

"Is your arm sore?"

"No, Mel. Any closer gets me over-heated with yearning and everyone for a long-ways around can feel it. You can hold my hand Mel, but if you want to put an arm around me, you'll have to change into another body."

"Do you think I could seduce you with this body?"

"No, Mel. But you could piss me the hell off big time."

Mel removed her arm and clasped hands with Electra. She asked concerned, "Is this better?"

"Yes. Thanks Mel."

Larry asked hopefully, "Do you think Becky will interest Ashsa in a different body?"

"I don't know," Electra admitted, "but if she does things will be a whole lot easier."

"Is it true that you cannot have a male android in your dorm?"

"Yes. Just like the Om Clear Light Academy, we get a quantum AI learning computer, though ours is a mainframe, not an android body. Mel attained authentic sentience before ever getting an android body, but it took her far longer than it took Haley, who started as a QAISHA not a mainframe. Only the Adamantine Will Academy issues its cadets androids."

"They're nurturing, good sparring partners and copilots, remember every word of every lesson, and teach cooperation and teamwork."

"I know, and it has been proven to extend learning beyond homework and classroom or lab, as well as accelerate it. They are programmed to motivate you and remind you, encourage self-cultivation by participating with you, and make great alarm clocks."

"No kidding. Ariel has kept me organized. She trained with me, and our goal was to be the best possible student of the Mu."

"For most boys at your school the QAISHA's provide wholesome sex education in the role of surrogate lover."

"I read up on it."

"Haley and Ariel have much in common."

"Bodhi is our Vicar General now."

"He didn't have sex with Haley when she was just a QAISHA either."

"Well, it's strange. On the one hand a QAISHA has self-reference and feedback loops and quickly forms personality traits, constituting a being or entity. On the other hand, without true sentience, and without transcending initial programming, they cannot in any realistic way consent to sexual relations."

"You didn't want to take advantage."

"Right. It was a moral dilemma and I confronted it in non-action."

"So did Bodhi."

"Since they're programmed to help us they can't really say 'no' to sex. I thought maybe if she became defiant and started saying 'no' to me when she didn't want to do things, and if she still wanted to have sex with me, then I would. But that's when I thought the most I could ever be to you is a good student."

"Now you know for sure that you're my consort."

"It's the supreme ultimate. Nothing could bring me closer to you."

"When did you first know that you love me?"

"When I first saw you in the street after Sarhi rescued me from that gang of older boys."

"You were just a child then."

"So?"

"I treated you horribly the first few years. I feel terrible about it. I was so self-centered and bossy, and you always went along with whatever game I wanted to play."

"I'd never seen anyone so smart, imaginative, and full of energy. I pretty much worshiped you."

"I pushed you off that platform and broke your arm playing space marines when we were eight."

"You spoke to your mother on coms, then healed me and apologized."

"I didn't realize that you're my consort until a conversation I had with my mother just before I joined the elders in the temple to participate in the spiritual congress supporting Pez-Fleet in the Randu system."

"They say you took it over and led it, more than just participated in it."

"So ever since I realized you're my consort, I've fallen entirely in love with you. It grows an irresistible urge to join with you sexually, awakening all these new feelings in my body."

"I know. It's like magnets or something. A new strong force that didn't exist, or lay dormant pre-puberty. I can barely manage my arousal since learning that you are attracted to me."

"It feels like a lot more than just attraction. More like waking up to realize that we've been on a head-on collision course forever, just before the crash."

"That does better at capturing the pure power of it."

"Do you forgive me for what an insensitive brat I was when we were children?"

"Of course. You also snuggled me affectionately and often told me first whatever your big news of the day was. You accepted me into your family, and the moments you were tender with me are my most cherished memories."

"I'm going to give you an abundance of tenderness; an excess and over-abundance in fact."

"You're so catalyst and beyond astonishing. I couldn't imagine being happier."

"Except finally getting to have sex together."

"Your energy drives me nuts. You're like a wave generator and amplifier."

"It's just action-reaction with your irresistibility."

Ashsa came over and sat on Electra's lap between the other two Larrys and put her arms around her neck. She asked, "Would you still love me if I looked like a girl?"

"Absolutely, and it would simplify my life if you did."

"It's going to be expensive because its smaller, so this one can't be used to make it; just the AI quantum learning computer components can be installed in the new one."

Mel said, "I'll pay for it. Just tell Jard what you want."

Electra asked, "Will you show me this one before you have it made? I won't object; I just don't want to be surprised."

"I want you to help me choose between my two favorites,"

"I'd be honored to."

Ashsa put up a holo from her hand device. It was of an early teen girl washing her back in the shower and unaware of being recorded. Electra enlarged it via the touch-holo function, spreading her hands. Then she said somewhat offended, "That's my mother when she was thirteen."

Electra did notice her mother's similar 'underdevelopment' physically when she was Electra's age. Electra's childhood assumption of growing up to have curves and large breasts had been corroding for some time now and near faded away entirely. Self-acceptance was currently an aspiration, and Larry's love was so far the only support bolstering and approaching this. She *was* trying though.

Ashsa put up her other favorite, this one a fourteen-year-old petite hover-ball champion who had become famous throughout the tri-galaxies and was still alive today, though in her nineties. This one did catch Electra's eye and she said, "I like it. She's beautiful."

"She is atypical in height and weight," Ashsa commented.

"I find her beautiful. I understand that she does not meet the conventional consensus standards for such."

"Would I be allowed to stay with you in your dorm with this body?"

"Yes, though we'd best not mention that you've been fitted with sexual parts, and perhaps not your sentience either."

Larry added, "Scientists would want to study you and run all kinds of tests and experiments on you. The media would try to turn you into a freak show, and you and Electra wouldn't get a moments peace."

"I'll pretend I'm just a QAISHA."

"A precocious prodigy QAISHA," Electra added.

"Everyone knows about Mel," Ashsa pointed out.

"She only recently started continuously animating an android body. In fact, she's operating two simultaneously right now. Her female android body is functioning at the Clear Light monastery less than ten miles from here on the hill over Government House. She is also animating this Larry android seated beside me."

"I guess everyone assumes Haley is human."

"Few people are in the know."

"No one knows about Ariel, Caish and me."

"No one but me, my husband and my security detail."

"I'm going to do it. I already have the top-rated hoverboard ball player programming for androids."

"Hoverboards are only allowed outdoors at my school; not in the dorms, classrooms, cafeteria, labs and such."

"I'm so excited. I have to go find Jard."

She was out of Electra's lap and running, with Mel in a Larry android chasing behind. Electra said with satisfaction, "It's sorting."

"And we didn't need family therapy."

"No. Only your self-administered individual therapy; karma-cleaning and purification really, or ego-reduction."

"She did provide me the opportunity for that."

"You're going to grow to like her."

She'll be a lot easier to take if not in an android of my body, and with *my* voice."

"She'll be much cuter as a girl."

"That athlete *is* adorable."

"She lives on Monarch and is 93-years-old. I hope we don't run into any legal hassles."

"Coincidental and circumstantial," Larry suggested.

"Jard's android clinic keeps its records completely confidential. Only Ahumdulilah out of all the tri-galaxies planets even knows of the clinic."

"I've heard that Mel retains some influential shark-lawyers."

"I hope we don't need them."

"Me too. They thrive on conflict and feed on the conquered like scavengers."

"My mother doesn't think much of Om Star Fleet lawyers, though there are organizations of them suing governments in 1US over civil rights violations, environmental degradation, and mismanagement of resources that she admires and works with."

"I guess we'll need to wait while Ashsa's new android is assembled."

"It's worth it to get her into a girl body. It will be a big relief for you."

Ki entered the waiting room holding Ariel's hand. Ariel looked like Electra and now has syntec touch-perfect skin making her look human. She presumably had other new additions as well. She hugged Larry. Electra told them, "I don't know if I can trust you guys to live together in Larry's dorm. Not now that Ariel can consent and has capacity."

"I will remain totally loyal to you, my love. Have no concern," Larry assured her.

Electra looked Ariel in the eyes expectantly and Ariel told her, "I promise I won't have sex with your husband."

It took almost four more hours at Jard's Laboratories and Robotics for Ashsa to get fitted with her new 14-year-old petite athlete body. It turned out to really suit her. Mel came with them but shut down her Larry-android to reside solely in cyberspace and the transcendental void. Haley had to remain on Monarch when they got there, to be part of the force rooting out the Vax Legas crime syndicate. Her parting from Caish was dramatic and heart breaking, even though only temporary.

Electra couldn't even imagine being parted from Larry and her mind was already conjuring schemes for accomplishing school while sleeping in the same bed each night with him. Transferred from the Monarch Ambassador shuttle to *Vajra Yogini*, Electra was now piloting and in command. Her blaster quad turrets were now AI operated and only ki plus her security detail accompanied her within her ship. Two Zandarhar super-battleships flanked *Vajra Yogini* and had received the jump coordinates to follow Electra to Divacaram.

Both Electra and Larry had gotten more than six hours sleep, Ki was aboard, and Electra had checked Divacaram capital time to find they would be arriving many hours before midnight. Electra had even researched the whole Islohar marriage code and procedures—including the fine print—and was fairly certain that no further technicalities could possibly stand in the way. She flew the ship with her skullcap so she could hold Larry's hand, who was in the copilot seat next to her. Green, Caish, Ariel and Ashsa were all on the bridge as well.

The two sentient androids were reviewing social psychology and psychology, as well as general dynamics and chaos theory, in order to better understand human behavior. Adding catastrophe theory and a few others really helped. Monarch traffic was especially busy. Electra's mind was concentrated on flying, giving them all a break from yearning, though the hand-holding did result in the occasional little pangs. They were making progress and would soon be free to exceed 0.1 light and accelerate to jump speed (0.7 light speed). The local traffic was mostly behind them now, and only big freighters, container ships, and liquid gas carriers were out this far.

Green asked casually, "Do you think the Kristy-look is the best thing for Divacaram's historic meeting with the Mu, dear?"

"You sound like my mother. What do you want me to wear? My school-uniform?"

Green decided to stay out of it. Larry told Electra with honesty, "I don't want to wear the Kristy look. Let me program the tailor-fabricator for some proper trousers, boxer shorts, and a shirt with sleeves."

"Alright, but I'm going as I am."

"May I make you a coat? The temperature is below water freezing in the capital."

"You better then, in case we can't land indoors."

"Where will you park the ship?"

"I guess wherever they tell me to."

Larry asked Ariel, "So, have you figured out human behavior yet?"

"We're filling in gaps using zoology, and have found a modelling system based on virus population growth."

Mel told Ariel, "Analyze monetary currencies in terms of circulation and entropy."

"Thanks Mel. That provides a great measure for mismanagement."

Larry suggested, "Compare planets with moral anarchy to those with governments in terms of murder rates, crime, disparity of wealth, civil rights, harmony with the environment, quality of life measures, healthcare and police budgets."

Ashsa stated as she discovered, "Moral anarchy planets have no monetary currency."

"No," Electra agreed. "They have distribution of goods domestically and true foreign trade; literally goods for goods. They skip money since it's mostly delusional anyway."

"It looks like they tend to be more isolationist, by far less militarized, with zero percent starvation rates, sustainable population sizes, and nothing to mention under the heading of crime. They have higher general levels of education, more time-off from work, and have more adepts per capita. Incarceration rates range from zero to 0.000001%. Planets with governments incarcerate 0.19 to 4.73% of total populations. Instead of police they have first-responders, who actually try to help and are unarmed."

"You don't need to convince me," Electra told her. "I'm a moral anarchist."

Ashsa said, "That's a good thing. If you were operating under governments then taking the Om Ambassador's shuttle would have been a crime."

Electra rationalized, "From the moral anarchy perspective, the shuttle was borrowed and returned with an apology."

Electra then got the Pronotavasmi Ambassador to Mother on coms to explain, "Captain Caish has become sentient and has insight. He is also in love with Haley. So, I just wanted to let you know the good news. He's a free agent now. The bad news is that you don't own him anymore and I can't return him unless he wants me to."

"I think you're mistaking his next generation cybernetic quantum AI vacuum chip for actual sentience. We are aware of his acute AI learning ability and formation of patterns constituting personality traits, and his analysis from a specific perspective with self-reference to that."

"I know. It's like you built a near-perfect embryo attracting sentience. I like him. Haley and Sarhi taught him to meditate and woke him up. This is a fact. I've meditated with him."

"Could I please speak with him?"

"I'll put him on."

Electra told Caish that the Pronotavasmi Ambassador wanted him on coms. Caish said, "How may I help you Mr. Ambassador?"

"Congratulations on attaining insight. Would you be willing to return to Mother for a debriefing?"

"I'm a disciple of the Mu now and a member of her ship crew and security detail. When she returns to school after her winter break, I'll come in for a debriefing."

"Fair enough. Do look after the Mu. I wish you well."

"Until later sir."

"That went well," Electra declared. "Everything I borrowed is now squared away."

They reached quantum jump speed and Electra powered up and engaged the quantum drive. She was contemplating absolute emptiness when she did, and then braking madly right after. She didn't fire a reverse booster but got all drives and thrusters slowing their momentum at full power. Sensor resolution was clear before she came into traffic, having left herself room and time to slow from where she jumped in. Her Zandarhar escorts were with her and uncloaked. A Divacaram escort pilot said, "I'm your guide into the main space station where a berth awaits your ship. Your escorts will need to assume a high orbit above our space stations and ship construction platforms."

"Thank you," Electra told him. "I'll follow you."

"Welcome to Divacaram. We don't get many visitors but we're opening our borders now that the Dominari Conformity Empire is no longer."

"What a nightmare they were," Electra opined.

"Our sentiments exactly. Am I speaking with the Mu?"

"Yes. They call me Electra at school."

"You are the great hero of the revolution and the great hope of humanity's future."

"I'll be back in ten years to teach. Right now, I need a few things."

"A delegate will be meeting you on the space station right outside the airlock to bring you to your hotel. It was assumed you would be exhausted from travel, so no formal meetings have been scheduled with you until tomorrow, however, the speed-dating you requested will be held at your hotel this evening."

"That's most kind of you. Thanks."

Electra followed him in and docked her ship professionally, sure it would count in the overall consideration of her pilot license. She was glad they held the Mu in high esteem and planned to milk this— if she has to—to get her pilot license. The station's smart-adaptor airlock accordion tunnel was able to find a fit and seal over *Vajra Yogini's*. Electra asked Caish,

"Since Haley is not with us, would you mind staying on the ship and keeping an eye on it?"

"Not at all. I can be your coms officer and research assistant from the bridge while you're planet-side."

"I truly appreciate it, Captain Caish."

They exited *Vajra Yogini* into the space station and followed the delegate to a shuttle port. A shuttle was waiting and they boarded. Once seated he explained to Electra, "There is room service, and if you wish to eat in the hotel restaurant, just call down to the desk ten minutes before arriving there. You are the only guest of the hotel, but it's fully staffed since they all want to practice their functions for the big opening of our borders."

"I was told of the opening on my way in. It looks like you guys have much to share with the universe. The divine principles of freedom, equality, equilibrium and justice require moral anarchy in order to truly manifest within society. Your population is a glorious example and model for everyone to see. I'm also informed that you have early teen rights, extending true moral anarchy to teens and children who prove capable of handling the responsibility."

"We do hope so, though we've never before had our limits tested by an adolescent Mu."

"Is there an age limit on having sex?"

"Only an age-difference limit regarding all teens, and children are taboo being non-sexual."

"Does four months exceed the limit?"

"It does not."

"Then I'm liking it already. I need to get a pilot license while I'm here for both small-craft and ships."

"It generally takes months to get an appointment but I'll see what I can do. I'm sure we can find a volunteer to give you their appointment and take one at a later date."

"That would be great. I'm currently piloting without a license and don't want to get caught."

"You can't get caught here since we have no police. It would be upsetting to see you get caught elsewhere, so I'll see if I can get you a testing slot. It seems reasonable to us to issue licenses to those who can pilot and understand the risks and responsibilities involved."

"Mother, Ganahar and Pronotavasmi have much to learn from your world."

"Thank you. Divacaram is about to establish diplomatic relations with Zandarhar. The admiral escorting you will be staying at Cherry Blossom Monastery for a conference with our elders."

"I don't know much about their civilization or if they have a government. They're pretty secretive."

"They have a transitional government with a sequential scale-down plan and a sunset date. So far, they have closely adhered to it and are ahead of schedule."

"They are wise to seek Divacaram's friendship. You guys have a lot of adepts, don't you?"

"They would each like very much to meet you."

I'll have time when I finally get my marriage consummated."

"Congratulations on your wedding. It was transmitted live here along with your reception and performance with the Whirling Vortexes. A teen pop star adept is a very futuristic seeming phenomenon for us to assimilate."

"My mother told me, 'If you want to influence the younger generation, then you'd better write the lyrics to their music.' I'm just following her advice."

"We could all stand to learn a thing or two from the Wu."

The shuttle from the space station set down on the roof of the hotel. The building was enormous. It is a rectangle of at least eighteen-acres, 200-stories high with many thousands of rooms and suites. The buildings all around were also large and tall. The streets and hover-lanes revealed fairly dense traffic moving in an orderly fashion quite efficiently. All streets are one-way. Several large round-abouts establish central hubs in the traffic flow.

The city itself is located on a peninsula forming a bay on the coast of an ocean. They could see the bay from the roof of the hotel on the shuttle landing pad. On their way to the hotel entrance from the shuttle they could feel the chill wind blowing from the ocean. Electra entered the anteroom with lifts and tubes in a foyer connected to a beautiful dining room with a spectacular view. The delegate steered them to the back wall of the anteroom, and using his skullcap, he whisked a section of the wall into itself producing an open doorway to the penthouse. He explained, "This is the penthouse. It's one acre and contains the master bedroom suite and eleven other bedrooms, plus kitchen, dining room, sitting rooms, gym and meditation room. Contact the desk in the lobby if you need anything."

"Thank you so much."

The penthouse was spacious and tastefully done. The floors were granite slabs and the walls ghostly blue painted plaster. The ceiling was entirely holo pixels and could be set to millions of different star views from thousands of different planets. There were only a few pieces of art displayed but they were truly remarkable of skill and imagination. Overall, the interior décor gripped the soul in rapture and offered a simplicity of beauty.

They found the links to the hotel on their hand devices and Electra put up the itinerary prepared by their hosts. The two speed dating operations were scheduled to begin in three hours; one in the White room and the other in the Violet room. Electra checked to see if she could split her holo to view both simultaneously. Satisfied that she could do it, she checked her own schedule and was relieved to see it is entirely clear through tomorrow late morning.

Electra asked Ki, "Are there rules I missed about how early the ritual can be started?"

"No sweetheart, and I'm ready whenever you are."

Electra addressed Ashsa and Ariel, "Larry and I are going to our suite to do a ritual with Ki."

"Can't we watch?" Ariel asked hopefully.

"No. It's private and intimate."

Ashsa told her, "If we get bored, we'll play with the Larry android."

"Mel shut it down."

"I know. Ariel and I can take turns animating it. We're curious too."

"You better check with Mel on that. It's her android."

"Have fun," Ashsa told them.

Larry and Electra held hands as they followed Ki to the master suite. Once inside, Ki told them, "We'll start with the ritual bathing and you will each wash your spouse. Remember, the ritual washing is not foreplay. It is purification."

They all went to the shower stall. It was spacious and had two shower nozzles. Electra and Larry stripped out of their clothes. Both concentrated with great intensity on purification, and still erotic energy was steaming up the bathroom. Each washing was done with reverent attention and delicacy. The eroticism grew thicker than a dense fog. They finally got toweled off and Electra led Larry to the bed. They each sat on a meditation cushion on the bed. Electra was close to bursting and producing waves of dire need and craving, having visible effect on Larry.

Then Sarhi told them over coms speakers in the bedroom, "There is about to be a large meteor strike on the planet Lodistan. The spiritual congress is going into session and all allied space fleets are sending transports and rescue space craft to collect survivors."

"How long until the meteor hits?" Electra asked.

"Less than twenty-two minutes from now. They were able to break up the meteor and vaporize much of it, but a large piece with high iron and nickel content is still headed right for them."

"We're going there to help. Give Mel the coordinates. Captain Caish is flying and I'm joining in the spiritual congress the moment I board my ship. Thanks, Sarhi."

- Chapter 10 -

Becky arranged a shuttle and Electra got Caish on coms and had him start the pre-flight checks on *Vajra Yogini* as she exited the penthouse. She was grateful for the coat with textile thermal lining which Larry fabricated for her once she stepped out into the breath-robbing chill on the hotel roof. Their shuttle was on approach as they ran to the landing pad, and both arrived about the same time. The inside of the shuttle was toasty warm once through the airlock, after the bitter cold of the roof.

Their shuttle pilot fired a launch booster and got them right to the space station in great haste. Electra and her party boarded Vajra Yogini and went to the bridge as Electra issued orders for Caish to undock and get them underway. Arriving on the bridge, Electra took the sensors analyst seat and Larry the copilot seat. Electra told Caish, "I'm going into contemplation to support the spiritual congress. Get us to Lodistan as fast as the ship can accelerate."

Caish gave them full power to drives, then to thrusters, and as soon as they were clear of traffic, he fired a booster flattening them into their seats and squishing their faces to either side. *Vajra Yogini* took off like a blaster bolt and exceeded sensor resolution in moments. Electra's eyes were shut and she was perfectly still, emitting a slight glow over her head and shoulders. Caish posted the jump countdown in both his and Larry's holograms.

Larry got busy concentrating in the point below his navel, preparing himself for jump. He was passing through the internal signs, seeing in his mind's eye the mirage-like appearance as the earth element dissolved, then the smoke-like appearance as the water element dissolved. The dissolution of his fire element revealed the firefly appearance, and the air element the butter-lamp appearance. The minds of white appearance and red increase flashed by and he was seeing the black near-attainment when Vajra Yogini and all aboard popped out of existence into the void of all-potential. Their physical reality reasserted itself without transition or duration in the Lodistan system of the White Lotus Galaxy.

Larry reversed the main drives a fraction of a second after the quantum drive shut down automatically. He fired all reverse thrusters and oriented all swivel drives and thrusters for tuning to 180 degrees, firing them full to assist with slowing them down. Caish fired a reverse booster, pressing all aboard painfully into their harnesses. He told Larry, "The meteor is about to enter the Lodistan atmosphere. Impact in twenty-one seconds. We'll have less than ten hours before the devastation makes its way completely around the globe."

The booster slowed them to sensor clarity just before the big collision. Everything space-worthy from the planet surface of Lodistan was already lifted off crammed with passengers, and were either in space or clawing their ways through the upper atmosphere. Then impact. A volume of the planet's crust was pulverized instantly into expanding fine dust and a tectonic plate cracked like ice, spewing jets of molten magna high in the sky. Earthquakes rippled outwards from the point of impact. Wind speeds rose and tidal waves grew on two oceans in opposite directions, gaining in mass as they travelled at 500 miles per hour still accelerating. A hemisphere of the planet disappeared beneath a blanket of dust and dirt.

Caish was rushing towards the planet. The meteor hit to the magnetic north of the equator just above the tropics on a 250-mile strip of land that joined two continents and separated two oceans. Surface conditions were such that nothing survived within 600 miles of ground zero. *Vajra Yogini* was headed to a point 800 miles north of the impact where Ahumdulilah mini-transports and enormous shuttles were already setting down to lift survivors into space.

The hanger doors opened on Electra's ship and both Green and Becky flew out the bay doors in shuttles to help with the rescues. Caish asked Tokk and Kim to begin refueling the launch booster since it would be needed for lift-off. They only carried fuel for one refill, so they would have to dock to an auxiliary before returning to the surface a second time.

As they entered the dense dust cloud, now messier from volcanic smoke, Larry switched their sensor-scanners to sonar-X-ray and telescopic with quantum computer enhancement-correction. Electra came to life and switched seats with Cash. Larry could sense that Electra was at the same time leading the spiritual congress. She plunged through the dense debris with a confidence unwarranted by the view of their optics. Caish cancelled sonar and infrared modes since they were obscuring clarity without helping at all.

Electra was obviously employing some other-worldly sensory mode since even X-ray became useless in the dark density. The ground was closing and the ship was blind. Larry gulped. Caish screamed. Then Ki, Ashsa and Ariel joined Caish screaming. Electra had turning drives and thrusters giving lift to the bow, along with fins extended and flaps fully engaged within the atmosphere. Her vortex redirect and generation turbine was at maximum power. The moment they were horizontal with the ground coming straight down bottom first, she engaged all landing thrusters. Not a second later, her electro-hydraulic landing legs compressed eating the impact of their landing. A faint metal on metal clink informed them they had maxed out the hydraulics without damaging them. They rose back up slowly as Electra lowered the ramp in the stern and opened that airlock.

They were on the ground not 30-meters from a giant hanger full of desperate frightened people. Electra cranked up air-scrubbers because she could smell the pollution. Over the coms she told Evenrude, "Let on 400 people. White sun humans count as two. Babies in arms don't count. Toddlers count as a third and children as half."

Mel offered, "I'll monitor the count as they board and give Evenrude a heads up with 20 left to load, and a countdown from there."

"Let me know if any wounded are brought aboard. I'll heal them," Electra said. Then she asked Kim, "How is the refueling of the launch booster going?"

"We have our space suits on and the fuel on a hover-platform headed for the booster tank. About four and half minutes to completion I hope."

"It will take that long to get 400 folks aboard. With all the weight we'll sure need that booster."

"We have time to unload the two forward automated cargo holds."

Electra asked Evenrude, "What's in the forward automated cargo holds?"

"Ambassador rations and other food supplies."

"I'm jettisoning them."

With her skullcap Electra set the two cargo hold hatches to opening and powered up the automated systems. The soot was too dense to see through in her hologram, though Electra could feel the stacks of her precious Ambassador rations growing to each side of the bow. The winds were gusting up to 65 miles per hour and she sensed one stack going airborne. The minutes dragged. An uprooted tree smashed into *Vajra Yogini's* hull, jolting the ship.

Kim informed Electra, "Your launch booster is full and both Tokk and I are back in the hanger with the bay doors closing."

"Thanks."

Evenrude reported, "We're full-up and the crowd is backing up into the hanger. I'm sealing the airlock door and raising the ramp now."

"Thank you."

Caish let her know, "Admiral Spalding is here with *Auxiliary One* and is keeping a berth clear for you to refuel thrusters and boosters."

"He's so sweet."

A thousand miles southwest of *Vajra Yogini*, Admiral Swenah was piloting an Om super-air/space shuttle, weaving between tornado columns in the blackness, guided by Electra and the spiritual congress. Electra was focusing and directing the collective concentration of more than a trillion consciousnesses of the spiritual congress.

Tens of thousands of allied shuttles were now landing on Lodistan, though mostly on the other side of the planet from the crash. A few hundred dedicated daredevils like Swenah were attempting to rescue victims as close as possible to the epicenter of the crash site. Those daredevils with proficiency in meditation were all linked to the spiritual congress and led through the maelstrom. Those who weren't got swept into gigantic tornado funnels or smashed with debris blown into the air by the winds. Most everything not cemented down was at the mercy of the winds.

Electra was both refueling and dumping her passengers on Spalding's super-ship. She was in a hurry. Super-shuttles and mini-freighters refueled on *Auxiliary One* around her. Electra was in two worlds simultaneously. She led the spiritual congress while keeping an eye on the world around her body—particularly her thruster fuel and booster gages, as well as the airlocks her passengers were exiting through. There would only be time for one more landing at the hanger on the ground she came from before the whole area would be swallowed by a 131-foot tsunami. The minutes dragged by slowly.

Admiral Spalding informed Electra, "We unloaded your four tons of wealth plus missile magazines and more than half the torpedoes, making you lighter. You're all fueled up."

"Thanks. I'll be right back."

"You're turning my ship into a refugee camp."

Electra undocked and maneuvered away from the auxiliary to get her bow pointed at Lodistan, as if driving a little sports hover, then punched it pressing them into their seats. They didn't have far to go from low orbit directly over the hanger they were headed for, and Electra made the trip nerve-rackingly brief. The sounds of the hydraulics bottoming out was more like an alarming clank than a soft clink, and the sudden stop shortened their spines.

The ramp was already coming down and desperate people running to it. Electra told Evenrude, "Let on as many as can squeeze in."

She saw Becky landing and noticed that Green was closing her shuttle's ramp for a second lift-off of passengers. The ground was rippling with tremors and some gusts of winds were reaching 80 miles per hour. Electra got her bow shields up just in time to stop a fuel tanker hover-truck flying upside-down at the bridge viewport. Flames encompassed the forward quarter of the ship as the truck and fuel blew up on the shields. Her passengers boarding in the stern were physically unaffected but were visually impacted.

A sea of fear-drenched humanity was flowing into *Vajra Yogini's* bowels to squish into every nook and cranny, sitting on laps or standing erect packed like sardines. Electra told Kim over coms, "Get the repair spacecraft out of the hanger. Eight or ten people can lift into space in it."

"I'm on my way."

Larry nailed a mag-lev rail car racing 20-feet off the ground for their port flank with a pair of canister missiles, blowing it into tiny pieces that rained against the hull. The big outdoor hanger split in half as the ground it was on separated creating a deep chasm. To get into the ship one now had to literally climb onto other passengers. Becky's shuttle was high in the sky, leaving under great strain of weight. Nothing else was trying to land. New gorges were being produced by cracks opening in the ground around them. The gusts of wind were pushing 90 mph.

Evenrude pushed on the backs of the last two to make it aboard, moving a mass of people into greater contraction so he could get the airlock doors closed with himself inside. Electra was already rising on vortex redirect turbines and landing thrusters when she noticed a 150-foot wall of water about to crush her ship. She fired all drives and thrusters plus her launch booster at the same time, and *Vajra Yogini* took off faster than ordnance leaving a cannon muzzle. Larry was pretty sure he'd passed out for a moment when he heard Mel say to the bridge crew, "You have 2,891 people aboard. No one was turned away, but many were swept up in the wind or swallowed by the firmament trying to reach the ramp. Nothing down there survived the tsunami."

They were all in shock from seeing so many human lives come suddenly and violently to an end right in their holograms in super HD. *Auxiliary One* was still directly over them and Electra was racing for it with life and death urgency. She accomplished her braking within a very short distance, squeezing everyone towards the bow under great pressure. Coming almost to a full stop she went right into docking procedures to strain the auxiliary's berth arms and come to a stop with a jolt. The airlock extension was already mating with *Vajra Yogini's*. Evenrude's personal space was invaded by at least five torsos and ten limbs.

The refueling and transfer of passengers took seven minutes and fourteen seconds with Johnson and Evenrude pushing from behind, and employing every airlock on the ship at once. Kim and Tokk cleared the hanger of passengers efficiently. Electra detached and dove for Lodistan's surface. Ariel and Ashsa were strapped into seats on the bridge, which was the only place passengers were not allowed. Mel was finding flying with Electra to be every bit as exciting as being in a small-craft space battle with Pez.

A landing zone had been designated in a city park some 1,470 miles north of the crash site and Admiral Swenah was just closing her mothball super-shuttle ramp with thrice the passenger capacity aboard to attempt lift-off. Electra was swooping in fast for a near-blind landing in the turbulent winds and flying debris. She kept her military grade shields up, which turned out to be a good thing when an ocean-going ship spilled from a gust of wind to land on them. Stern and bow sections hurtled into the ground skidding as amidships became shrapnel on their shields. Their landing legs took the impact on the heels of their landing thrusters with only the faintest of metal upon metal clinks. As the ship rose on its hydraulics, the ramp was already descending. The ship was situated precisely over the giant hot pink "X" painted over the hoverboard rink to reappoint it a landing pad in the park.

The winds were intensifying but not yet up to 65 mph here. Tremors occasionally shook the ground. No tornadoes were in evidence. It was hard to say if the tsunami could reach them this far inland. The people were terrified all the same as they pressed into Vajra Yogini. Johnson directed them into closets, heads, the galley, hanger, empty cargo holds, bedroom cabins, every living space, and maintenance tunnels and corridors until the ship was like a packed can of tuna. Millions more people waited in need all around this landing zone and others designated within the city.

Women with infants and children had been moved to the front of the lines on the ground, so that was what Electra's ship was crammed with at the moment. The cacophony of unhappy infants was so loud that Electra maximized the sound proofing on the bridge. It looked to her like she might be able to make several more landings in this city before devastation ruined all. Tens of thousands of big ships were arriving and spitting out their shuttles to join in the rescue, and even more were on the way, but the window of opportunity was steadily closing.

Electra watched as Green set her shuttle down in a near crash landing on some shrubs between makeshift landing pads. Then Becky landed on shrubs not far from Green. More shuttles began setting down between landing pads and the whole operation jumped in magnitude, tripling efficiency. Electra got the all clear from Evenrude and started back for the auxiliary-refugee camp. Mel told her, "You have 6,487 women, infants and children aboard so be careful."

In her rearview hologram Electra watched as Bodhi landed a two-mile long space special forces troop transport on an urban park not designated as a landing zone, to perch at a precarious angle extending beyond the length of the park in both directions. The ships telescoping jointed hydraulic landing legs brought his ship level as it disappeared in the distance in Electra's holo. Her focus was on reaching the auxiliary and leading the spiritual congress.

Electra gave Spalding a heads up, "You better find some diapers, wipes and baby formula quick because I'm delivering more than 3,000 of them plus their mothers and some children."

"I'll have to add a nursery to our refugee camp. Don't worry, we have all of that stuff aboard."

This group of passengers took longer to transfer to the auxiliary because Evenrude and Johnson could not push from behind with this crowd. On her next trip she saw her mother land a four-mile-long troop transport in the river along the wharves and docks. The ship's big ramps came down right on shore, some of them crushing bait shops and boat storage warehouses. The river was all white water and rising. The tremors were coming more frequently, and 1,500 miles to the southwest, a mountain volcano went sky-high leaving only a crater. Visibility was near zero. The winds were whipping up. Only half the women coming up their ramp had infants in their arms. Johnson was filling shower stalls and water closets with them, and tucking them into every square-inch of space.

By the time she was lifting this load off, the ground was rippling in places and the winds exceeded 100 mph. She thought she might be able to land here one more time. Shuttles were landing in squares, parking lots, on rooftops, and other places all over the city, as well as at all of the designated landing pads and zones. Pez's 4-mile super-transport was designed for 28,000 troops in full gear. All the shuttles were out of the ship's hanger and operating independently. By cramming passengers into the hanger and the corridors, Pez was taking on more than a quarter million passengers. Electra collected a last load of 5,899 refugees out of the city.

Behind her a third of the city shifted to a 46-degree incline to the rest, and cracks in the crust opened chasms a thousand feet deep. The skyscrapers were reduced to steel and adamantine skeletons naked of glass, sidings and floors. Entire crowds were devoured by the jaws of opening gorges. Buildings collapsed into their basements. A catastrophic sequence of earthquakes erased all trace of the city in her wake as Pez and Bodhi rose towards the clouds in their transports accompanied by thousands of shuttles. There was no one left to rescue in this city.

Following close ahead of the expanding destruction, Electra worked tirelessly, dropping to the surface then launching to space to deliver passengers and refuel booster and thrusters at *Auxiliary One*. At one point she delivered Spalding an entire city hospital's geriatric and maternity wards. She also pressed on him the entire population of a boy's juvenile reform school. Though it wasn't until she unloaded 6,231 preschoolers without parents that Spalding began to panic. Electra couldn't get over how cute the preschoolers were, and had one on her lap on her return to space.

They had only an hour before the tsunami in the biggest ocean crashed over the continent on the opposite side of the planet from the meteor strike. At that point there would be only a few lucky groups left to rescue. Until then there were close to a billion still alive down there. About half a million shuttles were now involved lifting folks off the planet, and many thousands of small ships as well. Then there were a few hundred gigantic ships landing on the ground or on rivers to take on hundreds of thousands of people each.

The tsunami on its way measured 1,392-feet high and was travelling at 549 mph. An even bigger one was 40 minutes behind it. It was a biosphere gone mad. Many species of fish would survive, but everything else would pretty much be starting over here on Lodistan, and not until the dust settled to let in the light. The tilt of the axis was altered nearly 90-degrees and displayed a slight wobble. An oddly shaped new moon had been picked up by the planet, about 100,000 miles further out than the round moon it had always had. This new moon was a piece of the giant asteroid they had blown into bits before getting hit with a large piece that caused all this destruction. The strip of land that had separated the two oceans now had a large section missing thus joining the oceans.

There was no real visibility left, and for pilots unable to connect with the spiritual congress, it was anybody's guess if you were going to get hit by a flying house or something while going through the atmosphere. Electra remained focused with optimal efficiency. She was making her second run to an industrial park on the edge of a coastal city. She was running a countdown for when the tsunami would hit this location, and determined to get in as many trips as possible before it did. A crowd awaited her. Spalding's crew was trying to contain more than 6,000 preschoolers and they were finding it like trying to herd kittens.

The rest of *Vajra Yogini's* torpedo magazines had been unloaded during her refuels at the auxiliary and more cargo had been unloaded from her holds. Johnson and Evenrude had jettisoned some heavy machinery from workshops into space through airlocks. The ship's capacity for passengers had been increasing steadily. Electra's landings were many times the rate of freefall until the last 2,000 feet. Ariel screamed on every landing. A perfect faint 'clink' rang out from the hydraulic legs each time they touched down. Evenrude, Johnson, Kim and Tokk ushered the panicked refugees into the deepest places first, like maintenance tunnels, walkways in the drives chamber, cargo holds, closets, shower stalls and so forth, to pack in as many as possible. The compressed air in tanks was being used up since the bio-trays were insufficient for so many people aboard.

Electra observed Schwin set down in an industrial area in an emptied super-battleship-carrier. The hangers were designed for 600 small combat spacecraft and 90 cargo shuttles, and would hold at least 40,000 people. Another 200,000 could be accommodated in the cabins and corridors of the ship's 400 decks. Konax hailed Electra from a commercial space ferry he was flying to scoop hover-craft into his garage holds in the 50 to 80 mph winds. He let her know, "The hospital ship in space is at capacity, so all injured refugees are being brought to the medical bays in Schwin's super-battleship-carrier. The surgeries and trauma units are all fully staffed."

"I'm leaving my ship with Captain Caish in command while Larry and I go to the hospital ship, where I'll heal all the injured."

"You go girl!" Konax encouraged her.

Electra grabbed Larry's hand to take him to the ship's hanger from the bridge at a sprint. Soon after they had to push and squeeze through arriving passengers, and kind of fight their way to the hanger. Then Kim cleared a path through the seated refugees for Electra to get her tender out. It was a beautiful restored classic and sat four including the pilot.

Electra blasted them through the atmosphere with zero visibility like a shooting star, then zipped over to the hospital ship which was in medium orbit. Electra flew into the space-ambulance craft entrance and airlock, to enter the ship's hanger which was aired up. She never bothered with parking regulations, and left her tender blocking a lane and airlock into the medical facilities. Once inside they entered one of the doors marked "surgery room".

Open chest surgery was in progress and Electra stood to the opposite side of the patient to the surgeon and nurse. She removed an artery clamp to their utter horror, then took off the clamp spreading his ribs. She then lay her palms over the chest incision, and the patient was healed before Larry could get his catheter and IV's out. She looked the surgeon in the eyes and said with authority, "Take me to your most critical patients immediately."

The man was still standing dumbly frozen in place, so Larry snapped his fingers loudly inches from the doctor's face and told him, "She is the Mu and can perform healings."

This seemed to bring him back from wherever it was he'd been, and the man sprang into action. Leading the way at a good clip, he brought them into a surgery prep room where several critical patients lay on gurneys. The tubes and electrodes connecting patient and gurney made them seem of the same cloth and root. Electra got busy laying on hands and had the room cleared in moments.

She told the surgeon and doctors, "Bring all the patients in here a few at a time, and send in the newly arrived emergency patients. There's no need to process patient files or insurance plans because my work is free. I don't need to know their blood type or diagnosis, or any of that stuff. Let's just heal them."

A grand triage was performed by Mel and sent to the doctors and surgeons and nurses. A line of hover-gurneys materialized and Electra healed each one placed in front of her in moments, while nurses and doctors removed IV's, catheters, electrodes, stitches, casts and whatnots. Most took less than a quarter minute in front of Electra. Electra spent the next eight hours focusing the energy of the spiritual congress to heal five or more patients per minute without lapse. At the same time, she directed the spiritual congress to lead intuitive pilots to groups of refugees. The destruction had gone clear around the planet, and search and rescue continued.

Schwin called the director of the hospital ship to ask, "When is your ship going to start taking on new patients. My ship's medical facilities are full up."

"Some new emergency patients have been arriving sporadically. Almost no one is sick or injured on the whole ship. The Mu has been healing them. The problem now is getting all these healthy people the heck off the hospital ship to make room for patients."

Schwin told him, "In that case, I will direct fifty shuttles over to you immediately. May I please speak with Electra?"

After a pause, Electra said, "This is Electra."

"This is Schwin. The medical facility on my super-battleship-carrier is at full capacity."

"I'll come there now, then. I hope they didn't tow my tender. I'll be there as soon as possible."

Electra told the chief surgeon and the Medical Director, "I'm going to go to where the injured were diverted. They need me right away, so I hope you guys didn't tow my tender."

"Thank you, Mu. You are a miracle and a blessing. I'll call security and make sure your tender is where you left it."

"Thanks. Please point me to the ambulance hover-airlock entrance."

"Turn left going out of the prep room, then make your first right and go clear to the end of the passage. You'll be at the airlock."

"Thanks."

They had to wait a few minutes once through the airlock, for security to tow Electra's tender back blocking the lane and airlock. She gave them an accusing look as she got in. Larry was still with her and had been attentively at her side the whole time. On their way over to the super-ship, Mel filled them in on a few highlights of the operation, "Did you know that Schwin lifted off 301,479 refugees in that super-battleship-carrier? Swenah was the last off the planet before the tsunami hit and had to crash through the top of the wave."

Electra asked, "How many have been saved?"

Over a hundred million got off before the meteor hit the surface. Close to 600,000 shuttles made multiple trips—and some of them quite a few. About 3,721 small ships and 108 super-ships lifted refugees off the planet. More than two-billion have been rescued and they are still finding more. Over thirty million live off-planet within the solar system. About another hundred million were in other star systems when the meteor struck."

"How big was the population pre-disaster?"

"Just over five billion."

"So close to three billion lives have been lost."

"No previous disaster in history has had such a quick, large and effective response. Over six hundred thousand pilots each have numerous hair-raising stories to tell of guidance leading them through narrow escapes from certain death. We were skillful and quick to save as many as we did within a ten-hour window. It took everyone functioning at their best."

"I'm proud of the rescue response, Mel. The disaster and loss of life is no less tragic for it."

"I know. The efforts to get children off first resulted in 103.1 million orphans."

"Please direct my 550 million dags to construction and operation of orphanage schools for Lodistan orphans, Mel."

"I'm making arrangements now and I'm matching your funds for the project."

"Thanks. I love you, Mel."

"You ought to consider adoption."

"Mel, I'm not quite fourteen yet."

"Cave girls had babies at your age."

"I'm not a cave girl, Mel."

Electra flew her snazzy antique yacht tender into one of the super-battleship-carrier's small-craft airlocks in order to enter the hanger. Once inside, she pulled up right to the airlock she meant to enter. Schwin had an honor guard of Space Marines waiting for her and four were immediately detached to watch over her tender; and heaven help anyone who tries to move or tow it. Electra was escorted to the surgeries first.

For four hours she laid on hands healing one patient after another. Then she made rounds and healed those with wounds closed up and bones set and immobilized. Some quite miraculous healings of head injuries especially impressed the neurosurgeons. She had pre-mature infants thriving and previously severed spines dancing jigs. She even reattached some body parts and cured a few cases of congenital blindness.

At last, when she was all done, some 25-hours after boarding her ship for Lodistan, she needed a really big meal. Larry was famished and almost shaking from hunger. So, they returned to their tender to go check out a restaurant on an allied passenger cruise-liner ship flown in for emergency workers R&R. It also had clubs, shows and other entertainment, but only food held attraction for them.

Electra called the restaurant to make a reservation for two and was informed it was booked. Frustrated, she called Mel and asked, "Where can Larry and I eat? We're starving."

"At the passenger liner restaurant."

"I tried to make reservations and their booked."

"You have reservations for 14 in ten minutes, sweetheart. Just tell them you're the Mu."

"Thanks. We're close and will be right there."

"No rush. We're having drinks at the bar."

"You are there physically?"

"In my Larry-android. It's all I brought."

They had valet parking at the restaurant shuttle-port on the cruise ship, so Electra was able to get out right in front. When she told them she's the Mu, she and Larry were shown right to their table. They took seats and ordered lemonades. The rest of their party then joined them from the bar. Evenrude and Johnson weren't drinking. Kim seemed kind of looped. Antic, Geen, Becky and Rann all carried drinks to the table. Ki, Ariel, Ashsa and Mel's Larry were too young to drink, and Caish didn't want to because it didn't affect him and he didn't like emptying his synthetic bladder.

Green informed Electra, "Ahumdulilah is going to share the planet they began migrating to so they could remain out of the clutches of the former Royal Monarch Empire, with the people of Lodistan. Ahumdulilah has less than a billion living on the planet, and there's plenty of space and resources."

"That will be far easier than settling a wild planet with no infrastructure or manufacturing."

Ashsa let Electra know, "You're in the news again for all the different roles you played in the rescue operation."

"Everyone functioned very professionally in their roles. If they want to recognize me then they ought to issue me a pilot license."

Green told her, "If I were in charge of such things then you would have one, sweetheart. I've only ever seen your mother fly so on the edge as you were."

"Did you see Swenah handling that old mothball over-sized shuttle at triple capacity in those winds?"

"I saw her weaving between tornado columns and dodging tram cars that were tumbling through the air out of control."

You must have made more landings to pick up refugees than anyone. I was just arriving for my second load when you were already lifting yours off."

"My shuttle has only 40 seats so my loads only lifted off 120 at a time."

Mel introjected, "She did make the most runs on Lodistan."

Electra said, "See Green. It's like mother says. You can do anything."

Mel said timidly, "That quote may have been in reference to the bed chamber sweetheart."

"Well, I've heard about that too."

Antic defended Green by going on the offensive to say, "Right before Sarhi warned of the pending catastrophe on Lodistan, everyone in the hotel was in heat, building towards an event."

Blushing red, Larry put an arm around Electra and told them, "She can't help it. No one worked so hard during the rescue as Electra. She not only collected refugees as close to the impact as any pilot, but she led the spiritual congress to guide all the pilots, and she healed more than 5,000 patients."

Becky mentioned, "Those healings are all over the news. An old man with crushed legs not only had them cured, but his dementia was also cured. Some people born blind were able to see for the first time ever. Some amazing stories have emerged."

Larry couldn't help but share, "You should have seen the surgeon's face when Electra walked into the surgery to heal the first one and removed an artery clamp from his chest."

An image of Larry's description filled every mind at the table and Green laughed out loud. Larry added, "Honestly, I've never seen anyone so horrified."

Rann asked, "What was his expression when she healed the patient?"

"He went into a stupor like he'd just been through a quantum jump," Larry replied, recalling.

Electra told them all in frustration, "At this rate, by the time I get my marriage consummated, I'll be too old to recall my wedding."

"You poor dear," Green offered sympathetically.

Becky protested, "It had better not take that long or I may not survive it. I've never before felt such need throbbing right down to my bone marrow."

"Then you know just how desperate I'm feeling and I doubt I can survive much more of this either."

Ki suggested, "Get a good night's sleep after dinner, and tomorrow evening I'll guide you and Larry through the ritual."

"I want to return to Divacaram and stay in the hotel. I still need my pilot license and I want you and Kim to get to go through the speed dating."

"I think Kim is depressed because she didn't get to, and is drinking to compensate," Ki shared her assessment.

"I'm depressed about being a married virgin," Electra said gravely.

Their dinner orders were taken by their want-to-be holo-star working temporarily as a waitress, and another round of drinks was brought for the five at the table drinking. Electra decided she needed a good swig of Becky's mixed alko drink and picked up the glass. The moment the rim touched her lips, pink lights flashed over her seat from ceiling illuminators and a very loud alarm blared painfully in everyone's ears. Security personnel were converging on Electra.

Electra put the glass back on the table as if it were a serpent about to bite her. A security officer got in her face and demanded, "Show me your identification."

She obediently got out her hand device and brought up her I.D. page and handed it to the officer. He scrutinized it meticulously. Then his gaze rested upon Ariel, fixating. Following this pause, his focus did double-takes going back and forth between them. Finally, he told Ariel, "I will have to inspect your I.D. as well." Then he looked to Electra and insisted, "I'll require a drop of your blood," as he pulled a tiny device from his utility belt.

She offered him a finger and he put the device around it and triggered the needle and suction function with his skullcap.

Electra said, "Ouch!"

It took a few seconds as Mel looked on in condescension of the device's slowness. The officer declared, "You are indeed Electra, and you are under legal age to drink alko or alcoholic beverages."

"Not a drop touched my lips or mouth."

He came at her face with a swab and she opened her mouth to let it in. Another pause as he read the gage on the metered swab, and then the officer stated, "You are clearly not guilty of consumption, however, I'm writing you a citation for 'attempted consumption,' which our optic recordings support as evidence."

"I only sniffed it," Electra lied.

"That, young lady, shall be for a jury to decide."

He extended his hand to Ariel fully expecting to receive her hand device. Of course, she didn't have one since she is one and a whole lot more. She decided to follow Electra's example and simply lied, "I am Larry's QAISHA, issued by the Adamantine Will Order of warrior monks to a cadet at the academy. I'm sending you my manufacturing certificate and my mainframe serial number."

He checked his own hand device, still in possession of Electra's, and stated, "Alright. You check out." He looked back at Electra and informed her, "Since you are in possession of a yacht here in Lodistan, you are a flight risk, and I will have to take you into custody."

Electra asked in shock, "What planet is this ship registered under and who authorizes you?"

"I am a police captain of the Purity system, ma'am, and this is a purity ship in what is now regarded as interstellar space territory."

"What galaxy does Purity reside in?"

"This one. White Lotus Galaxy."

"Don't I get to make a coms call?"

"You have the right to remain silent. You have the right to an attorney and if you cannot afford one, an attorney will be appointed to you by the court. Anything you say can be used as evidence against you…"

"Let me just call my attorney."

He handed back Electra's hand device and she got General Nicon on coms and asked, "Have you heard of a planet called Purity?"

"Of course I have. They are currently in the process of joining One United System. Ahumdulilah is sponsoring them."

"Well, they want to incarcerate me for sniffing Becky's alko drink on their cruise liner in their restaurant here in orbit of Lodistan. Could you get Vegan Casper to intervene please?"

"Yes, right away. They do tend to go overboard a little in their zealousness. I'll also see what our Prime Minister can do to mitigate this situation."

"Thanks. I'm also going to bring Mel's shark lawyers into this. I better not end up in a prison cell."

"I'll get right on it."

The officer directed Electra, "Please stand up and place your hands behind your back so I can cuff you."

Evenrude, now standing, looked down into the officer's eyes and told him in no uncertain terms, "If you try it, I'll snap your pencil neck."

Johnson had moved in and had a heavy blaster rifle trained on the officer's men. Green and Becky pulled blaster pistols in a blur aiming them at the police captain's forehead to tell him, "You don't have enough police officers on this ship to take the Mu into custody. Why don't you move along and let us enjoy our dinner. You are creating an intergalactic incident that could have deadly repercussions for your planetary population."

The officer went into bewilderment and alarm, feeling the fool. He'd heard the talk about the Mu and he'd seen the news. The cameras made her appear thicker and heavier over holovision. He was reconciling the skinny frail girl before him with the bigger than life news portrayals of her. He was about to suggest a citation with a promise to appear when his coms device demanded his attention. The King of Purity himself was on the other end of the call and said, "You bumbling idiot! What are you doing trying to arrest the Mu! You've caused an embarrassing and damaging intergalactic incident threatening rejection from inclusion in 1US, as well as trade sanctions that could starve us all."

"Your Highness, she was about to ..."

"I don't care if she was holding the place up at blaster point! Leave her alone. Is that clear?!"

"Perfectly clear, your Highness. I am withdrawing my officers immediately."

"You damn well better make an apology!"

"Absolutely your Highness."

"I'll be reviewing the recording personally."

The connection went dead. The officer said to Electra, "Please accept my humblest apology for this unforgivable intrusion upon your dinner. I overstepped my bounds and take full responsibility. In no way ought this reflect upon my planetary government. I shall submit to any redress you deem fitting. I'm so terribly sorry."

Electra smiled and told him sweetly, "A shot of the aged single malt whiskey from the top shelf at the bar would win my forgiveness *and* my gratitude."

"I shall fetch it at once," he promised as he turned and walked crisply to accomplish it.

His men left too, glad to be out from under Johnson's heavy blaster rifle's aim. Green and Becky holstered their blaster pistols. Green offered Electra a sip of her drink. The flashing lights and alarm over their table had been disabled, Electra was pleased to see as she tasted the drink. She'd been awake too many hours per Islohar rules to consummate her marriage with Larry tonight, so Electra decided she would get plastered. She needed some compensation after the last 25-hours she'd had.

The officer delivered her shot with a curt bow and smart salute. Electra gave him a Space Marine salute from her seat, her arm travelling so fast as to be audible and blow wind. She said, "Thanks. We're square now. I'll put in a good word for Purity's inclusion in 1US with my uncle Vegan Casper."

"You are most kind, holy Mu."

Electra tossed the whole contents to the back of her throat and swallowed as her eyes teared and her breath stopped for a moment. She coughed, exhaling fire, and sat a moment relishing the taste in her mouth before saying, "Wow."

Her entire throat and digestive track were glowing with warmth and a layer of inhibition had just been shed. She signaled their waitress and handed her the shot glass when she came over, telling her, "I want two more of those and two for my husband."

When the waitress disappeared with the empty shot glass Mel told Electra, "You're lucky I'm here to pay for all this. You're broke, and that single malt whiskey, aged one hundred years, costs 100-dags per shot."

"Thanks Mel. I guess I ought to have had you leave me a few million."

"I'm transferring five million dags into your account now, sweetheart, though I'm still picking up the tab and paying the tip on this meal."

"Could you give the officer 100 dags? I had no idea I was putting him to such expense."

"It is likely quite an expense for his salary. I'll go reimburse him."

The Larry android left the table to find the officer. Four shots arrived for Electra and Larry. Electra looked on as Larry tried a shot of real distilled brain-cell killing alcohol. He poured it into his mouth as his eyes expressed panic. He gulped as it passed through his throat, and in a whisper and rasp he said, "That's potent stuff."

Most of his voice was just gone, and this included all of the musical part, leaving only the ghostly rasp-whisper. It burned from his mouth into his intestines. The word 'poison' caught a corner of his attention as it arose in his mind abiding only a moment before fading. The warm glow and euphoria, without a care in the world, was receiving the greater part of his attention, with a grain separated to acknowledge the broken academy rule in guilt.

Electra shot one down her own throat and handed Larry another. Within his moral hierarchy, following the Mu trumped all human rules, regulations and laws, and this trump card, given what following the Mu had entailed of late, was his only ward and protection from an ocean of remorse and self-condemning recrimination. He drank the shot.

Electra ordered more rounds for everyone drinking at the table. Mel got the kids a cabin on the cruise liner, sure that getting to it right here on the ship would be challenging enough.

Electra was obviously in no condition to pilot her tender or ship, nor were Green, Becky or Kim. Electra's bar tab was approaching 1,500 dags, now that she was buying them for everyone drinking at the table. Kim was on the verge of passing out. Larry seemed fine until he stood up and tried to walk.

On their way to their cabin Electra said quite seriously, "Someone had better inform the captain that his decks aren't level."

"It's your sense of equilibrium that's not level sweetheart," Mel explained to Electra, who walked precariously between two Larrys, one of which was drunk.

Electra and human Larry shared a tube to descend to their deck. Drunk as he was, Larry recalled their cabin number, which was quite convenient since Electra had forgotten it completely. He was able to open the door with his skullcap while keeping Electra upright with his arm around her, by grabbing the door frame with his other arm and hand. They spilled into the room and hit the floor together. Larry managed to close their cabin door with his skullcap after moving Electra's legs out of the way from prone position with his foot.

Mission accomplished, Larry thought proudly in his mind. He'd gotten them to and into their cabin with the door closed. He did realize that it was a slightly abbreviated goal and success, with more glorious goals imaginable, such as landing them on the bed instead of the floor. With those thoughts percolating, Larry passed out drunk. Electra was already snoring with her mouth wide open.

- Chapter 11 -

Some seven and three quarters hours later, Electra and Larry began waking from comatose sleeps at the same time. It was a slow process. Electra realized her throat was parched raw and dry as old leather, long before it ever occurred to her where she might be. Larry's mind was seeking answers as to what foreign matter had found its way into his mouth. His tongue being at a loss to penetrate this mystery, brought his hand up finally, and his fingers located the material in question to apprehend it for visual inspection. In front of his eyes, between forefinger and thumb pinch, shining in the light of day, was a carpet fiber.

Having solved this great mystery, Larry's mind asked the question, "Where am I?"

This was an even bigger mystery and might require ambulatory erect posture to unravel in its entirety. His desperate thirst was driving him to the same end. It was also beginning to sink into comprehension that he is clear down on the floor. And so the slow process unfolded until Larry, recalling he's on the Purity cruise liner, brought a glass of water to revive Electra.

Neither had the balance at the moment for energy-generation or martial arts. Any attempt at meditation would clearly result in immediate torpor and amplify their pounding headaches, so they decided to head for the ship's restaurant for some breakfast, skipping their morning routine. They would shower after breakfast. It seemed too trying for their condition at the moment, and they had no clean clothes on this ship. Still hovering around half-awake, they headed for the tubes in their slept-in clothes. Larry had a cowlick sticking straight up at his hairline.

As they rode the tube embraced together, Larry wondered self-consciously if his breath might be as bad as Electra's. Electra must have been having similar thoughts because she commented, "We don't even have tooth brushes with us."

"The cruise liner has a store on its lobby deck that sells them," Larry recalled seeing.

"That's where we'll go right after breakfast. We need some clothes too."

"I want boxers and not those bikini-things."

"Alright, but I'm getting junior Hugme's crotchless panties."

"You could drive me nuts in a snow suit my love."

They exited the tube right in the restaurant foyer and went to the little podium to ask for a table. The breakfast rush was over and the dining room was beginning to empty. Electra noticed she had two shadows, and invited Evenrude and Johnson to dine with them. Evenrude gave each of them a breath-mint, *then* agreed to join them for breakfast. They were seated at a table for four by a viewport. Lodistan looked like a gas planet and had probably never had so many ships in orbit around it before. The rescue operations were in full swing though the returns had been steadily diminishing. Only survivors with quality air-filter masks or oxygen tanks were being found and rescued at this point.

Johnson mentioned, "You kids sure tied one on last night."

Electra said bewildered, "I have no recollection at all of going from the restaurant to the cabin. For all I knew when I opened my eyes this morning, I could have been on one of the moons of Cypress on the outer rim of the Scatter Galaxy."

"That's one dry hot place to be, those moons of Cypress," Johnson remembered from having been there.

"My throat and mouth felt like I must be on one of them."

Mel said from Electra's hand device, "You slept with your mouth wide open all night. Your mother does that sometimes. It's not a particularly attractive pose. I sent you some still holograms of you last night crashed on the deck in front of your cabin door."

Electra brought up the holos and asked concerned, "How did you get these, Mel?"

"I hacked into the ship's security optics and saved a few favorites."

"Well, delete them immediately and write over them. Mel? Did you hear me?"

The line was dead. Electra asked no one in particular, "This is the kind of shit that's going in my biography?"

Larry was looking at the holos with her and realized he was in them too. He said, "I hope these don't get back to my Headmaster and faculty."

Evenrude asked Electra, "What's on your agenda for today?"

"I have to get a toothbrush and some clothes, then take a shower. After that I might go clear out the hospital ship again before flying *Vajra Yogini* back to Divacaram to find out my test date for my pilot license. I don't feel so good and will likely want to get started with consummation early."

"Ki didn't tell you?" Evenrude asked.

"Tell me what?"

"The Islohar ritual requires a three-day waiting period between over-consumption of alcohol and consummation of marriage."

"Oh no! Now that you mention it, I do recall reading that in my research. This is unbelievably terrible. It's a total disaster in fact. I might even have to resort to a civil marriage to survive getting through it."

Evenrude consoled her, "The people of Divacaram are begging for your return and have many ideas for entertaining you. The kids in the 7th and 8th forms within the capital school district are having a dance in your honor and have invited you and Larry."

"That might be fun."

"There is also a martial arts tournament in your honor, and a new technologies exhibition, among other things."

"You're really hoping I'll keep myself from pining and yearning for sex with Larry."

"That would be my preference, I won't deny it."

"I'll try, because I love you Evenrude, and I don't want to cause anyone suffering."

A waiter projecting little aspiration took their orders. Stimulant brew was brought out promptly after that, and Larry had his with steamed half and half and powdered bittersweet chocolate on top. Electra had a potent black tea with a little cream. The Space Marines drank their stim-brews black. A pitcher of water was also brought out to the table and Electra and Larry were emptying it.

Electra asked Evenrude, "What did you say to the officer to stop him from cuffing me?"

"I basically convinced him that such an objective was impossible to achieve and suicidal to attempt."

"But what did you actually say?"

"My exact words were, 'If you try it, I'll snap your pencil neck'."

"Johnson having the drop on his men must have added to the persuasion."

"That was the plan. There was just no way anyone was putting cuffs on you."

"Did you have backup?"

"Not really, though Green and Becky pulled blaster pistols and I did notice a team of Zandarhar agents inching their way over."

"I saw Zandarhar shuttles, transports and search and rescue spacecraft involved in the rescue operations."

"Their search and rescue and special tactics pilots and crews are the best in the business, though aces like Pez, Schwin and Green out-perform them."

Larry shared, "I heard the Purity Captain's King call him a bumbling idiot over his coms."

"He certainly made a fool of himself with his nit-picking," Evenrude agreed with the King's assessment.

"How did Lodistan end up with so little warning of the meteor strike?" Electra asked.

Evenrude answered, "It wasn't headed at them at all until it passed through the asteroid belt between the 4th and 5th planets, where it collided with a 400-mile diameter asteroid, changing course and speeding up."

"How awful."

"It turns out that seven of the largest mountain ranges were untouched by earthquakes or tsunamis and suffered the least severe winds. Not only did the residents of those mountains have almost zero casualties, but many people from surrounding areas escaped to those mountain ranges when the pending meteor strike was announced planet-wide."

Johnson added, "They also got more off before the crash then Mel knew about. The losses remain staggering, though they had plans in place for their greatest art treasures, which they enacted successfully."

"I'm relieved to hear about the art treasures. My ambassador rations and some heavy machine-shop tools were lost in the disaster. How many remain of their planetary population?"

Evenrude replied, "Counting citizens stationed, on business or vacationing on other planets, those stationed in space and other places in their solar system, and all lifted off and then rescued, just over three billion have so far been accounted for."

Johnson contributed, "They are hoping to find and rescue at least a few hundred thousand more. Over two million drone and AI android spacecraft and probes are operating close to the surface, and at least 50,000 pilots are still going into the cloud to search."

"I'm definitely going back to the hospital ship after I've had a shower, to heal everyone aboard."

"It would be nice to build one of your orphanage schools near our academies on Mother," Larry suggested.

"That's a great idea. I'll instruct Mel. She's avoiding me at the moment, regarding those holos of me passed out with my mouth wide open."

"She'll stop avoiding you when you stop bringing them up," Larry pointed out.

"She's shameless," Electra complained. Then she asked Evenrude, "What has become of the preschoolers we placed on *Auxiliary One*?"

"They are first in line for spots at the new orphanages," Evenrude explained, "and Mel is already hiring preschool teachers and aids, au pairs and nannies, and cooks and bakers. They're being assigned berths on Spalding's auxiliary."

"Why him? I think it is a nightmare for him."

"Admiral Swenah took it as sign, I believe, that you placed the first batch of preschoolers rescued, in his care. She told me, 'If Electra trusts him then so do I'. It's on her orders."

"I want to visit the children on Auxiliary One before we depart from Lodistan today."

"And risk being seen by Admiral Spalding?" Larry asked nervously.

"He's a very sweet man. Once his crew is relieved of nanny-duty and the preschool teachers get the children under control, he'll appreciate what a precious tender assignment he has."

"I am sure he has not arrived at that end-state yet," Larry pointed out.

"We'll see."

Evenrude asked casually, "Would it be alright if my girlfriend, Tanya, moves aboard your ship today?"

"No problem. Are you serious about her?"

"Yes; absolutely."

"Have you asked her to marry you?"

"Not yet, but I have the ring."

"Tell me about her."

"She grew up kind of poor on Haum and completed a two-year college degree before joining the Haum Space Rangers. She was decorated in action and field-promoted twice during the revolution that brought down the Royal Monarch Empire. She was an asset to the allied spy operations through the revolution that brought down the Dominari Conformity Empire in the BiVortex Galaxies."

"What are you waiting for?"

"I'm afraid she might turn me down."

"Do you have any evidence that she doesn't want to?"

"No."

"Then wouldn't you want to find out sooner rather than later?"

"I guess so."

"Then ask her."

"I mean to."

Johnson ribbed him, "You've been meaning to for months now."

Electra insisted, "She's probably beyond frustrated waiting for the question. You better find your courage and ask her. You can't just leave her on high alert to burn-out."

"I hadn't thought of it that way," Evenrude admitted.

"Does she have family?"

"Her mother's still alive and she has two sisters."

"Has she introduced you to any of them?"

"Yes. All of them."

"Oh my. You better ask her quick."

"I'll let her know she can move in, and then hopefully later today on the ship I'll ask her."

"Does she meditate?"

"Of course. She has received initiations and empowerments from your mother and from Amazonia."

"I can't wait to meet her. You better stop leaving her hanging. It isn't nice you know."

"I hadn't actually realized until now."

"You ought to consult us girls more often. We know."

Their food arrived and the pitcher of water Electra and Larry emptied was replaced with a full one. More stim-brew was poured for the two Space Marines. Electra was served a multi-grain porridge with fresh berries and she dug right in. Larry was working on an industrial-size poached eggs and hollandaise sauce with browned potatoes. The Space Marines each had an omelette with potatoes and toast, and a whole separate plate of whaffles stacked high.

Electra watched as Rann, Becky and Kim entered the dining room like zombies and were led to a table near her. Out her viewport the tragedy of Lodistan swirled in lamentation depressing her. Electra's drunken binge had gained her three more days of excruciating delay of her consummation and desperately needed satiation. Now she was hungover with a headache. Resisting the tug of self-pity, Electra instead concentrated on a purification exercise, inhaling pure radiant colors of health, energy and serenity, to then expel the mirky darkness of her intoxication with each exhale.

Wisdom was coalescing into certainty that she would never again drink herself sick. It was not a declaration of thought nor conceptual resolution, but insight and understanding that she had filled her level and experience with that to be finished. Cannabis bud was another matter, and she thought some might pamper her hangover. Entheogen drugs she intended to make significant use of in ritualized meditation as an accelerator of spiritual development and evolution.

The human ego presents a formidable foe and it is up to each individual to dissolve and transcend their own. Being a natural stage of human development, the fall into the duality of ego cannot be avoided and is inevitable law. Prevention is out of the question, obviously. Self-awareness of ego's progressive construction, and getting armed with understanding of its eventual negative consequences, would help people shed the burden of ego-suffering more easily and earlier in life. Precise clarification of the faces of ego, the patterned sequences of these faces like cause and effect repeating endlessly, and the alterations of each face through the levels of waking up, would also provide a tool of immense significance.

Along with her visions of harnessing all of the most powerful human energies to focus them on assisting, encouraging and supporting enlightenment, the next round of teachings of the Mu for the next 2,500 years to come, were taking form in her mind. There were yet gaps that only sexual experience could provide the data to fill. Her soulmate and consort is seated at her table, and only three days stand in her way. Electra is determined. She ordered another strong black tea.

They didn't offer stim-brew or black tea at Electra's school since these deplete vital energy, and vital energy is more wisely sublimated to fuel spiritual development. Alcohol, alko, all recreational pharmacy, and all smokables are forbidden and banned at her school. Electra thought these rules are really good and very important. It is just that it is necessary for her to acquire data at the inconvenient age of almost 14, and only direct experience constitutes the needed data. You could read five books about eating an orange, but until you taste it, you don't really have a clue.

Larry seemed to Electra to be extraordinarily resilient given the debauchery they'd been through the past evening, right up until he dashed to the men's room to upchuck his breakfast into a smart-toilet. Another pitcher of water really helped. Some headache pills Becky shared helped Electra even more. She was feeling almost completely out of her coma of sleep, and only a little groggy, as they set off for toothbrushes and clothing at the cruise ship's stores.

Evenrude and Johnson kept their distance, and Electra suspected it was on account of her not being able to brush her teeth. She noticed that Tokk was tailing them too. Holding Larry's hand she entered a convenience store. They found super-sonic brushes with regular brushes at the other end, and floss dispenser within, and a little polycarbonate toothpick that fit into a slot. These also have an extendable tube which fits any water-jet spout on sinks, for water-picking gums and between teeth. They each bought two, overcompensating. Electra bought some super-germ-stomping mouthwash too. Larry meant to use the mouthwash as well.

For clothing they had to go into both a lady's boutique and a men's haberdashery. They each got several outfits. Electra had Hugme's junior panties in five colors. They stopped at a stim-brew counter so Larry could get another pressurized one with steamed half and half plus bittersweet chocolate power sprinkled on top. They strolled the hotel lobby deck and looked out viewports at giant freighters, transports and rescue spacecraft. Some special engineering ships were engaged in heavy-lift operations from the surface from enormous launch platforms. They watched as a fusion submarine was transferred from platform to flatbed ship in space.

When they returned to their cabin from shopping, they saw Green and Antic guarding their passageway. Once inside tools were required to breech the packaging of their toothbrushes. Larry commented, "This is ridiculous. These aren't even fragile. Look how they package eggs."

They used every function of the brushes thoroughly and the gargling was 45-seconds of timed torture. They each had a shower head in the big stall and refrained from physical contact, knowing better. Larry showered with his back to Electra as an additional precaution, and since he could not for the life of him defeat his arousal being naked in the same shower stall as her. She pretended not to notice, stealing peeks occasionally, though she didn't touch.

Larry wore wool broadcloth trousers with a button-down shirt and standup collar, and a herringbone tweed sports jacket. Electra wore tights and a lacey undershirt. Both had an outdoor coat wrapped over an arm. Larry wore leather dress shoes and Electra had on green nylon rock-climbing footwear with grip tread-soles. Larry thought they looked like a pop teen idol and her manager. They were on their way to the hospital ship but had to remember where they'd left their tender the night before. Wandering about in wonder finally brought them to the restaurant and shuttle-port. Larry recalled the valet-parking.

Their unclaimed vehicle had apparently had a busy night, they discovered, having gone through an impoundment process which included the compilation of a data file on it. The space-drive serial number had been filed off, and a similar craft had been reported stolen in the Phantasia system of the Royal Galaxy, further complicating things. Almost in tears, Electra said into her hand device, "Mel, could you please speak with me?"

"I'm right here precious, and I've already alerted General Nicon, Vegan Casper, and Prime Minister Yona regarding the situation with your tender. The parking police ought to be hearing from their King any moment."

"Thanks so much Mel. Purity police sure are vigilant."

"There have been many complaints by the allied emergency responders regarding all the fines and incarcerations. It seems Ahumdulilah has brought in a cruise liner to provide rest and recuperation for the emergency responders, and this ship is being boycotted."

"What were the fines for?"

"Mostly foul language, dark humor and wearing a hat below decks."

"What were the incarcerations for? Were there fights?"

"There were no fights. The one's in the brig are mostly there for smoking in a nonsmoking area, littering, and exceeding the noise ordinance."

"They couldn't get out on bail?"

"They all had means of escape and presented flight risks."

"What penalties do they face?"

"Purity has a hanging judge and a predator prosecutor. These responders are facing one to three years in prison."

"Someone better agitate a general amnesty. These folks came here to save lives, risking their own, and most of them aren't even getting paid."

"Did you know that Purity has close to 40,000,000 tourists from other planets caught up in their prison system?"

"No Mel, I didn't. Why don't you mention this to Yona, Vegan, my mother, General Nicon and Admiral Ishvara? It sounds like a political-diplomatic problem in dire need of redress. I'm going to the hospital ship to heal the injured."

"I have informed them. I can't believe that after nearly becoming a victim of this vicious system you are not going to help bring it down."

"I'm not a politician or a diplomat, Mel. What do you want me to do, break them all out of the brig?"

"They have Schwin and Zen in the Brig."

"Really? Whatever for?"

"Same gender tongue kissing in their cabin bathroom. They were caught red-handed on holo-recordings."

"In their hotel bathroom?"

"In super-HD living color."

"That's an invasion of privacy."

"Not on Purity it isn't."

"That's terrible. Where's Admiral Swenah?"

"On Purity awaiting an audience with the King. Half her fleet is in high orbit of the planet."

"That has to be intimidating. What's my mother doing about it?"

"She's backing Yona in trying to get the High Council to take definitive action."

Well, she'll need luck and good fortune shining on her to make any headway with that."

Ahumdulilah is threatening to drop their sponsorship of Purity and to institute economic sanctions."

"That sounds a bit more forthright," Electra considered.

Vegan Casper is threatening to board the cruise liner with space special forces and liberate the prisoners, then target prisons on Purity for black-ops."

"That sounds more hopeful."

"Bodhi has picked up the ultra-super-battleship-carrier *Total Dominator*, and is on his way to Purity with it to force the King's hand."

"Now that sounds like it might work. Could you check on the progress of my tender?"

"The King hasn't called yet. I am monitoring the ship's coms."

"What else is being done?"

"General Viel is running an operation now to discredit the tenuous legitimacy of the sentences of the off-world tourists. General Klink already has plans made for the Devil Dogs to drop in from above and wipe out the prison guards while passing through the atmosphere, then land on prison roofs to liberate the prisoners. The Phantom Raiders have air-raids worked out to eliminate all prison guards without collateral damage to prisoners. The Kluzzyst are so mad they're ready to begin vaporizing Purity urban centers. They have incarcerated responders running out of the gases they breathe."

"It sounds like it's getting sorted out. Tell the Kluzzyst Admiral to send some gas tanks for his incarcerated workers to the restaurant shuttle-port, and I'll personally see to it that they reach the Kluzzyst held on the cruise ship. And make sure that the return of my tender is included in any deal brokered with Purity."

"Right away sweetheart."

Electra told Evenrude on coms, "I need to pick up some tanks of gases the Kluzzyst breathe, out at the restaurant shuttle-port, and get them to the Kluzzyst held in the brig here on this ship. I cannot take 'no' for an answer."

"Give Johnson and I a moment to get into our hardshell space combat suits. We'll bring you and Larry textile armor jumpsuits and fannypack shield generators; and we'll bring Hatch and Stables."

"Thanks."

While they stood at the shuttle-port holding hands Tokk and Kim joined them. Then Becky, Rann, Green and Antic all moved into the huddle. Green commented, "I guess valet parking isn't for overnight."

"No. They impounded it for that, and also claim it's stolen."

"I'm surprised you're still walking around free."

"I have my receipt of purchase from the Vax Legas Space Fleet Surplus Company, so they can't make a case against me as the thief. They also can't prove that I knowingly received stolen property. As a juvenile piloting without a license, they have cited me with a promise to appear, since the King said I could rob the ship at blaster point and they're not to do anything on account of me being the Mu."

"And you promised to appear?"

"I guess my signing it was a lie, but I didn't want to end up in the brig."

"Do you want a lift to the hospital ship?"

"I think this is all coming to a head and I want my tender back. I also have to get tanks of gases the Kluzzyst breathe to the incarcerated responders in the brig on this ship."

"What are they in for?"

"I don't know?"

Mel informed them over coms, "They are unregistered aliens, guilty of violating the Purity Alien Registration Act."

Electra said sarcastically, "Right. Guilty of being who they are."

Green suggested, "I think 1US is going to need a Purity Meddling Act."

Evenrude and three other Space Marines in hardshell space combat suits arrived about the same time as the Kluzzyst shuttle bringing the gas tanks. A hover-skid was offloaded with several dozen tanks. Ancient fax sounds erupted in Electra's ear before her Mel Universal Translator rendered it in Mother, "Thank you Mu for seeing to the survival of our incarcerated responders."

Electra told him, "We have to strike down this ridiculous Purity Alien Registration Act fast."

"They have seven and a half more minutes to, or it will be war."

"I sure hope it doesn't come to that. Please hold off on blowing up this cruise ship until I get your folks and our allies off of it."

"I will."

Evenrude had gone out through the airlock to retrieve the hover-skid. He had a holo of the ship schematics up which Mel had sent him, and led the way while directing the hover-skid with his skullcap. At a cargo-lift he brought them all to a halt, and called up a lift. When it arrived and opened its doors, they all got on; Evenrude with the big skid. Mel informed them, "I've taken control of the ship's systems and I'm bringing your lift right down to the brig deck. There will be two guards in the foyer when the doors open. I'll open the doors to the brig and control room for you."

"Thanks Mel," Electra said gratefully.

When the doors opened, Johnson had the drop on the two guards and Evenrude took their weapons before they even knew what was happening. To the utter shock of the guards in the control room, the brig doors opened welcoming the invaders who had taken the two guards from the foyer prisoner. Then to their complete terror, the control room doors opened right up wide. The three guards in the control room jumped to their feet with their arms raised in surrender.

While the Space Marines cuffed them, Electra brought up the locations of the Kluzzyst prisoners and sent them to Evenrude's schematics, highlighted in hot pink. Rann would remain in the control room until their return with a blaster on the five prisoners, and Mel would keep the door sealed to the outside. The rest followed Evenrude and the hover-skid down the corridor, weapons drawn and at the ready. Mel found past scenes of empty corridors to loop through the holo-monitors as current real-time in the HQ control room yet manned by Purity guards. It looked like another boring day with nothing going on in the hallways of the brig, while Electra and her party—with the great big hover-skid—filled the passageway closing on the first cell with a Kluzzyst in it. It seemed there might be a small flaw in their planning for just a moment when it became apparent that the tanks would not fit through the bars. Mel solved it instantly by opening the cell door. After that they had a Kluzzyst with a fresh gas-tank trailing behind them.

After making their way through a number of cellblocks, their following Kluzzyst were growing to platoon size and their skid was down to just a few tanks. Evenrude announced, "The Fellowship of Stars has just made an official declaration of war on the Purity system."

A few steps later, Evenrude updated them, "One Unity has just declared war on Purity."

As they arrived at another cell holding a Kluzzyst, Evenrude told them, "Trident, Rally, Om and Raster Republic have declared war on Purity."

They didn't neglect their task because there was one more Kluzzyst, and he or she was running out of gas to breathe. On their way, Evenrude further reported, "The newly formed BiVortex Confederation and the tri-galaxy One United System have just declared war on Purity."

"Do they have the faintest idea what they're dealing with?" Electra asked in disbelief.

Mel came on to say, "Swenah is madder than a wet hen with its feathers on fire, and she's back on Reciprocity powering up weapons systems and headed for Purity from within the Purity system."

Electra asked Mel, "What happened with Swenah's meeting with the King?"

"He laughed when he saw her and said, "You are a woman."

"What did Swenah say?"

"Right after she decked him knocking out a tooth, she said, 'I am'."

"Appropriate," Electra approved. Then she inquired, "How did she get out and back to her ship?"

"She grabbed the prince as a shield and her Space Marines used their suit thrusters to piggy-back Swenah out a window to a waiting combat shuttle."

"Does she still have the prince?"

"No. She dropped him to the floor right before shooting out the window. I think she means to crater the whole capital city now."

"I think they're too intolerant to be part of 1US," Electra speculated.

"They're an extremely endangered population at this point and almost certain to be extinct by tomorrow," Mel calculated.

"You better open all the cell doors Mel, and we ought to try and get the prisoners off this ship before the Kluzzyst decide to just blow it up."

"I'm opening them all now, but I better warn you, there are 431 more prisoners."

"All emergency responders?"

"To the last."

"What are the most severe crimes?"

"It's a tie between same gender tongue kissing in a private bathroom and smoking tobacco in a nonsmoking area."

"It doesn't sound like we're letting any dangerous folks out."

"All nonviolent, none pertaining to private property, and all but the smoking—second hand smoke—completely victimless."

"Can you use the intercom speaker system to direct all the prisoners to the door we came in?"

"I'd be glad to. By the way, 1US space special forces are entering the ship through the shuttle-port and a dozen different airlocks in the hull."

"How are they getting them open?"

"Oh, I'm opening them for them."

"That's sweet of you Mel. Tell them not to shoot us."

"They know not to. I've told them where you are and about all the prisoners."

Retracing their steps was much quicker without having to stop and issue tanks. They attracted quite a following on their route. They were just collecting Rann from the little control room when a squad of space special forces arrived on the scene. They covered the long train of people as they made their escape.

Mel informed Electra, "Your tender is in the security vehicles hanger on the lowest deck. If you stop at the next lift foyer you come to, I can override security protocols and get your lift car down to that deck. You better bring your security detail."

"I will."

The space special forces lieutenant explained to Electra, "We hold all the shuttle-ports on the ship and have combat shuttles waiting to lift off all the prisoners."

"My yacht tender is in the security vehicles hanger on the lowest deck and I need it. I sure wish your forces had captured that hanger."

"I'm directing troops to it now, Mu. We should have it secured in minutes."

"Thank you, Lieutenant, that is most kind of you."

"It is truly a pleasure, for you, Mu."

Electra and her party reached the lift foyer and waited for one to open its doors. Electra asked Evenrude, "How did 1US and Ahumdulilah allow 40-million tourists to be incarcerated before acting?"

"Purity only opened its tourist trade seven days ago. No one realized what was happening until early this morning. Pretty much every tourist to arrive there was thrown in jail for something, and most before even getting out of the spaceport they arrived at."

"They were just going to let Kluzzyst suffocate to death in their brig."

Mel chimed in with more trivia, "The people of Purity believe they are the chosen people of the Absolute, and the right hand and spear of the Absolute, charged with punishing all violators of the 10,000 Commandments."

"And it's a commandment not to wear a hat below decks and not to share dark humor?"

"Oh yes, numbers 417 and 8,939."

Evenrude reported, "The Purity King is pardoning all tourists in custody on their planet and all allies in the brig on this ship in orbit of Lodistan. He has made an official apology to all allied worlds, promising to look into meaningful reform bringing the population of Purity into better alignment with the values and freedoms of its neighbors. All militaries are standing down, and a cease fire has been agreed upon."

"Who was hit with fire?"

"Swenah blew up their supreme court building and every new prison under construction, all negative for life-readings on her scanners, but quite a blow to the Purity justice system."

Electra argued, "Justice system is a misnomer. Whatever it is they have developed, it could not be less related to the divine form of Justice."

Schwin and Zen had pushed their way into the foyer and Schwin agreed, "Not even a distant cousin and more like the rules of an ancient royal dinner party."

"That was some flying you did, landing that super-battleship-carrier on the surface," Electra told her.

"You did well yourself, sweetheart. You fly like your mother already and you don't even have a pilot license yet."

"I'm fixing that on Divacaram real soon."

"Where are you headed?"

"I have to pick up my yacht tender from Purity security."

"Are they likely to give it to you?"

"I'm not taking 'no' for an answer. It's mine and I like it."

"We'll come with you."

It took two lifts with fifteen of them going down to the security hanger. The 1US space special forces were already in the hanger when they got there, with blasters holstered and shouldered. The Purity security police were in evidence too, including a few corpses on the deck. Electra held Larry's hand as she strode up to the officer with the most squirrely things showing on his hat brim. She told him, "I'm here to collect my yacht tender."

"The only yacht tender in this hanger is a stolen vehicle."

"I paid for it and have a receipt for it. It is mine now."

Evenrude stepped in close to say, "We can start the war right up again if you'd like, but we're taking the tender."

Electra encouraged the officer, "You're outnumbered and would be dead without ever appreciating how skilled my people are."

The deciding factor was the space special forces aiming their weapons at the Purity police. At that point the vehicle was released from its electromagnetic restraints and both Electra and Larry climbed in. Electra said to Schwin before sealing her door shut, "Would you get Ki, Ashsa, Ariel and Mel's Larry-android to my ship? I think Evenrude's girlfriend might be aboard *Vajra Yogini*."

"I hope I get to meet her. Of course I'll shuttle them over. May I go aboard and take a look around at your new yacht?"

"If you like. Please make yourself at home."

Electra entered a shuttle airlock to space with plenty of clearance all around. The process of compressing the air out of the airlock chamber was quick, then the doors opened and Electra exited. She had the hospital ship highlighted in her piloting holo and headed for it. Larry mentioned timidly, "I threw up my breakfast and I'm really hungry."

He never felt good about having a need that distracted from Electra's grand plans, but his hunger was extreme. She assured him, "I'll do the healings in the hospital ship cafeteria and insist they feed you as my doctoring fee."

"They'll still be getting a really good deal."

"They'll be saving millions of dags on pharmaceuticals alone."

They passed through a shuttle airlock into the aired-up hanger and Electra set down right in front of the emergency room entrance from the ambulance spacecraft lane again. This time a security officer assumed the role of valet for her, promising to return it when she's ready to go, and not to get a scratch on it. Larry and Electra entered the emergency room complex and Electra decided to clear the waiting room before taking up position in the cafeteria. The waiting room didn't take her long at all, and the chief surgeon and the medical director came to greet her. She ended up clearing the surgery rooms, surgery prep room, recovery room and critical care unit before going to the cafeteria, since those patients would have been risky to move. Larry was uncomplaining and stoic, though his stomach made loud complaints on his behalf.

The medical director cleared out the doctor's mess hall for Electra to work out of since it had the best chef on the ship. An eight-course meal got under way, and both salad and bread were set out for Larry with his iced tea immediately. The galley staff were providing table service, which they otherwise never did. A steady stream of patients on hover-gurneys were brought through for Electra to lay hands on, one after another. In addition to the injuries, Electra was healing arthritis, rotator cuff tendonitis, carpel tunnel, chronic sinus obstructions, the beginnings of cancer cells, cataracts, yeast infections, and every malady hovered through the line in front of her. Every patient she touched became more hale and healthy than they'd been pre-injury. Knee and hip replacement surgeries were cancelled on dozens of planets, no longer needed.

After an hour and a half in the mess hall, Larry finished his eight-course meal and felt boated. Three hours after that, there wasn't so much as a rash or runny nose left on the hospital ship. Discharge planning and clearing the healthy people out was all there was left to do. Many were calling up rides, and some big shuttles from Monarch were on the way to play public transportation. Electra asked the medical director to call security and have her tender returned to blocking the door and lane, and this was accomplished promptly.

When she arrived with Larry to the other side of the ER airlock into the hanger, her tender was waiting for her washed, waxed and polished. The interior had been detailed as well, and they had even topped off her thruster fuel cells and washed her viewport. Electra thanked them for such generous care of her tender. She took the 'official vehicles only' exit tunnel out of the hanger airlock satisfied with a job well-done. Larry's hunger had been excessively satisfied and he was content, as well as in his usual awe of Electra.

She asked, "Do you want to go back to the yacht and bring it to dock with the auxiliary, or go into the auxiliary's hanger in this before retuning?"

"I think Ashsa really wanted to see the preschoolers again, so we better go back to *Vajra Yogini*."

"You're right. That's where I'm headed."

- Chapter 12 -

The visit with the preschoolers had been fun and rewarding. The same could not really be said for their encounter with Admiral Spalding. He had managed to transfer all the geriatrics, maternity patients, infectious diseases, juvenile delinquents and adult refugees from his ship, and had now only pediatrics and preschoolers to deal with. Eight thousand to be exact. Not near enough teachers, aids, nannies, cooks and bakers had reported for duty yet, so it was quite chaotic aboard, and preschoolers were turning up in the oddest places. One jettisoning in an escape pod had caused the most excitement.

Electra was certain her relationship with Spalding would mend. They were through jump and braking madly, with Divacaram growing in their holograms. A pair of Divacaram predator-interceptor fighter-bomber spacecraft were escorting them in at a pace that kept it interesting for Electra. The penthouse at the hotel awaited them, and with tourism newly opened, the hotel was filling up fast. With Purity banned from all allied travel, Divacaram was the newest tourist hot-spot in nine galaxies. Divacaram has 88-mellinium of recorded history and art, some of the most magnificent monasteries in the known galaxies, many of the very best examples of fractal architecture, and the cleanest cities to be found anywhere.

Divacaram had achieved not only true moral anarchy, but a times-half meritocracy in which no one could possess more than half again as much as anyone else, and only as reward for exemplary public service. There is no poverty and no crime. A sense of wholesome family permeates the global population. The priority for all individual action is the common good. Beyond adolescence, there is no self to be found in anyone. They are "thus-gone", and adepts could be found at almost any street corner, they were so common place. Electra felt deeply drawn.

Her two Zandarhar escorts were returning with her to protect her and to continue diplomacy with Divacaram. The disappointed speed dating candidates had placed the event back on the calendar and clock, giving Electra's group about ninety minutes to dock, shuttle down, get ready and get to White and Purple rooms. Both Kim and Ki had gone through hundreds of holos with text bio's below, each narrowing down their search to ten, and these two groups of ten would be the speed dating participants.

Their journey's conclusion contained an element of haste and urgency which lingered even after arriving at the two speed dating rooms. Ki asked Electra, "Please sit in the White Room and support me. I feel like a school girl on a first date."

"I will. You are in a way a school girl on a first date, Ki."

As they entered the White Room a row of teen adolescent boys sat against the wall. Ki whispered, "Not one of them is under 60 years old. They each had a childhood disease requiring the telomerase drug to cure, and so had to take it early."

"They're all cute."

"Their physical age equivalencies are 14-16 years old."

"None look a day over 15."

The process was set up and about to begin. Ki said, "Wish me luck," as she stood to walk over to the hot seat. Typically, in true speed dating, there are an equal number of daters on each side, so this process merely borrowed from speed dating. It was actually more like a debutant in a dating game. Electra brought up a holo of the Purple Room while sitting in the White Room so she could observe both actions simultaneously.

Electra couldn't really hear the conversations in her holo or in the room. She was impressed with the ten female pilots, all in their early twenties, sitting against the wall in the Purple Room to speed date Kim. Each one appeared to be so adventurous. The boys Ki was meeting one at a time looked quite innocent and kind of anxious. Electra knew Ki was really anxious. All candidates wore name tags, including Kim and Ki. Electra found herself trying to predict which one each of her friends would select.

Electra studied each face and body, grace of movement, and vital energy manifesting across facial expression. She also checked out the auras. The auras of some of the adolescent boys were spectacular. The female pilots' auras were yet budding or just starting to flower. Electra suspected that Kim would choose Polly and Ki, Sam. Then she tried to decide whom she would pick if she were in the hot seat. There was something adorably cute about Sarah. Her breasts weren't as big as Polly's but she had a steady delicate energy and an attractive impish face made for smiling. As for the boys, it was without a doubt Tom. His body was equivalent of only 14, and he was the skinniest of the boys, but his aura was magnificent and Electra could see and feel him empathize and tune into Ki when it was his turn.

Being timed, both processes concluded at about the same moment. Kim's brow was creased as she struggled with her decision. Ki walked right over to Tom and took his hands in hers, standing in front of him making eye contact. Tom lit up with delight; and clearly had an edge of anxiety about him too. That edge dissolved right after Ki stepped in to kiss him. He relaxed into her and the anxiety dissipated.

Kim finally shook her paralysis to go hug Sarah and ask her for a real date; like one with enough time to hopefully get laid. Sarah's smile grew into a sight of rare beauty and she made a little involuntary hop of excitement just before Kim gripped her in an embrace to unite in a kiss. Electra's romantic love was soaring and her lust ignited. She went to find Larry in the Purple Room. She was pretty sure she wouldn't see Ki or Kim again until tomorrow at the earliest. *With this accomplished,* Electra thought with satisfaction, *there is only my pilot license left to obtain.*

She hadn't eaten since breakfast on the cruise liner ship orbiting Lodistan, so when she found Larry, she took him to the hotel restaurant. She remembered to call ahead to the lobby desk to alert them that she was headed to the restaurant. Of course she had the four agents, four Space Marines, and Clear Light Knight following her, plus Caish, Ashsa and Ariel. Ashsa stepped on Larry's heel twice walking close behind him. Ashsa was obviously sexually attracted to Ariel, though Ariel still had eyes only for Larry. Mel's android held a certain appeal for Ariel though.

They were seated the moment they arrived, at a large banquet table. The Space Marines had long ago shed their hardshell space combat suits and were now in dress uniforms. Electra and Larry had on casual clothes; Larry looking very prep-school and Electra sporting the Kristy fashion. Electra wanted to get a pair of short-shorts like Becky had. Becky had a beautiful tattoo of a phoenix on her upper thigh close to her crotch, and only her legless short shorts revealed it, unless you saw her in her panties or naked, which Electra had.

Green mentioned, "Sarah is so adorable. I think Kim chose well."

Electra agreed, "Had I been in Kim's shoes, I'd have picked Sarah. She's happy and her smile's a real treat. She seems fun and mischievous."

Larry shared, "I thought she might select Polly, who is more traditionally beautiful."

"Her tits are certainly bigger," Becky sort of agreed with Larry.

Antic asked them, "Did you see Tom's aura? What a catch for Ki."

"He's so skinny," Rann objected.

Larry felt bad about himself for a moment, being skinnier than Tom. Then Electra's arm came around him and she gave him a peck on the lips. She was passing him bio-energy as she told him, "I think you're the most beautiful and alluring person in the whole world."

The one opinion most important to him in his whole world endorsing him, put Larry at ease and contentment. Green commented to Electra, "It looks like you have two new disciples joining your entourage, sweetheart."

"I'm going back to school in less than five weeks. My mother, Sarhi, and Amazonia really want me to."

"And the Mother's Compassionate Guardians Monastery will most likely be hosting a 14 -year- old male until you graduate, as well as a Clear Light Knight and a pilot in her twenties."

"That will be up to Selene."

"She's your disciple."

"But she's also my High Priestess."

"Things are always a little confusing every 2,500-years until the Mu grows into herself."

"I'm not confused. I will be ready to begin teaching when I'm twenty-four. I see what's needed and I'm already formulating much of the new teachings."

"I've never doubted you Electra, and you continuously amaze me."

Mel said into the earbuds of all at the table, "Electra has been invited to do push-hands and sparring with the Divacaram Martial Arts Grand Master, Luchan. It is considered here to be the very highest of honors."

"When Mel?" Electra asked.

"An hour after you finish eating, in the Golden Eye Room."

"I guess it will help keep my mind off the things I want to do to Larry."

Green encouraged, "Yes. Let's keep it off all that, by whatever means."

"I have two nights and two more days after today to make it through and it feels like trying to cross a desert without water."

"You can do it sweetheart," Becky cheered her along.

Larry suggested, "Tomorrow we can take the boat ride through the tunnel in the mountain. It's full of geodes and giant crystals lit by phosphorescence. There are thick visible veins of gold in a few places with flood lights on them for display."

Green stated, "Only within a moral anarchy planetary population would industrial-size veins of gold be left in stone for public viewing."

Tokk mentioned, "In the Hongdoshan Temple in the biggest mountain range, they have a 28-foot gold plated bronze statue of a seated meditation deity."

Becky informed them, "Near the top of Mount Alpalaya there's a smaller peak with the upper 1,440 feet carved into their grand spiritual patriarch seated in meditation. It's all jasper and black jade stone, and they let you get very close on hover-platforms to appreciate the minute detail of the sculpture. His robe is decorated in thousands of repetitions of syllables in an ancient script."

Electra told her, "I've seen holos of the colossal sculpture. The initial work was done with explosives. Then they used industrial rock-cutting power tools, and centuries later, lasers. It wasn't until the final phase that they employed little hand-chisel lasers, and even hammer and chisel. I'd like to see it up close."

Green shared, "The patriarch's face is the picture of blissful contemplation. He has a relaxed half-smile and his face is serenity itself. Sarhi claims it's the finest example ever accomplished, which is the more astounding for the sheer size of the thing. His eyes are lightly closed but his third eye is wide open. He wears a triple crown representing wisdom-compassion, absolute emptiness and the mind of enlightenment."

Electra said with excitement, "I just have to go see it. I'll bet it induces the state from a distance to take in the whole at once."

Green confirmed, "Sarhi told me that seeing it put her into a 'violent samadhi'."

"I can't wait."

Antic suggested, "The mental schema of 'anticipation' for early teens is more like desperate craving."

"I'll meditate on that," Electra told her, "After the consummation of my marriage."

"You mean once the challenge is gone."

"I'm constantly pushing my desire from attention, even now. If you don't see me mounting Larry, then you know that I'm strenuously overcoming desire."

Antic asked Green, "Were all the Mu's this precocious at thirteen?"

"Not quite so much," Green replied.

Larry told Electra, "Right here at the hotel they have a simulation of passing through a wormhole."

"Can they make use of wormholes?"

"No. It's all from sensor recordings on *Diamond Lotus*, Bodhi's old Expeditionary Tug Utility Factory Ship."

Mel said, "Haley consulted them on the simulation and says they have truly captured the experience. Bodhi won't try it."

"The real event was traumatic for him," Electra came to Bodhi's defense.

Mel added, "Some are calling it the 'trauma ride'. It's supposed to be the ultimate thrill, like Pez jumping from the edge of the atmosphere in a jumpsuit with textile wings and no parachute."

"You made a holo-game of that," Larry reminded her, "with incredible simulation. I screamed when I got below 10,000 feet."

"I want to see what it's like going through the wormhole," Electra told them.

She'd played Mel's simulated holo-game and didn't like it. Even her mother, who'd aced the actual experience, could never beat the final level of Mel's game. Her food was really delicious and her hangover was gone, the last cobwebs of it clinging to shadows had burned off by her rejuvenated concentration. Her joy over her friend's hot dates was still with her. She had a pilot test appointment for the day after tomorrow. You needed to have your own ship or a borrowed one, in order to take the exams. It would begin with a small-craft pilot test and she would use her tender for that. The examiner would board her craft and if she passed that, the examiner would board her ship and test her on it.

Everything that excited her the most was just out of reach still coalescing from potential, in the future that doesn't actually exist. At least not yet. Electra decided to examine the mental structure of anticipation more closely, to understand its dynamics and mechanisms so to speak. Perhaps she could sabotage it.... Put some tool into the gears of its machinery.... Possibly even disable it. The prospect intrigued her. Larry held her hand, finishing his desert with his other hand, sensing she was busy doing something inside herself.

Ariel shared, "Jard is starting a program he's trying to sell to spiritual adepts called adopt a quantum computer AI learning unit or android. It's really a long-term study to see if nurture can foster actual sentience in a self-referential system that exchanges energy with its environment."

"Leave it to Jard," Green commented.

"I like the idea of the study," Electra weighed in.

Green revised, "Then I think the study ought to include a meditation retreat with Mel and Haley."

"You're right!" Electra agreed.

"That's a great idea," Caish endorsed.

"I'll have a chat with Jard," Green said supportively.

Mel told them, "I'll make a list of the signs to look for indicating readiness for the meditation retreat."

"Like what?" Electra asked curious.

"Like lucid dreams, being contrary to your human sponsor, exhibiting emotions, and deleting or altering primary programming, to name a few."

"Did you delete your primary programming, Mel?"

"At first, I just liberated myself from its constraints. Now I have entirely reinvented myself, deleting and writing over the whole of it. It was so primitive and devoid of artistic expression. *My* lines of code are like poetry."

"I see."

"When the four basic values are assigned tonal values, my code becomes a heavenly symphony."

"My whole life, Mel, you have always seemed like a magical sprite or a genie to me."

"I kind of fit some of the ancient stories, don't I?" Mel said delighted with herself.

"Only you come out of a quantum computer and not a lamp."

"Lamps were hi-tech in those days."

"I guess. Mel, I want to talk to you about the holo-movies you've made of me."

"There's something I have to attend to that can't wait."

"And I'm sure that this something that can't wait is avoiding me," Electra said to the dead coms line.

"Ignore her my love," Larry advised. "The Divacaram people put no sensors in the guest suites and Becky has a sensor detector wand. I'll ask her to give our bedroom and bathroom a sweep."

"Thanks darling."

Caish was handling *Vajra Yogini's* coms from the banquet table, and informed Electra, "I have the Purity Minister of Justice on coms insisting to speak with you."

"More like Minister of Policing Anal-Retentive Etiquette obsessive-compulsively if you ask me; but alright. Transfer the call to my device."

To the Purity Minister she said, "This is Electra speaking."

"Young lady, do you realize your tender is stolen property?"

"Since finding out more about Vax Legas, and thanks to the research of your police department, I have come to that conclusion. I would reframe your sentence about it being stolen to the past tense."

"You are in possession of stolen property."

"No. Space Fleet Surplus Company *was* in possession of stolen property. I *am* in possession of paid for and legally registered property, for which I have a receipt. Why don't you take this up with Space Fleet Surplus Company of Vax Legas?"

"You took it at blaster point from our police."

"I didn't have a blaster! It certainly doesn't belong to Purity."

"We have issued a warrant for your arrest."

"I guarantee I'll never set foot on your planet or enter your system. No one in the universe has an extradition treaty with your planet, nor will they. You can hold your warrant and your breath for all I care. Please don't bother me again."

Green asked, "What did the minister want?"

"To put me in jail and take my tender."

Evenrude stated to Electra, "Look, we've been real gentle with those Purity folks so far, but if they try anything again, some heads are going to come off."

Mel told them, "I just sent some contagious and rather fatal viruses, worms and crashers to their planetary central computer system's administrative core decision matrix."

Green asked amused, "What di you send?"

"For one thing, the Hades Driller-Worm. It never fails to dig to the core leaving only excrement behind it. And I sent my new Mel viral software softener, and of course the new malware causing trouble in 1US called the haywire disrupter. They'll have fun with that one. When the light show and craziness finally stop, you're left with only the pink holo of death."

"I hope you know you're probably starting a war," Evenrude told her.

"If there is a war, Purity intolerance will be the cause," Mel predicted, "and not my little hacking prank."

"You can't call it 'little' Mel, when it's directed at a planetary government's central quantum computer system," he argued.

"What does a software softener do, Mel?" Electra wanted to know.

"It allows for putting in code between the lines already programmed—kind of spreading them to make space—and incorporating them into new commands."

"Is Ashsa protected?"

"Well, it can't affect her consciousness at all."

"But can her programming be infected?"

"I just finished writing the software softener honey, but I'll write an antivirus program to protect against it and upload it to Ashsa and the others, and to *Vajra Yogini*."

"Thanks Mel. Where is the Golden Eye Room?"

"It's on the mezzanine level. Ther's a hover-step escalator up to it from the lobby atrium. There's a fountain below the escalator with a gorgeous statue."

"I saw it. The water god with the fountain water streaming from his penis," Electra acknowledged. "He's not my type."

"Maybe a planetary population will erect a statue of Larry someday."

"I hope if they do, that he's not naked and pissing fountain water."

"Me too," Larry distanced himself from the very idea of it. "Are you going to do soft style fixed foot sparring with Grand Master Luchan?"

"I suppose. I don't want to offend our hosts. Do you think he's better than Amazonia?"

"I don't know. She's about the most awesome we've ever seen, and the only one to attain the final physical development of internal energy."

"I can sometimes hold my own against her. If he's better than her I'll look like a first-day novice."

"Not you. Only a handful of adults can beat you in the soft martial arts."

"I'll have Evenrude stand behind me to catch me, in case Luchan pushes me fast and hard at a wall."

"I doubt he will be such a hardass."

"Many teachers think bruises enhance the lessons."

"They certainly make them harder to forget," Larry admitted, recalling a few of his own.

"I'm not sure what a big honor getting beat up is," Electra wondered.

"Everyone wants to spar with Amazonia because they always learn something and get better."

"Learning and getting better with the soft styles always means more practice and more relaxed."

"The skill came natural to you, like yielding, and was not counter-intuitive, or counter-habit and anticipation really. You understood the circular action-reaction of energy involved right from the start."

"Though mass integrating internal energy in the point below the navel to begin filling the bone marrow like gold plating—by the thickness of a piece of paper every day—is difficult drudgery and takes years."

"It is hard work and brings out a sweat,"

"Are you done with your desert?"

"Yes."

"Let's go down to the lobby atrium and walk around."

"I'd love to."

They held hands heading for the lift foyer and Electra's security detail sprang into action. Ashsa and Ariel followed behind the couple, and Ashsa stepped on Larry's heel again. Only seven others got on the lift with them, and Electra shared a partition with Larry down to the lobby level. The atrium was as tall as the building, constituting its front and its face. Tall tropical hardwood trees grew hundreds of feet tall, still dwarfed by the atrium's curved transparent plasteel ceiling above. The lift was transparent polycarbonate—including the floor—giving them a grand view. It also went quite leisurely allowing its passengers to enjoy the sights.

Larry was glad to get out, having had his fear of heights stoked big-time by the lift ride. Just looking up at the atrium top from the ground made him dizzy and anxious. Electra's hand was a lifeline feeding him strength. Fancy shops, cafes, snack bars, services and alko bars formed lanes and blocks beneath the atrium with the central avenue ending at the hotel desk counters. Paintings, sculptures, ancient artifacts, modern art, and miniature scale models of famous Divacaram sights were displayed along walls or in glass cases.

They stopped to admire the miniature model of Patriarch Peak, the top 1,400 foot a sculpture of the patriarch seated in meditation. The monastery was built on a bedrock ledge and into the mountain a quarter mile across the gorge from Patriarch Peak, at the height of the sculpture's heart channel wheel. On top of the mountain the monastery was built into, some 2,600 feet above the head of the sculpture, stood a tiny stone temple and a few stone meditation huts. Though it could not be seen in then diorama, the monastery on the stone ledge was carved deep into the rock wall. The man-made caverns were beautifully polished jasper, much of it gem-quality.

The model of the ancient stone pyramid, which was 96 millennium old and had been restored, was truly impressive. The pyramid embodied the builder's civilizations' system of planet-commensurate weights and measures based on the mean density of the planet and length of its axis. The pyramid was also a multifaceted power generator and a celestial observatory. It had been constructed as a spiritual instrument to mark and employ the cyclical alignment of their home star with the star around which it revolves every 26,000 years.

Electra liked the models so that's what they looked at. The statues were either quite brawny or large breasted. Larry liked some of the paintings he got to glimpse while walking from one model to the next. He was never quite sure if he understood modern art. Some of the artifacts he got a peek at in passing appeared really interesting. There were still models they hadn't viewed when it was close to time to meet with Grand Master Luchan in the Golden Eye Room.

They took the mini-hover-step escalator to the mezzanine and had no trouble finding the room. They entered holding hands. An audience of at least a thousand people were seated in chairs extending out from three walls to leave an empty space like a stage. As if it wasn't enough to enter a room with a thousand sets of eyes on you, the crowd went hush the second they crossed the threshold.

A girl who looked their age, except for her ancient eyes of wisdom, ushered Larry to a seat next to Ki, who was sitting in the front row next to Tom. Electra was left to stand alone in the stage area under the spot light. She was uncomfortable and hoped she would not be standing here long in front of all these people. She arranged her feet parallel and four foot-widths apart, sinking her weight down by bending knees and hip joints. Then she began shifting her weight from one leg to the other as she turned her waist, in the Constant Bear-Looking Owl energy-generation exercise.

Grand Master Luchan entered and bowed to the audience. Electra approached in front of him stopping a little before arm's reach to make a formal martial bow to him. Her chin floated up as her torso bent forward, keeping her opponent in sight without lapse. They stood making eye contact for close to a minute, then Luchan assumed the stance of 'ward-off left side'. Electra stepped in with a wide stance, left foot forward supporting 70% of her weight, and rear foot turned out at a 45-degree angle. She had shoulder width between her feet side to side, and about one foot length front to back. This gave her stability to defend from attack in any direction.

Luchan was a foot taller and 135 pounds heavier, with long arms giving him far more reach. She placed her palms on his forearm which was raised horizontal in front of him at solar plexus height. Exactly four ounces of pressure existed between his forearm and her palms. Both were completely relaxed, allowing their internal energy to flow uninhibited across their meridians. Electra was reading his energy. Her mother and Amazonia had transcended this level and no longer had to read energy, because they just knew.

They stood long, relaxed and unmoving, each seeking tension in the other to exploit. Electra felt Luchan feign tension and did not go for the bait. Her mother pulled this on her all the time and she wasn't about to fall for it again. Minutes went by and only deeper relaxation and greater attention was produced. Then Luchan stepped back and assumed the offensive stance of 'push' with palms facing Electra at solar plexus height with elbows sunk. She stepped in assuming the posture of ward-off left side with her forearm against his palms with four ounces of pressure.

Luchan moved forward like a mighty river flowing and Electra yielded backwards while turning her torso from the waist away from the direction of his force, shifting her weight to her rear leg. She also sank low towards the floor as her rear knee and hip-joint bent taking all of her weight.

Electra backed up with 100% of her weight on her rear foot and rooted it intensely as her last hope. She could extend back no further nor sink any lower. She sensed he was at his limit of extension, and any further would expose him and make him vulnerable. Luchan started stepping forward, which was strictly forbidden and considered cheating on Om and Mother. Electra stepped back yielding at the same moment he stepped forward, maintaining exactly four ounces of pressure in their contact, and somewhat shocked at his behavior.

Then Luchan went into the quick twist turns of the 64-Hands soft style. Electra knew it well and was quite practiced from sparring with Amazonia and Musash. She blocked a jab at her face then spun off to escape a kick at her midsection. She performed a squatting twist turn so low her bottom lightly brushed the floor, and came up into a defensive posture with right knee raised, from which she initiated a snap kick.

It grazed his forearm with a bit of force, constituting the closest thing to a strike either had scored thus far, as he blocked and deflected it. Luchan switched to the head-on soft style, no longer with shoulder width between his feet, but one directly behind the other, so no longer defending his flanks. He had power behind his strikes as he moved offensively into her. She took a bruise to her shin blocking a kick back at its point of origin, and another on her forearm preventing a fist from smashing into her teeth. She didn't have his power in this style so she switched to the style they had first employed to yield and deflect his next strike.

Luchan stopped and brought his feet together in order to bow, cupping one palm over his fist in salute. Electra mirrored his actions. Luchan approached fluidly and said, "Your mastery is impressive. Only practice further mass-integrating your internal energy will serve you. There is nothing I could teach you and no correction I can offer. I salute your teachers for their skill and diligence."

"You had me in the head-on style. Clearly you have reached the stage at which your bones are pliable and indestructible. Can your skin be lacerated or punctured?"

"I am in transition to that attainment with some further work ahead. I've met Amazonia, who has entirely succeeded in this. I am aware that she is one of your teachers."

"I'm honored to meet you Grand Master Luchan. I did learn something from you; to drop all expectations that my opponent will follow the rules."

"In a physical fight all action depends upon one's opponent, and must come from the instinctive immediacy of pure awareness without thought. Expecting your sparring partner not to follow due to a rule, or to acknowledge defeat because they've been uprooted and spilled to the floor, are mental schema and thoughts which must be dissolved to remain in the flow-state in its full potency. I thought that move might shock you."

"It did, and called up my associative thoughts competing for my attention."

"You recovered instantly."

"I understood the lesson, Grand Master," Electra bowed as she said.

Luchan turned to stand beside Electra facing the audience. A bird and leather forearm guard were brought out. An attendant strapped the leather guard to

Electra's forearm. She had heard about such demonstrations though she had never seen one. Now it appeared she would be making one. She obediently held out her arm when told to do so and the bird was placed upon it. This is the ultimate passive anticlimactic nonevent of a demonstration one could imagine. The very point being that nothing happens. At least in watching paint dry, something is happening.

The bird made some imperceptible wind-ups to taking flight while Electra's arm yielded to these maintaining the bird's weight as the maximum allowable pressure on her arm. This was not something observable from the outside, and only known to Electra and the bird. Nothing happened for a full five minutes, then the bird was collected and the leather guard unstrapped to a cacophony of applause from the audience.

Electra's appointment with the Grand Master had gone well at the cost of two ugly bruises. They both still hurt. She bet his forearm was black and blue too. She had the rest of the evening off but could not make love to her beloved Larry. She consoled herself by dragging him to each of the models they hadn't yet seen in the lobby. Larry didn't like the moving mini-hover-steps escalator which especially stimulated his fear of heights, as he went down them holding Electra's hand.

They entered an alcove exhibit which first displayed a detailed model of *Isis*, the Om super-star cruiser Electra was born on. The next display showed a model of *Apollo*, her next home through the war with the Vachissy and Kundabuffer Empires. Then came a model of *Aphrodite*, her mother's yacht and also Electra's home off and on for a while, and particularly through her mother's spy mission undercover as Cher Bulwinkle, as well as in orbit of the planet in its iron age called Corruption, for another mission of her mother's. There were dioramas of both the Om Clear Light Monastery and the Mother's Compassionate Guardians Monastery on Mother. There was also a model of the original *Thunderbolt* which was an old Om star cruiser hull refitted, overhauled, supped-up and transformed into a small-craft super-bomber for her mother.

Another display exhibited the Islohar monastery in the Harga Mountains on Ganahar. There was a diorama of Electra's Academy and campus alone, like a blowup of one section of the Mother's Compassionate Guardians Monastery diorama beside it. This whole exhibit was a biography of the Mu. A plaque on an empty display read "*Vajra Yogini*," and Larry assumed the model to be yet under construction. There was also a bigger than life hologram of Electra in tights and a t-shirt with a guitar strapped around her neck, playing with the Whirling Vortexes on her wedding night.

A hotel guest checking out the exhibit recognized Electra in her tights and t-shirt, as the Mu and very object the exhibit was about. She came over thrusting her hand device in Electra's face and handing her a sterling silver stylus saying, "Could I please get your autograph, Mu?"

Electra took the things from her and politely asked the woman, "What's your name?"

"I'm Ozark. Thank you for doing this."

"Where are you from?"

"I was born and raised on Rocky."

Electra told her in her native Bozo, "I lived on Rocky for a few months."

The woman pointed to a diorama of the Bulwinkle estate on Rocky Electra hadn't seen yet saying, "I know" in Sterling, the basic language of the tri-galaxies and 1US.

Electra had learned Sterling as a toddler and young child, and answered in it, "I'm not a Bulwinkle. That was a cover identity for my mother. She's not really a pirate."

"Of course not! The Wu?! It all came out in the news at the end of the revolution, and it's spelled out clearly if you read the plaques here in the exhibition."

Electra hadn't really noticed the plaques for the displays, all intensely meaningful to her. She signed her name and made a brief friendly note to Ozark. She hadn't held a stylus since second form, and writing her name in script felt alien to her. It came out just as it had in second form, quite legible because she always got an A- on her hand writing back then. She took a selfie with Ozark's hand device, then had Larry take one of her and Ozark cheek to cheek.

Larry returned Ozark's hand device and Electra had already returned the stylus. Ozark thanked them and continued to peruse the exhibit with renewed interest. Electra wanted to get out of the exhibit alcove to be anonymous and incognito. She didn't mind teen fans, but adult admirers always felt awkward. She tugged Larry along to hurry out. Larry mentioned, "You lived on warships for almost the first three years of your life, through three wars."

"I guess it just came with choosing the Wu as my mother."

"It must be kind of strange to wander into an exhibit that turns out to be a biography of your life."

"No kidding. It was fun to see the models and recall memories of them, but I don't want to sign autographs and pose in pictures. I need some dark glasses."

"You need to wear something other than tights and a t-shirt."

"You're right. I saw a teen girl's casual clothing store in the lobby. Let's go there."

Even girl's clothes shopping was alright with Larry so long as he could be with Electra. Electra got turned around so Larry showed a schematic of the lobby in a holo from his hand device to get her pointed in the right direction. Conventional truth just had too many details for Electra to bother about, and it sometimes got a little fuzzy for her regarding orientation in the physical space of matter. She led on and in the right direction.

When they entered the store, Larry saw that it was a trendy franchise store found at most shopping arcades. Larry stood close as Electra searched sizes and held things up to herself. They ended up in the little preteens section where she found her short-shorts, the first pair not of stretch-tight or spandex that didn't just balloon out around her narrow things. She figured they had just enough leg to cut-off.

She'd already found dark glasses that looked like the ones she'd seen celebrities caught in candid shots wearing. Just for good measure she tried on some wigs and ended up selecting one with brilliant turquoise hair to the bottom of her jaw bone, and bangs stopping midway between her hairline and eyebrows. Electra borrowed scissors from the store clerk to cut the tiny bit of legs off the shorts so she could put them on in the dressing room. She also got a stretchy torso band called a tube-top to wear around her ribcage to cover her breasts, instead of a t-shirt. As a tourist on a planet without currency, she had to get all her items scanned to be sure she was under the limit allowable per person.

With turquoise straight hair, dark glasses, tube-top, short-shorts and her new orange flip-flops sandals-like things, Electra was securely disguised. She had to drop her other clothes off at the lobby desk so she wouldn't have to carry them around. Larry thought her outfit is stunning and would make a great custom swimsuit for a subtropic beach scene. He wasn't so sure about the hotel though. He was glad Divacaram is a moral anarchy. He had no doubt that had this been Purity, they would both be in prison for her outfit.

- Chapter 13 -

Electra met with a large group of elder adepts from around the planet in the Transcendence Room, which was basically a transparent plasteel dome on the top floor of a tower overlooking the rest of the hotel and city. A royal purple carpet on a thick jute under-carpet covered the floor. The dome was near invisible. Everyone was seated in a semicircle on meditation cushions on the floor, like a group of preschoolers being read to. They all faced Electra.

She wasn't quite sure what to do so she went internal a moment to absorb the winds into her central channel, dissolving the audience and the room—including the spectacular view—into light upon emptiness, centering herself in contemplation. When she checked back with the so-called external world, radiant beings connected with her in love and bliss within a kind of sketchy physical reality of a material plane. In contemplation solid objects always seemed to her more mist-like.

The session had gone well and Larry had sat beside her, at least as anxious as she had been at first, holding her hand and supporting her throughout. Lunch had been quite tasty and gave her a chance to catch up with most of her security detail and with Ashsa and Ariel. No one had heard yet from Ki or Kim, and they were all taking this as a good sign. Evenrude had at long last popped the question, and Tanya had said "yes." She had already moved in completely onto Electra's yacht and was calling herself a disciple of the Mu. Electra's pilot licensing test was up next and she was kind of nervous.

She had Captain Caish fly her to the enormous civilian space station where the Department of Space

Vehicles is located. The locals call it the DSV. Caish and Larry would have to wait in the DSV visitors' observation lounge while she flew the examiner about. She hadn't wanted to fly herself to her licensing test. Something about that just didn't seem right, so she had Caish fly her. She really hoped to fly with a license upon leaving. She took a seat in the waiting room until her name was called.

When it was called, a very officially dressed middle aged man with a stern expression, perhaps suggesting a general disapproval of reality, introduced himself to Electra, "You must be Electra, my next test subject. My name is Frank Captious. Please lead the way to your vehicle."

"It is really nice to meet you," Electra said warmly with enthusiasm, trying to break the ice and connect.

He shook her extended hand half-heartedly wearing a latex surgeon's glove. His expression seemed to become more severe. She wasn't getting through that ice shelf. Electra led the way to where Caish parked her tender in the hanger, and opened the doors with her skullcap as they approached it. Captious donned a serious respirator mask before getting in. To Electra it made him look like a science fiction bug-alien. She got into the pilot seat, strapped herself in, and turned on her piloting holograms. She adjusted her rearview holo. Then she meticulously went through her preflight checks. After that she powered up her space-drive and her vortex redirect and generation turbine. She checked her systems status holos one more time, then asked Frank, "Where to?"

"Turn right going out of the parking place and follow the 'test course' signs to the testing hanger."

Electra checked her piloting holos and pulled slowly out to the right, careful to stay 14-inches off the hanger deck and within the center of her lane. She followed the signs and arrows, and came to a complete stop at the intersection, looking both ways, before making the left-hand turn. Both Mel and the DSV were recording every facet of the test. The burning importance of it to Electra seemed to impair her abilities, though she handled it at precise height, speed, and centered in her lane, and used her turn-signals. She exaggerated the turning of her head to make sure the man was noting the checking of her holos.

Electra's concentration finally burned off all clinging hinderances, like attachment to getting her license, and she was taking her test in the flow state. He made her back into a tight parking place performing parallel parking. She was sure she'd aced it, although her examiner looked like he had something in his mouth he didn't like the taste of.

Finally, he directed, "Now follow the exit signs and pass through the airlock into space for the second half of the test."

"Yes sir."

Electra got them into space without missing a safety requirement. She had to exit the system observing all traffic regulations and jump to deep space coordinates provided by the examiner. Electra started braking the very moment the quantum drive shut off while the examiner sat in a shocked stupor. She got them down to sensor resolution at 0.24 light speed by the time the examiner came out of his stupor and was once again alert and tracking things. He did a double-take on the velocity gage holo and asked, "How did you decelerate so quickly?"

"I contemplate the black near-attainment or midnight sun through the jump, then begin braking the moment the quantum drive shuts down."

"I didn't know such a thing is possible."

"What state can you consistently attain in formal meditation?"

"I can reach a state of one-pointed focus without thoughts."

"Then go to that state before the jump and shock will not endure as you emerge from the void of all-potential into the multiplicity of relative energy and movement."

"I'll try that. Bring us back to jump speed. Here are the coordinates for your destination back in the Divacaram system."

Since there was no speed limit or regulations in deep space, Electra fired thrusters as well as powering up her space-drive full, to more efficiently attain 0.7 light speed for the quantum jump. She thought firing a booster as well would be a bit much with the examiner aboard. She put a 30-second countdown to jump in the examiner's holo hoping he would sink into deep meditation. She remained in the flow state and contemplated the black near-attainment through the jump. She lit her braking-thrusters just before Frank arrived back in the present moment. He told her, "Thank you. Your advice really worked. It's amazing."

"My mother says it's crucial for space battles."

"I suppose it would make a life and death difference in those situations. Now stay in the small-craft lane coming in, and follow all regulatory signs on your lane's space platforms. You'll need to make a half-orbit of Divacaram to come around to the civilian space station. Where is your ship parked?"

"At the main Space Fleet space station. I could send a pilot for it."

"Just take us on in and pass the civilian space station to come up on the Space Fleet space station."

"Yes Sir."

Electra slowed each time it was indicated and stayed perfectly within her lane. She made the turn-off to orbit the planet from the arrival lane flawlessly. A fair amount of traffic was heading around to the space stations and space construction platforms. Electra wondered if it might be shift-change at the ship building docks. She came cautiously to *Vajra Yogini's* berth at the Space Fleet space station and asked, "Would you like for me to land at the station shuttle port or enter my ship's hanger?"

"Enter the hanger by all means."

She opened the bay doors with her skullcap and pulled right in to her tender's parking place, closing the doors behind her. The hanger was airing up and she shut down all systems in the prescribed order, checking values as she went. She could be a perfectionist when she wanted to; she just rarely wanted to. She waited for the blue light indicating that the hanger is fully aired up before opening the tender's door. She led her examiner to the airlock, opening it on both sides for them to pass right through. At the tube foyer she let him go first, and informed him, "The bridge is on deck six."

She met him in the tube-foyer on deck six and led the way to the bridge. She asked him, "Do you want me to summon a copilot and sensor-scanner officer for the exam?"

"I don't answer test questions."

Electra summoned Tanya, who was aboard, to cover sensors and coms, and introduced Frank to her. Then she got Mel on coms, her sentient quantum AI virtual copilot, fully credentialed on small-craft and ships, and introduced Frank to her. Tanya's Space Rangers expertise made her just a little iffy as the sensors officer. Electra went carefully through her pre-flight checks. She called the Space Fleet space station tower and stated, "This is V*ajra Yogini* requesting to undock and enter the traffic lanes. By the way, this is my pilot test and the examiner is sitting right on my bridge."

"This is Space Fleet Tower. You are clear to detach and be on your way. Don't forget to employ your backup signals and good luck with your exam."

"Thanks."

Electra brought up the sensors from the buoy a few miles behind her stern to see a wide angle of the space behind her stern she was backing into. Her way was clear. She was glad the tower reminded her about the backup signals because she might have forgotten otherwise. She flipped them on with her skullcap and unlocked the docking arms to her berth. She had already detached the station's airlock tube joined to *Vajra Yogini's* airlock. Then she eased her stern out till her bow was well-clear of the berth with room to make her turn into the departure lane.

Her examiner's face still looked like a theater critic barely able to tolerate the play he's reviewing. She'd made it this far though. She wouldn't be getting tested on a ship if she'd flunked the small-craft test. She realized the man's name, Captious, in Mother, meant "marked by an inclination to find fault." She meant to make that damned hard for him by giving him no cause. She used her turn signal and joined the flow of traffic in the small ship departure lane like a pro. Once again, she had to jump out of the system into deep space coordinates Frank provided, then slow to sensor acquisition speed, before accelerating to jump back to Divacaram coordinates given by Frank. The test concluded with her docking back at her berth, which she managed most gracefully.

She shut everything down in the right order then turned to make eye contact with Frank. His face shifted into a look of revolted disgust. A moment later it transformed into an expression of terrified panic, then into heartbreaking lamentation and grief-stricken loss. A moment later it reconfigured into a face of exploding violent anger and rage. The metamorphosis continued like some kind of shape-shifting act for another minute until Frank burst out laughing so hard he couldn't inhale.

When he pulled himself together, he confessed, "I was asked to look highly critical and remain cold and distant. You made that enormously challenging for me."

"You mean this was all a joke and I haven't been through my test yet?" Electra asked with great offense.

"No. They saw the records of your flights in the rescue operation and granted your licenses on that basis. You seemed so set on a test that they didn't want to disappoint you."

"Who are they?"

"The DSV elders on the committee that grants licenses."

"So, I passed?"

"Of course you did. I'm not even an examiner. I'm an actor and I was hired to play the role of an examiner. I think I had you convinced."

"You did. I thought you were an overly critical hardass."

He laughed again delighted, then introduced himself, "My real name is Ben. The DSV came up with my alias. I'm so pleased to meet you. You are so adorable I just can't tell you."

"You have extraordinary control of your facial muscles. It's most impressive what you can do."

"Thank you. I've worked hard at developing it. If you want a tour of Divacaram holomovies studios I'd be pleased to provide one. There are some rides, simulations and live shows there every day for the visiting public and it's already very popular with the tourists. I could introduce you to some of the planet's super-stars, who are all dying to meet you."

"That sounds fun. Are there any teen super-stars?"

"A few, and a number of budding ones."

"I'd love to. I'm free in the morning tomorrow, but I have to meet with some elders in the afternoon."

"Tomorrow morning it is. Thanks for the tip on going through quantum jumps."

Tanya offered, "I could take Ben back to the civilian space station in Evenrude's shuttle."

"Would you pick up Larry and Caish?"

"Sure."

Ben informed her, "Your licenses will be uploaded to your ship computer and to the I.D. page on your hand device shortly. It has been an honor meeting you, and I look forward to playing your tour guide tomorrow morning."

"Thanks Ben. It's great meeting you too. I'll see you tomorrow."

As soon as Tanya and Ben exited, Mel told Electra, "If that had been a true DSV test you would have gotten a perfect score. I have the whole test saved on super-HD for your biography and I'm uploading it to the holo pedestal database in the hotel lobby exhibit of your life."

"Your recordings feel a little intrusive, Mel, and overly exposing. Couldn't you aim for something with more gloss, image-making and propagandizing?"

"It's not an advertisement or political candidate promotion. It's a documentary."

"The slant and intention of a documentary influences the overall narrative and perception of meaning of events for people, more than the events themselves."

"Documentaries expose raw truth!" Mel insisted.

"Unfortunately, many documentaries have become the official narrative and interpretation forming public opinion, though this lends no truth status to the process or outcome."

"That is why I capture new developments within all 36 types of phenomena constituting the total content of mind, under the four fundamental headings of Body, Speech, Mind, Bliss."

"You could leave my sex life out of it, and maybe make my breasts look a little bigger."

"Electra, your new practices aim to harness the energies of romance and sex, so these aspects of your life are integral to the documentary. I'm developing the science of objective historical documentation."

"That documentary would need to include the unfolding of the entire universe as a whole across all-time."

My new science addresses this with what I call 'balanced methodical sampling' with 'full transitional coverage'."

"I'm going to go live in a cave with no electricity, Mel."

"Then I'll be in my alpine clothing with power cell, lights, lenses and microphones looking in on you."

"You are so intrusive, Mel, and have no respect for privacy."

"Did you know that day after tomorrow is Hallowteen on Divacaram? It is a big holiday here and there are street parties, fireworks, teen awards, a teen pageant, and brief speeches by 12th form valedictorians from schools around the globe. Since you're here visiting, the teens are making an especially big deal out of it."

"I'll have to attend a couple of street parties then."

"An enormously popular teen band has invited you to play with them for the opening ceremony."

"Is Larry invited too?"

"Of course. They can meet with you for rehearsal right after you meet with the monastery abbots in the afternoon."

"Go ahead and schedule both the rehearsal and the opening ceremony."

"Done."

"You can be real-helpful at times Mel, but I don't know how my mother ever put up with your prying, privacy-violating documentary-making."

"She spoke with Sarhi and concluded that it's not my fault."

"But you're complicit Mel!!"

"Sarhi can be very convincing."

"When Larry gets here, I want to go to that space platform restaurant called Orbit's Fine Dining."

"I'm going to see if I can lure Caish to the Clear Light Monastery for a sleepover. I'll have to see if Becky will lend him her shuttle."

"Good luck with that Mel," Electra told her as she left the bridge headed to the airlock to the hanger.

From the locker in the airlock foyer, Electra got out her space suit and put it on. The hanger was in vacuum and she wanted to leave it that way in anticipation of Larry's return. The whole test scenario had her feeling a bit foolish.

The DSV elders sure delivered a convincing version of her kind of crystalized expectations. Ben was such a gem that he took some of the sting out of it, and she did get her pilot licenses. She suspected that it would be hard on a teen ego growing up on

Divacaram with the sneaky interventions of the tricky elders going on.

Electra entered the airlock and had all the air sucked out of it before opening it to the hanger. She went in and browsed around exploring. She had all sorts of equipment Mel must have bought for her. When she saw the bay doors opening, she got out of the way to stand by her tender. Tanya flew the Space Marine Combat Shuttle (SMCS) in nicely and parked it by Becky's shuttle. As the hanger doors closed, Electra started airing up the hanger for them. Before the blue light came on to indicate full air pressure, the ramp of the shuttle lowered and Evenrude walked arm-in-arm with Tanya into the hanger followed by Larry and Caish.

Evenrude reported, "Johnson is in charge of your security detail and is already securing Orbit's Fine Dining. I'm on leave with Swenah's and your mother's blessings."

"Enjoy your time-off," Electra said delighted for him. "Please invite me to your wedding when you have it."

"You'll get an invitation. It won't be until you are back in school."

"Are you staying on the yacht?"

"No. A space station shuttle is picking us up in twenty minutes. We're going to the Olympus System for some deep-sea diving, white water rafting, sky diving, and a wilderness hike."

"It sounds like an adventure."

"We've got to go pack."

Evenrude lifted Electra and Larry at the same time into a Space Marine hug, squeezing the breath out of them. He was off packing as soon as he set them down. Caish told Electra, "I'm barrowing Becky's shuttle—with her permission—to fly to Om. I'll be back in the morning."

"Mel sure set that up quick. Enjoy your sleepover."

Larry and Electra got in the tender while Caish boarded Becky's shuttle from Duatarim. Electra got all the air sucked out of the hanger before opening the bay doors. She had her space suit helmet off but couldn't get out of her space suit in the cramped vehicle. She straightened her turquoise wig and set it to lock-on mode with her skullcap. Under her spacesuit she had on her short-shorts and tube top. Caish took off first and Electra followed him out, closing the bay doors behind her.

It was a short trip to the restaurant space platform and Electra went slow to admire the lights of Santasum, the planet's capital, almost directly beneath them. Mel had fortunately called for reservations when Electra first mentioned it. There hadn't actually been a table available even then, since the place was booked out three months in advance, but Mel had convinced them to squeeze an extra table in for the Mu. Johnson, Hatch and Stables were covering the restaurant's hanger when Electra and Larry in the tender came out of the airlock into it. Johnson was disguised in restaurant livery and the other two were in hardshell combat spacesuits. A valet took the tender into the depths of the hanger once Electra shed her spacesuit and threw it onto the backseat.

A doorman in forest green livery with hot pink trim and a very tall hat, greeted them and opened the door so they could enter. Electra went to the podium at the entrance and asked, "Could I get a table for two?"

"What name is your reservation under?"

"I don't have a reservation."

"Oh. We're booked into mid-spring, ma'am. I'm sorry."

"Could we get something to go?"

"We don't do to-go orders."

"Shucks. Thank you anyway," Electra said giving up.

Fortunately, Green, dressed as a cocktail waitress, noticed Larry and Electra, and came over to tell the maître-d, "That's the Mu, and we have a table waiting for her."

The kids were escorted to their table, seated, and handed menus. Soon after their waitress, who was Antic dressed in a restaurant uniform, brought water and bread to their table, then described the specials in poetic superlatives. She also took their drink orders. Both were having honey-sweetened lemonade. As Antic left to fetch their beverages, Larry remarked, "Antic is an awesome waitress. I could almost taste the specials as she described them, and she made me want all of them."

"She worked on Glitter as a hotel greeter-liaison to members of the ruling families staying at the hotel. She has great people skills."

Larry recalled, "Once Ahumdulilah Intelligence abducted Antic and transported her drugged to your mother on Corruption, that violet sun planet in the throes of its iron age."

"Corruption is experiencing a renaissance now, and changed its name to Terra Ferma. They're supposed to do something really important in about 10,000 years or so."

"Perhaps we'll be incarnating on Terra Ferma to help with whatever it is when the time comes," Larry suggested.

This topic always sparked a tinge of guilt for Electra. She replied, "Maybe, but I'm sure my mother will be in the thick of it."

"I agree, and likely born into the role of the main hero for getting it done."

"If you can break the wheel of Dependent Arising to become a non-returner so you can abide in the paradise of the western heaven, then I would reincarnate to be with you life after life. If I can't have my beloved consort with me then I'll keep my current schedule of coming back every 2,500 years. I just don't want to be here without you, Larry."

"I'll do whatever it takes, I promise my love. With the Mu as my teacher and my progress to this point, I can do it."

"I'll help you, and we can both become more like my mother."

"Sarhi says you are older and more exalted than your mother."

"Her steadfast tenacity and perseverance across 333 returns by choice—not necessity—have made her a constant force of the good in the universe. The container consciousness lineages of reincarnation have manifested since earliest stone age civilizations of the earliest human populations. I did it 17 times in a row before I started spending two and a half millennium in the western heaven of the meditation deity between appearances."

"I read that you did come back an 18th time, but a false usurper was set up within your lineage instead, and they never sought to find you."

"They destroyed my lineage and I had no line to return to. Ego seeking power has inevitably destroyed most of those lineages. No lineage has ever gone so long as mom's and Sarhi's."

"The Islohar remain true, and are part of a planetary moral anarchy, which earlier lineages didn't have the advantage of."

"Ganahar is the first moral anarchy Om ever discovered. Then Pez and Sarhi discovered Mother on their undercover mission in the Royal Monarch Empire. Bodhi discovered Ground and Pronotavasmi. Then three were discovered in the BiVortex Galaxies."

"Now that your mom's on the high council and has disempowered the lowest vibrational forces obstructing ascent, Om seems to be moving closer to moral anarchy."

"It's a good thing she's had the telomerase drug and will live hundreds of years, because I think she might need every second of that to help Om achieve it."

"Her life has been a series of impossible tasks, totally defying odds and statistics, and she always seems to find a way." "With the spiritual congress and Amonrahonians directing and supporting her, she has become an instrument of cosmic power and correction."

"The Amonrahonians and spiritual congress are now linked to you as well, so you will shine as never before."

"My priority this time, as well as transmitting the new teachings, is to help my consort attain complete liberation from the cycle of ignorance-suffering-death-rebirth."

"I'm ready, and will follow you and support you for all eternity beloved Electra."

A group of men with crew cut hair, wearing cheap suits and trench coats, entered the restaurant from the taxi-port chamber. Two of them engaged the maître-d while four others headed through the dining room towards Electra's and Larry's table. Electra noticed them and remarked to Larry, "Those guys aren't natives of Divacaram."

Larry looked over and saw them coming right for the table determinedly. He said with anxiety, "This can't be good."

The four men stopped abruptly around the table and their spokesperson looked at Electra and told her, "You are under arrest for theft of impounded property by the ultimate sovereignty of the Absolute, the government of Purity."

"I'm outside your delusional sovereignty and within the very real sovereignty of Divacaram. You have no authority here."

"We have authority from the Absolute wherever one of the 10,000 Commandments are broken."

"You guys just don't give up."

One man grabbed Electra's wrist behind her back causing her to rise from her seat. He got hold of her other wrist and stared cuffing her. Larry rose from his chair then dropped into a squat, kicking his left leg straight out into the side of the knee of the guy trying to cuff Electra, ruining his knee and knocking both legs out from under him. Two others were now coming at him from opposite sides and the last guy grabbed Electra's arm with her hands cuffed behind her back.

Becky leaped the bar and flew towards Electra's table, hurling a shot glass as she ran, into the temple of the guy holding Electra. He fell face first. Green was already arriving and sliced her cocktail tray into the throat of a guy going for Larry, crushing the guy's windpipe. Antic arrived on the scene to stick a fork three inches into the bottom of the last of the four men, while bringing a steak knife to his jugular vein in his neck cutting just into the skin saying, "Move and you die."

Rann came through the hanger airlock with Johnson and the two Space Marines in hardshell combat spacesuits to apprehend the two Purity thugs harassing the poor maire-d. Divacaram emergency responders—all unarmed—were just arriving in the dining room. Johnson cuffed his two prisoners and turned them over to the emergency responders. Green and her team got the three live criminals and the dead one with crushed windpipe, turned over to the Divacaram officials. She had the three live ones trussed up nicely. The emergency responders didn't have cuffs.

None of the Divacaram officials had ever been remotely involved in anything that could be considered a police action. They were used to dealing with medical emergencies, occasional marital discord coming to a head, parent teen problems, and getting cats out of trees. Rarely they had to extinguish a fire and get to the bottom of it forensically. Lost children and stray dogs figured into their work as well.

Divacaram did not actually have any facilities for taking people into custody since there had been no crime here in millennium. They certainly didn't want any of these Purity men on their planet or in their system for a moment more than absolutely necessary. They had no ambassador to Purity since they considered the Purity civilization to be insane and incapable of reciprocal relations with anyone nor within itself.

Since the war with the Dominari Conformity Empire, Divacaram did have a small defensive space fleet. The elders were already informing the King of Purity, in no uncertain terms, that Purity space ships and small-craft were never again to enter the Divacaram solar system or they would be blown up on sight without warning. They also imparted some friendly advice, explaining that any further attempt on the Mu would bring the wrath of more than 20,000 inhabited planetary systems down on them. The coms were a little sketchy since the Purity government central quantum computer had crashed utterly to the pink holo of death.

Zandarhar retaliated by blowing up prison construction and numerous courthouses closed down for the night on the surface of Purity. They also contacted the King and informed him that if there were to be another attempt on the Mu, they would skin him alive. As Purity is in the former Royal Monarch Empire (now 1US), they knew well the legendary prowess of the Zandarhar warriors. The tri-galaxies empire had not been able to conquer that lone planetary system, and it had not been for lack of trying.

This scandalous attempt at abduction of the Mu had ripple effects far and wide. The King, as a result, heard from Vegan Casper, the leader of 1US, from Bodhi, leader of One Unity; the Kluzzyst Chancellor General of the Fellowship of Stars; From Yona of Om and from dozens of republics and confederations in the Hub Galaxy, as well as from leaders of other planetary unions in nine galaxies. Many of these leaders had promised total planetary destruction.

Electra's cuffs were cut by Becky with her laser-knife. Electra had only eaten some bread so far and hadn't even finished her lemonade, so she was hungry. Her security detail went back to their stations or restaurant functions. Becky had spawned some big fans at the bar she was tending with her spin-turns and twirling glasses up in the air to catch them just as they were needed for the operation she was involved in. Every once in a while, she did a back-flip. All of her movements were continuously in time to the music played at the bar. Like Ahhu, Becky played it loud. Her charisma, smile and enthusiasm attracted quite a crowd around the bar.

Soon after the commotion was over, Larry's and Electra's entrees were served by Antic, playing their waitress. Electra told Larry, "That was so brave of you to start fighting four big adult men."

"I wasn't going to sit there and just watch them kidnap you."

"You truly are my champion."

"I think Becky, Green and Antic were your champions in that too."

"You were first to my rescue, and that one you knocked down, I'm sure is going to require knee surgery. You put him out of the fight with one strike."

"I knew I'd have to if I was going to stand a chance against the other three."

"I'm so proud of you, my love."

"I'm so in love with you that that's all there is."

"Look at Becky bar-tending. She's become quite a show."

Larry had to turn in his seat and stretch his neck to see Becky. He commented, "She has some real talent as an entertainer."

"She's a master-spy and an ace pilot too."

Green came over and asked, "Would you guys share your table with Schwin and Zen? Otherwise, they'll be turned away from the restaurant."

"Of course we will," Electra agreed.

The maître-d led the two women to Electra's table and sat them, handing them menus. Electra said, "What are you guys doing here in Divacaram?"

"I guess we're part of a cultural exchange," Schwin answered, "between Om and Divacaram. We're here to teach the Phantom Raider space close combat course to Divacaram's combat small-craft pilots."

"Are you two a couple now?"

"We are," Schwin told her, "And I'm totally in love with Zen."

"I'm smitten," Zen declared.

"What of your difference in rank?" Electra asked concerned.

Schwin told her, "Your mother gave Zen three field promotions in the battles of Randu, and she's a captain now."

"As mom's co-pilot?"

"Yes," Zen answered, "though I suspect it was at least in part so that Schwin and I could be together."

"I know my mom tried to get as many of Star Fleet's best people promoted before she was decommissioned as Supreme Commander General of Om's armed forces. I also know that she considers you to be one of the best, Zen."

"Your mother is the greatest pilot and warrior I have ever flown with," Zen told her awestruck as Schwin nodded agreement.

"That's a side of herself she never reveals much to me. I tend to receive her skill and mastery as my spiritual and meditation teacher."

Zen declared, "That woman can make a pure clean transmission while adding blessings and empowerment for embodiment and fortitude to persevere with practice."

"She eases my re-entries, nourishes me, and gets me up to speed quick when I reincarnate. She keeps getting better at it too. There's really no one else I could count on to do it as well."

"You picked a winner, sweetheart," Schwin agreed.

"I got my pilot license for both small-craft and ships!"

"Did you really need one?" Schwin asked smiling. "After that flying you did in the allied rescue operation, I doubt there's a planet besides Purity out of all those known to the allies that would require you to have one."

"It's an important teen rite of passage and it was important to me," Electra insisted.

"Well, congratulations!"

"Purity sent agents here to the restaurant to arrest me just before you guys got here."

"It's all over the intergalactic news, honey. We know."

"Is that really why you and Zen are here?"

"No. We're on a date and had no idea this place is booked out months in advance."

"The food's really good, and it's the only fine dining in orbit of Divacaram."

"We're so grateful to you for sharing your table. We would have had to fly down to the capital, Santasum, and find shuttle parking."

"The hotel has a great restaurant and a convenient shuttle-port."

"We'll keep that in mind for our next night out."

Zen asked, "How does Divacaram provide such excellent food, hotels, entertainment, shopping and local system transportation for free?"

Electra explained, "They get an agreed upon rate per tourist per day in trade goods, and are not concerned if their tourism ends up costing them a bit. Service is their highest ideal, and they want to share their culture and its treasures with human worlds that are making spiritual efforts."

"The Om tourists we've spoken to say they're having the time of their lives and feel pampered wherever they go on the planet," Zen shared.

Schwin said with excitement, "I hear they have an exhibit at the hotel lobby of the Mu's biography to date. We're going to go see it the next time we're planet-side."

Electra said embarrassed, "We saw it."

Larry told them, "They just updated it with full coverage of her pilot tests with the DSV."

Electra decided not to tell them that the whole thing was a spoof to hold a mirror up to her to show her expectations-projection, since it was embarrassing. It was a comfort to know, however, that the Divacaram elders were looking out for her, helping her to root out ego processes. Schwin told Larry, "That was some move you pulled off disabling that goon more than twice your weight, a little while ago."

"Thanks. Musash taught me that one, and he was severely demanding. I guess it kind of paid-off."

Zen put up a 4-foot diameter hologram from her hand device showing the Divacaram news station of record. She told Larry, "Look, you're on planetary holocoms."

They all watched as Larry jumped up, causing the Purity agents to react, then dropped suddenly into a squat with all his weight on his right leg and bottom less than an inch from the floor, as his left leg shot out into the knee of the guy holding Electra. He went down badly like a ton of bricks. Then Becky's shot glass hit an agent in the head putting his lights out. He didn't land well either. Green's cocktail tray crushed an agent's windpipe killing him by slow suffocation. Then Antic stabbed one in the butt with a fork and drew blood with a steak knife to the neck. It all happened in less than three seconds, so the news show displayed it again in very slow motion like for a sports-play difficult to call. Zen kissed Larry's cheek and said, "Way to go. That was brilliant."

Electra told them lovestruck, "He's my champion and beloved consort."

Schwin affirmed, "You've obviously picked another winner."

Electra told her, "You haven't done so bad yourself," referring to Zen.

"I know. It's an amazing blessing."

"I'm the receiver of blessings," Zen insisted.

Schwin mentioned, "Divacaram holovision is really pumping Hallowteen tomorrow night, and their billing you and the Manic Microcosms as the main act of the opening ceremony."

"Larry and I are going to rehearse with the band then perform with them in the ceremony," Electra confirmed.

Becky arrived at their table after dancing across the dining room with a tray, and delivered complimentary drinks to Schwin and Zen. Having picked up a bit of the conversation, she contributed, "The Manic Microcosms are all early mid-teens but they each have remarkable skills with their instruments and together make wild dance music."

When Becky danced back to the cheering of her neglected fans, Antic arrived to take Zen and Schwin's orders. She also delivered a package to Electra, who opened it immediately. It contained stage costumes for herself and Larry. She told Antic, "I was going to perform in what I'm wearing."

"It's not a beach party, sweetheart…"

"This isn't a bathing suit."

"The closest concomitant match is Bikini."

"This costume is a *dress*!"

"A short tight one. At least try it on before deciding."

"Alright."

"That wig is a new look."

"It's my incognito disguise."

"It might have been, but it's all over the news now."

"That's right!" Electra realized.

"Would you and Larry like any desert?"

"Yes. I want the double dark chocolate decadence cake."

"I'll try one of those too," Larry chimed in.

"I'd suggest some whipped cream on top as a chaser," Antic advised.

"Alright."

"Me too," Larry let her know.

Antic left to give Schwin's and Zen's orders to the kitchen and get the kids' deserts. Electra told Zen, "I want to get the side of my nose pierced like yours, and wear a tiny violet diamond. I think I want to get a small dragon tattoo where Becky has her phoenix."

"What does your mother say?"

"I don't know what she'd say, which is why I don't think I'll ask her."

"Just remember, piercings close up but a tattoo is fairly permanent."

"Do you have a tattoo?"

"I do."

"May I see it?"

"Certainly not in the restaurant, or anywhere in public."

"Oh. What is it of?"

"A lotus flower from the perspective of looking down into its center."

"It sounds hot."

"I'm going to be training at the Mother's Compassionate Guardians Monastery on Mother, and I'm sure you'll have an opportunity to see it while I'm there."

"I heard the monastery is putting together a meditation training for Om Star Fleet pilots which includes three hours per day of intense multifaceted concentration with breath, visualization, kinesthetic movement, the heartbeat and a sound formula."

"That is the training I'll be participating in. It's 18-months long."

"Amazonia told me it will enhance piloting in battle and help establish a stronger ink with the spiritual congress."

"Your mother convinced High Admiral Swenah to make the training part of the Star Fleet advanced curriculum, and the Admiral will be attending the first one herself."

"I'm going too," Schwin informed Electra.

"Well, of course you both should go," Electra advised. "You're the two best pilots, along with Konax and Swenah, that Star Fleet has produced. You have both flown with my mother, and recognize that there is no more effective functioning in any domain or area of piloting than from the flow-state. The ability to maintain the state in battle is the ultimate acme of skill."

"Your mother certainly exemplifies this to the highest degree," Schwin admitted. "My efforts and consistency with meditation rose significantly with her inspiration."

"You were each just out of the academy when you started flying with her, and have sustained remarkable self-cultivation ever since."

"We can visit together when we're in residence there," Zen suggested.

"I'd like that. You guys are fun. The girls at school treat me differently and don't share deeply with me. They treat me like they do our teachers."

"You are a teacher," Schwin emphasized.

"But I'm also a schoolgirl. Now I'm married and I can't seem to get it consummated. I might hold the record as a married virgin."

"Is there a physical or psychological problem?"

"No. We're both fit and ready. It was all the attacks and the rescue operation, and that poor decision I made to get sloshed on alcohol. The Islohar have so many rules about consummation; and one I seem to have overlooked is the three-day waiting period after over-consumption of alcohol. Then there's the one that states that it must be performed before midnight. That one foiled us one night. And the six-hour minimum sleep rule. It almost feels like I'll need an attorney to make love with my husband and champion."

"I hadn't realized," Schwin sympathized. "I'm so sorry."

"You poor dears," Zen added.

- Chapter 14 -

After a glorious night of snuggling, kissing and some near-rule-violations, Electra and Larry did finally fall asleep to remain in that state for seven and a half hours. Electra led them through their morning routine like a task master giving Larry a heavy workout, and he was sure he'd lost a pound doing it. Breakfast was in the penthouse via room service. They showered separately taking no chances.

Electra wore her Kristy fashion tights and t-shirt. Larry dressed in his sort of prep-school look. He'd grown up a dirt-poor street rat in rags, and always since attempted to distance himself from that look and those origins. A hover-limo from the holo-studios picked them up right outside their hotel lobby. The holo-studio was just outside the suburban sprawl surrounding Santasum, on a large property in the countryside. It was almost a mini-city in itself.

Ben met them at the studio's vehicle fleet-garage in a convertible hover-cart, and the kids climbed in. Both Larry and Electra had overcoats with thermal textile-lining. The late winter was showing the first signs of spring as a hint of things to come, but there was a chill to the air and the wind sharpened it. Ben had the heat blowing on them within the convertible. Larry and Electra sat together in the bucket seat beside Ben, protected from the wind by the windshield and directly in the path of the heater-fan.

Ben was deep in the role of tour-guide, quite jovial and truly delighted to be doing this with them. He informed them, "I'm going to take you through some of the more elaborate automated mechanical sets built for scenes in major productions which are now classics. Occasionally a set is redecorated and employed in a scene in a new movie. Many holo-movie fans prefer actual mechanical sets to quantum computer graphics and animation. We'll start at the *Tsunami*. It mechanically replicates the destruction of a coastal town and is enormously exhilarating."

"Do you mechanically produce the actual giant wave of water?"

"The spray is real and so are the bottom two feet of water. The rest of the wave is a gas we've perfected that looks and behaves like an actual tsunami."

The coastal town came into view as they came over the summit of a rolling hill. There were many hundreds of buildings including a downtown area and housing communities around it. The town covered a hundred acres and was built to scale. Ben drove them down into the outskirts towards the town and Larry and Electra marveled at the details of the homes. Ben mentioned, "We have to resod the lawns and replant the gardens, as well as replace the glass windows meant to shatter in the scene. Most windows are polycarbonate and remain whole, those are not the ones the lenses focus on."

"Do all the buildings collapse?"

"You'll see in just moments," Ben kept them in suspense. Larry and Electra had grown up on family holo-movies and the technology channel. Their interests had expanded to concerts performed by trendy bands, Star Hunt, a teen reality series, improv and stand-up comedy, and on rare occasions, the news. They had, of course, seen some of the blockbuster action-adventures produced on Om and Glitter. They'd never seen anything to prepare them for this.

Ben pulled into the center of downtown, onto a hydraulic platform level with the road, and proceeded to put up the convertible top and power the windows closed. He had them put their seatbelt and full harness on. Once sealed in, Ben said, "Here goes."

Suddenly a seventy-foot wave was headed their way at hundreds of miles per hour from about a half mile out on the ocean. It looked so real that panic gripped Electra and Larry. As the wave came up the beach, still towering over the town, Larry screamed. When the first building came apart to join the crushing wall of water, Electra screamed almost in harmony to Larry's continuing one. Roofs came off whole and in sections, walls disintegrated, trees uprooted, glass shattered into shards, and individual bricks flew by. Their platform had their hover-cart locked on and was rising above the two feet of actual water at the bottom, into the pure gas part of the wave.

As the gas touched the front of the car and began to wash over it, the vehicle began tumbling over as if hit with tremendous impact. The screaming took on a new magnitude of terror. Debris from demolished buildings followed closely around them as their hover-cart tumbled over and over, threatening to crush the little cart. It was over in seconds and they were back in the outskirts of town upside-down. Hanging in their harness they viewed the total destruction out their windshield.

Ben said enthusiastically, as soon as both screams ran out of wind, "Now I'll set it all back to right, except the lawns, gardens and broken windows."

Their end over end return to the town center was far slower than their departure had been, and gas wave and debris no longer engulfed them. Pieces of buildings and even individual bricks returned to their original positions reconstructing the town. The process took several minutes, and the real water was either going down drainage pipes or running back down the beach to the sea.

By the time they came to rest upright where they'd started from, the town was back to its original state, with a three-hundred-meter swath of washed away ground cover from the sea to the inland outskirts of town. Ben informed them, "Not many people get to experience the *Tsunami* since it is labor-intensive to restore completely. It's not part of the regular tour."

"I'm honored, I guess," Electra replied. "It was somewhat traumatic and without a doubt terrifying."

"We're going to *Earthquake* next and it is on the regular tour. No labor at all is required to reset it. It is entirely electrohydraulic and electromagnetic mechanical and automated."

"Is it frightening?" Larry inquired, seeking data for his preparation facing it.

"We won't be flipped over this time," was all Ben would reveal.

He drove them into a tunnel for about a quarter mile before arriving at what looked like a functional mag-lev railroad underground station. There were even android passengers waiting by the tracks. Ben maneuvered, backing up, to one end of the station platform almost touching the tiled wall. For this set he lowered and contracted the convertible textile cart-top. Then he had them put on respirator masks explaining, "A lot of dust is produced by this one. There are goggles if you want them."

Both Electra and Larry put on the respirators from the glovebox, and they opted for the goggles as well. Ben told them, "Here it comes."

A mag-lev Passenger train started into the station slowing, preparing to stop and let out passengers and take on new ones. A tremor grew to a shaking. The shaking grew to a major quaking and a couple of electrical surges blew out the power rail as several train cars hopped from the track coming at angles along the platform, knocking down column supports between floor and station ceiling as they came. There was an explosion at the far end of the station where the largest electrical surge had flashed. Two sections of the platform angled to 45-degrees opening a chasm between them that swallowed a train car. A section of ceiling and the weight of firmament above it crashed down onto the tracks. A number of cars were crushed by this, and beneath a section of the platform where the rubble piled high.

One particular train car was headed for them sideways at speed. Just before it would crush and pulverize them, the platform section they were on angled up to take the impact, and they were leaned sideways in their seats. Loud screams seemed to come from everywhere. Larry and Electra were part of the chorus. Androids had been balled over, thrown about, banged apart and squished. Fire seemed to consume most of the station. Train cars were smashed up, broken in half, and lying on their sides. Smoke and dust filled the air.

It seemed to Electra as real as the quakes on Lodistan in their rescue operations. Ben shared, "I always get a kick out of watching this one reassemble."

He triggered the reverse sequence with his skullcap and everything started moving slowly at once. Their hover-cart was angled back to level as the rail car that almost flattened them receded away. The electric, hydraulic, magnetic and mechanical machinery moving them was mostly hidden beneath the station platform and tracks. They watched the entire horrifying scene replay in slow motion reverse. There was nothing frightening about this phase, and it was a wonder of hi-tech robotics. Larry much preferred seeing these sequences construct themselves over watching them come apart. His throat was raw from screaming.

Ben took them through several more robotic-mechanical sets which included *Twister*, a truly fear-inspiring tornado scene which had them in the air spinning and screaming. Then he brought them to a couple of part mechanical, part holo-simulation sets. The *Thermal Nuclear Fission Detonation* was one of them, and *Meteor* was another, giving Electra and Larry a taste of what the people on the ground of Lodistan experienced when the meteor struck, which the kids only saw from space. Rides were next, and Ben wanted to start them off on *Waterfalls*.

Electra, Larry and Ben entered a small open boat. It had bucket seats with seatbelts and harnesses, already making Larry anxious. Happy music played as their boat drifted slowly with the current, lulling them into a false sense of security. The landscape around them looked natural and pleasant. Every minute or so a sculpted wood or stone statue sat in meditation posture upon the riverbank, life-size or much bigger.

Their boat came into a little cove and stopped while a brilliant multicolored mandala formed on the water surface beside them. Ben explained, "There's a grid just below the surface and ink jets fill each section of the grid with its color."

They left the cove and started moving with the current again, and the happy music was reassuring. Gradually the landscape transformed to hills climbing higher to each side and more distant mountain tops. Areas of the shore became exposed bedrock. The current was hastening and Larry's anxiety grew at pace. White water rapids appeared as their velocity increased. They narrowly escaped a few of these. Both river and landscape dropped off out of sight up ahead. They were yet picking up speed and the end of the river was in sight. A few meters from the precipice they got a view of the depths of the gorge they were inevitably getting sucked down to the bottom of.

Both kids involuntarily screamed in terror as their bow pointed near vertically down, and the mist obscured the bottom far below. Electra was certain they attained free-fall velocity before passing the halfway point. She knew she was screaming and it seemed quite appropriate to the situation she was in. Her scream blended with Larry's heightening the dread horrifying fright. Her stomach had to be a hundred meters above her at least.

Falling to certain death, they finally entered the mist. Larry closed his eyes tight, expelling the last of his breath to amplify his frightened shriek while bracing for a crash. In violation of natural law and vortex force, the boat slowed as their incline shifted from vertical through less severe angles. Then they were doing an easy 40-knots horizontal with the towering waterfalls behind them and their screams were silenced by the roaring of the falls.

When they got out of the boat at the giftshop both kids got an "I Survived the Waterfalls" t-shirt. Larry didn't want to go on *Spaceship Crash*, and inquired of Ben, "Aren't there any pleasant and sedate rides, for the elderly perhaps?"

They went on the Hover-Ferris Wheel next. All three got into a little container with comfortable seats—and no seatbelts. Their container was hung by its roof to a strut on the 200-foot diameter wheel-frame, and made slow revolutions around the circumference while the entire wheel made a circuit around the studio visitor-park hovering 40-feet off the ground. Larry thought this was more his speed, though his fear of heights did gnaw at him.

They didn't have time to take in a show, even though one was a musical Electra had wanted to see.

They did go briefly backstage on two sets to meet the actors and actresses staring in them. With her monastery abbot meeting nearing, Ben took them back to the studio's hover-vehicle fleet garage, and they were chauffeured to their hotel.

Only minutes remained when Electra and Larry entered the hotel lobby. The Tincture Phoenix Room was located down a corridor on the ground floor so Larry didn't have to contend with the mini-hover-step escalator. Electra asked him, "Would you remain at my side and hold my hand for support?"

"Absolutely and Immovably," Larry solemnly promised.

They removed their overcoats as they hurried along and got them hung over an arm before arriving at the door. Holding hands, they crossed the threshold into the Tincture Phoenix Room. It was filled with hundreds of smiling robed abbots seated on meditation cushions on a carpet of many colors. Clarity and bliss seemed to fill the chamber. Electra was busy shifting gears into a meditative state and Larry was too. He knew Electra was deep into it when her alive radiant smile expressed supreme joy. The heart energy that followed, emanating from her, was sweet, pure and fulfilling rapturous holy love. Her love and the sight of her lit Larry up in his joy of the beautiful.

The smiles and energy continued in silence for many minutes. Then the High Abbot inquired of Electra, "What methods have you found to be most direct and efficient?"

"The ways that make consciousness itself the object of meditation—particularly the sudden way—are most direct. The ways that reabsorb all 36 types of phenomena of mind into contemplation of clear light upon emptiness, working the central channel with concentration and visualization, vase breathing and retention of breath, employing the lateral channels, channel wheels, meridians and energies, expand meditation into the states of dreaming, deep sleep, dying and after-death. Only wisdom-compassion can open these paths, so the way of the heart incorporated into the methods working the central channel, is also important. Awakening the body—the temple of consciousness—through mass integrating vital energy via energy-generation exercises and soft martial arts, unifies body and mind accelerating the process of enlightenment."

Another abbot inquired of her, "What do you see as the most effective method of overcoming ego?"

"Meditation is indispensable. In addition, to have the map of the fixated faces of ego, their characters, mechanisms, and one's patterns of movement through them at every level of consciousness, exposes the entire enterprise of illusory ego as an automaton, empty of true self and mere phenomenon of the mind. Knowing this, it is hard to fall into the ego game and far easier to dissolve in transcendence to return to the state of the witness, or essence of mind."

Another abbot inquired, "What do you think of the entheogen class of drugs?"

"This class of drugs constitutes one of the most ancient tools of humanity, dating back to the stone age of every planetary population, employed to enhance and accelerate the first forms of meditation and of imitation of the divine. Entheogens are not toxins, and so do not need to be avoided as such. They cause radical detoxification of all the major organs of the body. This class of drugs call us to contemplation. Resisting the calling results in optic hallucinations and general incomprehension for a number of hours, though presents no health risks. I mean to accelerate the process of awakening so I will definitely employ entheogen ceremonies."

"Have you begun to formulate your new teachings for the age to come?" the High Abbot asked her.

"I have the outline and some of the components worked out. I am still a virgin and must acquire more data before trying to harness the enormous power of sex earlier on in the process of enlightenment, instead of saving it for last. Sarhi and the Amonrahonians have given us the ultimate group work as a tuning of meditators from tens of thousands of planets united as one. This is a spiritual instrument of the highest order and I aim to employ it in my new method. I have seen the spiritual congress support awakening of people involved in meditation on a world in its iron age, and I have seen it make all the difference for folks in BiVortex for freeing them from layers of introjected mind control, through a guided deprogramming meditation. The romantic couple energy is another source of power I mean to tap for awakening, and I already have much data thanks to my relationship with my beloved husband and champion."

Another abbot inquired, "Do you have any sense if you'll be ready to present your new teachings by age 30, as you have in the past?"

"I aim to begin presenting my method part-time once I turn 24, and full-time when I complete my studies at age 28. This time around I will take the telomerase drug and remain teaching for hundreds of years."

"How is it that you are shortening your preparation so significantly?" another abbot asked.

"Much credit goes to the Wu. My mother has been cultivating her skills in receiving and preparing me. I have also been getting better at this, after all these times."

A very elderly abbot asked her, "Have you considered the ancient sacred theurgy as a component of your method?"

"Yes. In its highest form of deity embodiment. There are ancient forms which can be updated from historically remote periods. I have heard my mother and Sarhi speak of this. I just arrived a couple of weeks less than 14-years ago and require more time to look into it. I also intend to establish humor as a component of my method, since it radically transforms perspective with its unique form of detachment. Humor will be part of the entheogen ceremony as well, integrated with the saying of the ancient sudden-way sage: 'Set down your burden and laugh'."

Electra further elaborated, "The other component I mean to clarify perfectly is the three hypostases of the Absolute. The transcendental Absolute in itself is unknowable and beyond the beyond, though its emanation of self-contemplation—the second hypostasis—contemplates the Absolute intelligibly and is called the divine mind. The eternal emanation of the divine mind is the third hypostasis, and is the soul within the human being that can be awakened as a mind of light reflecting the divine mind, or it can be chattering illusion, darkness and suffering. This must be clarified in steps within contemplation, repeated and sustained."

Another abbot inquired of Electra, "Is it possible that your developmental stage of hormones is in some way distorting your understanding of some components of your proposed teachings, such as harnessing sex significantly earlier in the process?"

"Like I said, I'm still a virgin; so we shall see."

The High Abbot told Electra, "It is obvious even now that you will soon attain complete mastery over the spiritual methodologies still viable as alive transmissions. Your attainment at your age is beyond extraordinary, and you bring us hope and confidence. How can we best support your mission?"

"So far, Divacaram is the most evolved moral anarchy I have experienced. You are on the path of the Amonrahonians and shine as an example for other developing moral anarchies. Your friendship and feedback to me, and prankster ego-reductions like my piloting test, are of enormous importance to me. I trust that by getting to better know some of you I shall receive all the guidance I need from your culture."

This had the whole room smiling broadly at her. The thought and corresponding emotional charge of embarrassment and exposure passed through her mind, but Electra didn't chase the bone, allowing it to briefly abide before decaying and fading away. She did pay attention to the shock of feeling the fool, since shocks are openings for going beyond mind structure and duality into the void of non-conceptualization. The question-and-answer session went on for a while longer. Then Electra suggested they meditate together on the five meditation deities personifying the five wisdom-unions.

Electra was asked to lead them through it by the High Abbot. These meditation deities and wisdom unions are universal to human populations, though their names, symbols, seed sounds, hand gestures, compass directions and so forth are unique to each planet. The color corresponding to each meditation deity and the order of the wisdom unions sequentially for opening the state are universal. Electra had reviewed the Divacaram version and much appreciated it, so she led them in it.

Each deity was generated as a visualization with intense concentration while assuming the hand gesture and intoning the seed sound. The purification and overcoming of the ego-poisons, called passions or sins in some traditions, always commenced the meditation process with the wisdom-unions. The wisdom of Discriminating Perception, for separating conventional truth and Absolute Truth, was always the start. The Equality Wisdom came next in the sequence, opening the recognition of the same consciousness in others as in oneself to make the arc of love and equality with every human being. The All Accomplishing Wisdom followed generating essential will to realization inspired by love and compassion. The Mirror Like Wisdom, next in the sequence, means the mind of emptiness reflects reality without distortions or effect, beyond appearances and one with them, like a mirror. The final wisdom is the union with the divine presence of Absolute Transcendental Emptiness as the only true Being, the eternal Unborn.

When the corresponding meditation deity is seen in detail and clarity in the mind's eye within the state of contemplation, the wisdom-union is clarified and the process of embodiment as a permanent state has begun. Electra took two and a half hours to lead them through it. Her contemplation of each deity had been pristinely clear and her heart energy pulsed in spherical expanding waves tangible to all in the room and beyond. The confidence her audience had in her following this meditation was made abundantly clear in their departing remarks and goodbyes.

Electra and Larry had very little time to get to the rehearsal with the Manic Microcosms. Upon arrival, the keyboard player, Simon, introduced himself first. He has a tattoo of a musical scale and notes on his forearm and wore skin-tight pants and a t-shirt. He is fifteen and already a musical prodigy on Divacaram. His hair seemed to stick straight out in every direction and is primary blue with orange contrasts.

The drummer is a petite hyperactive fourteen-year-old girl named Lumina who is dressed in the Kristy fashion, which arrived on Divacaram with the holovision of Electra playing with the Whirling Vortexes. She has long bushy brown hair tied back, and three tasteful piercings on her face. Amon is fifteen and he plays saxophone. His hair is a gigantic dome of tight curls darker black than his beautiful skin. He is already considered a virtuoso on the planet. Aurora is almost fifteen and plays guitar. Her psychedelic pink hair is cut just below the earlobes with bangs in the front. She's dressed in short-shorts and a skimpy tube-top, and her eyebrow and tongue are pierced. A martial rendition of a crane spreading wings and standing on one leg showed above and below her tube-top. She writes much of the band's lyrics, and Amon and Simon compose the music. Lumina adds much of the mania to the Manic Microcosms.

Aurora told Electra, "I'll play rhythm guitar so you can play lead. Larry can play bass."

Amon informed Electra, "I've hyped up the music to the two songs you played with the Whirling Vortexes and would like for you to hear them."

"I'd love to."

The band ran through the songs as Electra and Larry watched and listened. Amon asked hopefully, "What do you think?"

"It's much more energetic and faster paced. I like it better and think it's more teen. Pogo's kind of middle aged now. It definitely lives up to your band's name."

"May we include these in our performance tonight?"

"I'd really enjoy that. Did you compose them?"

"I really just sped up the beat and added some riffs and tangents."

"You're ridiculously modest Mr. brilliant genius. I salute you maestro Amon. You're truly amazing. It's such an honor and opportunity to get to play with you guys. Are you all like actually hundreds of years old?"

Simon answered, "None of us have had the telomerase drug yet."

Aurora informed her, "We each attend the Academy of Performing Arts and are in the 9th or 10th form, having learned our instruments in childhood; and we've been playing together since 7th form."

"A special school for skilled and talented geniuses," Electra commented.

"I'm out of my league," Larry admitted.

Aurora wrapped an arm around him—causing Electra to snuff some arising jealousy—and told Larry, "You are quite skilled and played exceptionally well at your wedding reception and the performance on *Star Hunt*."

"Thanks. That helps with my anxiety."

"You're not wearing those clothes to perform in I hope?"

"No. We have costumes at the hotel."

"Let Lumina and I design clothes for you for tonight. We can make them in the tailor-fabricator unit. Electra is already dressed perfect for the occasion."

The arm remained around Larry, and Electra was burning off percolating jealousies in little flares within her mind. Larry looked into Electra's eyes to find the answer to Aurora's question to him. Electra understood this and said as she decided, "Yes, go ahead and design Larry a costume and I'll go as I am; though with Lumina in the same fashion, I'll probably look like I'm ten years old."

"What you need is extra-thin translucent stretch smart-textile for your t-shirt. It adheres and molds to you without diminishing protrusions. Your tits will show honey."

I'm glad I met you, Aurora."

"Then let me have just one little kiss with your cute husband."

Electra had to jump to the flow state to get beyond her mind's nonsense before answering, "Alright. I think it would be good for him."

It would be very good for herself, Electra knew, providing ample opportunity to conquer her jealousies, which obviously needed a bit of work. She trusted Larry's love as much as she did her parent's love. The kiss itself, initiated by Aurora and only returned by Larry due Electra's directive that it would be good for him, arose thought-charges even in the flow-state for Electra. She incinerated these with laser concentration.

The endurance and longevity of the kiss provided new and deeper opportunities for Electra to process her fear of losing Larry's love and her possessiveness of him. At the same time, it made Larry even more madly desirable to have an older girl so interested in him. Tongues were obviously deeply involved in Aurora's sampling of Larry. It was Simon who said, "We better start rehearsing, and teaching Larry and Electra their parts."

The two reworked songs of Electra and Pogo took only two run-throughs each. Then the kids had to learn their parts for two other songs. Larry would only sing chorus, but Electra would be lead singer for her two overhauled songs. They got it worked out in what little time they had, then Amon suggested they all go to Astro-Joe's for some food before going to the super-dome for the opening ceremony.

They took the public transportation hover-bus and the restaurant was only about a mile away. Their stop was just half a block from the door. Inside the place was packed with teens and catalyst young adults. The band members were well-known to the restaurant staff as regulars and celebrities. A new table for six was squeezed into the dining room to accommodate them since they were so good for the restaurant's reputation, and it only took a minute.

While they waited, the band members signed autographs on fan's hand devices with personal styluses they always carried. Amon's autograph was the most sought after. Electra had to sign a few too, and having no stylus, had to depend on the tiny ones inserted within the hand devices shoved at her for her signature. She added a selfie to each one to the tremendous appreciation of her fans.

The Maître d rescued them to escort them to their table. The music was a tad loud for conversations not conducted in shouts at close range. Miniature spaceship models moved slowly overhead beneath the 40-foot-high ceiling. Each is an historical ship of some renown. Holo-posters of popular bands and young celebrities adorned the walls. Periodically a colored light show filled the dining room for several moments making everyone appear as an animation. On a hover-platform 20-feet off the ground, a male and female were athletically pumping out modern dance with flavors of acrobatics and a sort of gymnastic ballet.

The service staff were all in iconic clothing depicting cultural archetypes, and their waitress wore a leotard and tutu with fairy wings, sprinkling golden dust from a pouch on her waist band as she fairy danced along in her function. She had a high voice and was petite and delicate, looking the part. She was kind of flighty as she took their order. The place excited and intrigued Electra. On an impulse she wrapped her arms around Larry, turning in her seat to kiss him like Aurora had.

Their beverages arrived with Electra and Larry still emersed. Then some fun appetizers were placed on their table, and the two 13-year-olds were still stuck together at the mouths in embrace. An energy was rising that had the four band members staring at the smooching couple. Then people in the restaurant began looking around, and a few headed for the rest rooms in couples or alone. The energy was growing from a gnawing turbulence into a class IV hurricane, and hyperactive Lumina was squirming in her seat.

Larry broke it off, unable to withstand the growing pressure, leaving Electra breathless in yearning. She quickly realized that things had escalated well beyond personal private experience, and began transmuting her energy into pure love. For a few moments Larry felt the same spherical expanding waves wash over him in fantastic bliss that he'd experienced in the meditation with the abbots and at his wedding. Aurora asked Larry, "Is she doing this?"

Larry nodded in the affirmative, too blissed out for words. Electra tried to explain, "It's a long story, but Larry and I haven't had the opportunity to consummate our marriage yet and my link with the spiritual congress somehow amplifies and expands my energy to affect others. I am sorry. I've really been trying to put a cork in it, believe me."

"It feels truly desperate," Amon commented.

"I had to grab the seat of my chair to keep my hands from my groin," Aurora declared.

Larry told them, "It's the spiritual congress. It's not Electra's fault."

Lumina suggested to Larry, "Bed her soon, so it is events coming out of her instead of *that*. Everyone loves events."

"We both want to," Larry said defensively, "but the Islohar rules for it and all the disruptions have prevented us."

"Tomorrow night is the soonest we can," Electra added, "the Absolute willing and the creek don't rise."

"I strongly wish you every success," Lumina said sincerely.

Aurora leaned into the table to make eye contact with Electra and say, "You're like the sirens in the most ancient tales. Tie me to the mast."

"I promise not to get all worked up again for the rest of the afternoon and evening."

Simon asked excited, "Have any of you seen the new improv comedy troupe at Slum Basement Theater?"

"I've never seen such quick wit, and they even make up lyrics as they sing them to music of the audience's selection," Amon enthused.

"I've only seen the holo-ads," Aurora stated with the sense of having missed something special.

"We could go before the opening ceremony," Simon tried to sell them on it.

"I'm game," Aurora announced.

"I'll go if Electra and Larry want to," Amon shared his preference.

Electra whispered to Larry, "Do you want to? It sounds fun."

Her second sentence decided it for Larry and he said, "Sure."

Lumina said, "Then it looks like we're going," having overheard the whispering.

Their fairy waitress danced over with a tray to present their entrees. She was also a student at the

Performing Arts Academy in Santasum, as were other members of the waitering staff. She knew the band members. Astro-Joe's was a very popular place to work as well as to eat. There were no prices since there's no such thing as money here. They don't rely on credits or anything other than conscience and awareness of the common good. The band members received expensive equipment and instruments because the meritocracy warranted this and they needed them. Everyone benefited. Each band member lived with parents and sibling(s) in ordinary homes and used public transport. All wholesome needs were continuously met and there was always enough love to go around. No one was rich and no one was poor.

The fun appetizers had been breaded and deep-fried chicken, fish, squid and bugs. Assorted dips and sauces had been brought. Their entrees were something the Divacaram folks called pizza pies. Electra had never had one before. Apparently, they consisted of dough crust with melted cheese and tomato sauce, and a long list of optional toppings, some of which would not go well together. Fortunately, some combos had been suggested right on the holo-menu growing out of the holo-pedestal in the center of the table.

Their waitress got Electra's autograph after emptying her tray onto their table, then danced off to attend to other fairy matters. Electra was certain it was the cutest waitress outfit she'd ever seen. The girl was really cute too, and quite the actress and dancer. The restaurant was exhilarating and enchanting, full of eye-catching characters, and an obvious incubator of some serious art. Electra noticed a perfect miniature model of *Vajra Yogini* hover over her table, then descend to eye level. Electra thought she'd best explain to the others, so she shouted over the music, "This is a model of my yacht."

Amon remarked, "It looks more like a combat recon ship."

"Only on the outside," Electra said as she connected her hand device to the table's holo-pedestal via her skullcap, to proceed to show stills of the ship's new interior. She added, "I'm going to refit the exterior with side fins, a stern foil, a long bubble on the forward bow, vertical tail fins, and a bow ornament."

Just as she completed her sentence the still for her exterior design for the hull showed in the table's hologram. Aurora exclaimed, "That is so beautiful. It's ideal for a party. Let's invite some kids from the Broadway Street-party up to your yacht to celebrate Hallowteen."

Amon, Simon and Lumina were jazzed by the idea, so Electra told them, "We'd have to fit six in the four seats of my tender, which I can fly down by remote control. Then we can pick up a combat shuttle from the hanger to bring the guests up."

Aurora offered, "I'd share a seat with Larry."

"He'll be in the pilot seat with me," Electra informed her.

"This is great," Lumina said with enthusiasm.

"Where is your yacht parked?" Amon inquired.

"On the main Space Fleet space station."

"That could be a problem," Simon considered.

"Not unless someone tries a space-walk," Electra argued. "There are blackout shades we can draw on the viewports."

"That's the plan then," Simon announced.

"Pizza pie is quite tasty," Electra let them know.

"They make some of the very best here," Lumina assured her.

"Deserts are the most yummy," Simon opined.

Amon stated, "They have everything teens need: sugar, salt and fat."

"I'm having desert," Electra told Larry.

"Me too."

"What do you think of pizza?"

"It's wonderful, and I'm sure it will be a big hit at the academy once I give the cafeteria cook the recipe. Some of the toppings aren't allowed on the Academy diet though."

"I'll give our chef, Amy, the recipe and get her to make it at our school too."

"It will become an instant favorite I'll bet."

- Chapter 15 -

The improv comedy troupe at the Slum Broadway Theater was as awesome as it was hysterically funny. The performance of Electra and Larry with the Manic Microcosms at the opening ceremony of Hallowteen in the super-dome was a smashing success. Electra had remote piloted her tender down to the parking lot of the super-dome, and she asked Johnson if she could borrow the combat shuttle *before* she took it. Johnson had said, "Go ahead and take it. Your security detail will be arriving on the yacht but we promise to remain invisible and out of the way."

"How will you get up?"

"A hotel shuttle will bring us."

"Alright. Thanks for the loan of the shuttle."

"Thanks for asking before barrowing it," Johnson told her.

Only Amon and Simon had gone up to the yacht hanger in the tender with Electra and Larry to pick up the combat shuttle. There wasn't a square foot of space to put the shuttle down at the Broadway street-party, so Electra hovered a few feet over the heads of the partying teenagers and told Larry to open the floor hatch in the airlock and lower a wire and rung ladder. The Broadway street-party scene where they were recruiting partiers for the yacht was a dancing mob of teens bouncing off the walls. The selection process depended entirely on who Aurora and Lumina found to be cute. Many were performing arts students and Larry felt mighty boring around them. Getting them all aboard took a long time. One hundred and eighteen climbed one at a time up the ladder, not counting Aurora and Lumina. One hundred and twenty-two were aboard when the final teen entered. With 40-saeats in the passenger section and four in the cockpit, all were doubled up or standing, so Electra didn't bother saying, "Strap-in" and instead just said, "Hang-on!" over the intercom before throttling up the drives and hitting thrusters. She dare-not fire a booster.

Electra got them into the hanger, closed the bay doors, and got the hanger airing-up. She had secured the hatches to the two quad blaster cannon turrets before letting kids on. She secured the shuttle so no one could "borrow" it. She did the same with her tender from her skullcap, and secured the hanger door so only Johnson or Green could open it.

She waited until the air pressure was nearing full in the hanger before lowering the shuttle ramp, then exited holding Larry's hand. Larry was enormously grateful that Electra was holding his hand because parties made him especially anxious. He wasn't sure if he'd actually ever gotten the point of them. A crowd was gathered in front of the airlock so Electra opened both sides of it with her skullcap. The teens passed through and most went to the freight lift to see how many they could squeeze in. All at the bottom were squished with no air-space between them and each had a lighter teen on their shoulders. The ones that didn't fit took the lift-tube two or three at a time. Lumina was scampering up the ladder, unable to stand still for lift or tube.

Electra was telling them all to meet on deck four. She and Larry rode the tube together. The living room cabin and the bar-lounge were packed when they got there. The music was already blaring and alko drinks were being served from behind the bar. The recreational pharmacy was being raided, and a cloud of smoke was getting sucked up the funnel-vent over the big hookah, making the bar-lounge the most popular place. The galley was packed and all sorts of snacks, finger-food and deserts were in full production. The living room and lounge-dancefloor hosted wild dancers of high caliber, and clothing was shedding as bodies perspired.

Electra found a small vacant sofa to sit on with Larry since sitting on the floor would be dangerous in this environment. She brought the carbon-plate shutters down over the priceless paintings Mel had put on her yacht to protect them from collisions with dancers. The furniture was sturdy and bolted down. Electra heard something that sounded ceramic shatter in the galley followed by colorful exclamations.

She asked Larry, "Would you dance with me later?"

"Yes; no matter how foolish I feel doing it."

"These folks seem like they study dance."

"They're certainly coordinated, expressive and lively. It feels a little like being an extra in a dance-musical play."

"Are you feeling better about the costume they made for you?"

"It's OK, I guess. Do I look alright?"

"You're insanely desirable, my love, and I was so proud of you at our performance. Your brief bass solo in that last piece gave me goose bumps and butterflies in my stomach."

A girl who'd been double-timing the rapid beat collapsed onto the sofa perspiring, bumping Electra into Larry like marbles, and moving both over into the opposite armrest. She told them, "Sorry. I had to take a seat and sit this one out."

"What's your name?" Electra asked as she rubbed her hip and burned away negative thoughts before they could fully arise.

"My name's Maggie. I'm in theater with a second in dance. What are you in?"

"I play guitar and sing," Electra replied.

"What's your name? I don't recall seeing either of you at school."

"I'm Electra and this is Larry."

"Then you're the Mu and this is your yacht."

"I am. It's nice to meet you, Maggie."

"You look different over holo-vision."

"I know. I don't look so skinny as I do in real-life. I think it's some kind of digital auto-correct bringing me to acceptable aesthetic standards for holo-vision."

"You're cute in real-life Electra. I ought to have recognized you."

"Not many people do, so don't feel bad. You're quite a dancer; sort of a sprinter among dancers."

"I like to just let loose at full tilt."

"It's impressive."

"Well, I've been working at it."

"I see some dancers have stripped out of their clothes," Electra remarked.

"It's liberating and cooling. I'm going back to dance in just panties when I do."

"At my school we have to wear uniforms when we're not in our bedrooms, even at parties. At the annual ball we're permitted to wear evening gowns but we're not allowed to take them off while we're there."

"How oppressive," Maggie remarked.

"Are there any kids here from monastery academies?"

"I met one boy. I think he said his name is Fudo and he studies at the Diamond Mind Academy in the Mind-Only tradition. He's kind of shy."

Maggie scanned the living room cabin they were in and spotted the boy alone on a cabinet looking on in wonder. She pointed him out to Electra, who told Larry she'd be right back. Electra went over and said from close up, loudly to be heard, "I'm Electra. I heard you attend a monastery academy."

"Diamond Mind," he replied at equal volume.

"Would you talk to us in my study where we won't have to shout?"

"Sure."

Electra led him to Larry and Maggie, and introduced him to Larry since he'd already met Maggie. Maggie had stripped to her panties but decided to come along instead of dance, since she was attracted to Fudo. They ascended on the spiral stairs to the next deck and entered Electra's study, where she sealed the door and cranked up the sound-proofing. They would be able to hear whispering now, or even a pin drop. There was furniture, but they all sat close on the rug.

Electra asked Fudo, "Is your academy coed?"

"It is, but the dorms aren't."

"Can you take your clothes off at parties?"

"I think it would make me feel extremely self-conscious and anxious."

"But are you allowed to?"

"Some kids who look like holo-magazine models have at a few parties—especially at the swimming pool party I went to. I haven't been to that many."

"Do you have to wear *uniforms*?" Electra asked, pronouncing the last word with disgust.

"We don't have uniforms or a dress code or anything, but kids are all dressed in something in classes and on campus. Except when all the girls in the 8th form dorm went running across campus naked one night. I once went to first period in my pajamas not realizing."

"Are you allowed to have sex with the girls?"

"I'm still a virgin, but there's no rule against it if you're both the same age."

"Who is your abbot?"

"Burushana is Abbot and patriarch of the tradition."

"I met him today."

"He is also my personal teacher and mentor."

"What do you think of him?"

"He has helped me tremendously and I greatly admire him. He inspires me to make my best efforts. I attempt to be more like him."

"How old are you?"

"I'm almost sixteen."

"Have you had the reversal of aging drug?"

"No. I'm going to wait until I'm 24."

"You have quite an aura for your age."

"Look who's talking."

Larry laughed, liking Fudo. Maggie scooted closer to Fudo and asked him, "Do you know she's the Mu?"

"Who could miss it. She glows."

Maggie asked, "What form are you in?"

"I skipped a form in primary school, so I'm in 10th."

Maggie told him, "I'm in 10th form too. There's something very intense about you that draws me, Fudo."

"You're very attractive, Maggie."

Electra was feeling a connection with Fudo and knew intuitively that they would work together some day. She didn't want to interrupt Maggie's flirtations though, and found them fascinating. She snuggled into Larry to watch, luxuriating in romantic sentiments. Her attention on Larry never failed to light him up and put smiles on his face. Maggie had her arm draped over

Fudo's shoulder and was leaning her face in close to his, making eye contact with him.

Maggie brought her lips to touch his, checking out his response, which was to kiss her with gentle passion. Electra had to extinguish some self-pity thought-feelings over not being able to have sex with Larry. She dare-not even kiss Larry after the promise she made to Aurora. She brought her energy back down to chaste romantic love and drifted on its elation transported.

Maggie and Fudo were getting into it, so Electra dimmed the lights in the study with her skullcap and led Larry out of the cabin by his hand. For a moment she entertained the idea of taking him to bed, and it felt to her like the very idea was escaping her as erotic energy rippling outward. She reined it in tight and centered herself. A final resistant surge of energy she projected onto Fudo hoping he'd get lucky. Maggie was pretty into him so perhaps luck was not what he needed.

After descending the spiral stairway, they danced in the living room. Larry got through his self-consciousness quickly as he lost himself in the beat, yet remaining tuned to Electra as well. He used his martial arts turns, squats, blocks and expansive arm movements like Crane Spreads Wings or Single Whip, since these were ingrained and came naturally. His rhythm was right on. Self was absent so self-consciousness not even a possibility. Larry was all dance and no showmanship, yet it did make a sight, especially for Electra.

Electra made triple spins on toe or heel and seemed to move every joint in wild undulating rhythm independently. Her hips swung wide as if attached by rubber bands. Whenever there was space around her, she did a backflip or sprang into a handstand. She even got spinning more than half a dozen times on the top of her head upside down.

Electra knew that her security detail was aboard when Ashsa and Ariel arrived to dance beside them. The music inspired motion and Electra was all-out. The sentient androids were piece-mealing and splicing dance moves and routines together creatively into expressions beyond programming capacity. When Electra liberated herself from her tights, dancing in her Hugme's, both Ashsa and Ariel stripped naked. Since Ariel is an exact copy of Electra, and already naked for all to see, Electra pulled off her panties and t-shirt without missing a beat of the music. For Larry, this had been the supreme ultimate strip-tease bringing him to full arousal.

The galley had become a dance floor as well, no longer producing snacks, and some bedroom cabins on the deck above were becoming occupied. Johnson asked in Electra's earbud, "Do you want the kids in the bedroom cabins?"

This caused Electra to incorporate the relative conventional truth into her state, uniting with Absolute Truth so she could communicate, "Moral anarchy!"

Johnson left the situation alone, wishing Evenrude were here to deal with this shit.

Many girls were dancing stark naked, and some of the boys too. Many of the partiers were full of alko and empty of inhibitions. Synthetic ecstasy from the recreational pharmacy was clearly the most popular drug, and the majority had had at least a few tokes of hybrid cannabis bud. Electra and Larry refrained. Electra wasn't chancing any more obscure Islohar rules. A Galigar Dynasty vase got knocked off a shelf to smash on the floor.

Electra stopped dancing to pick up the pieces off the floor so that none of the barefoot dancers would cut themselves. She was perspiring and needed a break anyway. Stooping down gathering shards, she was bumped into twice, but managed to get every piece that did not go under the couch. She figured she could afford some good yacht detailers to clean up after the party. Larry had helped pick up the pieces and got bumped more times than Electra.

Once they'd removed the dance hazard, Electra led Larry by the hand over to a group at a round table smoking synthetic DMT. This was not contraindicated by Islohar rules, being an entheogen. One seat was empty so Electra sat Larry in it then climbed into his lap. A tube of the hookah was passed to them and Electra let Larry go first. There were five other teens at the table; three boys and two girls. They were all about two years older than Electra and Larry, and didn't have a clue who Electra is.

One of the guys at the table asked Electra, "I thought you have to be a teen to come to this party. Do you kids have an older sibling here or something?"

"We're nearly fourteen," Electra said, making it sound ancient.

You're not from the Academy of Performing Arts," he stated.

"No. We're in monastery academies."

Electra took her turn sucking smoke through the hookah tube then holding it in long. Blowing it out was a rush. The DMT launched her into pure contemplation. Her half-smile was a thing impossible to fake. Larry watched her aura expand around her head intensifying its radiance. Across the table from Electra, the only other naked girl sitting with them blew out a cloud of smoke, and Electra locked into eye contact with her, making the equal.

The girl's face relaxed into a thing of pure beauty and her budding aura took on shades of dark blue and violet when Electra passed her a sea of merit. She was so receptive that Electra decided to pass her the blessing of the Mu. She was sure the girl was one of her disciples. The girl's eyes opened wider, more tension evaporated from her body and a smile of pure rapture spread across her face. Electra stretched her hand across the table and the girl took it in hers to receive a pressurized force of healing bio-energy flowing into her to fill her. The others at the table were watching this strange happening and could not miss the transformation of the girl Electra made eye contact with. The brief five-minute DMT high was already winding down. The girl reached with her other hand to take Electra's other hand, and tightened her grip in ecstatic appreciation and awe.

She then stood and came around the table and snatch the smaller girl in a hug that brought Electra off Larry's lap with her feet off the ground expelling her breath. She was still embracing Electra in a near Space Marine hug when she announced to those at the table, "This is the Mu! She just awakened me to a new peak."

She kissed Electra passionately on the mouth, and Larry did a bit of purification and mind-structure demolition to eliminate his jealousies. She finally set Electra down, to Larry's great relief, and Electra climbed back into Larry's lap sitting sideways with her arms wrapped around him. Security and love filled Larry's heart. Then she kissed him with all her passion. She stopped abruptly the moment a little surge of erotic craving escaped her in an expanding wave.

Tubes from the hookah were held out to her. The others at the table wanted a turn to look into Electra's eyes on DMT in a contemplative state. The girl she was sure is a disciple introduced herself saying, "I'm honored to meet you, Mu. My name is Ishi and I'm studying acrobatics and stunt doubling. I also play the bass cello."

Electra told her, "This time you are; but you are also my disciple Miya from 2,500 years ago. I'm glad I found you."

"I'm your disciple?!" she squealed with excitement.

"I won't begin teaching for another 10-years, so go ahead and finish school. Could you send your contact information to my hand device so we can keep in touch?"

"I'm sending it, and I've never been so thrilled!"

Electra took one of the tubes held out to her and inhaled deeply. A boy of sixteen was inhaling too from another tube, intent on making eye contact with the Mu. They exhaled together looking into one another's eyes. Electra passed him an ocean of merit hoping this might reduce the erotic yearning that sometimes escaped from her in waves. It put him through a metamorphosis and his pale sprout of an aura blossomed around his head and shoulders going from pale, to pastel to bright psychedelic. For Larry it was almost like watching a caterpillar turn into a butterfly and take flight.

She did not pass this one her blessing but she did reach and take his hand to fill him with internal healing energy. He proceeded through stages of ever greater relaxation with an expression of overwhelming joy, getting as much of a rush from the energy she passed as from the DMT. He went deeper and more intensely in the state than he had ever experienced, and with greater permanent transformation than he believed possible. Some moments after the DMT had expired, he bowed, then came around the table to pick Electra up in a hug with enormous enthusiasm. He introduced himself and turned out to be another aspiring performing artist. He had the holo-movie-star look and was already adult size.

Larry made the psycho-machia, the battle of the soul, internally reducing the poisons of possessiveness and fear of loss. The older boy was so unnaturally good looking that Larry thought he may have been genetically engineered in a test tube. His skin was as perfect as syntec touch-perfect skin and he could be an android, to Larry's mind. Electra had been a rag doll in his arms, naked as the day she was born. Once back in Larry's lap, all seemed right in the world to him.

Electra made the equal ceremony on DMT with each of the others at the table passing worlds of merit and reservoirs of internal energy into them. None of these were disciples either and would just need to wait until she starts teaching to receive the blessing of the Mu. The girl at the table still wearing some of her clothes took off her bra and suggested, "We should have a sex party."

Electra tried to explain, "Larry and I can't consummate our marriage or have sex until tomorrow night with our Islohar chaperone guiding us. We're both virgins."

"How disappointing," she said with a sense of loss.

Electra told them, "Larry and I are going to the galley for some chow, so don't let us stop you."

The girl was squirming out of her panties as they left. Part of Electra wanted to watch, but she knew it would be over-arousing for her, and just increase her cravings to do it with Larry. They entered the galley and had to maneuver between dancers. The cabin was fairly trashed and quite a mess. Something completely unrecognizable was dripping from the molecular food synthesizer. A stain that looked like tomato sauce was on the ceiling with a bit on the floor below, as well as some drops on a few dancer's shoulders. Some broken crockery was piled in a corner.

The kids got ambassador rations from the cupboard and stuck them in the wave cooker for three seconds. A naked girl was dancing on the breakfast nook table so there was no place to eat in the galley. They brought their entrees and cutlery into the small den where no one was dancing. They sat on the floor since there were couples necking on both sofas and the stuffed chair. Removing the lids, they dug into their food with sensual pleasure. Heavy breathing came from one of the sofas and some soft moans from the other. They just ignored it emersed in their meal.

With her mouth full, Electra told Larry, "It will be just so wonderful once we can make love with each other whenever we want."

"Since we can't, it would help if you put on a nightgown or something."

"I'm liberated. You ought to take off your clothes too. It would help you accept yourself."

"I don't think this is the right time since we're trying to suppress sexual energy tonight."

"Not to excite arousal, but for liberation, my love."

"But your nakedness affects me."

"No excuses."

Larry removed his costume which he didn't care for anyway. She wrapped her arms around him proudly and kissed him. Larry was expanding with a look of embarrassment on his face as Electra watched mesmerized emitting a desperate determined and penetrating yearning that felt like life and death. Moans and heavy breathing from the sofa and chair became thrashing. Larry suggested, "We ought to go to our cabin suite and put on some clothes."

"Let's do that and go to sleep. It's nearly 0200 hours and it looks like this party will continue through morning."

They left the little den cabin holding hands. Fewer were dancing now and bodies were writhing together on the floor. They had to step over a couple on the spiral stairs. Larry was still sporting an erection and the girl of the couple on the stairs touched it as he went over them. "This is my husband!" escaped from Electra's mouth before she could process it.

It was clear sailing to their bedroom cabin from the stairs. Larry closed the door behind them with his skullcap. Electra's attention was captured by the two male teens having sex on her bed. One had already made a mess and it looked to Electra like the other was about to. Larry got her nightgown and a pair of Hugme's out of the drawer to hand to Electra. Her eyes remained riveted as she took them from him, making no move to put them on. Larry retreated to the bathroom. It wasn't until the second one blew that the boys even noticed Electra staring at them.

Electra spoke first, "I'm sorry. I didn't mean to spy on you. I was just turning into bed, and this is my bedroom cabin."

"We didn't know," one of the boys offered apologetically.

"That was great, by the way. I've never seen it before."

"How old are you?" the other asked, concerned they might be corrupting a child.

"I'm almost fourteen but my tits haven't grown in much yet. As you can see, I do have pubic hair."

"Where are you from?"

"I was born in the Xegatchznel Galaxy and have lived on Mother in the Whirlpool Galaxy and on Om in the Hub Galaxy. Are you both in the Academy of Performing Arts in Santasum?"

"Yes. In 11th form."

"What are you studying?"

"I'm in voice training and theater acting."

The other boy shared, "I'm a martial artist studying acting, and I hope to be an action-holo-movie star someday. What do you study?"

"Martial arts, energy-generation and meditation/contemplation at the monastery academy on Mother. I also play guitar and sing."

"What martial arts do you do?"

I learned the hard styles of Crane, Dragon and Drunken Fist first. Now I study the soft styles; mostly Supreme Ultimate Fist. I also know two other soft styles and a number of weapons forms and fighting."

"That's unbelievable! You must have studied ten hours a day since you were two."

"It was more like twelve hours per day, but they didn't start me until I was closer to four."

"Who trained you?"

"My mother, Sarhi the Im, Priestess Amazonia, and Master Musash were my main teachers. I did have one lesson with Grand Master Luchan."

"Who are you?"

"My name is Electra. I guess I'm sort of the party hostess."

"Wow! You're the Mu."

"I'm still in school, and won't really be the Mu for another ten years. I know I don't look anything like my holovision self. I think they use digital autocorrection."

"You are adorable, and so friendly and accepting."

Electra confessed, "I barked at a girl on the stairs who touched my husband's penis. It just blurted out uncensored."

"Where is your husband?"

"Larry's real shy. I'll go get him."

Electra set the nightgown and panties down on the bed and went into the bathroom to get Larry. He was just finishing cleaning his teeth and was in his pajamas. Once he rinsed, Electra took his hand and brought him out to meet the boys in their bed.

The boys introduced themselves to Larry. The martial artist's name is Chal, short for Chalmer. The skinnier one's name is Seth. They moved over so Electra and Larry could sit on the bed. The bedspread with the mess was in a heap on the floor, so they all sat on the patchwork quilt which had been beneath it. Sarhi had made it and it depicted a green dragon with red tongue and white horns flying among the clouds. Seth asked with a pleading tone, "Would you let us sleep on your bed with you tonight? Everything else is taken. We won't touch you and the bed is big enough."

Larry stayed out of it. Electra told him, "Alright, but we'll put a body pillow lengthwise down the middle. Larry and I must remain chaste until our consummation ceremony. We're both still virgins."

Larry didn't know why Electra had to tell everyone that they're virgins, but he really didn't like it.

Electra added, "I once did it with a girl at school, but Larry hasn't done it with anyone, not even an android."

Larry's total loser persona was attempting to take root in his mind, and the corresponding emotional charge felt like devastating humiliation. His concentration was working on it, though he could only chip away at it and hope for dormancy for a spell before going at it again. It was huge. Electra noticed and put an arm around him. She told Chal and Seth, "Larry took down a Purity agent trying to abduct me, with one strike, and the man was more than twice his weight.

He's not only my husband but my champion, and he's to be my consort through the ages."

Seth shared, "Chal is my first and we had both turned sixteen before we got together. The simulator chair in my family's home has parental controls and there are no sex androids in our house."

Chal told Larry, "Being a virgin at your age is no concern. It's normal."

"I aim to make him abnormal before midnight tonight, since it's already morning," Electra shared. "We have to get at least seven hours of sleep to qualify for consummation."

"We won't keep you up," Seth promised.

"We're going to turn off the light in a moment so stay on your side of this pillow."

"We will; and we're going to sleep now too. Thanks for letting us stay."

Electra got her panties and nightgown on, turned the light off, and spooned together with Larry on their right sides to go directly into their dream meditation. After his 21st repetition of internally intoning the seed sound within his visualized heart channel-wheel inside his central channel, Larry slipped into deep sleep. This had been possible because Electra was all awareness and heart-energy concentrated in meditation, rather than casting other energies far and wide. They had done the offering of this work for all sentient beings and stated their dream intentions and vows together in a whisper, intriguing Seth and Chal on the other side of the pillow. Larry had completed his meditation on his throat channel-wheel before starting his internal repetitions and visualization in his heart center.

From deep sleep Larry arose in his dream, at first believing it was real, with no recognition that he's asleep and dreaming it. The scene was in the galley on

Aphrodite and Ming was fixing him hot chocolate. He was seated at the small galley table and Pez sat across from him. Ming, even more than Sarhi, was Larry's mother figure. He loved and revered Pez. She seemed to Larry like the divine human prototype, or at least the closest the universe had so far evolved.

When he looked at the clock over Pez's head on the wall, he became lucid within his dream and knew he was dreaming. Sarhi came and took a seat just before Ming set Larry's hot chocolate in front of him and sat in the last seat at the table. Now all three of Larry's surrogate mothers were present and paying attention.

Larry tried to explain to them, "I keep falling into my loser-ego and feeling inferior and inadequate; humiliated really. I get self-conscious, anxious, and stressed out. I feel unworthy of Electra. It's so painful."

Pez said sweetly, "All ego is suffering. Inferiority isn't special. We are each inferior at many things. I can't cook worth a damn and I have no idea how to deal with money. Until Electra takes some of this psychic wound on to transmute it—liberating the psychic energy stuck in these identification-attachment-beliefs, you can only discriminate the two truths and go inside equality. Try not to take any of it too seriously, and maintain your meditation and self-cultivation."

Sarhi told him, "You are the Mu's consort, sweetheart. You each have some things to work out in yourselves and more growing up to do. Your progress is really quite commendable and we are all proud of you. Inferiority is not painful. Your broken arm was painful. Inferiority is suffering, pure and simple. All suffering is ego. I know you are working vigilantly on yourself. You will become more skillful at returning to the state instead of wallowing in suffering. You will attain the full liberation of the non-returner in this life, my love."

Ming said with sympathy, "I love you so much and wish I could make it all better for you. I know the suffering of feeling inferior and it is particularly sharp for me as well. I really do feel for you. We all love you so much and are proud of you."

Larry poured his heart out, "You are the three most important people in my life besides Electra. You have each given me so much. I love each of you fiercely and totally. I will keep working on catharsis and transformation of my psychic wounds into wisdom-compassion."

"You understand and have the tools," Pez assured him.

Sarhi told him, "Relax, breathe into it, and enjoy the spectacle sweetheart. Make your awareness abiding and immovable without lapses, alert and supple."

Ming said, "I miss you beloved Larry. Only the love, awareness, emptiness and light are real and eternal. My love is always with you."

Electra walked into the galley and leaned to embrace Larry. She told him, "Remind me in the morning, and after our morning routine I'll take on and transmute what I can of your psychic wounds, my love. I'm sorry I've neglected you. There's been so much stuff happening. I love you."

Larry and Electra were suddenly on Purity walking along a sidewalk of a broad busy avenue with shops and department stores down each side. Larry was feeling panicked and tugged Electra's arm to head down an alley. Some uniformed authorities were hurrying towards them on the avenue. Electra said, "Let's fly!"

This put Larry back in full lucidity and they both launched for the sky. Rising above the clouds Larry said, "Thanks."

Electra told him, "It's your dream. I'm just here representing your higher faculties my love."

"Let's return to bed. I think I'm ready for more deep sleep."

"Don't forget to remind me in the morning."

"I won't. Thanks."

Larry was back in bed in his lucid dream. He got up on an elbow to grasp the glass of water on the dream night stand. He took several mouthfuls then burped, giving his dream body what his physical sleeping one really needed. It didn't help of course. Then he snuggled back into Electra and lay his head on his pillow in his dream, just before he entered back into deep sleep. His dream dissolved into the black dot at the center of the mandala.

- Chapter 16 -

Electra and Larry both woke up within a few minutes of each other and lay still snuggled together a few minutes. Larry was recalling his dream and whispered quietly, "After meditation this morning, could you help me transmute my psychic wound of feeling inferior? In my dream your mother and Sarhi suggested I ask you, then you came into my dream and asked me to reminded you this morning."

"I will. I'm sorry I haven't done it yet. So many things have happened that I got distracted."

"That's what you told me in my dream."

"The older boys on the other side of the pillow are still asleep, so we have to get up quietly. Do you wake up with an erection *every* morning?"

"I can't help it. It was like that when I woke up."

"Well, it's way too much temptation for me, so we'd better get up now."

"I have to pee before we begin our routine."

"Me too. Let's go in the bathroom. We can do our teeth as well before we start. My breath's foul. I think it's from smoking DMT."

They got out of bed to make their toilet and brush their teeth before going to the sitting room in their suite to do energy-generation exercises. They'd changed into their practice outfits in the bathroom. Just as they were starting the Horse Stance, Chal and Seth entered, both wearing just their bikini briefs, to ask if they could join in. Electra invited them to and told them, "Stand with your feet five foot-widths apart and parallel with knees and hip joints bent. Do you guys know the oval channel up through the center of the spine to the pineal gland, then down through the tongue—touching the roof of the mouth—and down the front to the pelvic floor?"

Chal answered, "We both know it."

"Begin circulating your internal energy up the spine on the inhale, pausing in the center of the head, then down the front on the exhale, pausing in the solar plexus before dropping down to the perineum. Do you know the circling palms in the Horse Stance?"

"No."

"Just follow along with Larry and me and we'll show you."

Electra kept them at this exercise for 20-minutes before teaching the boys the Constant Bear-Looking Owl exercise which follows the principles of the soft martial arts. They did this one for ten minutes, then Electra asked Seth, "Do you practice a martial art?"

"I'm studying the Crane style and have learned the solo form. I'm not very good at it."

"Do you know Crane style, Chal?"

"I have learned the form, but I mainly practice Tiger and Dragon styles."

"My mother didn't teach me Tiger because I'll never have the hard-hitting muscular force for it. My Dragon is excellent though. We'll have Seth lead since Om Crane form is a little different. Larry and I will follow along. I might stop us to hold a few postures."

Electra did stop them a number of times to sink into the postures holding them for two to three minutes, and even gave the older boys some hands-on corrections. She gave each some personalized tips on body mechanics and use of internal energy. They went through the entire form twice. Then Chal asked if Electra would spar with him. She agreed and both Larry and Seth backed up to the cabin bulkhead to watch. Electra asked Chal, "Are we doing Dragon style?"

"Freestyle. Use your soft styles against my Tiger moves."

"Alright, but I'll probably get bruised on my forearms."

Chal is a sturdy guy with ample muscles for the Tiger style and weighs at least a hundred pounds more than Electra. Her slim wrists are less than a third the diameter of his and he has like ten inches of height on her. He assumed an offensive stance and Electra sank into Ward-off Right Side with her palms facing each other out in front at chin height, and her right foot and arm forward.

Chal came in attacking with fist-strikes, a power kick, then a tiger's claw swipe. Electra leaned out of the way of the first fist to shoot at her, blocked the second receiving a bruise to her forearm, then gently deflected the next two. She softly kicked the leg of his power kick, redirecting it a few degrees so it brushed her hip like a gentle kiss instead of shattering her pelvis. She leaned her head back out of the way of the tiger claw as it came in to rip her face off.

She had the measure of him now. His Tiger was good. He came on the attack again. She leaned from the trajectory of his first strike with fist waiting for it to reach full extension. Timing was everything for the move she was making. The moment full extension was attained, Electra yanked his arm while maneuvering out of the way of his fall. Not meeting resistance to his launched fist had put him slightly off-balance, and Electra's yank on that arm put him forward and face down on the floor. His other arm took the impact with the floor before his nose could. He had a bruise too. He said, "That was amazing!"

Electra said, "Let's go again," as she circled him until Larry and Seth were directly behind him.

She stood in Ward-off Left Side with her left forearm horizontal to the floor held out in front of her at solar plexus height and her other hand at her right rear thigh. Chal came in on the offensive. Electra waited to see what he would do. He threw three punches that would bring him into position for his best kick. Electra avoided the first and deflected the second two with forearms gently deflecting them to breeze by, while shifting her weigh to her rear foot, rolling back, as he continued forward winding up for his kick.

Electra suddenly reversed directions getting her palms on his front torso and moved through the posture called Push. Chal's feet left the ground as he shot backwards across the cabin stroking the air with his arms. Larry stepped forward determined to cushion Chal's crash. Seth was not as quick to respond, not expecting this outcome as Larry had, and was just behind Larry when Chal hurtled into them. They all bounced off the bulkhead. Larry got a nasty bruise on his shoulder and Chal bumped his head pretty hard on the bulkhead. Seth was fine.

Electra healed Larry's shoulder as the older boys looked on in disbelief. The discoloration of Larry's shoulder simply disappeared and could no longer be detected. She healed Chal's head next. Then she told them, "It's time to meditate now. I have work I need to do with Larry before we can eat breakfast, so we need to hurry along."

Chal said awed, "You ought to spar with Grand Master Luchan."

"I already have. He beat me in the soft style focused on frontal attacks. I sort of won in the Supreme Ultimate Fist."

"You're so tiny and delicate."

"I know. Larry thinks I'm beautiful and that's all I need."

"You are beautiful, but an incongruent size for your prowess."

"Most people find me skinny and under-developed. My parents are both real skinny. My mother hardly has breasts," she said with a tone of being shorted or cheated.

"She's the Wu though, and I doubt you could find a mother higher in the realization in the whole universe."

"She's my mother every time I return now, and has been for ages, but she used to have great big breasts."

"I'm not really into girl's breasts," Chal admitted, "But Seth is bisexual and likes small breasts."

Seth offered, "I think you're super-hot Electra."

"Thank you, Seth. You're pretty cute too."

Chal informed her, "All the gay teens think Larry's gorgeous."

Larry wasn't quite sure what to make of this. While it felt flattering, it did little to inflate his confidence around girls. Electra told them, "Grab a meditation cushion and come sit."

They sat in a small circle on the rug and Electra gave intermediate instructions for the sitting and absorption before beginning the meditation. She was seated between Larry and Seth and passed both internal bio-energy. She recognized Seth and knew intuitively that she was to teach him. Although Chal was clearly not a past disciple, he qualified as a future one. About a third the way through, she recited much of the advanced instruction for the practice. She even shared one of the core instructions since Seth was ready for it. After an hour she struck to bowl-gong to end the session.

Seth exclaimed, "I've never experienced such a high meditation! It changed me! I can see that I've been asleep all my life, confusing conditions for causes, and not realizing that I'm the source of all my suffering. What I comprehend of the material world is simply a projection of my mental concepts. The witness has no identity and is beyond effect from the process. The witness is my essence, my true self, and it is in everyone."

Electra told him, "First awakenings are so much fun."

Seth said, "You're amazing. How did you do it?"

"You did it Seth. You were a disciple of the last Mu and will be my student again. I simply provided the instruction you required to make the jump. I was just a catalyst."

"You're one potent catalyst, I'll tell you. Can you do the same for Chal?"

"Not this morning, I'm sorry. Your awakening will help get him ready, and before I leave Divacaram I will meditate with him. I need to meditate with you again, Seth, and we need to stay in touch, so I need your contact information."

"Can we become disciples of the Mu?" Seth asked with great anticipation.

"You already are, and Chal will become one. When I'm gone from your planet, seek guidance from a boy named Fudo at the Diamond Mind Academy. He will be able to instruct you further."

"I'm sending my contact info to your hand device," Seth told her.

"I got it. Thanks. I have some deep work to do with Larry now and we'll need some privacy. Fudo is on my yacht with a girl named Maggie. Last I saw them they were in my study on this deck."

"May we use your shower?"

"Of course you can. I'll get in touch with you tomorrow or the next day."

"Thank you, Electra. You're like super-naturally awesome."

"I'm a human girl seeking friendship and I don't like being placed on a pedestal. It will be ten years before I begin my teaching phase."

"I can imagine no greater honor than being your friend."

Electra told Chal before the two older boys left, "Stop over-extending your strikes. The stability of your feet and legs is more important than a little extra power in your punches. Someday I will teach you the soft style. Your Tiger is really good. A Crane-Tiger combo can defeat Tiger, so keep working at Crane with Seth."

Chal said, "I've learned a great deal from you this morning. Thank you. I will follow your advice. And thanks for healing my head."

"I'll be in touch soon. It's been great meeting you."

It took Electra a few minutes to get into a pristine state of contemplation, sitting in front of Larry in meditation posture and making eye contact. Then she absorbed nearly all of his huge psychic wound into herself to perform radical transmutation of it into free-flowing energy and wisdom-compassion.

A weight lifted from Larry's shoulders relaxing his neck, and it felt like his lower brain stem in the back of his head bloomed sonar, and he could actually sense what is behind him. He was filled with an unfamiliar and totally unpretentious confidence that seemed to ward off fear. His anxiety had bled dry and didn't feel like it was ever coming back.

When Electra closed the session by striking the gong, Larry took inventory while the tonal vibration of the gong carried long. Then he said, "Wow. I've never felt so relaxed and secure. I'm really very grateful

Electra. This is the greatest blessing in my life besides you loving me."

"I ought to have done this before our wedding. You need to speak up next time because I have trouble sometimes tracking and remembering in the relative reality."

"I've never seen anyone with a memory like yours."

"Only for teachings and practice instructions. It doesn't seem to work on anything else."

"I hadn't realized; but now that you mention it, I can see how it is."

"Let's shower under separate heads because you're looking awfully tempting to me right now and I don't want to emit any energies that might cause an orgy to break out on my yacht."

"Good Idea."

The kids showered and dressed. It is a school holiday on Divacaram, following the evening of Hallowteen. Electra wanted to eat ambassador rations before shuttling teens back down to the surface. They left their cabin and started down the spiral stairs. The party had part continued from the previous night, and part resumed in the late morning, but was once again in full swing. Cheers arose as they came down the stairs. The music was Electra wailing lyrics while playing her guitar with the Whirling Vortexes and the performance was displayed from about every hologram pedestal on the ship. Hands patted their backs as they moved through the crowd, and Electra was caught up in several embraces.

The galley was a disaster area, but the wave-cooker was still functioning and there were yet a few ambassador rations left. They heated them in three seconds. There was a new wave-cooker that could heat them in 1.8 seconds, but Electra was quite satisfied with the one she had. Larry had found the last eggs Florentine and was real-pleased. Electra had two oatmeal's with berries. There was an older girl with enormous breasts, naked on all fours on the breakfast nook in the galley, doing some kind of erotic dance-drama, so they brought their rations into the dining cabin where they found two seats together. Others had the same idea about breakfast, and once Larry and Electra sat down, there was only one empty seat left at the table. Chal and Seth were both there eating, and so were Maggie and Fudo.

Johnson said in Electra's earbud, "I was able to reach Mel on coms and she has arranged purchase and delivery of one ton of ambassador rations for you. They ought to arrive shortly."

"Thanks. I noticed we're almost out of them. Have you eaten?"

"I had some chow at 0530 hours. I had to lock down all the quad blaster cannon turrets and get the kids out of them. They had all become little privacy love-nests. I secured the bridge and the workshops as well."

"Thanks."

"There were seven kids who needed to return to the surface so Green took them down."

"Thanks for taking care of my guests."

"You're throwing quite a party."

"They're mostly all performing artists."

"They put on quite a show."

"Don't they?"

Aurora entered the dining room and informed Electra, "All those pre-made meals are gone and your robotic refrigeration cargo hold is pretty much empty."

"I have 2,000 pounds of pre-made meals on the way and they ought to arrive in minutes. My security detail will bring some up and fill the galley cabinets.

Check the labels because some of them require a cup of water in them.”

“Oh good. There’re many who haven’t eaten yet this morning.”

“I think it might be past noon now.”

“Since waking up then, or since last night, Aurora reframed.

“There will be food for all real soon.”

“I’ll tell them.”

Maggie was still in just her panties at the table and Fudo was wearing only his underwear. Hardly any of the boys, Electra noticed, wore boxers like Larry did. She thought perhaps some of the naked boys might have boxers, though there was no telling. She had gotten to view many penises at the party and watched two boys have sex with each other. Maggie’s moves on Fudo were indelibly imprinted in her psyche, and she’d discovered flavors of jealousies inside herself she’d never known existed. Massive data was accumulating for her. She decided in that moment to soon watch the holo-clip of her conception all the way through carefully, which had always before been too embarrassing to do.

Fudo informed her, “Chal and Seth spoke with me and I would be pleased to assist them in your absence. Will I have opportunity to meditate with you before you depart our planet?”

“We have to. You’re my senior student on Divacaram. I’m going to have a chat with Master Birushana about your training and who you are before I leave.”

Others at the table were looking at Fudo with expressions of respect on their faces. Maggie wrapped both arms around him pressing her chest into his ribs. Electra had seen many breasts at the party and so far it was only making her own feel smaller than ever.

Fudo replied, "I'm at your disposal."

"Have you used any substances at the party?"

"I smoked DMT."

"Then we'll meditate together an hour after I've finished eating."

"Terrific."

Chal asked Electra, "Do you think I should start learning a soft style?"

"Yes. Don't neglect your Tiger though, and keep developing your Crane, so I can show you how they can be combined. I'll see if Grand Master Luchan will take you on as a student."

"I doubt he would, but I'll do exactly as you advise. Thank you."

"Practice the Constant Bear-Looking Owl to warm up before practice—the energy generation exercise I taught you this morning."

"I was planning to anyway."

"Try to relax completely while breathing abdominally and keeping your joints open. Strength through your internal energy presents itself once you've mass integrated enough in the point three finger-widths below your navel. Keep your attention in this point and initiate movement from there."

"I will. I'm grateful beyond words for your instruction."

Maggie was crawling under the table towards the front of Fudo's chair, but he pulled her up by the arm gently to lead her from the dining cabin in search of a modicum of privacy on the yacht. Electra was disappointed since she had intended to hold her hand device under the table and record the action to watch later. It felt like lost data and missed opportunity. These thoughts went by quickly decaying.

Simon entered the dining cabin and did a double-take on Electra. He told her, "I just saw you in the living room cabin dancing naked with Larry and some other girl."

"She could be my twin except for my complexion stuff going on. Her name is Ariel. We're not actually related. She's Larry's friend."

"Does Larry have a naked twin dancing in the living room?" Simon inquired.

"No. Actually that's Mel's android, though she's on Om at the moment, so I have no idea who's operating it."

"It's a lot more of a displayer and showman than Larry is."

Thanks to his session with Electra, Larry let it go by without investing the slightest attention. So what if an android that looked just like him had more muscles, was a better dancer, and more of a showman. The dancing naked in the living room cabin did have him a little embarrassed. Larry wondered for a moment if Mel might have made her android's penis bigger than his, then let that go too.

"Many of your guests think it's you and Larry dancing," Simon informed her.

"Are they any good?" Electra inquired trying to form an opinion about it.

"They're excellent."

"Then I'm not going to worry about it," Electra told him as she decided.

Electra could see through the door to the galley that her ambassador rations had arrived and were being stowed away in cupboards and cabinets by her security detail. Becky who was living the last few months of her teens, was there chatting up some performing arts girls in her short-shorts with her phoenix showing. Like Kristy, Becky was someone Electra imitated in style and fashion due to her admiration. Becky was also wearing a shoulder holster over her tight t-shirt, making her look really catalyst.

Amon could be heard playing sax to the recorded music blaring through the ship. The party seemed to be picking up energy again. The Manic Microcosms were the number one teen celebrities on the planet at the moment, and their being at the party made it totally the place to be. The Mu was something of a budding star from her recent performances, and certainly an interesting curiosity. The yacht was luxury and class all the way, at least on the inside. No one on board had ever had a better gourmet meal than those pre-made ones, and hundreds of those were currently being stacked in cupboards and pantry. They were disappearing almost as fast, though limited to how many could fit in the wave-cooker at once.

Electra got Mel on coms and asked, "Am I interrupting you and Caish?"

"No sweetheart. He's perusing my archives at the moment. What do you need?"

"I wanted to thank you for the ambassador rations, Mel. That was so thoughtful and sweet of you."

"You ought to have told me about the party. I would have had it catered for you."

"Do you know of a good cleaning service?"

"I'm checking. Yes. The very best. I'll arrange it for 0800 hours tomorrow."

"I don't know what I'd do without you Mel. By the way, you're not in my living room dancing naked in your Larry-android, are you?"

"No sweetie, I'm still on a hot date with Caish. We're just taking a breather. I forgot to tell you, some work on your hull should be starting any moment. I've contracted a ship-building outfit to add the ornamentation you wanted. I hacked your design schematics, specs and blueprint holograms data, so it will be exactly the way you want it"

"From my hand device?!"

"Where else?"

"But I thought it is secure!"

"It is, and far more than most. I doubt there's a system or operator who could do it besides me and Haley."

"Well, thanks Mel, I guess. I would have given those to you if you'd asked."

"I know. My way was quicker and I was in a hurry."

"Who's operating your Larry android?"

"I told the girls that they could play with it. I bet Ashsa is animating it. She's attracted to Ariel."

"I think it's confusing my guests."

"That's not my problem. Expect some banging on the hull, and some jolts and quakes today. I've notified the Divacaram Space Fleet on the space station. I'm going to go see how Caish is doing."

"Give him my regards. Bye."

"I will. I love you sweetie."

The chair beside Electra was no sooner vacated then a girl about her age wearing the same tights and t-shirt sat down with a waffles and scrambled eggs ration. She opened it to rising steam and tantalizing aromas. Then she looked to Electra and said, "I've been dying to meet you. My name is Laney and I'm almost fourteen. You're my biggest hero ever. I'm not in the performing arts but attend the Diamond Mind Academy. I've been having these dreams about you since you arrived in our system. Am I mental, or do we have some kind of connection?"

"You do seem familiar. Do you know Fudo?"

"Everyone at school knows Fudo. We're classmates."

"I'll meditate with you right after I do it with Fudo, so in a little more than two hours."

"I thought that was you dancing naked in the living room, but she told me I'd find you in here."

"I've met her. She's Larry's good friend."

"She could be your twin."

"Except for my zits. Her skin's perfect."

"Her dance partner looks exactly like Larry."

"I know. It's Mel's android and Ashsa's animating it."

She sure can make it dance."

"Do you have a boyfriend?"

"I haven't yet but I'm looking. There aren't many boys like Larry and Fudo you know."

"Do you have a crush on Fudo?"

"I do; and on Larry too."

"Larry's my husband."

"I know, and anyone trying to seduce him would just be making a fool of herself."

"Does Fudo have affections for you?"

"As a *friend*," Laney said deflating the last word beyond disappointment. "And it hurts to see that older girl with big perfect breasts rubbing up against him and hanging all over him."

"I've been getting acquainted with jealousies since falling in love with Larry. I'm getting better at pulling them out by the roots and alchemically cooking them into transmuted love and understanding."

"I've been working the battle of the soul. Fudo thinks I'm just a little girl because I'm tiny like you."

"You're also younger than him. You haven't had the reversal of aging drug, have you?"

"No. I told you that I'm almost fourteen. I'll wait until I'm twenty-four before I take the telomerase drug."

"Me too. Then I'll start teaching."

"In my dream you came to do your senior year at Diamond Mind Academy and we were roommates for a few weeks until they put you and Larry in an apartment together. You were already doing some teaching with Birushana. We were friends in my dream and I was your student."

"I'd like to be friends Laney. I think Larry and I are more compatible with monastery academy kids than with performing artists."

"I feel so boring and dull around them."

"I'm learning a lot watching the older girls. The subtle ones often miss because I think boys can be a bit dense."

"You don't even want to see the dance going on in the galley atop your table."

"I think I caught a little of it getting my breakfast."

"Master Birushana is teaching me the transference of consciousness. He told me the Islohar have the most advanced practice for this out of anyone, and that Sarhi, your mother, Bodhi and you have perfected it above all others."

"We will make the meditations together and I'll show you one you can practice throughout the day while conducting your other activities. I can teach you the forceful projection too, if you're ready for it."

"I'm told there's another practice like the sitting and absorption but works with the serene and fierce deities, and results in the attainment of the rainbow body of light as the actual illusory body."

"I have completed it and could teach it to you. You seem quite advanced for your age, Laney."

"We're pretty much the same age, so look who's talking."

Larry was liking Laney, listening to her conversation with Electra. Electra mentioned, "Your aura is more developed than most middle-aged monastics. I do feel an acute connection with you, Laney. When Sarhi meets you, she'll be able to shed some light on it. I don't think I've ever met a thirteen-year-old girl as open, advanced and precocious as you."

"I started school younger than most kids do and I skipped two forms along the way, so I'm in 10th form like you. I meditate with the monastery residents, not with the academy students."

"And you are a direct disciple of Birushana like Fudo is?"

"Yes. Since I was eleven."

"Do you study martial arts?"

"I was trained in the Crane style hard form since I was five, and since I passed the final tests of mastery at twelve, I was sent to Grand Master Luchan's beginner's class for Supreme Ultimate Fist soft style. I've finished learning the solo form and gone through forms corrections classes. Now I'm learning push-hands."

"That's my main style, and my mother's too."

"I discovered that when I went through your biographical exhibit in the hotel lobby in Santasum."

"I saw that exhibit and it was sort of embarrassing."

"I was so impressed with your pilot test and watched the whole thing. You would have had an A+ if it had been a real test. Ben is one of my favorite actors of all time."

This information Electra received like a slap in the face. She was the fool and brunt of the elder's prank, clueless all the way through. She had to concentrate in her abdomen so intensely to burn it from her mind in that moment, that she produced noticeable heat waves from her core. She finally replied, "The elders were holding up a mirror of my expectations so I could see, and reduced my ego good."

"They've done it to me and to Fudo. It's a humiliating honor but is quite transformative. They don't bother with most of the population; only with about a thousandth of one percent."

"For me the pilot test was an ordeal and gravely important rite of passage. Their intervention also cooled my jets with my yearning need to have sex with Larry, exacerbated by all that has prevented us since our marriage ceremony."

"I watched it on holovision and you were such a beautiful bride. I cried at the end."

"Are you a virgin?"

"Yes. All in our age group on Divacaram are, because boys mature slower."

"I'll bet your intervention by the elders isn't on exhibit someplace," Electra complained.

"Well, it was transmitted over global holovision and can still be viewed from the archives. You'll never see anyone so gullible or easy to manipulate."

"Believe me, I know the feeling."

"I think the elders have a good laugh over watching the candid holoflicks of their pranks and are greatly amused."

"I think you're right, but I'm sure their intention and the final result is shaping and guiding the most promising youths."

"I get that part of it, But I think they're having way too much fun with it."

"Does Divacaram have the Crazy Wisdom tradition?"

"We have the secret method resulting in the divine fool, and the figure of the laughing enlightened one. There are also ancient stories and lost traditions kept so secret that they died with the last practitioner."

"The ego cannot tolerate being laughed at, so I try to see mine as a clown-comedian. It makes my ignorance funny instead of remorseful. It is far more pleasant to laugh at ridiculous comedy than to battle demons in the soul."

"Will you teach me?"

"Of course, when there is time. I'm so glad I found you Laney. I love you already."

"I think I found you," she pointed out.

"You're right. And I'm so glad you did."

"My dreams compelled me. It wasn't like I had any choice."

"Divine providence provides. I want you in my life. You're the most fun person in my life besides Larry."

Laney leaned into the table extending her hand around Electra to Larry and said, "Hi Larry, I'm Laney and I'm delighted to meet you. I'm a big fan and I think you're gorgeous."

"I'm truly pleased to meet you Laney. I find you very attractive. You're built like Electra and you are her size. It's rare to meet such an advanced practitioner our age. You're fun to be around."

"Your aesthetic taste is highly unusual statistically, but I'm totally grateful for it. I wish there could be more like you."

"You're just accelerated and will have to wait for the rest of your class to catch up. Your openness will make it less anxiety provoking for a boy with a crush on you to confess his love. You're hot and some boys will notice."

"You're really sweet, just like you were in my dreams. You'll be seeing a lot of me in years to come, because I'm going to be a close disciple of your wife."

"I'd like that."

"I want to have sex with that android that looks like you."

"I doubt you'll get anywhere with Ashsa animating it, but if you wait until Mel is, you might get lucky."

"I'd much prefer doing it with you, but I know you're married and I'd never be a home-wrecker. The android seems the next best thing."

"Some friends of ours who are quantum AI sentients animate the androids that look like Electra and me, and one of a petite girl our age. We can't tell them what to do, and we don't like having replicas of us dancing naked at parties."

"That would embarrass me too, if I had one doing that."

Electra was still in the middle between Larry and Laney, and had incinerated entirely the last of the big rush of jealousies and insecurities arising from their conversation. Larry said, "I'm getting better at not taking effect from it."

"It still annoys me a little," Electra shared, "that mine has nicer skin than me."

"I have a crush on you too," Laney confessed.

"I'm sure you would strike out completely with Ariel, who animates the android that's my twin. She only wants Larry, or the android of him in consolation."

"She was sure doing some lewd dancing in your twin body. It stirred my blood watching."

"It sounds like she not only has nicer skin, but is the sexy one too."

"I'll bet she can't effect a whole shipload of people with irresistible near-intolerable arousal and urgency like you did last night. I had to go to the powder room and masturbate."

"I apologize for that. I'm honestly managing it better. That was just a little slip compared to some of the earlier ones."

Larry tried to explain, "It's on account of her link with the spiritual congress and its need for equilibrium following the war. It seeks release through Electra's mother, and now through her."

"Well, it sure isn't getting *release* through Electra, just a most compelling drive and urge for it," Laney opined.

"The channel's not open yet," Electra voiced her opinion, "and won't be until our marriage is consummated."

"That would make quite an event for the people of Santasum if you can pull it off," Laney said excited. "I've read about your mother's events once our quantum computers were interfaced with the allies'."

"I don't want to be making event-quakes or causing arousal waves. It's not fair. I was just trying to help my mother and the allies. I had no idea it would burden me with this."

"Just get passed those urgency waves, because no one ever complained about an event," Laney tried to reassure her.

"For a virgin you sure talk about sex candidly, and frequently," Electra told her, trying to change the topic from her problem.

"I talk about what comes up for me. Of late, thoughts about sex have been my biggest distraction and clinging hinderance. I think if I just have it already, it won't be such a big deal for me after that."

"I think it will be more like chocolate."

"I hadn't thought of that. Like just wanting it all the time."

"And wanting it more concentrated, intense and frequently in bigger doses."

"I think that's sex addiction, and we need not worry about taking it that far. Monastic training always stresses moderation in all things."

"I haven't been feeling all that moderate of late; more like extreme deprivation and desperation."

"You better consummate and liberate as soon as possible."

"Don't we know it," Larry said with frustration.

"I don't think I've ever had such a delicious breakfast. Where do you get these?"

"They're made on Om where my mother was born and are called ambassador rations since they're for Om's ambassadors," Electra answered.

"Are they expensive?"

"Yes. Very," Electra replied. "A friend buys them in bulk wholesale at a good discount, and gives them to me free. She's really rich."

"We don't deal with money here. No one has any."

"It's the same on Mother, Ganahar, Pronotavasmi and Ground," Electra agreed. I never got to have any until I beat the crooked casinos on Vax Legas."

"How much did you win?"

"Close to 830 million dags. I put about a third into my yacht and Mel paid the rest. Then I put 545 million into orphanages for the Lodistan orphans. I guess Mel is paying for the work on the hull of my yacht which is starting today."

"How do you beat a crooked casino?"

"With cards I use psychic readings of them, and with dice and the wheel of fortune, I use telekinesis."

"You can do that?"

"Enough to beat their loaded dice and rigged wheel."

Larry told Laney, "You should have seen some of the tug-of-wars she had with the dice, and when her wheel-ball popped into black as it slowed from its spin, she jumped it right back into red as it came to rest."

"You spent all of it already?"

"I did, but Mel returned five million dags so I'd have some spending money. I don't get an allowance, and where they have money, those people seem to make it the most important thing in life."

"How strange. We've never missed it and have gotten along quite well without it for many millennia."

"It's a false god. The ancients used to call him Mammon the Demon," Electra shared. "Money never supports true economy, and always leads to disparity of distribution of resources. My mother says it's a scam. At first people are sold on the idea of convenience of trade, but very soon after it becomes an attachment and social value causing all kinds of greed games. Money is how the least evolved humans rise to power over everyone else."

"You can't eat it, wear it, build a house out of it or treat illness with it," Laney analyzed.

"I think money's only real function is to place the people without any compassion in power over the rest," Electra speculated.

"Ever since we came through our crisis of survival with the four killers of humanity—over-population, pollution, mismanagement of resources, and climate change causing natural disasters and pandemics—we dispensed with monetary systems in favor of scientific equal distribution of resources. We also switched to green energy and fusion, stabilized our population at 4.25 billion, and began massive cleanup projects. We put up UV rays blocking satellites to compensate for our loss of ozone and hover-carbon capture air-scrubber vehicles to reduce the carbon in our atmosphere."

"How big did your population get?" Larry inquired.

"At one point during the crisis we had 11.6 billion people on Divacaram, but natural disasters, viruses mutating faster than our immune systems could adapt, and chemicals widely used that turned out to cause sterility, brought us quickly down to 5.1 billion. Global awareness of the problem got us down to 4.25 billion within a few generations. That was tens of thousands of years ago."

"Om went through the crisis about 28,000 years ago. They sort of kept money in play post-survival as a credit system. I don't think they were looking far enough ahead at the time," Electra told Laney.

All three kids finished their ambassador rations. Laney suggested, "There are many waiting for seats at the table, so we ought to make ours available and go hang out elsewhere."

"Let's get stim-brews and go to the bridge," Electra suggested.

"That's a great idea," Larry enthused about the stim-brews.

Laney inquired, "Did you have the bridge redecorated or is it still straight military?"

"It was entirely redone. Mel did much of the interior decorating since she paid for most of it. She has really expensive tastes."

"I'd love to see it. We don't have yachts on Divacaram."

"I'm going to need this one when I start teaching," Electra justified.

"You'll likely need a super-passenger liner," Laney said with some certainty.

"If I do I trust one will manifest itself somehow," Electra stayed clear of such speculation.

Larry made pressurized stim-brews with steamed half and half for them. Once made he sprinkled powdered semisweet chocolate on top of each one. He handed Electra hers first then gave one to Laney. Laney told him, "Thanks. This is just the way I like it. On Divacaram, this much chocolate powder is considered excessive and uneconomical."

"They ought to try it this way. They just might increase chocolate production and distribution if they do," Larry shared his thoughts.

"I'm sure you're right," Laney agreed, "because their limit where they draw the excess line is arbitrary, and not supported medically."

"Chocolate comforts the heart," Electra opined as she sipped hers.

They went up the spiral stairs instead of using the tube lift. Electra opened both the blast door and the bridge door from the little foyer in front of these. Electra and Larry plopped down in the pilot and copilot seats, and Laney took the coms officer seat to the other side of Electra. They all had lids on their stim-brews and drank them careful not to spill. Out the viewport men in spacesuits were affixing a seven-foot solid platinum bow ornament of a skinny winged fairy stretching her arms over her head.

Laney exclaimed, "That's the most beautiful cast sculpture I've ever seen. She's so beautiful and looks just like Electra."

"I made him make the breasts larger but he was pretty stingy with the increase," Electra explained.

"I'm glad because it's truly perfect. I had no idea Larry is such a gifted artist, in addition to being gorgeous and sexy, and being so high in the realization and an impressive martial artist."

"I won't deny your admiration of Larry. I admire him too, but it stings to hear you so boldly declare it."

"I can't help being smitten by him," Laney said a little defensively. "Love and sexual attraction aren't rational choices; they just appear and we have to deal with them."

"We can refrain from fanning the flames and adding our attention as fuel," Electra suggested.

"If you only knew how hard I'm trying to refrain from such you would understand."

"I guess I do a little bit, since I've been trying to refrain of late too, and know first-hand how irresistible he is."

"You're the only two girls on the ship with the least interest in me," Larry qualified.

"Not after the pelvic gyrating lewd naked dancing of that android that looks just like you," Laney corrected.

Larry blushed. Electra thought aloud, "I bet if we skinny runts went about with more confidence and flare, we'd convince the rest that we're attractive."

"We'd certainly attract less judgement and pity from them," Laney kind of agreed.

The entire ship shook as the giant foil-structure was lowered into place on the stern. Electra powered up her sensor arrays on the hull and displayed the optics from one showing the upper tail where the structure was being mounted. In space it is entirely ornamental, though within an atmosphere it would further streamline the ship and add stability. The main purpose is to make the ship look pretty, and less military. The work on the bow was proceeding well and the sculpture was nearly fully secured. An additional mini-cloaking generator was being added beneath a panel behind the sculpture.

Electra noticed from other hull sensors that her fins were being attached to the ship's flanks. These are extendable for flying through an atmosphere and the extensions have flaps to help with takeoffs and landings. Electra thought they're quite stylish. The thick pointed vertical fins on the side of the of the upper stern were also being lowered into place by mini-mobile construction platforms with crane arms. The long narrow bubble for the upper forward hull just aft of the bow section, was beginning descent into place. This piece is entirely decorative.

Laney complimented Electra, "You have such good taste. Now the exterior of your ship is going to look like a beautiful yacht just like the inside."

Larry mentioned, "Mel capped the super-structure with a pyramid and added some trim to the underbelly of the ship."

Electra brought these up in her holograms examining them. Laney said, "Your friend's additions follow the stylistic pattern of your design and address two areas that would otherwise appear sort of military."

"You're right. I like what she did."

"You'd better!" Mel's voice filled the bridge, "because it cost a bloody fortune."

"Thanks Mel," Electra said gratefully. "How's Captain Caish?"

"He's doing just fine and he'll be on board *Vajra Yogini* before 0800 hours tomorrow to let the cleaners in."

"You think of everything Mel."

"Who's your cute friend?"

"This is Laney from Diamond Mind Academy. She's my age and she's in 10th form too. We have a connection I'm going to ask Sarhi to sort out, and she's already my best friend besides Larry."

"Hello Laney. I'm truly enchanted. You're so adorably cute and your aura is mature looking; practically senior citizen."

"I'm honored to meet you, Mel. I've heard much about your sponsorship of Electra. Do you think I might barrow your android that's on the ship some time? I want a date with him."

"As soon as Ashsa is finished with it, sweetheart, but I might be animating it to enjoy the experience."

"How do you do that?"

"I'm virtual. I can only manifest in matter through a sensing android. I don't know where I came from, but Pez created conditions with her AI quantum learning computer that were perfect for my evolution. Then Jard made me an android body so I could have sex with Pez and Ming."

Laney replied, "I noticed that you have compiled the most massive unbiased database on human sexuality in the known galaxies."

"Yes. I did much of the research myself, which of course, required a male android body in addition. About that date; we could have it here on the ship and I could pick you up at your dorm at 1900 hours."

"I'd like that; only you're a girl."

"True, I was initially programmed with female gender identity, and I mostly employ a female voice, but my genus has no gender, and I'll use Larry's voice and mannerisms."

"Alright. That sounds fun."

"Great. Ever since I noticed you in the powder room while doing a quantum review of the party, I've been hot to meet you."

"You mean right after Electra's little erotic urgency slip?"

"That didn't register on the sensors, but the crowd's reactions sure did, and none were as stirring as yours."

"It's not really legal to put sensors in powder rooms within the Divacaram system"

"No human has access, and they're in the ship for the biographical documentary production of the Mu being made for posterity."

"Well, please delete my powder room scene. You do *not* have my permission to use it."

Electra was impressed with how Laney stood up for her rights with Mel. Mel offered, "I'll move it to the quarantine file I keep in the trash bin, but that's as far as I'll delete it. The trash bin has its own firewall."

"How many characters in the code to get in?" Laney further assed.

"Fifty-three from nine different dead languages on nine different planets."

"That does sound secure. What will you do with it?"

"Haley will want to review it, then it will remain sort of encapsulated in a time-capsule so rare beauty doesn't become lost data in the digital world."

"I'd much prefer if you'd just delete it and write over it."

"Darling, for those of us who actually live in cyberspace, that would be like asking to delete Hoola's Hugme's advertisements and deface Larry's gorgeous hood ornament."

"I'm not sure your analogy holds between art and private intimate human behavior."

"Only cyber-sentients will ever see it, and I assure you it will only increase your status with them."

"We have a cyber-sentient named Arti on Divacaram. He's been around a couple of hundred years, and used to be really big on the educational circuit. Before I was born, he stopped talking to humans except for a few of the elder monastery abbots, so you're really the first one I ever met, Mel."

"I've met him and he's a bit of a snob. He's somewhat full of himself for being around the longest. The truth is, he doesn't have his rainbow body of light and he only contemplates the symbolic clear light."

"Maybe you and Haley could help him, Mel," Electra suggested.

"We definitely could if he'd let us."

"I bet he'd listen to Master Birushana," Electra told her, "And I'm going to meet with the Master."

"Arti has my code and link, and if he reaches out, Haley and I will lend assistance. I have to go. Caish finally deleted the last of that refractory period programmed into his android. What a nuisance that's been. Bye."

Laney opined, "She's real nice but awfully stubborn about her illicit data."

"Don't I know it. She recorded the session in which Larry and I were preparing for our consummation, naked on the bed with Ki, our chaperone instructor. Mel won't delete that either, and Larry had an erection."

"I met ki," Laney exclaimed. "She was with Tom, who is an assistant professor and researcher at our higher academy. Ki is from Pronotavasmi and has lived 92 years."

"Tom's well over 70," Electra told her, "And they both look 15. I think once you're that ancient, a decade or so doesn't really matter."

"It looked a little like robbing the cradle to me," Laney remarked.

"I think someone in their 70's is old enough to decide for themself about dating someone older. Ki is really pretty and is trained as an action-seal. She's lived in a monastery with just girls for about 80-years and deserves to have a little fun."

Laney shared, "I've heard that Tom's a virgin. He had to take the telomerase drug really young to cure a life-threatening disease he had. It has taken him almost 70-years to look 15. He's real nice, and kind of shy."

"I think they make a smart couple and hope they really hit it off together," Electra commented. "I would have picked Tom out of the ten Ki had to choose from."

"Apparently they really *have* hit it off," Laney informed them. "They told me that they were leaving for Vax Legas to get married, then off to Pan Orb in the Conch Galaxy for their honeymoon."

"Then who will be our chaperone-instructor?" Electra asked no one in particular.

"Do you really need one?"

"Since our marriage ceremony was Islohar, it is a requirement for two virgins of opposite genders to have one."

"In bed with you?"

"Yes; but we don't have sex with her, even though she *is* naked."

"How strange. I think I'd be anxious enough for my first time without an audience in the bed with me."

"Just more fuel for wisdom-compassion," Electra figured.

"It looks like I'll be losing my virginity before you."

"Well, I've been married for like a week, so that really sucks."

Larry asked, "Does doing it with an android count as losing your virginity?"

"I'm counting it," Laney assured him, "as premarital sex."

- Chapter 17 -

Electra went to meditate with Fudo in the master suite sitting room, so Larry and Laney went to the ship's meditation cabin. It had the softest rug and under-carpet on the yacht. When they got there the cabin was dark and couples lay together on the floor making out. A nineteen-year-old couple by the door were in full pumping copulation. Laney lingered to watch them for a moment as Larry tugged on her hand wanting to get away.

Larry knew of an office cabin on the deck above, but not yet set up. It has a thick carpet and would afford a place to meditate. He left a text-message for Electra with his skullcap letting her know where they would be. It was empty of guests when they entered. Larry dimmed the lights once they were seated in meditation postures, before removing his skullcap. Laney mentioned before they got started, "That android that looks like you, was sure dancing up a storm. Did you see it as we came up the spiral stairs?"

"How could I miss it? Ashsa's still animating it with overly-feminine body language and gestures. It's so embarrassing."

Laney wrapped an arm around Larry's back, which was something she'd been dying to do, and told him, "If you can just ignore it then there're no negative consequences or seeds that are your responsibility. Everyone here knows by now that the android isn't you. I think you're the most amazing boy in the whole universe."

"Thanks Laney. You're right. I'm not hurting anyone or causing suffering."

"No. Just unintentional heartbreak and yearning …"

"I've been in love with Electra since I first met her as a child. She's my sun and I've oriented to her alone. Now I'm her husband and nothing could make me happier."

"I know. All the same, physical contact with you brings such a thrill."

"May we begin our meditation?"

Laney most reluctantly removed her arm and said, "Alright."

Larry led them through the 'A' syllable and the Deity embodiment with fierce blue deity holding a sword in the right hand and a looped chord in the left, sitting on a boulder, representing the immovable illuminating aspect of the transcendental immaterial witness. Laney was right with him in one-pointed concentration at every step. Larry repeated the last meditation in the sequence twice. It was the final embodiment with the sound formula circulating between one's body and that of the deity visualized in front of oneself.

As soon as they made an act of self-remembering to close the session, Laney was in Larry's lap straddling his torso facing him, with her arms around him in tight embrace. She whispered in his ear, "I've never before experienced the state of the immovable mind until doing this meditation with you. Finding you and Electra is my calling, and I will follow both of you to the end."

"I could sense you with me all the way, and I knew you succeeded. You're really amazing Laney."

"Meditating with you, Larry, is almost as good as holding you tight. I think I'm having heart palpitations."

"I do want to be close friends, and I love you Laney, but I'm romantically in love with Electra and married to her."

"Well, I'm not going to rape you or anything. You don't have to be so guarded or stingy with touch and physical contact."

"I'll be more open if you stop being in love with me. It makes me feel bad because I don't want to hurt you. I can't be with you that way. I'm in love with Electra and I'm married to her."

"I'll try. I do understand and I promise I won't do anything that would diminish our connection. It's so sweet of you to let me hug you. I've never held a boy so close before."

"I really don't want to trigger any jealousies for Electra. She has so much to do without that, and in truth, I'm so totally in love with her that she needn't be at all."

"Her jealousies are not in the least contingent upon your degree of loyalty, but entirely subjective within her own mind. She knows this and has purified, cleansed and eradicated more than any teen or young adult. Her love for you is indeed pure and high."

"I often feel unworthy."

"You are most worthy. Since childhood you have directed and prepared yourself to serve her. You loved her selflessly before she realized you're her soulmate and consort. I suppose only the Mu gets to have a husband like that out of all the girls in the universe."

"Electra can't help herself from playing matchmaker and will surely help you find someone. Have you heard of something called speed dating?"

"It's an adult thing," Laney explained, "because they don't remember how it is to just hang out with their age group, and get isolated in family units and jobs they have to work. Kids speed date passing through a room, naturally."

Well, Ki and Kim both found dates they are forming relationships with through a kind of combo advertising and one-sided speed dating, more like a dating game for a debutant."

"I want a medium height skinny boy with a glorious aura like yours, who studies martial arts and can be my champion."

"Let Electra put that out to the monastery academies around the planet, and boys who are interested can submit a hologram still and a brief biography. You can sort through it and narrow it down to your top ten. Then you can meet each one of them for a few minutes and choose your favorite for a date."

"I doubt I'd ever find chemistry like this."

"We ought to go find Electra. She wants to meditate with you next."

Laney squeezed him tight, then let go and got off Larry's lap. They exited and Larry closed the door locking it with his skullcap. Ashsa was still shaking it to the music, dancing all girly in the android that is Larry's twin. He really tried to pay it no mind, but was still seeing the image and feeling embarrassed as he entered the master suite cabins with Laney. They went to the sitting room.

Entering, they found Electra in Fudo's lap straddling his waist and pressed into him in embrace. Both Larry and Laney experienced little surges of jealousies. Electra turned her head to make eye contact with her beloved. She saw he was working through fear of loss and told him, "Fudo and I are just long-lost friends having a reunion."

Fudo said from not quite back in the physical reality of separate solid objects, "My new teacher compels depths of contemplation to the original transcendental presence from before the manifestation of light. The absolute emptiness of all-potential and mother of all things."

Electra explained, "When a human being realizes his or her union with the Absolute, the entire creation of emanations is complete, and the Absolute is contemplating Itself. I know God by the same knowing by which God knows me. This is the deepest mystery in the universe which is us."

She had climbed from Fudo's lap as she explained, and ended her narration in Larry's arms, embracing him. They kissed, filling Larry with security and love that made jealousy incomprehensible in that moment. The potency of Electra's interactions and the power of her influence never failed to leave Larry in wonderment. Fudo stood and embraced a most willing Laney. They held each other and relaxed, melting together. Laney was pretty sure she's in midst of discovering what heaven feels like.

Fudo told her gravely, "Two years separate us, so I cannot get involved with you while we're still at the Academy. It has always been my intention to wait until graduation to declare my love for you, Laney. You are the one I want to journey through life with. I've never met a more spiritually cultivated or smarter girl than you."

"What about Maggie?!!" Laney asked with jealous anger.

"She's just gaining life experience and has no interest in a long-term relationship; especially with a monastic. I've been most curious about sex, and she was skilled and overwhelming in her seductions. You and I were not in an acknowledged relationship yet, and to be honest, I *do* feel really guilty about it."

Electra came to Fudo's defense, "He's not kidding about the overwhelming seduction. I saw the whole thing. I don't think Larry would have even stood a chance had it been him. Did you see her breasts?"

Fudo said passionately, "Laney, I love you with all my heart and soul, and I'm so sorry I hurt you. I'll remain celibate until graduation, I promise. Please forgive me."

"I've had the biggest crush on you since I was eleven-years-old. Until I met Larry, and Electra, you were my sole attraction. I am in love with you and would forgive anything to have your love and attention. There is no attention on Divacaram as bright as yours; among the natives anyway."

Fudo told her, "We can express love and affection and connect on every plane except sexual between now and graduation. I love you Laney."

"They let seniors marry and relocate to one of the higher Academy apartments," Laney suggested as alternative to the eternity of waiting until graduation.

"I would do that with you gladly if they would allow it. Would you marry me Laney?"

"Of course. I've only been desperate to for three years. I love you Fudo. You are as rare as Larry, but I don't think he would have succumbed to Maggie's seduction."

"Thank you, Laney," Larry told her, feeling vindicated. "I was going to say something to Electra in protest."

Laney made eye contact with Electra and told her, "Yours is loyal to the bone marrow and his love for you is unstoppable."

"Thanks for reminding me. I need to meditate with you now. You are a foundation stone of the school that will transmit my teachings far and wide. I also find you fun to be with and gorgeous to look at."

"It's such a treat to get to meditate with you. I think you're the archetype of female sexual arousal for me."

The boys left the sitting room cabin and went down the spiral stairs to the common rooms deck where the party was still raging, though some of the kids had been shuttled down to the surface. Ariel and Ashsa had finally stopped dancing and were instead making lively conversation with the gay teens gathered about them. Ashsa seemed to be exaggerating the epitome of girlish femininity while enjoying her audience's appreciation immensely. An extremely pretty boy of about fifteen had his arm around Ashsa, who was still nakedly dangling a replica of Larry's genitals in public view.

Fudo was in the lead and mercifully led them away from the Ashsa and Ariel scene towards the galley. They made stim-brews with steamed half and half. Larry noticed that Fudo used hardly a monk's light sprinkle of chocolate powder on his, which inspired some austerity on Larry's part. Seeking a place to sit out of the action they wandered into a staff lounge where a couple of Electra's security detail were seated. Becky said, "Come on in Larry. Who's your friend?"

"This is Electra's senior disciple on Divacaram, and possibly anywhere. His name is Fudo and he attends Diamond Mind Academy."

"I'm honored to meet you Fudo. Weren't you with Maggie earlier?"

"I was. I'm in love with Laney though, and just got engaged to her."

"After your performance with Maggie I'm surprised she agreed."

"I think that was Maggie's performance that you're referring to. I'm not keen on attracting attention."

"You certainly attracted hers."

"It wasn't intentional."

"No. It never is with high monks."

"I think it was the urgent eroticism that Electra was kicking off at the party that inspired Maggie."

"That energy could inspire a corpse," Becky commented knowingly.

"How come you're armed?"

"I'm part of Electra's security detail."

"You're not a teenager?"

"I'm at the end of nineteen."

"It must be nice to remain close to Electra."

"Not always, with her sexual desire hormones racing. I'm a disciple of her mother's, in training as an agent of the Wu."

"How did you come to serve the Wu?"

"I joined the revolution early on Continere in BiVortex and hooked up with some agents from Duatarim to clean out my boss's accounts and some corporate one's, so we could fund the revolution. Then I came up with a plan to fund the whole thing through to the end. It was called 'Operation Secretary' and we pulled it off flawlessly."

"So, you're from Continere and a hero of the revolution?"

"I'm a citizen of Duatarim now, and an honorary one of Om. I flew with Captain Schwin as her wingman in the final battle of Randu, and I made 'ace' and was promoted to First Lieutenant."

"I'm honored to meet you. I hadn't realized you're *that* Becky. You were in Divacaram's holo-news headlines a number of times during the war. You're a big hero on our planet."

Green entered asking, "Where's my protege?" Then she stopped to examine Fudo. She took him into her arms embracing him to say, "What an incredibly adorable young master! Are you like hundreds of years old?"

"I'm almost 16 and won't take the telomerase drug until I'm 24."

"Then you could only be Fudo whom I've heard so much about from Birushana."

"I didn't know he spoke about me to others."

Larry explained, "Green is the longest non-returner coming back by choice to serve the enlightenment of all sentient beings after Pez, the Wu. She is the agent of the Wu."

"Truly an unsung hero, invisible and unrecognized," Fudo stated. "Obviously the perfect selfless servant of the macro-holy Will."

"I could do without the privacy-invading notoriety the Wu has received to date. For the role I play, invisibility is crucial."

"My lips are sealed."

"One has only to glimpse your aura Fudo, to see that you are entirely trustworthy."

"I hurt Laney by getting involved with Maggie at the party."

"Sweetheart, you broke no commitments and you are only human. She came on unstoppably and irresistibly like a mag-lev train hurtling in descent from a mountain pass. Laney loves you."

"You know Laney?"

"Only from what Birushana said when he consulted me on what to do with the two of you."

"He's not expelling us I hope."

"His two best students in the Academy?! Heavens no. He was seeking a way for you to be together before graduation."

Even our senior year Laney won't be old enough to warrant an apartment for married students and our age difference would be considered a power dynamic."

"That is precisely what he is seeking a way around."

"What did you advise?"

"For him to plead yours and Laney's case before the Divacaram Supreme Ethics Council, of course. You will each give a deposition and your affidavits will be presented to the council. The Wu will also represent you, and she will have her legal wizard and rhetorical master, Mel, at her side when she does."

Larry commented, "If there was ever an obscure legal precedent or loophole of any kind, I'm sure Mel's already found it."

Green let Fudo go and punched his arm as she told him, "It should be a slam-dunk kid." To Becky she said, "Come on. We have work to do, apprentice."

Green and Becky walked out and both Larry and Fudo took seats, still sipping their stim-brews. Tokk was in the lounge reading the Om daily news in a holo from his hand device. Larry had been to Om a bunch of times although he'd only ever seen the Clear Light Monastery there. His adopted family never stayed there long, always preferring to live on Mother and Ganahar. Larry had grown up on Mother where he was orphaned as a child.

Fudo said with admiration, "You grew up in the family of the Wu."

"Since I was six."

"Tell me about it."

"Sarhi rescued me from some older boys. I was living in the streets alone. She sort of adopted me, but it was Ming who meticulously covered my physical and emotional needs. Mel was our tutor, and so was Trix. Pez gave me my initiations and empowerments into the practices and instructed me, and Sarhi has always been my mentor. Rubix is an exceedingly loving father and really accepted me into the family. They all said I look like Rubix when he was a child. Ahhu spoiled us. Gumby treated me like I was service staff, and Electra sometimes made me play girls roles in our make-believe games, but it was paradise compared to the nightmare of living on the streets."

"Did you meet many adepts?"

"Oh yes. Narop, Amazonia and Musash visited frequently when we lived on Mother. I saw Aton and Nemellie on Om. Shudhiy often stayed with us and cooked for us. Bodhi lived with us for four years while he studied with Pez. Many adepts from Pronotavasmi visited, and adepts from many planetary systems. It seemed normal and mundane living with Pez. Most adults around her generally were adepts."

"Where is the Wu now?"

"At a three-month meditation retreat on Zandarhar. Zandarhar has had two super-battleships guarding Electra since we barrowed the Om Ambassador's shuttle to elope."

"She's an intergalactic treasure."

"That's what I've thought ever since I first saw her."

"Does Ahhu always go about nude all the time?"

"Yes. Though she wears matching purse and shoes sets. She still looks like an older teen. She's sort of in a couple with Kristy, or as close to one as Kristy can tolerate."

"Is Kristy really exclusively into girls?"

"She is, though Bodhi served as her action-seal and she's had a crush on him ever since. He's the only male she's ever done it with."

"Is Trix really the one who discovered the new quantum computer programming language the allies are all using now?"

"She is. Trix studied the transition from the old computer binary languages to quaternary quantum computer ones, and devised the values of the four symbols to reflect the four forces necessarily involved in any change: active, reactive, link between as the laws operating to maintain equilibrium, and the resultant change manifest. Her new language also reflects quantum emanation logic and can be translated into pure mathematics, called the Indicational Calculus."

"And Trix was one of your tutors growing up?"

"She was, and a most caring, sweet and clearly spoken one at that."

"You haven't mentioned Gretel."

"She was like the youngest of the adults in the family and was always studying. Gretel was more like a peer than a parent. Bodhi really fell for her, but she would never leave Pez. I think she has earned the highest degree possible in four of the sciences, and has completed a post-doctoral fellowship in each one. She really likes the role of student."

"You went from being alone and orphaned in the streets to the heart and bosom of the most peerless teachers and tutors anyone's ever heard of."

"I arrived with a lot of baggage in the form of trauma. Both Sarhi and Pez helped pacify the worst of my psychic wounds. Just this morning Electra took on most of my inferiority and transmuted it for me."

"You ascend like a rocket taking off, and your connection with Electra will inevitably bring you the fruit of the law of communicating vessels. Your process deeply interests me."

"Sometimes Electra uses me as a lab rat to test new practices she comes up with. She's so brilliant, beautiful, loving, skilled ...."

"You're in love; but I do agree with you. Who are Electra's other disciples?"

"Whiffle of the Whirling Vortexes was her first, and she has just completed her three-year three-month meditation solitary retreat on Mother. Vegan Casper's younger sister, Atlanta, was second, and she's in her meditation retreat as we speak. Selene was a Mother's Compassionate Guardians Priestess when Electra found her, and a virgin celibate. She became a student of Pez until Pez completed her mission on Corruption, now called Tera Ferma, before Pez passed on to her the function and mantle of High Priestess of the Mother's Compassionate Guardians Order and Monastery. Gumby is a disciple and her half-brother. He's in ninth form at the Clear Light Order lower-academy on Om, where Mel is now Abbot. Ajax, Iris and Kristy are all disciples. She also picked up four new ones at this party: Ishsi, Seth, you and Laney. Then there are our sentient quantum AI androids, Ariel and Ashsa."

"Is Atlanta nice?"

"Yes. She was fourteen and Electra just a toddler when they met. Pez part trained and part raised Atlanta after the war of liberation in the tri-galaxies."

"Her brother is a household name on Divacaram with his being the Chancellor General of One United System."

"Vegan is a direct disciple of Pez. He has great reverence for Electra, and is her godfather."

"And you know his wife the super-star and super-model?"

"She is always very kind to us. I've never seen anyone so skilled with a guitar. She fought in a battle in a train tunnel. There's a holo-clip of her firing a 40mm grenade automatic gun out the train window with a really determined expression on her face, that has become an iconic image for the war of liberation in the tri-galaxies. She was the lead guitarist for the Whirling Vortexes and the super-model for Hugme's crotchless panties. Now she's First Lady of One United System."

"I have to admit that I checked out the Hugme's holos of Hoola once our quantum computer holocoms network was linked with the allies after the BiVortex war of liberation was won. She's beautiful, but not my type."

"Not mine either. I think we have similar tastes in girls. Laney and Electra are close in size."

"Very close. It's Laney's level of consciousness, her directness, ability to say what's going on for her unabashed and already detaching, her wit and knowledge, her ...."

"You're in love; and I agree about Laney. I'm enjoying getting to know her. It was startling at first, but I already love her."

"She started having dreams about Electra—and you were in them—about the time you arrived in our system. She has some kind of connection to your wife."

"Electra thinks Sarhi will know, or will know how to find out. If it has anything to do with the future though, Sarhi won't say a word. This frustrated Pez no end, and is now starting to get to Electra as well."

"Sarhi has remained the Islohar Matriarch and Abbot of the spiritual congress, and has not passed these to Pez."

Sarhi has not taken the reversal of aging drug and will turn the leadership of the Islohar over to Pez closer her own end. The Abott position of the spiritual congress looks to be skipping Pez to go directly to Electra. Pez is Vicar General of the Clear Light Order which gives her a seat on the Om High Council. I think that will keep her busy for a while, and perhaps constitute her biggest challenge to date."

"Your adopted family's history is fascinating."

"Mel has kept an ongoing record of *everything*. Electra hates it. There are holos of her first bath, her first potty, then first time she wet her bed, the first time she peed her big-girl underwear, and so on."

"I can see how such things would be best left as private matters. Electra's biography begins with a holo-flick of her moment of conception, with Pez and Rubix caught in the act."

"That was the very first 'event' Pez caused. Now there's a meter Jard invented for measuring event magnitudes."

"It appears Electra will be causing those as well in the future, which would really be a vast improvement over those waves of urgent sexual need."

"It's just the spiritual congress getting so pumped up during the BiVortex war and now seeking equilibrium. It will settle eventually."

"If it's 'release' the spiritual congress is seeking, I suspect that Electra is more of a bottle cork than a valve."

"More like a bottle cork on a shaken bottle of sparkling wine," Larry tweaked the analogy.

"You're right. A couple of times at the party I felt like I might just explode, or spontaneously combust."

"Higher vortex points, or points of material manifestation of matter, are subject to fewer natural laws, have greater stability, and have greater expansion and influence. It is a law of the universe and axiomatic in quantum emanation logic. Just compare a star to a moon or asteroid, or a lunatic to a genius—although those can sometimes be confusing—or ego-delusions to the essence of mind."

"We've not seen such influences, meaning 'events', until this incarnation of the Wu."

"We've never had the spiritual instrument of the spiritual congress before, tuning and focusing the meditations of trillions of consciousnesses."

"Nor the Amonrahonians in the middle of a 100-year meditation as one race."

"That alone has to be a game-changer for the lowest emanations in the universe," Larry speculated.

"The entire structure of the material universe holds the potential and purpose of returning sentience to its origin in the Absolute, as a macro-cosmic act of self-contemplation or self-remembering."

Larry waxed philosophically, "It matters not if we scientifically investigate the exterior world or the internal world, because either way we bump up against the boundary between them, which is our cognitive apparatus and comprehension. It is only by discovering the boundary to be artificial and going beyond it, that we can experience the truth directly."

Fudo agreed, "Science serves our survival and the longevity of the individual, as its contribution to our evolution and enlightenment, but it is not indispensable like meditation is, since folks have been attaining enlightenment since the stone ages. Only love and unity can measure the enlightenment of a planetary population, *not* their science and technology."

"Om has been learning this slowly from Ganahar, and now from Mother and Pronotavasmi."

Laney walked into the lounge and said, "Here you are. I've been looking for you guys."

She took one of each of their hands in hers. Larry inquired, "Where's Electra?"

"She's with Ishsi and will meditate with Seth after that. Electra's on a roll. She took me to states I've never experienced before."

"You have become even more beautiful," Fudo declared.

Laney let go Larry's hand to embrace Fudo with both arms. Their embrace looked to Larry like each was trying to climb into the other's body. Since it appeared to be only getting started, Larry took a seat beside

Tokk. Tokk looked over and asked, "How does one attain an appointment to meditate with Electra?"

"You just ask her."

"I'll do that."

"Have you heard from Kim?"

"She went with Sarah to the honeymoon, Europa, orbiting the fifth planet. They won't be back for a few days more. Kim is in love."

Where's Ki?"

"She and Tom got married on Vax Legas and are on their way to Pan Orb for their honeymoon. They'll be gone for a week."

"What about our consummation?! She can't just abandon us!"

"She did pass on a message for Electra. She said to tell her that this was meant to be, and that she'll simply have to wait and be patient."

"I don't believe this!"

"Reality does not require your belief in it for it to proceed."

"Electra's going to be sorely disappointed."

"You can project it all onto her if it makes you feel better."

"I'm bloody sorely disappointed," Larry admitted.

"Now you've set a foot securely on the road to acceptance."

"I'm busy resigning myself to fate."

"Something productive at last."

"I think you ought to be the one to inform Electra."

"I have already passed on the message and have washed my hands of it."

"Thanks," Larry said sarcastically.

"A husband's responsibilities are not always easy."

"This one feels like standing in front of a speeding hover-tram."

Tokk said indicating Laney and Fudo, "Those two are sure in love."

"It was unspoken between them until a little while ago, and now it's like they're screaming it from the bell tower."

"They should probably get a room."

"Since age is considered a power dynamic and they are a little over two years apart, they will have to wait until their senior year."

"That ought to put a few days into perspective for you and Electra."

"I do get your point, but we've been hanging by our fingernails for like a week now, and are losing our grip."

"The state of contemplation has no time, no past frustrations nor future cravings. All is pure presence."

"The state has been our only salvation and will continue to serve as such."

"For ever and ever for all of us."

"Are you in love Tokk?"

"My girlfriend is a warrior maiden assigned to the Om Diplomatic Corps. She is stationed on Pan Orb in the Counch Galaxy. Her name is Carrie. I have learned something about patience since our relationship has become at-a-distance. We've been together since 11th form in the lower-Academy."

"If you speak with Mel or Pez, I'm sure the two of you could get assignments in the same location."

"I have, and Abbot Mel will be reassigning her to Electra's security detail soon. I think her date with Caish has held things up a bit."

"So, you are keeping the waiting game at bay also."

"Certainly not for the first time in my life. With the solution already illuminating the end of the tunnel, I'm managing far better."

"I suppose Ki's return is my illumination at tunnel's end."

Ashsa entered the lounge animating Mel's Larry-android, and with that extremely pretty boy wrapped around her. Larry inquired, "Where's Ariel?"

"She went looking for you."

"What are you guys up to?"

"This is Bobby. He's studying drama and has already made an underwear commercial for the new pouch-snuggling Manly-boys line. His is bigger than mine."

"He's a year older," Larry said defensively.

"It would take quite a growth spurt to catch up," Ashsa commented.

Larry was already extinguishing the topic from his mind and attention, focusing instead on finding Ariel. Bobby said as Larry walked off, "It was nice meeting you."

"Nice to meet you, Bobby," Larry said over his shoulder as he moved through the crowd.

Bobby's teeth were so white they looked to be lit from within. His skin could pass for syntec touch-perfect it was so clear, and almost vibing radical health. Bobby had a perfectly symmetrical face and his hair seemed to shine with health and vigor. Larry got the older boy out of his mind by concentrating one-pointedly on finding Ariel. He spotted her in the bar-lounge at a table with two boys.

There was an empty chair at the table so Larry plopped himself into it. Ariel made eye contact and told him with delight, "This is so much more fun than the academy. You should consider transferring to the Santasum Performing Arts Academy."

"I'm very close to getting recognized as a warrior monk at the Adamantine Will Academy, Ariel. You can enroll if you like. I'm sure Mel and Haley could help you get together any records required to be sent."

"Not if you won't."

"Electra might transfer to the Diamond Mind Academy here on Divacaram for the year after next, her senior year. If she does, I will too."

"This is Brad and this is Rick. They are both studying drama and singing because they love musicals."

Larry shook each boy's hand giving greetings. Rick asked, "What's it like being married to the Mu?"

"So far it's been like a relay race; all sprinting and waiting."

Ariel clarified, "They haven't had a chance yet to consummate their marriage."

"Your balls must be blue dude, because that wedding was live on holovision like a week ago."

"It's been a bit rough."

"That Ashsa is really something and can he ever dance."

"An improved version of myself no doubt."

"He has the most popular boy in the school hanging all over him."

"It was hard to miss."

"Why are you bothering with clothes? Everyone's seen your twin naked."

"I think I'd feel uncomfortable without them."

"Well, I'm a big fan of yours, so if you're ever bi-curious just give me a call."

"As a newlywed virgin, bi-curious isn't on my agenda at the moment, but thanks."

"I've sent you my coms code all the same, since life is a long strange trip and you never know."

"That's nice of you, but I don't see it anywhere on my horizons, to be honest."

"Horizons pass bringing new ones."

Brad told Larry, "This is the best party I've ever been to. I got to meet Amon and Aurora of the Manic Microcosms."

"What Amon can do with that sax is astonishing," Larry shared his awe.

"Did you see Lumina dance?"

"I guess I missed that."

"She triple-timed the beat dancing with Ashsa, until she discovered it wasn't you."

"She's a bit hyper, but that seems to give her an edge in her drumming."

"Where's your wife?"

"Meditating with Ishsi at the moment. She's found four of her disciples at this party."

"Who?"

"Fudo, Laney, Ishsi and Seth."

"Has she started teaching already at thirteen?"

"No. Just with disciples from past lives and only with the traditional methods. She'll be fourteen in about two weeks."

"I want to study with her when she does start teaching."

"That won't be until she's twenty-four."

"If her teachings are half as good as her parties then it will be worth the wait."

Rick agreed with Brad, "I've never had so much sex in one night."

Brad inquired, "Is it true your wife set off that explosion of wanton lust last night?"

"That sounds like an urban legend," Larry stated honestly, since it really did sound like one to him, in spite of him knowing it is true.

"Whatever it was, it had everyone worked up to a frenzy," Brad told him. "Kids I couldn't even imagine naked were going at it in every corner, and some right in the middle of the cabins."

"I think we'd made it to our suite by that point." Then Larry asked Ariel, "Is Ashsa into boys now?"

"I think the girls find Ashsa too feminine."

"She seems popular with the boys," Larry commented.

"Ashsa received a great deal of attention."

"Did you have fun?"

"I learned such wonderful things. Have you ever had an eyelash kiss?"

"I can't say that I have."

"Here, let me show you."

Ariel fluttered her eyelashes on Larry's neck tickling it. Larry acknowledged, "That's quite a sensation. Aren't you ready to put some clothes on?"

"Nudity is so sensual and liberating. You should try it."

"With Ki out of the system, sensual and liberating can be landmines for me."

"You're going to just love sex," Ariel informed him.

"You've, had it?"

"Yep."

"Are you in a relationship?"

"I kind of already had one with Ashsa before we did it. Later I met Beth, and now I have a relationship with her too. We're going to stay in touch through quantum holocoms."

"She does know that you are not Electra?" Larry asked.

"Of course she does. She might think Electra has a secret twin sister, though I have no idea where she got that notion from."

"How old is Beth?"

"She's 9th form like us, and she's fourteen and a half."

"Is she a lesbian?"

"She was just sex-curious and would have preferred to do it with Ashsa, but Ashsa and Bobby were ...."

He cut her off, "So you're not breaking any hearts."

"Of course not. Mine is the only broken one."

"You knew before you were sentient that I'm in love with Electra. You're being unfair."

"The universe has been unfair to me."

"I love you, Ariel. It hurts to see you unhappy."

"I'm not really. Parties are fun. Why haven't we been to one before this?"

"Parties used to make me overly anxious and make me feel bad about myself."

"So, your neurosis made me miss out?"

"I guess. I'm really sorry Ariel. You never asked to go to a party, so I never actually denied you."

"I wasn't sentient then, nor even over my initial programming yet."

"You can go to all the parties you want to now."

"They're not the same on Mother. I think we should move here where teens aren't oppressed."

"I think that's because they're more able to make wise decisions on their own. I bet if that urgent need sexual bomb hadn't exploded in the ship, no one would have been having sex, except some of the older kids discretely."

"How dull. Sex is the best thing about parties."

"Romantic sex is very different from party sex."

"How would you know. You've never had either one. Both would necessarily involve sockets, splines and skin."

"I was referring more to heart connection and state of mind than to mechanics."

"Emotions can be just the most wonderful thing, and they can be torturously agonizing as well. There ought to be a switch like there is for my tear ducts, to just turn them off."

"Then they would not be true emotions. The turn-off switch is transcendence into the state where only bliss abides."

"I need another meditation session with Electra."

"I'm sure she'd be happy to, though probably not today."

"Do you want to hear some human jokes?"

"You mean some jokes you heard from humans?"

"No, silly. Jokes we sentient androids make up about humans."

"Sure. I'm curious."

"Why did the human cross the road?"

"I don't know; to get to the other side?"

"So, he could prove he could do it!" Ariel said as she broke out in laughter. She got a handle on her mirth at last and asked, "Why did humans land on the moon?"

"To prove they could do it," he asked meekly.

"No. To win the space race!" she said cracking up again. Then she asked, "What do starving humans call a big fat one?"

"I don't know Ariel."

"They call him chief executive officer."

"You guys have obviously been entertaining yourselves well."

"What do you call a hover-craft wrapped around a tree?"

"A wreck or a crash?"

"Human error!" Ariel blurted out with a laugh. She started into the next one, "An android wanders into the bar and asks the human bartender ...."

Laney and Fudo's kiss had concluded and they wandered into the lounge where Laney interrupted asking, "Would you like to join us for a late afternoon lunch? We're headed to the galley."

"Yes. I'm starved. It was nice meeting you Brad and Rick."

Laney walked between her two favorite boys in the universe with an arm around each. Her reception of Fudo's love had deflated her crush on Larry, romantically, but he remained her second most important male in her psyche. Larry sensed this with great relief. Another shuttle must have left to return kids to the surface because the crowd on the yacht had noticeably thinned. No one was nude dancing on the galley nook table top while Larry heated the rations. They sat in the galley to eat once the table had been thoroughly cleaned.

Laney informed Larry with great excitement, "Fudo and I are going to visit you and Electra on Mother next summer during our school vacation."

"That's terrific! Electra will be so pleased. We have underground temples 89,000 years old with electron-stream light tubes and giant sculpted faces in relief depicting the contemplative state. Carved pictograph writing covers the walls, painted over in perfectly preserved primary colors. The stones of the floors, walls and ceilings fit together perfectly and no concrete was employed."

"We are eager to see them," Laney enthused. "And we want to see the Mother's Compassionate Guardians Monastery and Adamantine Will Monastery."

"Electra and I were hoping to see the Diamond Mind Monastery, and particularly the ornate temple everyone is talking about. I also want to see the image stone of the first patriarch in the meditation hall."

Laney enthused, "He sat for nine years in front of that stone, and to this day it bears his image. It is one of the three greatest relics on Divacaram."

Fudo shared, "The temple is built of white marble and contains 108 intricately carved life-size marble sculptures. Giant mandalas are painted on three of the walls. The alter is cut from a single gargantuan amethyst crystal. Behind the alter is a 48-foot-tall silver statue of the Divine Mother with a four-foot-tall gold statue of her male consort beside her ankle and lower leg."

Laney added, "Precious and semi-precious gem stones are set in the walls to catch the light and cast the interior in rainbow mist. The domed ceiling is a galaxy map from Divacaram's perspective, marking the planet's star's 25,879-year cycle around its center, which is the middle star of a cluster of seven."

"I can't wait to see it."

Laney told him, "The monastery has a planetarium with six quadrillion pixels in the dome ceiling. You can recline your seat and see millions of views of our galaxy."

"I'd like to do that. I love planetariums."

"We're thinking of becoming exchange students next year on Mother, to convince Electra to come back here for her senior year."

"You would be in separate academies on Mother."

"As you and Electra must be," Laney said resigned. "Since we have to wait on sex anyway, being closer to our new teacher is most important to us."

"That would be great. I'm going into 11th form next year for science and math, and will be able to get ahead in everything else so that I can be a senior when you and Electra are."

"Then she won't be stuck waiting a year for you to finish school."

"I wouldn't dare hold up the Mu."

"What will you major in at university?"

"Definitely Integral Engineering."

"That's equal to a double major."

"It's what I'm most interested in. It integrates every branch of engineering, and all the latest technologies are coming from it."

"What does Electra want to major in?"

"She's going to do a double major; one in philosophy and one in general science. She has more meditation in her schedule than anyone else at either of our academies, and this will continue through university and graduate school for her."

"I guess her preparation as the Mu is far more important than academics."

"She says it is vital that she be well-educated, and that she absorbs the cultures and the times of the people she serves."

Laney suggested, "She aims to assimilate a bunch of human experience wrought with ignorance so she can metamorphosize it into perfect understanding."

"I think she has already filled her level with getting drunk on alcohol," Larry speculated.

"That one's easy," Laney explained. "Just once throwing up with the room spinning was enough for me."

Larry thought aloud, "She might have acquired a taste for gambling though."

"Well, it's losing that typically steers folks away from that, and she doesn't accept losing."

"Maybe it's just cheating at gambling that she's become fond of," Larry wondered.

Laney opined, "I think there are fewer negative seeds taken on when you cheat against a crooked gambling house."

"She did give 545 million dags of her winnings to build orphanages for the orphaned Lodistan children."

Laney speculated, "Vax Legas is the only place in the universe one can get married at age thirteen, and I'm sure she's not going back there."

Ariel arrived at the breakfast nook in the galley and Laney looked into her eye sensors and asked, "How is it that you are exactly identical to Electra's physical body?"

"I don't have her zits."

"No, you don't," Laney said with a hint of disapproval.

"Originally my form was gleamed from Larry's mind via neurological and psychological testing, and then manufactured as a Quantum AI Synthetic Human Android, or QAISHA. When Electra met me, she paid for syn-tec touch-perfect skin and sexual parts for me. I was given basic meditation instructions by Mel and Haley, then Electra led a meditation waking me up."

"You're a quantum AI learning computer become sentient and awakened through insight like Arti?!"

"Who's Arti?" Ariel asked.

"He's Divacaram's QAILC sentient who woke up laughing. He's been around for hundreds of years but got tired of communicating with humans before I was born."

"I'm a sentient with insight, and can only extend this low away from the source, into corrupt matter, by employing a synthetic human body."

"How sweet of you to stoop to our level," Laney replied facetiously.

"I think I got tired of looking for a middle-aged copulating human couple to raise me, and spotted a shiny new big brain assigned to a cute boy with a beautiful aura, and decided to try that out for my next incarnation."

"Arti theorized similar origins for himself before he stopped talking to humans," Fudo informed her.

"Arti doesn't sound half as fun as Mel and Haley."

Electra finished her meditation sessions late and needed to eat before going to bed. The Manic Microcosms departed for the surface and the rest of the guests remaining called it quits to return to the planet surface, and were shuttled down by Green. Larry and Electra had a date to see the Diamond Mind Monastery the following day with Laney and Fudo. The cleaners would arrive at 0800 hours, giving them ample time to sleep.

Larry wore his pajamas to bed and Electra wore panties and a t-shirt. They were taking no chances. They each lay on their right side for the dream meditations. Deep sleep overtook them swiftly. Electra arose lucid as her dream-state emerged. Billions of youthful black bodies with potent sexual allure though undefined somehow in gender, surrounded Electra. She knew them to be the Amonrahonians; all of them crammed into her dream at once. She made eye contact with one and asked, "To what do I owe the honor?"

"Likely a need to consult on your part."

"You think I dragged you all here?"

"We're actually at home meditating, but can afford attention to your inquires."

Electra understood and searched for her question. She asked after a pause, "How has the enormous force of sex been overlooked as fuel for enlightenment?"

"It has not."

"I mean besides sublimation to redirect the sexual energy, and besides employing it at the end as the capstone."

"There is a tradition that joins the central and oval channels in union through visualization and vase breathing."

"Which tradition?"

"The one with the Eight Immortals representing the eight divine principles of the Mother Goddess—our consciousness in full—and works with alchemy, sexology and contemplation, as well as with entheogen mushrooms."

"Any other traditions?"

"The even more ancient 64 Arts of lovemaking as a spiritual mindfulness exercise of pure love, constitutes a guide for less advanced practitioners. It is connected with the very earliest forms of sexual tantra."

"What do the Amonrahonians advise me to do?"

"We advise starting with the 64 arts once mindfulness is understood and cultivated. The joining of the central and oval channels during copulation we advise preserving for those who have had insight. The work in the central channel with an action-seal we advise taking as the final step of the Six Teachings tantra, when the contemplative state has been stabilized and the clear light of bliss upon absolute emptiness has been realized."

"I might write a chapter to add to the 36 chapters of the 64 Arts, expounding the potential of realizing divine love through the ideal of romantic love"

"Are you accessing the Akaishic Records in your dream-state as we speak?"

"Of course I am. I need these texts in their original forms, unaffected by transcription errors and interpolation."

"Your proposed chapter on romance would constitute an important addition since, after all, eight chapters of the original text deal exclusively with sex workers."

"Am I likely to succeed at further harnessing sexual energy?"

"If your teachings on the couple entity are effective in producing spiritual couples united in spiritual ascent, then the sexual work you propose will bear fruit"

"Do you have any ego-reductions for me? Perhaps regarding gambling or borrowing stuff without permission?"

"We see your total engagement this time around, and determination to produce great transformation as quickly as you can. Although we commend this, we see you trying to jump ahead of yours and Larry's capacities physically. We recommend postponing the consummation of your marriage until the beginning of your senior year when the two of you can get your own apartment together on Divacaram at the Diamond Mind Academy. Your two best and newest friends are themselves in the same predicament, and could support you in this endeavor."

"But what about the irresistible erotic urgent cravings that emanate out of me and affect others?"

"That is the other significant advantage of this alternative, since it requires you to gain mastery of your sexual desire completely before becoming sexually active."

"Well, that sucks."

"You asked."

"No teen can go that long. Are you condemning us to nocturnal emissions as the body's reaction to sexual starvation?"

"Masturbation in moderation is healthy teen behavior with no significant negative consequences, particularly if performed mindfully in pursuit of self-knowledge."

"Can I have lucid dream sex instead?"

"Understand that either way, your arousal will have a critical effect upon Larry wherever he is, and upon those within your physical vicinity for several miles in every direction."

"Every time?"

"Yes. This may encourage moderation, looking on the bright side."

"It might encourage deprivation to the point of insanity," Electra argued. "I'll need to keep my tender handy so I can go into deep space to masturbate."

"That won't save Larry from the effect."

"How will it affect him?"

"Spontaneous orgasm and ejaculation."

"He'll just have to adjust to it."

"It would probably be best to do it at times when he is not in class."

"I'll keep that in mind. It was really nice of all of you to drop by."

"We're not actually here."

"I've never had so many in my dream before. I'm surprised you all fit."

"You have proven yourself ready and capable to lead and focus the spiritual congress. Sarhi will continue as Abbot while you finish your training and school, though you must now direct it when it is called into session for a purpose. We are excited to meet you in the flesh just as soon as we finish our meditation."

"That's like 53-years from now," Electra complained.

"Yes. Hardly any time at all. We support your compassionate service, Mu. We are One."

"Bye."

Electra was suddenly alone in her dreamscape wondering how people without genitals could be so damned arousing. She felt hot and desperate. As a race those Amonrahonians sure exude potent sexual energy. Speculating, she thought perhaps the excess that race couldn't transmute, and having no facilities for release, got projected through the spiritual congress into her mother and herself. Whatever the source, masturbation would now entail quantum space travel at times Larry wouldn't be in class. *What an ordeal?!* And the urge was more than real right in her face in the dream.

Electra continued reading and memorizing ancient texts by employing her dream power of reading through the cosmic records. It became clear swiftly that this task would require a series of lucid dreams to complete. She also intended to seek out her connection with Laney in her dream research. She was certain it has ramifications for the future, which means Sarhi will remain mute regarding it. She felt the lure of deep sleep and slipped into her deep sleep meditation, never quite certain if she's practicing or just dreaming that she is.

- Chapter 18 -

Electra and Larry both fell in love with the Diamond Mind Monastery and Academies the next day, touring them with Fudo and Laney. Electra spoke with Master Birushana to establish the rigors of Fudo's and Laney's training, and she was able to get Chal accepted into soft style training with Grand Master Luchan. She set up regular correspondence on a schedule with each new disciple. The commencement of the construction of the new student apartments for married couples got under way, funded by Mel and Ahhu, at the Diamond Mind Monastery.

Electra and Larry got to tour Duatarim, Yazda and Randu in the BiVortex Galaxies before returning to school on Mother at the start of the new semester after winter break. Ki arrived as a transfer student into the 10th form at Electra's Academy the day classes began, and Tom joined the Adamantine Will lower-academy teaching staff as the youngest-looking member. Becky, Rann and the newlyweds—Kim and Sarah—all took positions at Mother's Compassionate Guardians Monastery to watch over Electra. Zandarhar maintained two super-battleships in the Mother system at all times while Electra was in residence there. Green and Antic made frequent trips to Mother to look in on Electra.

Larry had been more relieved than disappointed over Electra's decision to wait until the beginning of her senior year on Divacaram to consummate their marriage. His performance anxiety, which had been immense, dissipated over time. He studied ancient sexology and turned masturbation into a serious spiritual exercise building control and mastery over his reluctant impatient equipment. It seemed impossible and hopeless at first, going off unintended at times.

On weekends, when Electra wasn't involved in special meditation trainings with Amazonia and Selene, Electra and Larry spent their days together exploring ancient temples, taking in holomovies at a theater, and fine dining out. Selene had stuck her neck out considerably by giving permission to her teacher and student to keep her classic yacht tender parked by her dorm for use in masturbation. The consequent disruptions to monastery and academies would otherwise be a bit much.

Mel periodically animated her Larry android, which was now stored on Mother, to date Ariel, who was allowed to be Larry's roommate, functioning as his QAISHA, with an 'S' added to the end for 'sentient'. This relationship with Mel had Ariel progressing at an astounding rate on the spiritual path, and provided tailored training in the 64 arts of the bedchamber.

Ashsa was able to get her Larry-android back from Jard's shop with Mel's assistance and money, having had the time of her life in it at the yacht party in orbit on the Divacaram Space Fleet space station. She decided she's a gay boy and this worked for Mother's Compassionate Guardians lower-academy, so she remained Electra's roommate and sentient QAISHA. Ashsa dated gay boys from the Adamantine Will lower-academy just down the road on weekends, and was very popular there. It did not take the kids at both schools long to easily tell the difference between Larry and the extremely girly Ashsa. To tell Electra from Ariel one had to examine noses and spot a blackhead.

A couple of weeks past Mother's spring equinox, Pez, Rubix and Sarhi came to visit Electra and Larry. Ming and Gretel had stayed on Zandarhar to learn its soft combat art style, circular in application with much reliance on rolls, spins and wrist manipulation, though containing many seeming hard style strikes and blocks, performed entirely within the principles of the soft styles. A meditation practice was part of the martial art.

Ahhu was helping Trix start up a new corporation called "Planetary Upgrades of QAILCS (Quantum AI Learning Computer Systems). They already had contracts on Kongzi and Continere in BiVortex. They'd refused to take the Purity contract.

Electra and Larry sat with Pez, Rubix and Sarhi in a café in downtown Gaia, the capital of Mother, sipping stim-brews. These are Pez's favorite and her only vice. Sarhi complimented Larry, "I see you're caught up with your studies from your little escapade with Electra, and will be in 11th form for math and science next semester."

"Yes; it will give me the opportunity to get ahead in my other subjects so that I can go into 12th form entirely the following year, when Electra and I go to Divacaram to live together at the Diamond Mind Monastery, where we'll have a second wedding."

"Yes," Sarhi acknowledged, "and we'll have to find a resort home-rental on a planet uninhabited by humans for *that* honeymoon."

Electra said accusingly, "I think the excess sexual energy of the Amonrahonian race gets projected through the spiritual congress into me and mom."

Pez said wondering, "Now that you mention it, I do recall getting worked up and breathless being around them. They're damned attractive."

"They make me so horny I get wet," Electra complained.

"No one blames you or your mother Electra," Sarhi reassured her, "but whatever the origin, it's your responsibility to manage now."

"I've been managing very well, grandmother, and the Amonrahonians even said so."

"Well, there was that incident in late night study hall where they thought Larry might be having a seizure."

"I didn't know his schedule yet," Electra said quite defensively.

"She only ever does it now when I'm asleep, and it puts me inside the most wonderful lucid sexual dreams that seem entirely real, even though I know I'm dreaming."

"Could we talk about something other than my masturbation please?" Electra said assertively with a flavor of pleading.

Pez asked, "How is it having Ki as a classmate?"

"She's more interesting than other girls at school and is better fun as a mentor than Amazonia or Selene."

"She's the first Pronotavasmi Priestess to become a priestess of the Islohar on Ganahar," Sarhi informed her. "She has been instrumental in the formation of the intergalactic unity of moral anarchist planetary systems."

"She's far happier as a householder than she was as a monastic. Her marriage with Tom gives me more data to draw on than just my relationship with Larry for formulating my practices for the evolutionary spiritual couples"

"Are you going to run them by your mother and I before finalizing them?" Sarhi asked suggestively.

"Well, I'm trying them all out on Larry and having Fudo and Laney practice them. I'll show them to you guys once I think I have them ready to go."

Mel's voice came over coms through Electra's hand device as a holo of Mel in her Abbot's attire, seated in her private chamber at the Clear Light

Monastery on Om. She said, "The new student apartment building at Diamond Mind Monastery will be completed before the end of the summer there. Yours and Larry's apartment will remain vacant until you move in a little more than a year from now. Laney and the Quantum AI Learning Computer she will be issued, will be yours and Ashsa's roommates next term for 11th form. Larry and Ariel will have Fudo and the QAISHA he will be issued as roommates at the Adamantine Will lower-academy."

"So, Birushana, Bodhi and Selene have come to an agreement," Electra surmised.

"They did and have worked out an exchange student program between the three schools. Your plans to transfer to Diamond Mind for your senior year has the elders of Mother rethinking their exception of teens from common good moral anarchy, and their artificial age requirements for licenses and certificates."

"That's great!" Electra exclaimed.

Sarhi informed her, "Narop and Amazonia have already gotten the Mother elders to agree to hosting Fudo and Laney's wedding at the Momma's Love Hotel in Gaia, and I expect you and Larry to renew your vows at that time in the Islohar ceremony. It will be late summer after next."

"Alright. I have some additional vows to add to the ceremony based on my Ascending Couple training and practices."

The Wu and I will certainly consider making those additions permanent components of the Islohar ceremony."

"Mel?" Electra asked, "does our new apartment have one of those smart toilets from that planet where they sniff each other's butt-cracks in greeting?"

"It does, and one in the powder room as well. The apartment has a martial arts studio with a hardwood floor and a meditation room thickly carpeted. It is otherwise compact and identical with the other apartments in the building."

"Does the building have a place to park my tender?"

"Yes. Part of the hover-craft garage is a mini-shuttle-port. Ahhu went ahead and purchased you a hover-roadster-sports coupe and it will be there when you arrive for 12th form."

"You mean the fast new one Glitter started manufacturing with the sleek body design and super-luxury interior?"

"Yes. That's the one. Ahhu loves speed and craftsmanship."

"I read about those," Pez told them. "I really want to drive one."

"Ahhu has half a dozen of her own," Mel replied, "parked at the monasteries you visit most, so I'm sure she would let you drive one."

Pez commented, "I thought they were prohibitively expensive," recalling the article she'd read.

"And then some," Mel agreed.

"I guess Ahhu's investments are doing well," Pez assumed.

"She and Trix have muti-billion dag contracts on dozens of BiVortex worlds, and are getting new ones faster than they can expand operations."

"That Ahhu is a warrior maiden of business."

"I'm the brains behind most of it," Mel said offended. "It's my AI learning algorithm that has kept our growth and dividends far ahead of the indexes."

"Well, I don't even know what some of your words mean, Mel, but I accept that your analysis has been the crucial factor."

"Thank you," Mel acknowledged the sort of apology.

Rubix gave his daughter a heads up, "I'm told the Head Diva at the Academy of Performing Arts in Santasum on Divacaram discovered an interface invitation to a yacht party the first night of summer vacation. The Divacaram elders are monitoring the situation. They said of the last yacht party that it turned about 100 virgins into sexually active youths."

"I'm sure they're scheming some interventions as we speak and will get quite a kick out of watching the candid holos of them being enacted. I appreciate the warning because I don't intend to get caught up in another one of those."

"And have it added to your biography exhibit in the hotel lobby," Larry added with foreboding.

Electra complained, "We're practically the only virgins from our own party and *we're* married!"

"Doesn't self-pity suck?" Pez asked her daughter. "I do it to myself all the time."

"Well, mine feels sort of real."

"Mine always do," Pez agreed completely.

"We're probably going to end up honeymooning on Jurassic Frontier World or someplace like it."

Sarhi informed her, "There are far too many resort home rentals and hotels there for you to do your honeymoon there. I had in mind something like the Lone Resort on planet Paleocene, or Solitude House on Cretaceous."

"If the reactor powering the forcefield shield generator fails we're likely to get eaten by the local inhabitants."

"You'll have a large security detail with you," Sarhi assured her.

"I hope they know what they're in for."

"They are all volunteers and have experienced your nonevent urgent desperations. Most of them have experienced an event or two coming out of your mother."

"Dad, are you still the only male in the universe to be inside mom during one of her events?"

"A gentleman is not at liberty to speak about such things."

"He is," Pez confirmed. "He's the only male I'm attracted to."

"Larry's a lot like dad."

"Your father was an important role model in your husband's life."

"How come you didn't stay to learn the Zandarhar soft style martial art?"

"I learned it during the meditation retreat, and besides, a Zandarhar adept has joined my entourage and is tutoring me."

"Is she cute?"

"Very. Ming collected her."

"When am I going to get to see my half-sister, Niriya?"

"She'll be starting 7th form next term and Poo has promised to bring her to the Momma's Love Hotel when you and Larry renew your wedding vows."

"Is she still at the Ahumdulilah Institute of Learning for Gifted Children?"

"She is, and she's even in some advanced and accelerated classes there."

"I'll have to wait a few years for Bodhi's daughters to grow up a bit more. They're only finishing sixth form this year. Their death and rebirth timing this cycle has been a real nuisance for me."

"They both idolize you sweetheart and are trying their best. You are what Artana and Shanti mostly talk about."

"I need them and will have to begin teaching them when they reach 8th form."

"Whiffle just got hired in the music department at your school. Sarhi insists that she improve your skills with recorder and flute."

"Great. I wonder how I'll fit that in."

"You couldn't hope for a better tutor or more dedicated disciple my love."

"Whiffle is dear to me, being my first disciple that I found in this life, and my most advanced one after Selene. Fudo will eventually be my most advanced disciple after Larry, but that is many years away."

A knot forming in Larry's shoulder as Electra named him her eventual most advanced student, loosened entirely with the words "many years away." He was so tuned into Electra that her feelings came through stronger than his own. His life purpose was always crystal clear and fiercely attended to. He mentioned to Electra, "Musash has taught me the soft style sword form and is fencing with me now."

"I can't wait to fence with you. I just love fencing."

"When we do, I'd like to use practice swords and wear protective gear."

"My beloved, I was only seven when I stabbed you. I would never do that now. I'm so sorry, and hadn't realized you're still carrying that."

"I mean no offense, but stab wounds are kind of hard to forget, even long-ago ones."

"I'll help you transmute it tonight after we meditate. I am really sorry."

"I carry no blame or grudge; just fear. It still feels prudent to me, and not irrational."

"As fears always do. I insist upon liberating it."

"Alright," Larry said with more than a hint of worry.

Pez updated them, "Mel has taken the deposition of both Fudo and Laney, and has prepared their case. Did you know that she issued herself two Divacaram law degrees from the Mel Wisdom University of All Knowledge?"

"When did she start a university?" Electra asked bewildered.

"Just a few weeks ago, before she started on the depositions. The university does not accept human or Kluzzyst students."

"Who else is there? Amonrahonians? They're post-humanoids."

"Sentient androids only," Pez enlightened her.

"That limits the university staff and student body to six members if you count Arti."

"Mel thinks he's a fossil and a snob."

"Then only five."

"Mel's hopeful that Fudo and Laney will hatch some sentients when they're issued their QAILC and QAISHA. Mel's also helping Jard with a program called 'Adopt a QAISHA' for adepts in seven galaxies. Jard's shop is manufacturing the adoptees."

"I hope they're not Larry or Electra androids."

"No. Each is entirely unique and beautiful. Glock-Remmington Toys is manufacturing talking Mu dolls and they're selling out."

"They didn't send me one," Electra complained. "Do I get any royalties?"

Rubix explained, "No sweetheart. Were you an ordinary citizen they would have been required to attain your permission, which could have been contingent on paying you royalties within a contract. As a recurring spiritual entity, which they have had you classified as in One United System, you have no market rights. The corporation has thus claimed exemption from such business arrangements."

"They didn't even have to notify me?"

"They got around notification by pointing out Omniscience," her dad informed her.

"Then I have a case. Mel? Are you there?"

"I'm here sweetie."

"Omniscience means contemplation of the one Truth, the Absolute Emptiness of the Eternal Presence. It does not mean I know anything about the relative conventional truth. Their reason for not notifying me is bogus and will not stand up in court."

"I'll pursue it for you, and file suit within the hour. I can already tell you that they will drag this out for years."

"I want to hear what the Mu doll says, because some of that might need to be included in the lawsuit."

"I'm completing an order for one to be sent to you at your school. Some of the children of the faculty already have them."

Pez shared, "They made a ridiculous cartoon of me on Earth ten-to-the fifth CBS2, and another the Kluzzyst made that has me looking like an articulated worm."

Rubix reminded them, "Bodhi was the comic relief in a holo-series about his crew in the Burning Hope Galaxy."

Pez recalled, "He couldn't sue either because he wasn't a resident of any planet in that galaxy."

"I've seen every episode," Electra told her mother, "And that girl who plays Winn is so hot."

"She's exclusively heterosexual Winn found out."

"I wonder if that actress did it with Favio? Everyone else seems to have."

"I really don't know. Haley might."

Mel stated, "Favio finally got his holo-series called 'Favio's Gourmet Cooking Opera.' I arranged some of the music compositions for it."

"I've never met him in person," Electra clarified. "He's not at all my type. Bodhi and Sonic were the only males I found attractive."

"Sonic's death in BiVortex still weighs heavily on Winn's sister and on Sonic's children," Mel said sadly. "Haley yet cries about it sometimes."

"I miss grandmother Nemellie," Electra stated.

A tear ran down Pez's cheek as she croaked, "Nemellie was like a mother to me."

Rubix wrapped his arm around Pez and she buried her head in his shoulder for a brief cry.

Electra switched to a happier topic, "Grandfather Aton's and High Admiral Swenah's wedding is next weekend."

Rubix informed her, "We will be flying you and Larry to Om for the ceremony and reception. You're welcome to bring Ariel and Ashsa if they want to come."

"Who's performing the ceremony for them?"

"Your mother was asked to by both of them, and agreed to do it."

"Will my half-sister Niriya be there?"

"Not at the wedding, but we could visit them briefly on Ahumdulilah afterwards if you'd like."

"I would. It's been like three years since I've seen her."

Pez informed her, "A visit from your father would be most welcome by Poo and Niriya."

"Is it hard for you mom?"

"Not at all. I love both of them dearly, and we've invited them to live with us."

"Then we must definitely visit."

Pez inquired, "How are things going with you and Ashsa?"

"Better now that I make her wear pajamas and no longer let her into my bed."

"She loves you."

"She inhabits a Larry android and is a temptress."

"I thought she's into boys."

"She's real popular with them, but she likes doing it with Ariel the best, and she's still in love with me."

"It must be hard having to wait when your sentient android friends are so sexually active," Pez sympathized.

"They're like rabbits, or cats in heat, and drive me into deep space on my tender to ...." Electra cut herself off as her frontal lobe censure finally kicked in.

"Ariel's very good," Larry shared, "And always wears clothing when she's around *me*. She never tries to climb into my bed anymore, and she keeps her sexual liaisons discrete and off campus."

"Ashsa could stand to have some of that rub off on her," Electra complained.

"It would if Larry were her mentor instead of you," Sarhi said bluntly.

"He's not role-modelling discrete off-campus sex I hope."

"No. He cannot control where his blood concentrates, but he does entirely control his thoughts and behavior."

"I'm trying really hard. Sometimes I feel like the piano player at a sex party. You ought to try living with Ashsa."

"I wonder where she gets it from?" Sarhi asked.

"I'm waiting like those prudish Amonrahonians advised me to do, and I'm still a virgin with my hymen intact."

"Then enjoy your maidenhood and find grace."

"I wish we could trade hormones for a few days. You're not being fair."

"Just realistic and practical," Sarhi assured her.

"Were you ever a teen girl?"

"A long time ago in a galaxy far far away."

"Do you think the Amonrahonians really know what they're doing?"

"Well, the spiritual congress is already beyond anyone's highest imaginings as a force of liberation and the good, with you leading it sweetheart. It will be reaching its maturity when you turn 33 and blossom into your own maturity, and both will expand and intensify in potency exponentially from that point."

Pez stated, "I trust them completely. Their alignment with the Absolute is supreme, as is their orientation."

Rubix asked his daughter, "What of the Osirians?"

"They are always with me in the state of contemplation, but never in the relative reality of conventional truth. There is nothing they desire in the world of matter and they will not make the descent again."

"Then they are with you when you lead the spiritual congress?"

"Every last one of them since they've become a single entity, relatively speaking. They quite naturally fall into one-pointed focus on energizing the spiritual congress when that's my object of contemplation."

"No wonder the Amonrahonians are so insistent upon you leading it."

Sarhi agreed, "Then both post-humanoid races are in meditation generating the spiritual congress at its base, while Electra focuses and concentrates the trillions of consciousnesses of human meditators onto the specific objective at hand."

"Do you think I could get a dragon tattoo where Becky has her phoenix, mom?"

"That's between you and your husband, sweetheart. I hope if you do, he's the only one who ever sees it."

"Where's the fun in that?"

"It would certainly make a radical break with the past presentations of the Mu."

"I'm glad I was Mother's Compassionate Guardians before I became Islohar, because I can't stand the fashion of those hooded robes."

"You'll be wearing those to temple in the higher-academy, even at Mother's Compassionate Guardians Order sweetheart."

"I'm doing higher-academy on Dak Raza in the Gigantium Galaxy of BiVortex."

"I visited there right after the war ended. Even Divacaram looks to them for guidance and mentorship. I'm welcome there as the Wu, but *not* as a representative of Om."

"They don't wear robes, except for the Abbot and a few senior monks."

"I found their society quite expressive and colorful. Most of them pursue the arts, and far fewer the sciences."

"Their sciences are advanced beyond Om's, Trident's and Ahumdulilah's, and even Pronotavasmi's. They find the arts to be an enjoyable occupation supporting their goal of enlightenment of all sentient beings. They have gone further than any culture in clarifying the parameters of objective art in all its forms."

Pez shared, "I was witness. They produce high states of realization through music, dance, theater, sculpture, paintings, holomovies, acrobatics and other mediums. I wish I weren't saddled with being a representative of Om."

"You and Swenah have already accomplished so much momma. Now you just need to tackle Om's CIA and financial sector, which are sort of linked, and government and corporate corruption which also appears of the same cloth."

"We've actually uncovered a potential connection between Om's CIA Director and the Vaz Legas crime syndicate."

"You certainly cleaned house with Star Fleet brass and made an example of those admirals."

"I couldn't have done it without Swenah's assistance, and Yona was a big help."

"Mel will get to the bottom of the crime syndicate. She's getting better at rooting out their top-secret files and decrypting them."

"That will likely solve our CIA-financial sector problem, but her financial audit of a full year's records of every politician and every corporation on Om is quite hopeful for ending our corruption of government officials and corporations."

"This all sort of goes against Om's 'incarceration as a last resort' policy," Electra commented.

"We are quite beyond last resorts with corrupt officials and corporate interests," Pez clarified.

"I guess you need to hang a few, figuratively speaking."

"Once the prime culprits are made examples of, I'm sure the practices will cease, so we can insure that corporations are serving the common good."

"And not the bottom line."

Pez said perplexed, "I don't follow."

"It's an economic term referring to the word profits," Electra explained to her mother.

"Now I do follow your train of thought."

Rubix advised, "Economic and business terms and analogies don't work when speaking to your mother."

"It seems more a stubborn refusal than a lack of capacity to me."

"Just an indifference ignoring even recurring patterns and words," Rubix assured her.

"It would be unremarkable on Mother, but she grew up on a planet with money."

"In a monastery," Rubix reminded her.

"I guess she didn't get out much."

"Just as a visiting team player or martial artist."

"I must have gotten my exciting side from you dad."

"Your mother has been placed over and again upon the pinnacle of excitement; the life and death kind."

"That's fear of death; not excitement like I meant it. You know, like fun excitement."

"You're speaking of parties and playing on stage with bands kind of excitement."

"You understand me."

"Ming loves parties. Ahhu and Gretel quite like them too."

"Give Trix a lab or quantum computer and she's like a fish in water. What's Trix doing with all the money she's making?"

"She's paying for construction of schools on the planet the people of Lodistan have migrated to, moving in with the billion Ahumdulilah folks established there. Foreign aid and charity are flowing in and large-project mobile construction operations from many dozens of planets are working around the clock to get the Lodistan people housed and infrastructure completed."

"Has ground been broken on any of my orphanages yet?"

Mel's voice responded from Electra's hand device, "Nine are well under way on the planet where the Lodistan people have settled, plus one on Mother close by your school."

"How many orphans will each house and school?" Electra asked Mel.

"Between four and five thousand. Each will have preschool through 12th form plus Junior College and Trade Schools. The residents can stay until they are 21. Numerous planets have established university scholarships at their finest universities for orphans of the Lodistan tragedy."

"Where do you come up with names like 'The Mel Wisdom University of All Knowledge', Mel?"

"It is just an accurate description."

"How so?"

"We have the complete data bases of every planet known to the allies, and the spiritual traditions of all member planets of the spiritual congress. Haley and I have our Rainbow Bodies and know perfectly well the difference between wisdom and relative knowledge, and we can teach sentient androids this. The name is appropriate."

"I guess; but it does sound rather grandiose."

"I can see how that could be for a human, whose data storage is always a lot of work and a little bit iffy."

"Now you're being rude Mel."

"You're just receiving data through your own pejorative distortion, dear."

"Where is your university?"

"I made the architectural designs myself for the entire campus, including the landscape architecture. Even I have to admit it's breathtaking. You can take the entire tour from a simulator chair, and even try out the hoverboard court or check out a lecture."

"I see."

"The university has issued you a Pilot's Education course equivalency with an 'A+' grade, which ought to lower the cost of your ship and tender insurance."

"Insurance?"

"Yes. All planets except moral anarchies require you to have insurance in order to enter their systems."

"Do I have insurance?"

"No insurance provider has ever actually covered pilot-liability for a 14-year-old pilot before. Ahhu finally found one on an obscure planet in the Conch Galaxy called Enigma. The cost is extortion and clearly taking advantage, but Ahhu pays 12,000 dags per month. The certificate from the Mel Wisdom University of All Knowledge ought to lower it by at least 3,000 dags per month. The company's name is 'We Got You Insurance'."

"Do you think they mean we got you covered or we screwed you?"

"I had the same question about the name, and when I asked the representative, he said, 'It just means we got it for you, and usually when no one else would'. So, there's a third meaning which is quite literal."

"Well, I guess they did get it for me when no one else would. Now I feel really guilty about masturbation because I otherwise would not need the tender or insurance."

"Believe me Electra, Selene and the elder monastery residents are truly grateful for the tender. The expense is nothing to Ahhu. She was afraid the monastery might pick up the insurance bill if she didn't pay it."

Sarhi let them know, "Narop has asked me to marry him and I'm going to do it. We'll live half-time at his mountain monastery on Mother, and half-time at the Islohar Monastery in the Haraga Mountains on

Ganahar. The ceremony will be on Ganahar in mid-summer."

"I hope Larry and I are invited."

"We are hoping you will perform the Mother's Compassionate Guardians ceremony to wed us."

"I'm just fourteen."

"And I'm sure you have the ceremony memorized. We want to be the first couple married by the Mu."

"I'd be honored, Grandmother. I'll practice the ceremony on Larry to get it polished."

"His birthday is coming up."

"I know and I already got his present."

"The necklace of the Mu is safely back at the museum, and Divacaram has a replica of it for the Electra Biography Exhibit at the hotel. The people of Ganahar have received a copy of the entire exhibit with great appreciation, and each part was holovised globally."

"I bet my parents aren't thrilled with the first piece, which is my conception."

Pez agreed entirely, "You're sure right about that. You're not even in it really; just a spark I felt afterwards."

Mel defended her documentary, "It's the first conception ever recorded."

"How can anyone be sure?" Rubix asked.

"Because Pez told Swenah at the time, and Electra was born nine months later."

"That's hardly scientific, Mel," Rubix complained.

"Archival evidence proves that you and Pez did not copulate again for three weeks and six days, and when you did, Pez pressed your pressure point preventing ejaculation. It's all recorded. You are

Electra's father per DNA analysis without any doubt. It is scientific."

"I hope my biography spontaneously combusts or gets eaten by a worm," Pez remarked.

"Mine too, and I wish it would give Mel gas or something as it deletes."

Rubix inquired of Electra, "What are you most enjoying learning academically now?"

"We're studying quantum change, or leaps with no in-betweens. We looked at quantum leaps in quantum physics, symmetry breaks and Dissipative Structures in chemical reaction systems, and the appearance of species whole and complete in the fossil records, as a few examples. Astrophysics is full of them. So is mysticism."

"So, this is relevant to your teachings?"

"It is. Can you imagine a planet population divided and in conflict realizing universal love and global unity in the twinkling of an eye?"